Praise for Patricia Gaffney and her novels

"Patricia Gaffney . . . is one of the finest writers to come along in years."

—*Romantic Times*

To Have and To Hold

"Compelling and sophisticated."

—Virginia Henley

"Patricia Gaffney writes with power and passion."

—*Romantic Times*

To Love and To Cherish

"Magnificent! Powerful, beautifully written, and as deeply moving as it is richly romantic . . . destined to become a classic."

—Mary Jo Putney

"A beautiful story that tugs at the heartstrings. A powerful tale of love and faith."

—*Romantic Times*

Forever and Ever

"Simply glorious."

—Nora Roberts

"Lovely writing and a story that is honestly and passionately told."

—*Romance Forever*

continued . . .

The Saving Graces

"Anyone who's ever raised a glass to toast her women friends will love this book—its raw emotion, its rueful humor, its life lessons."

—*The New Orleans Times-Picayune*

"This ode to the friendships between women could easily become the northern version of *Divine Secrets of the Ya-Ya Sisterhood*."

—*Booklist*

"A jewel of a book and every facet sparkles."

—Nora Roberts

"Rich, lovely . . . an intimate portrayal of friendships through the eyes of four unforgettable women. I hated to put it down!"

—Michael Lee West

Sweet Everlasting

"A romance of immense beauty and emotional power . . . exquisite!"

—*Romantic Times*

"A beautiful, tender love story, evoking your senses and stirring your emotions. It will renew your faith in unselfish love."

—*Rendezvous*

Wild at Heart

"Delightfully different . . . *Wild at Heart* brims with laughter and passion."

—*The Literary Times*

"Wonderful and enlightening. . . . Ms. Gaffney once more stretches the bouhdaries of the genre as only a premier writer can do."

—*Romantic Times*

Outlaw in Paradise

"Lively, exceptionally well-written."

—*Library Journal*

"Sophisticated, humorous . . . a delightful, mature romance that brings readers a unique look at the Wild West."

—*Romantic Times*

Crooked Hearts

"With a lyrical voice and keen wit, Patricia Gaffney weaves compelling stories that echo in the human heart."

—Nora Roberts

"Absolutely marvelous. . . . It's been a long time since I read a book this wonderful. I loved it."

—Joan Johnston

"Poignant and exciting. An unforgettable read. There have never been two more wonderful and memorable larcenist lovers."

—*Romantic Times*

"Heartwarming and delightful . . . the best matched hero and heroine since Hepburn and Tracy . . . pure pleasure."

—Elaine Coffman

"Wickedly delightful. You'll never meet two more outrageous, endearing characters."

—Margaret Brownley

"Sexy, funny, and wildly entertaining."

—Arnette Lamb

"A refreshingly unique and humorous romance."

—*Affaire de Coeur*

"Fabulous . . . unusual and beautiful, warm and witty . . . one of the funniest and most entertaining stories I've read in a long, long while."

—Rebecca Paisley

To Have
and
To Hold

Patricia Gaffney

NEW AMERICAN LIBRARY

NEW AMERICAN LIBRARY
Published by New American Library, a division of
Penguin Putnam Inc., 375 Hudson Street,
New York, New York 10014, U.S.A.
Penguin Books Ltd, 80 Strand,
London WC2R 0RL, England
Penguin Books Australia Ltd, 250 Camberwell Road,
Camberwell, Victoria 3124, Australia
Penguin Books Canada Ltd, 10 Alcorn Avenue,
Toronto, Ontario, Canada M4V 3B2
Penguin Books (N.Z.) Ltd, Cnr Rosedale and Airborne Roads,
Albany, Auckland 1310, New Zealand

Penguin Books Ltd, Registered Offices:
Harmondsworth, Middlesex, England

First published by New American Library, a division of Penguin Putnam Inc. Previously published
in a Topaz edition.

First New American Library Trade Paperback Printing, March 2003
10 9 8 7 6 5 4 3 2 1

 REGISTERED TRADEMARK—MARCA REGISTRADA

LIBRARY OF CONGRESS CATALOGING-IN-PUBLICATION DATA:

Set in Fairfield LH Light

Printed in the United States of America

BOOKS ARE AVAILABLE AT QUANTITY DISCOUNTS WHEN USED TO PROMOTE PRODUCTS OR SERVICES. FOR
INFORMATION PLEASE WRITE TO PREMIUM MARKETING DIVISION, PENGUIN PUTNAM INC., 375 HUDSON
STREET, NEW YORK, NEW YORK 10014.

In memory of Major Tom.
After many years of faithful service,
our golden boy has been promoted.

I

"But it is too rude of you, Bastian! How can you send me away like this? Don't you like Lili anymore?"

"I adore you," Sebastian Verlaine avowed, prying away the grip of his mistress's tiny white hand, clamped to his thigh like a nutcracker. Through the carriage window, he watched the chimneys of Lynton Great Hall, his dubious inheritance, recede behind a screen of ancient oak trees. He couldn't help liking the look of his new house. But it was hard to sustain admiration for its rough granite grandeur when he thought of everything that was broken, peeling, crumbling, smoking, or leaking, and how much even rudimentary repairs were going to cost him.

"And have we not had a nice time? Did we not play lovely games in your new *baignoire*? Eh? Bastian, listen to me!"

"It was paradise, my sweet," he answered automatically, kissing her fingers. They smelled of perfume and sex, an essence he wasn't capable of appreciating just now, at least not in any way that required virility. Enough occasionally was enough, and four days and nights in the intimate company of Lili Duchamps was, as the lady herself would put it, *plus qu'il n'en fant*—more than enough.

"*Oui, paradis,*" she agreed, insinuating her index finger between his lips and tapping his teeth with her fingernail. "Put off your silly men's business and come to London with me. We have never made love on a train, *oui*?"

"Not with each other," he conceded after a second's thought.

He bit down on her finger hard enough to make her snatch it away and glare at him. It would have been amusing to say, "You're beautiful when you're angry," but it wouldn't have been true.

"Oh, you are cruel! To send me off all alone to—to—*Plymouth*—" she made it sound like *Antarctica*— "and make me ride on the train to London all by myself—*c'est barbare, c'est vil!*"

"But you *came* by yourself," he pointed out reasonably, "and now you just have to do everything in reverse." Past her lavishly styled, champagne-colored hair, he watched the quaint parade of thatched-roof cottages glide by as the carriage bumped and rumbled up Wyckerley's cobblestoned High Street. The cottages were charming, he supposed, with their fat dormers, profuse gardens, and pastel fronts; but his aesthetic appreciation was tempered by the thought that his own tenants probably lived in half of them. Then they weren't so charming. Then, like the manor house, they were just a lot of old buildings that needed his money and attention.

"But *why* can you not come with me? Why? Ooh, I hate you for this!" She drew back her hand, but he grabbed it before she could strike him. By now he knew her shallow tempers; she rarely caught him off guard anymore. "Take care," he said in the soft, menacing tone with which he'd originally seduced her; the fact that it still worked was one reason their affair was growing stale. "Do not try my patience, *ma chère*, or I'll have to punish you."

The lurid flare of excitement in her eyes made him laugh—spoiling the mood. "Oh!" she cried, thumping him on the chest with her fist. "Beast! Cad! Ungrateful bitch!"

"No, darling, that's *you*," he corrected, holding her hands still in her lap. Lili's English wasn't fluent, and sometimes she called him the things her own spurned lovers called her. "Now, kiss me and say good-bye. Justice is waiting for me."

"Who? Oh, your silly court business." Suddenly her peevish scowl lifted. "I know—Bastian, I will come with you and watch!"

2

"No, you will not." The good souls of Wyckerley already worried that their new viscount was a degenerate; one look at Lili and their worst fears would be confirmed. He wanted to save them from that, or at least delay the awful truth a little longer.

"*Mais oui!* I want to see you in your black robes and your *perruque*, sending poor criminals to the *guillotine*."

"Ah, darling, what charming blood lust." He leaned across the carriage seat, intending to retrieve his walking stick. Lili intercepted the move by seizing his hand and pressing it to her powdered white bosom, inhaling to inflate it to the maximum—a needless augmentation of an already prodigious endowment. In fact, Lili's bust was what had first attracted Sebastian, four months ago at the Théâtre de la Porte, where she'd made her debut in *Faust* as the living statue of la Belle Hélenè—a good role for her because it didn't require her to speak. Despite her reputation as one of the most heartless of the *grandes horizontales*, she'd proven an easy conquest: one intimate supper at Tortoni's, absinthe afterward at the Café des Variétés, and then the *coup de grâce*, a pair of diamond eardrops in the bottom of a bottle of Pontet-Canet—*et voilá*, they were disporting themselves on the black satin sheets in her gaudy rue Frochot apartment. She'd been his mistress ever since, but she wouldn't be for much longer. They both knew it—how could they not? They were professionals, he as keeper, she as kept; they knew how to recognize the first stirrings of ennui before it could blossom into full-fledged contempt.

With a little shimmy, Lili got her left breast into the center of his palm; he felt the nipple harden into a warm little peak. She uncovered her teeth in a carnivorous smile and slipped one of her knees over his.

The carriage had just stopped at the entrance to Wyckerley's exceedingly modest town hall, or "moot hall" as they still called it, inside of which two magistrates and who knew how many poor criminals were waiting for him to help dispense justice in the petty session. Pedestrians were passing on the street, staring openly at the new D'Aubrey brougham, while above, the coachman waited patiently for his lordship to alight. Satisfying Lili didn't take long, Sebastian knew from experience, and sending her away happy would be the better part of discretion. But the logistics, not to mention a disinterest that might be temporary but was nevertheless profound, defeated him. With a sigh, he gave her luscious breast a soft farewell squeeze and withdrew his hand.

Predictably, her eyes flashed with anger—"eyes like multifaceted marcasite, their soft glance more stimulating than a caress," according to a so-called critic in one of the Paris theater revues. Not so predictably, her dainty little hand drew back and slapped him hard across the cheek; he barely caught her wrist before she could do it again. *"Pourceau,"* she spat, her long-nailed fingers curving into claws. *"Bâtard.* I loathe you." But the lascivious look was back, and it grew heavier, lewder, the harder he squeezed the bones in her wrist. All at once the carnal gleam in her eyes irritated him. They'd played this game too often, and now he was mildly repelled, not aroused by it.

She must have seen his disgust; when he pushed her away she made no protest, and except for one brief, longing look at his cane, she seemed to be through with violence. *"Au revoir,* then," she said airily, pulling up her low bodice, patting her hair, every inch the insouciant *coquotte* once more. "Darling, how do you say *'je m'embête'* in English?"

" '*I'm bored,*' " he answered fervently.

"Exactement. So I will leave you to your so *bourgeois* business affairs. When you are next in London, you must do me a great favor, Bastian. *S'il vous plaît,* do not come to see me."

"Enchanté," he murmured, privately amazed that she was letting him off this easily. The Comte de Turenne had been foolish enough to break off his liaison with Lili while dining at the Mai-

son D'Or, where she'd retaliated by dumping a plate of Rhine carp *à la Chambord* in his lap.

He opened the door and sprang down to the pavement, breathing deeply of the unperfumed air. "John will take you to the posting inn where the Plymouth mail coach stops, Lili. I'd let you have my carriage, but then, how would I get home?" He gave a Gallic shrug, enjoying the tightening of her carmine lips. "You'll be fine," he said more kindly. "John will wait with you and see that you're safely ensconced and on your way." He reached into the inside pocket of his frock coat and withdrew a jeweler's box. He flipped it to her in a quick underhand lob she couldn't have been expecting. But with the dexterity of a cricket ace, she threw her hand up and caught it—*chunk*. Like lead to a magnet, Sebastian analogized; or a lure to a great, hungry bass. "I wish you well," he said in French. Less truthfully he added, "I treasure our time together. You may be sure I'll never forget you."

Mollified by the gift more than the words, she lifted her chin and her theatrical eyebrows in what she no doubt intended to be a regal look; he could imagine her practicing it in front of one of the dozen or so mirrors in her boudoir. "Good-bye, Bastian. You are a terrible man, I do not know why I put out with you."

He grinned. "That's put *up* with me, darling—although your way is closer to the mark." She was softening, she was all but ready to forgive him. To forestall her, he swept off his hat and made a low, fatuous bow. "*Adieu, m'amour*. Be happy. My heart goes with you." Before she could respond, he slammed the door, sent John a discreetly urgent look, and backed away to the curb, keeping his hand on his breast as if overcome with feeling. The carriage jerked away, and he had a last glimpse of her scowling face, cheeks just beginning to flush with anger as she realized he was mocking her—for whatever else Lili might be, she wasn't stupid. But it scarcely mattered now, and all he could feel as he watched the coach turn the corner and disappear was relief.

5

There wasn't much to downtown Wyckerley. Like most English villages, it had the requisite old church, picturesque cottages, inn and alehouse, a few shops, and of course, the village green, complete with dilapidated, lichen-covered cross. Two happy accidents of nature lifted Wyckerley out of the ordinary, though, and made it genuinely charming. One was its aspect: it sat on a lush green hill overlooking not only Lynton Great Hall a half mile to the east, but the south Devon coast and the dark, brooding wastes of Dartmoor to the north. The second natural gift, even more delightful, was the Wyck, a cunning little river that ran right through the town, side by side with the High Street, spanned at convenient intervals by stone slabs or humpbacked bridges built by the Romans fifteen centuries ago. In April, violets and marsh marigolds covered the river's steep-sided banks, and strawberries and watercresses and wild daffodils. "O, to be in England now that April's here," Browning had mooned from Italy, and Sebastian found himself in unexpected sympathy with the sentiment as he sniffed the clean, crisp breeze and watched the colored wings of birds flicker in the plane trees across the way.

A man passed him on the narrow sidewalk, bowing respectfully; another tipped his hat and mumbled, "Afternoon, m'lord," as he hurried by. Sebastian was surprised they even recognized him, considering the largely absentee nature of his landlordship up to now. He'd been the Viscount D'Aubrey for more than a year, since the death of his second cousin, Geoffrey Verlaine; Geoffrey's widow had lived on at Lynton Hall until her marriage last Christmas to the village minister, a man named Morrell. Since then, Sebastian's actual residence at the Hall had been brief and sporadic, wedged in between more gratifying entertainments in London and abroad. (Although how gratifying they really were was a question, considering that rewards like the acquisition of Lili Duchamps for a mistress had been the dubious fruit of more than one such entertainment.)

The church bell ringing the quarter hour reminded him he was late. Town hall was a low, squat building of red Devon stone, with two chimneys and a slate roof. An unprepossessing structure, to say the least, and for a moment he was in sympathy with Lili's incredulity when she'd heard he meant to join two other town worthies on the bench as a justice of the peace. How respectable, how stolid and squirelike of him, how Fieldingesque—how utterly unlike Sebastian Verlaine. He'd been called many things—rake, sensualist, seeker, dilettante, degenerate. What he had never been called was "Your Worship," a magistrate's title. All that could account for this odd turn of events was a momentary lapse of reason, a brainstorm, a transient fit of insanity brought on by the simultaneous importunities of three city fathers, the mayor, the curate, and his own bailiff, all ganging up on him in the guise of a social call while he'd been, to put it delicately, "in his cups." (Putting it candidly, he'd been howling drunk. But they couldn't have known it, since he was a past master at feigning sobriety.) When the civic triumvirate had finished enumerating their concise, cogent, and compelling reasons why he ought to serve as a justice, he'd been in deep sympathy with them, and ready to don robe and wig that very minute.

Reason had come crashing back, but too late: it was time to pay the price for his folly. Ah, well, who knew, it might even be diverting, a bit of droll fodder at someone's dinner party the next time he went up to London.

The proceedings had already begun, he perceived upon entering the building. A windowless cloakroom preceded the hall of justice, and from its shadowy vantage he heard a voice—the mayor's, he thought—asking questions, and another man's voice, soft from either reverence or fear, answering. From his angle behind the doorway, Sebastian could see three-quarters of a squarish room, not large, dimly lit by the sun streaming in through high, dusty windows. The justices were out of sight to his right;

in front of him was a compact gallery, rough benches behind a railing with room for about thirty spectators, all taken today by sturdy Wyckerlian burgers. A woman sitting at the end of one of the benches stood out from the others by virtue of being better dressed. She wore her yellow hair in old-fashioned ringlets; in her lap was an enormous square of black wool, on which she was knitting fast and furiously. She saw him out of the corner of her eye and looked up, startled. His hiding place was found. Keeping his stick but not his hat, Sebastian made his entrance.

The proceedings came to a halt and every eye fixed on him as he strode unhurriedly to the top of the room. Mayor Eustace Vanstone and his fellow magistrate, a burly, bewhiskered gent with a florid face and stiff military bearing, were seated behind the long side of a rectangular table. "Don't get up," Sebastian admonished when they started to rise, aware that others in the room were standing, too. "Sorry to be late. Glad to see you've gone ahead without me." He shook hands with Vanstone, an elegant, silver-haired man with shrewd and rather ruthless eyes. The other justice was Captain Carnock, whom Sebastian hadn't met before; he had a kinder face, but a handshake that almost shattered his knuckles. Both men had on black robes, but only the mayor wore a wig. Sebastian wore neither; his frock coat and trousers were black, though, and he deemed that judicial enough.

There was an empty chair next to Vanstone's. The mayor was clearly the one in charge, with important-looking papers and documents scattered on the table in front of him. He made a half-hearted show of giving up his place to Sebastian, who said easily, "No, no, stay where you are, I'm fine here," and sat down in the third chair.

Vanstone indicated he wanted a conference; the other two men leaned toward him, and the mayor spoke in a confidential undertone. "Lord D'Aubrey, the case we're presently hearing is that of Hector Pennyways, miller's assistant, charged with lewd conduct and being a public nuisance." He inclined his head toward a fellow standing eight feet away behind a waist-high wooden bar. Dressed in a smock-frock of dirty white drabbet, the accused looked unrepentant but harmless; he had a large, full-moon face, and he waited for his punishment with the stolid vacancy of some bulky farm animal. "To wit," Vanstone went on, "he became intoxicated at the George and Dragon, went outside and relieved himself in the river—in full view of several passersby, including a woman—and finally fell unconscious against the Maypole on the green, where he remained until the constable was summoned."

The image of it had a coarse, Rabelaisian charm that made Sebastian chuckle—inappropriately, he saw at once, as Vanstone and the captain looked identically unamused, civically dismayed, and judicially set on dealing with this affront to public decency without delay, and certainly without levity.

Without mercy, either. "Sixty days in the lockup and a guinea fine for damages," decreed the mayor, and Carnock nodded in agreement. They glanced perfunctorily at Sebastian, taking his concurrence for granted.

His long legs wouldn't fit comfortably under the table; he swung them to the side and idly tapped his walking stick against the toe of his left boot. "Sixty days?" he mused. It seemed harsh for a crime that wasn't vicious, only inelegant. But Vanstone had the look of a man who knew exactly what penalty matched what crime, plus he had two thick, intimidating law books on the table in front of him. Sebastian shrugged his shoulders, and the case of Hector Pennyways was closed.

The parish constable, a man called Burdy, was tall and raw-boned, with an enormous pink nose inked with a map of purple capillaries. He took the defendant by the elbow and hustled him toward a closed door at the back of the room, presumably leading to a holding area of some sort. Minutes later, he reemerged with a new prisoner, a woman this time, accused of stealing her neighbor's laundry from their shared wash line. After her came a few civil suits, boundary disputes and the like, and then they went back to criminal matters: two more public inebriates, a suspected Peeping Tom, a brawler. Nobody had a lawyer, which made self-defense all but impossible; under English jurisprudence, the accused wasn't allowed to speak on his own behalf. An indefensible system, Sebastian had always thought, and one on which the Americans had clearly improved.

The caliber of crime in Wyckerley was nonviolent, venial, and definitely not worth repeating in humorous anecdotes for the delectation of his jaded friends. What surprised him was that he wasn't altogether bored. No matter how trifling or ludicrous the offenses, the people who had perpetrated them were interesting, in their way—at least to look at and speculate upon; closer acquaintance would probably not be edifying, and Sebastian was a firm believer in the axiom that familiarity breeds contempt. But from this distance, and for a little while, their stories entertained him, and he even got an old moral lesson hammered home anew: the poor go to gaol for the same crimes with which the rich aren't even charged.

Eventually the sameness began to wear on him, though. Under the mayor's subtly reproachful eye, Sebastian brought out his watch for the second time in ten minutes. Only four o'clock? This game wasn't fun anymore. Then, too, he and Lili had had champagne instead of food for lunch, and what he could really use right now was a little nap. "How much longer?" he inquired bluntly of the mayor, who leaned toward him and murmured, *sotto voce,* "Only one more now, my lord."

He grunted, watching the constable make his last trip to the prisoners' waiting room. Behind the gallery railing, the woman with all the black knitting began to roll up her handiwork and stuff it into her workbasket with nervous, jerky movements. Around her, the other spectators sat up straighter, whispering or clearing their throats.

Aha, thought Sebastian, *it's the last prisoner they've come to see.* He turned to Vanstone to ask why. But before he could speak, the door in the back of the room opened and the constable came through, ushering a woman before him.

II

"ACCUSED IS RACHEL Wade, Your Worships, widow, charged with indigence and no fixed abode. She was released six days ago from Dartmoor Convict Prison, whereupon she made her way to Dorset, the county of her birth. In her home parish of Ottery St. Mary, she was detained on the twelfth of this month and taken before the magistrate, who declared her an undesirable and ordered her to quit the county. Accused came to Devon, on account of it being the county where her marriage took place. On sixteen April, she was taken up again, in Wyckerley, St. Giles' parish, for not having a place."

The constable stopped reading from his writ and added on his own, "She were found in Jack Ratteray's root barn, claiming all 'er money was stole in Chudleigh. Four apples was found in 'er effects; accused admitted she stole 'em, but she weren't charged."

The room had gone absolutely still, every eye trained on the tall, slight woman standing alone at the bar. Sebastian peered at her more closely, trying to discover what about her unremarkable form could have elicited such fascination. She was dressed in a gown of grayish worsted, shapeless, styleless, essentially colorless except for the mud stains at the hem. No hat or bonnet. Her figure was youthful, but he judged her to be middle-aged because of the silver in her dark, too-short hair. She kept her head bowed and her eyes on the floor, shoulders slightly hunched. Nevertheless, in spite of her posture, the aura she projected wasn't abject or furtive; only hopeless. She struck him as a woman beaten down so thoroughly that even servility had gone beyond her.

"Will anyone speak for her, Constable?" queried Vanstone. A few of the defendants had had witnesses to testify for them.

"No, Your Worship."

The mayor cleared his throat importantly. "Then the court has no—"

"What was Mrs. Wade in gaol for?" Sebastian asked negligently, never taking his eyes from the woman. He thought she might look up at him then, but she didn't. The room grew even quieter.

Vanstone leaned toward him and murmured, "My lord, she served a ten-year sentence for the crime of murder."

His cane stopped its restless tapping on the toe of his boot. If Vanstone had said she'd gone to prison for flying around the village green on a broomstick, he couldn't have been more surprised. *Murder.* He narrowed speculative eyes on her again, trying to believe it.

"Court orders the accused remanded to the Tavistock lockup until her case can be taken up at the May assize." The mayor bunched his fist, preparatory to smacking it lightly on the table like a gavel, an affectation Sebastian suddenly found irritating.

"Wait," he commanded softly, halting the judicial fist in midair. "If no one will speak for her, how can she answer the charge?"

"My lord," the mayor began with careful deference, "it's not our concern. If she has a representative, she can answer, but that's in due time. This hearing is not evidentiary, you see. Our powers are prima facie; in most cases we arraign, we don't try."

"I know that," Sebastian snapped, and the mayor's sleek, clean-shaven cheeks reddened. He softened his tone. "But you see, I don't feel sufficiently conversant with the case in order to adjudicate it responsibly," he said, enjoying the turgid, magisterial sound of the words. "And I'm sure you would want me to adjudicate it responsibly."

"Of course, certainly, my lord," Vanstone raced to assure him, and Captain Carnock echoed his agreement, both men nodding vigorously.

"Then you'll give me leave to address the accused?" He felt Vanstone bristle, but didn't look at him; his attention was on the woman again. Unlike the majority of her predecessors, she didn't hang onto the bar with nervous, white-knuckled fingers; she stood a full foot behind it with her hands at her sides. A center part made a straight white arrow down the crown of her head, which remained bowed. He wanted to see the face of a convicted murderess. "Mrs. Wade."

"My lord?" she answered in a low but clear voice, audible in the farthest corner of the hushed room.

"Mrs. Wade, look at me." His tone was sharper than he'd intended, but she didn't jerk her head up in startled obedience. She lifted it slowly, with unconscious drama—he assumed it was unconscious—and looked him full in the face.

For one awful, shocked instant, he thought she was blind. Her eyes, so pale they looked like crystal, were wide and unblinking, almost unreal, like a doll's luminous, painted-on eyes. She had a high, pale, intelligent forehead, sharp cheekbones, a small nose. An intriguing mouth, full but stern, the lips compressed in a defensive straight line, as if to keep in check any wayward utterance not absolutely required for survival.

She was younger than he'd thought, and yet her unlined, unblemished face was, strangely, not youthful; it seemed more blank than young, and not innocent but . . . erased. She might be twenty-five or thirty-five, it was impossible to tell, the criteria by which he judged people's ages were simply missing in her case, irrelevant. He took note of her long, angular body, more thin than slender, her femininity all but eradicated by the ugly dress. All but. But it was her eyes that drew him, again and again, back to her extraordinary face.

A whole minute had passed since she'd spoken. Vanstone began to tap the end of his pen against one of his law books in a soft *pat, pat, pat,* discreetly restive.

Sebastian asked the question uppermost in his mind, although a dozen others seethed under the surface. "How old are you?"

"Twenty-eight, my lord."

Twenty-eight. The bloom was definitely off the rose, then. With a slight shock, he realized she'd been in prison since the age of eighteen. "And whom did you murder, Mrs. Wade?"

They both ignored the quick, stifled gasps around them. She didn't drop her eyes, but she was rhythmically clutching and unclutching small handfuls of skirt at her sides. "I was sentenced for the murder of my husband," she replied, in the same low but carrying voice.

He waited, assuming she would add that she was innocent. She didn't. He laid his stick on the table and leaned back, folding his arms across his chest. "Have you any family here?" There was a broken-off exclamation from somewhere in the gallery of onlookers, but he didn't look away from the woman to see the source.

"No, my lord."

"Friends?"

"No, my lord."

"There's no one who can help you?"

"No, my lord." Her voice had absolutely no inflection; no defiance, no hope, no self-pity, not even matter-of-factness. Just— nothing. She bent her head; immediately she was anonymous again, a tall, slight nonentity, and he was left to wonder what about her had been so compelling only a second ago.

He asked, "Can you read and write, Mrs. Wade?"

"Yes, my lord."

"You've searched for employment, have you?"

"I have."

"And?"

She looked up. Her unearthly gaze riveted him again. "I could not find a place," she answered, still without any emphasis, weighting all the words equally.

"How much money was stolen from you?"

"Nine pounds, four shillings, my lord."

"Indeed? And how did you come by such a princely sum?"

"I earned it in prison, my lord."

"Doing what?"

She took an audible breath, as if all this vocalizing were wearing her out. "I worked most recently in the tailor's shop."

"You're a seamstress?"

"No, I was the bookkeeper."

"The bookkeeper." He raised his brows to show that he was impressed, but it didn't persuade her to say more. "But no one would engage you in that capacity upon your release?"

"No, my lord."

"Did you try for other employment?"

"Yes, my lord."

He made an impatient gesture with his hand, telling her to keep going.

"I sought employment as a clerk in a dressmaker's shop, a draper's, a—tobacconist's. After that, I tried for work as a domestic servant and then as a laundress. But I could not get a place."

"Because of your past, is that it?"

She bowed her head in assent.

He watched her, brooding, aware that time was passing. Her passivity irked him. He thought of Hester Prynne, facing down the indignation of her Puritan judges. The two women were in roughly similar straits, both confronting a community's censure and abandonment; but Mrs. Wade lacked the adulteress's cold, fierce, trampled dignity. Mrs. Wade had simply erased herself.

He felt pity for her, and curiosity, and an undeniably lurid sense of anticipation. Against all reason, she interested him sexually. What was it about a woman—a certain kind of woman— standing at the mercy of men—righteous, civic-minded men, with the moral force of public outrage on their side—that could sometimes be secretly, shamefacedly titillating? He thought of the hypocritical justices from England's less than glorious past, men who had taken a lewd pleasure in sending women to the stake for witchcraft. Watching the pale, silent, motionless figure behind the bar, Sebastian had to admit a reluctant but definite kinship, not with their sentencing practices but with their prurient fervor.

"If the vicar were here," Vanstone spoke up, "something might be done for her. But as you know, Reverend Morrell is in Italy and not expected to return for several more weeks."

"Isn't there anyone else who can help her?"

"Help her?" The mayor chose his words carefully. "We are not an adjudicatory body—as you know, my lord," he tacked on hastily, "—and as such our task is not to find places for the indigent or the luckless who come before us. Our mandate regarding the deserving as well as the undeserving poor is simply to uphold the law."

"And what law was it Mrs. Wade broke?"

Vanstone blinked rapidly. "Beyond murdering her husband, you mean? She is indigent, she has no address—"

"Yes, but what—"

"I beg your pardon—and she is not the responsibility of St. Giles' parish, my lord. Her own village in Dorset expelled her to save the drain on their poor law allotment, and now she's here, asking to be a drain on ours. She's unemployed and unemployable; in my view she ought to have been transported after her conditional release, not dumped on the tax rolls of citizens who aren't legally responsible for her in the first place."

Captain Carnock nodded his large head several times and said, "Quite right, sir, quite right."

"We don't judge this woman," the mayor went on in more modulated tones, seeing he was carrying the day. "We only propose to remand her to the county gaol in Tavistock until the assize judges sit next month. No doubt they'll determine her appropriate residence. If it's here, we will, of course, take her into our charity house, assuming no alternatives present themselves in the interim. But for now, I think we must do our duty . . ."

Sebastian stopped listening. He'd seen something in the woman's face when Vanstone spoke of the Tavistock gaol, and he thought it was fear. No, more than fear; panic. But it was so fleeting, replaced so quickly by the blind-eyed mask, that afterward he felt confused, almost disoriented. Had he imagined that look of terror? No. All his preconceptions vanished. She'd piqued his interest before because she appeared to have only one dimension: nervelessness, emotional torpor, impassivity to the point of numbness. Now she fascinated him because—maybe—that was a lie. She had her head down again, shoulders hunched in the chary, wounded posture of self-effacement that seemed second nature to her. But he knew what he'd seen, and the quick flick of panic in her disturbing eyes somehow changed everything. He stood up.

Vanstone broke off in the middle of a sentence, gaping up at him; Carnock's mouth fell open in surprise. They thought he was leaving. "My lord," Vanstone began, but Sebastian ignored him and walked across the short space of dusty floor between the magistrates' bench and the prisoner's bar.

Mrs. Wade kept her eyes on his feet; when he was within an arm's length of her, she looked up briefly, lashes fluttering with nerves, as if she expected some affront, a curse or a slap. Otherwise she stayed still, palms pressed to the sides of her thighs. While he studied her, a faint pink flush began to bloom in her prison-pallid cheeks. At the base of her throat, above the narrow collar of her cheap dress, a fast, erratic pulse hammered. Still, despite her physical vulnerability, she managed to convey an attitude of remoteness. *You won't touch me*, her body said, *because I am untouchable.*

"What were you before you went to prison, Mrs. Wade?"

She hid her confusion by keeping her eyes on his knees. "I was . . . a girl. That is, I had finished my studies and I—was living with my family. I was . . ." She drew a shaky breath. "My lord, I don't quite know what you mean."

"Quite" sounded extravagant on her lips; until now she'd limited her short, declarative sentences to nouns and verbs. "Were you a respectable girl?"

"My lord?"

"Were you a lady?"

Inquisitive murmuring sounded all around them. But after only a slight hesitation, and in a tone of voice that was, for once, adamant, Mrs. Wade answered, "Yes. I was."

"Yes," Sebastian agreed. He let his gaze roam over the length of her tall frame, rather enjoying her reaction, which was to stop breathing. "So. You can keep books, you say?"

"Yes, my—"

"And when you were a schoolgirl you were very bright, weren't you? Top of the class and all that? Come, Mrs. Wade, answer me."

"I—yes—I—"

"Quite. Do you think you could manage a household?" Everyone, including Mrs. Wade, stared at him in disbelief. "Mine, I'm speaking of," he clarified, turning toward his fellow magistrates but still addressing the woman. "I happen to be in urgent need of a housekeeper, my former one having retired only this week. I'd pay you whatever she earned, and naturally you'd have your room and board. It's no sinecure, I assure you; the place is in chaos—I'm having difficulty entertaining my friends." That was all true, and came out sounding perfectly rational, he thought. Strange, since his real motives for offering employment to this woman, this murderess, were murky in the extreme and would undoubtedly prove, if a light were shone on them, to be the reverse of rational. "Do you know who I am?" he thought to ask.

"Lord D'Aubrey—they told us."

"Right, and my house is Lynton Great Hall, which is unfortunately not nearly as grand as its name. You'd have your work cut out for you, as the saying goes. Well, madam, what is your answer?"

"My lord!" sputtered the mayor, coming to his feet. He had to pound on the table for order because the whispering among the spectators had become full-throated exclamations of surprise and excitement. "I beg you to reconsider this—this—perhaps hastily made offer, which I'm sure you've made in good faith, out of your kind and generous nature."

Sebastian bowed gratefully, smiling. His motives might be murky, but one thing was certain: they had nothing to do with either kindness or generosity.

"But perhaps it is a little too hasty? The woman is a convicted felon, my lord, the crime she committed a terrible one—"

"For which she paid a high price and has presumably repented. Have you repented, Mrs. Wade? Ah, she's speechless. Well, we will give her the benefit of the doubt. Tell me, Mayor, are you a proponent of the retribution theory of penal servitude, or the rehabilitation theory?"

"What? Why, I support both, to some extent. I suppose you would say a judicious mix of the two."

"Yes, very good, very diplomatic; one might say mayoral, even.

Under either theory, sir, do you think it was intended that a convict prisoner pay for her crime indefinitely, without regard to the length of the sentence she's served already?"

"Certainly not, but with respect, my lord, is that really the point?"

"No, you're quite right. The point is that Mrs. Wade wouldn't be here if she had been able to find a job after her incarceration. Would you agree with that—that she's committed no actual crime?"

Vanstone couldn't seem to answer. It was Cannock who finally said, "No, my lord, other than indigence, which is more of a condition, I suppose."

"Thank you, sir. And that being the case, you'll also agree that the remedy for her unfortunate condition is *employment*, not imprisonment. I'm as eager as anyone here—more so, I daresay—not to tax our charity allotment with the addition of aliens and undesirables. By hiring Mrs. Wade, I can save the parish the cost of supporting her in the workhouse, save the overburdened judges the trouble and expense of trying her at assize—for what we've concluded is not a crime to begin with—and offer gainful employment to a woman who we have no reason to think was not rehabilitated by our modern and enlightened criminal justice system. And I get a housekeeper in the bargain. Gentlemen, what could you possibly find objectionable in this ingenious solution?"

Mayor Vanstone found many things objectionable in it, but what they all boiled down to was an aversion to the thought of the lord of Lynton Great Hall employing a felon for his housekeeper. Since Sebastian wasn't prepared to explain that, either to himself or to Vanstone, and certainly not to the sharp-eyed spectators who were following the debate as if the future of civilized life in Wyckerley depended on it, he resorted to tyranny—the favored fallback of English aristocrats when democracy wasn't going their way. "Right, then," he said, "it's done."

Occasionally the rewards of viscountcy were extremely gratifying.

He turned back to Mrs. Wade. Rachel, her name was. She looked dazed. Now that he had her, a hundred misgivings assailed him. What if she were stupid? What if she proved incompetent? What if she murdered him in his bed?

She'd been following the exchange in a kind of frozen fascination, and the swiftness of the resolution had caught her off guard. "Oh, I say," he exclaimed, as though the thought had just occurred to him, "you haven't said whether or not you agree to my proposal, Mrs. Wade. Well?" he prompted when she couldn't seem to speak.

"A housekeeper," she said carefully, as if needing to make certain she had the exact nature of this astounding *deus ex machina* straight in her mind.

"That's it. We can put you up in the Tavistock lockup for two months, after which the assize judge will send you to the workhouse, probably for the rest of your life. Or you can come home with me and manage my household. Which do you choose?"

She didn't smile, not so much as a twitch of the lip. But a desert-dry look of appreciation flickered briefly in her eyes, and it set his mind to rest on two out of three scores: she wasn't stupid, and she wouldn't be incompetent.

"My lord," she said with appropriate solemnity, "I choose the latter."

III

THE SHORT CARRIAGE ride back to Lynton Hall was accomplished in virtual silence. Sebastian could have broken it, could have chattered all the way home if he'd cared to torment his new housekeeper. Had she not been allowed to speak in prison? It would explain why the simple utterance of words seemed to exhaust all her resources. Instead of talking to her, he watched her (not an activity calculated to set her at ease), bothered only occasionally by the strangeness, the enormity of what he'd just done. Since he couldn't justify it, he decided to put off thinking about it.

They were facing each other on opposite seats of the brougham. Once their knees bumped when the carriage swung round a curve, and Mrs. Wade shrank back as if from a sparking fireplace. To keep from meeting his eyes, she looked out the window and watched the village go by, then the newly plowed fields, then the greening oaks and alders bordering the carriageway to his house. Her one and only possession, a tapestry bag, lay on the seat by her thigh; she kept a protective hand on it at all times, seemingly out of habit. She'd been robbed in Chudleigh, he recalled. He studied her sharp, clean-edged profile, in pale relief against the dark seat cushion. Shafts of the blinding sunset struck her in the face, making her squint. She lifted her hand to shield her eyes, and he saw that the nails were short and broken, the palm calloused. Her shabby dress had a faint stain on the bodice that looked as if it had been washed, futilely, more than once. The constable had said they'd found her in a barn, surviving on stolen apples. Impossible; it was a picture he could not make his mind form. Even with her derelict clothes and deplorable hair, she looked like someone's upper-class governess fallen on hard times. Or . . . a nun. That was it, she looked like a nun, who'd suddenly been yanked out of her dark, safe cloister and shoved into the chaos of real life.

Lynton Great Hall came into view through the carriage window. Her pale-eyed gaze sharpened and her face lost its shuttered self-consciousness. Sebastian tried to see the house through her eyes, the three E-shaped stories of weathered Dartmoor granite, mellowed to the color of honey in the waning sunlight. It wasn't particularly grand, and the interior, as Mrs. Wade would soon find out, was a minefield of domestic inconveniences. But it had a rough-and-ready elegance that he liked, as if it couldn't make up its mind whether it was a manor, a fort, or a farmhouse. Lili had ridiculed it—which had instantly enhanced his fondness for the old pile. Steyne Court, his father's estate in Rye, was much bigger, a palace compared to Lynton. Sebastian would inherit Steyne, too, one day, but in the meantime Lynton Great Hall was perfectly adequate. Especially since he didn't plan to spend much time here.

They rolled over the short, graceful bridge spanning the Wyck, not fifty yards from the west front of the house, and for a second he thought he saw pleasure on the face of his new housekeeper. But when she glanced at him and then quickly away, no hint of a smile leavened her somber features. The carriage passed under the gatehouse arch and clattered into the weedy flagstone courtyard, upsetting a flock of rooks roosting on the battlements. Sebastian jumped down and reached for the woman's hand to help her negotiate the step. She looked confused for a second; then her face cleared and she took his hand, as if remembering something old and long forgotten.

"This isn't the formal entrance—that's on the other side; we passed it in the carriage—but it's the door everyone uses," he told her, gesturing to the studded oak portal with "A.D. 1490" chiseled in the stone block overhead. Inside, one of the maids—Susan, he thought her name was—was lighting the lamps in the hall. She looked startled, as well she might; a couple of hours ago he'd left the house with one woman, and now he was back with another. She dropped a curtsy and began to turn away. "Wait," he ordered, and she halted. "It's Susan, isn't it?"

"Yes, sir." She curtsied again; she had a pretty, freckled face, and bright orange hair under her mobcap.

"Mrs. Wade, meet Susan, one of your charges. This is the new housekeeper," he informed the maid. "You'll report to her, just as you used to do with Mrs. Fruit."

A comical look of amazement came over Susan. She stared at Mrs. Wade, at Sebastian, back to Mrs. Wade. She gave a little nervous laugh, then blushed beet-red when she realized he wasn't joking.

As for the woman, it was impossible to tell what she was thinking. She might be embarrassed, and there might be a flicker of sympathy in her eyes for Susan's discomfort; but otherwise her reserve was too opaque to penetrate.

"You'll have Mrs. Fruit's old rooms on this floor," Sebastian said shortly, suddenly out of patience with her unvarying reticence. "You'll dine with me tonight, and we'll discuss your duties. I keep country hours here—dinner's at six. Please be punctual. Susan, show Mrs. Wade to her quarters." Not waiting for an answer, he left the two women standing in the hall and went off to get a drink.

By six o'clock, he'd consumed enough rye whiskey to restore his good humor. He was hungry, and his French cook, whom he had brought down from the London house, had made spiced prawns, quails stuffed with cranberries and truffles, and a fillet of beef. Sebastian took his seat at the dining-room table, waved away the footman and poured his own glass of wine, and sipped it thoughtfully while he waited for his housekeeper.

By six-ten, she hadn't come. A bad beginning. He rang for a servant. Susan appeared, and he told her to go and fetch Mrs. Wade. She returned in five minutes with a message that Mrs. Wade was just coming. Sebastian grunted and drank more wine. Ten more minutes passed. He threw his napkin on his empty plate and stood up.

Her rooms were in the far corner of the east wing, near the library and the musty, unused chapel. It was a long way, but there were only two turns; she couldn't have gotten lost. Was she primping? Vanity was the last vice he'd have accused Mrs. Wade of possessing. No one had lit candles in the long, windowless corridor. He was mentally cursing the incompetence of his staff and his own unexplainable impetuousness in hiring an incompetent housekeeper—when a soft sound halted him in his tracks.

In her colorless dress, she was only a blur against the dark gray of the wall to which she seemed to be clinging. He went toward her until he was close enough to touch her. Close enough to smell the fresh scent of soap and water on her skin. "What's wrong? Are you ill?"

"No, my lord, no, truly, I'm not ill." She spoke quickly, fearfully; if she were ill, she would lose her new "place."

"What, then?"

"Nothing, only a—a weakness; and it was just for a moment. Now I'm all right."

"Oh, I can see that." He could see very little, but there was enough light to make out the faint line of perspiration over her top lip. "How long were you in the lockup before your hearing today, Mrs. Wade?"

"A day. And a night."

"Did they feed you?"

A pause. "Yes."

"Mm. Something more than pilfered apples, I hope." She was incapable of smiling, or of acknowledging his jest in any way. "Permit me," he murmured, sliding his arm around her waist. If she'd been stronger, he was sure she'd have stiffened; but as it was she could only bear the intimate contact with a wan, speechless dignity. They began to move slowly down the hall, back the way he'd come. She kept her hand at her side, and sometimes he felt it brush against his thigh. She was tall, but so slim he could have gotten his arm around two of her. She felt a little boneless by the time they reached the main corridor; he stopped under the lighted sconce and looked down at her, keeping her in the crook of his arm. "Not going to faint on me, are you, Mrs. Wade?"

"Oh, no." But her face looked pearly white in the candlelight, and she'd gone so far as to let her temple rest lightly on the shoulder of his coat. They stood still for a period of two full minutes. "I'm all right now," she said positively at its conclusion, pulling away from him to prove it.

She looked a bit better, not quite so ghostly. He offered his arm; she took it, and they made a slow, stately procession to the dining room without further delays.

He sat her at his right so he could keep an eye on her—or catch her if she started to slide under the table. As each course was served, she stared at it for a moment, as though assuring herself it was really food, and then consumed minute bites with great care. The fillet was tough. Without asking, Sebastian took her plate from her, cut the meat into small pieces, and handed it back. "Thank you," she murmured, disconcerted. He kept topping her wineglass, but she barely touched it; she scrutinized it as she had the food, holding the glass in front of the candle, taking an occasional sip, inhaling the bouquet. She kept her eyes down, so he could only imagine what she was thinking. The less she revealed, the more he wanted to know about her.

By meal's end, she was a new woman. Her cheeks had natural color, and her lips weren't set in the straight, grim line; she'd even relaxed enough to let her shoulders sink against the back of her chair. Studying her over his glass, Sebastian smiled to himself, thinking she had a little of the look of a woman after sex: tired but satisfied.

"We'll have that in the drawing room," he informed a maid who came with the coffeepot on a tray. "Mrs. Wade?" Wordless, they walked together out of the dining room into the hall. All her movements and gestures were scaled down, designed to attract the least amount of attention. It was self-deprecation refined to an art form. He thought of nuns again. Silent as a cool draft, Mrs. Wade glided rather than walked, the movement of her legs barely discernible. As if the goal were to go from point A to point B without disturbing the air.

In the drab drawing room, someone had lit a fire in the fireplace. He glanced around at the faded curtains and thin carpets, the dingy, outdated furniture. Everything in the room, the whole house, needed refurbishing, but so far he hadn't been able to work up enough energy or enthusiasm for the task. The sole domestic improvement he'd commissioned was a second-floor bathroom, complete with bronze tub and gold fixtures, cast by Chevalier and shipped over from Paris. Lili had loved it.

The new housekeeper was standing with her head bowed, hands folded at her waist, evidently waiting for him to sit down first.

"Mrs. Wade, you have an extremely annoying mannerism. You won't look at me, even when I'm speaking to you. How did you come by it, and how do you propose to get rid of it?"

She was stunned. In her agitation, she looked away—then quickly back, remembering herself. "I beg your pardon," she blurted, blinking fast, keeping her silver eyes wide on him with an obvious effort. "I didn't intend any disrespect. I believe it's a—a habit, my lord, nothing more."

"A habit."

"Yes. Acquired in prison. We—were not allowed to look at the wardens, my lord. Or indeed, at each other. It was against the rules."

He could hardly believe it. "Why?" he demanded, irrationally angry with her.

Some emotion clouded her luminous eyes for a second, then disappeared. "Because—because—I don't know why! It was part of the punishment."

They looked at each other in mutual wonder and disgust, and for those few seconds, Sebastian saw her as a person, an equal, not just a woman he was planning to seduce.

Then the maid came in with the coffee. He told Mrs. Wade to sit down on the sofa in front of the fireplace, and she obeyed with a soft-spoken, "Yes, my lord." He couldn't imagine her issuing orders to anyone, but that was her lookout now. He sat beside her, angling his body to face her. She sipped her coffee the way she'd drunk her wine: experimentally, as if she weren't quite sure what it was. Out of the silence he heard himself ask, "What was it like in prison?" It wasn't at all what he'd meant to say.

Her face turned haggard while he watched. She looked old again. Her mouth worked, but she couldn't get any words out. Finally she bowed her head, defeated.

As if he'd never asked the question, he began to tell her about her housekeeping duties. There were twelve indoor servants, he thought, more or less, and they would all answer to her. He wasn't fanatically neat, he wasn't interested in military order; he just wanted things to run smoothly, preferably invisibly, with the least amount of effort from him. "I expect I'll be away a good deal. There's a bailiff who manages the estate in my absence, a man named William Holyoake. You'll meet him tomorrow.

"As for your wages, I'll have to check to see what Mrs. Fruit earned. I'm sure it was adequate, but in any case I'll pay you what you're worth." She listened with grave attention, nodding in the right places. "Have you anything else to wear besides that dress?"

"No, my lord." She smoothed her hands over the wrinkled folds of her skirt self-consciously. "This is what they gave me on my release."

"Well, it won't do."

"No," she agreed. "I'm good at stitchery, I could make something else as soon as I've earned—"

"Go to the village tomorrow. There's a shop that sells a few things ready-made. The gowns aren't much, but they're better than that. Get one."

"Yes, my lord."

He smiled dryly. He could have said, "Get your skin flayed while you're there," and in all likelihood she'd have dipped her head and said, "Yes, my lord." She was in his power, a virtual slave. The situation was unquestionably provocative, but it ought to have been more so, more stimulating. He hadn't really gotten to her yet. She simply didn't care enough.

"You're tired," he said solicitously. "We'll speak again, but now I'll take you back to your room." Mild words, innocent of implication. But she colored, rising slowly, as if summoned to a punishment, and the glance she sent him was a study in resigned unsurprise. He hadn't planned to do anything with her tonight, but her blasted fatalism was insulting. She seemed to have come to an extremely cynical understanding of his intentions. Come to it, in fact, even before *he* had. Fine; he would try not to disappoint her.

He'd never been in the housekeeper's rooms. Mrs. Wade lit the candle on the mantelpiece, and by its light he was glad to see that, although they were small, the rooms were clean and comfortable. The sitting room had a desk in front of a window overlooking the courtyard, a table with two chairs, and an armchair in front of the cold stone hearth. The bedroom beyond was even smaller, and unremarkable from what he could see through the low doorway. Mrs. Wade had no visible possessions; whatever had been in her tapestry bag had been put away, out of sight.

She was standing by the mantel, watching him. He tried to imagine her in a prison cell. Locked up in it day after day, night after night. Ten years of her young life in a cell as small as this room. No, smaller. Not allowed to look at anyone. Not allowed to *look* at anyone.

When he went toward her, she didn't drop her eyes, even when he drew close. But her nostrils flared when he lifted his hand and brought it to the side of her head. Her dark brown hair was silky, much softer than it looked. He sleeked his fingers into it, above her ear, watching the candlelight play over the silver strands. "I don't like your hair in this style," he murmured. "Don't cut it again." She gave a slight nod, but he thought he saw bitterness in her eyes, or humor, maybe both. "What?" he demanded softly. "Tell me what you're thinking."

"Just that—my hair is longer now than it's been in ten years. This is . . . luxuriant." Her lips twisted with irony; she was making fun of herself.

"Have you always had the gray?"

"Not always."

"Only since prison," he guessed.

She nodded again. "There's less now than before. It . . . seems to be fading."

"Good. You're too young for gray hair."

Because of her reserve, touching her seemed a daring encroachment, almost like the breaking of a taboo. But wasn't that what made her irresistible? The top of her ear peeked through the hair, pale pink and delicate, nearly transparent. He followed the dainty curve with his fingertip, pressing against its springy coolness. The hollow behind her ear was warmer, much softer. Her body shook slightly with every heartbeat. Otherwise she didn't move, not even when he slipped his fingers inside the high collar of her dress, soothing the overheated skin there lightly. "Look at me." She turned her head, and with the movement her throat brushed the back of his hand.

The look in her opal-colored eyes stopped his slow caress. Cooled his ardor. Nothing he could do, the look said, no matter how callous or capricious, could touch her.

Good; then they understood each other. Her attitude was hardly flattering, though. He admired her stoicism, but not when it was directed at him.

He let his hand fall away and stepped back. "Sleep well, Mrs. Wade. We'll speak again in the morning."

"Good night, my lord." As expert as she was at hiding her feelings, she couldn't disguise her relief. He would enjoy making her pay for it.

A faraway bell was tolling midnight. The church bell in the village, she supposed. The lingering, deep-throated peals were soothing and sad, the very sound of loneliness. Time passed slowly, was the message in the bell's leisurely pace. But time in the world and time in a convict prison were not even in the same dimension. And the church bell's lonely knell was infinitely preferable to the cruel shriek of a prison bell, whose dreadful note was the tonal embodiment of everything brutal and despairing.

Throwing off the covers, Rachel rose and sat on the edge of her bed. Her bare feet looked strange on a carpet. She burrowed her toes in, testing the softness. The mattress was *too* soft, as if a mistake had been made. The air was indescribably sweet; she'd left the window open, even though the night was chilly, so she could smell the air. Last night, she'd sat on the brick floor in the

Tavistock lockup, a nine-foot-square cell, airless and lightless. A pailful of filth in the corner, left by the previous occupant, had kept her company all night.

She fumbled with matches on her bedside table and lit the candle in the brass holder. The little thrill in her chest at this elementary but powerful act—controlling light and darkness in her own room—would probably fade soon, like her awareness that the bed was too soft. How quickly one could adjust to the unspeakable luxuries of freedom.

She put her hand on her stomach, which felt queasy. She hadn't eaten much for dinner, scarcely touched any wine, but the food had been so rich, it had made her nauseated. And afterward she'd drunk coffee. Real coffee, the taste so powerful and exotic she'd only been able to take a few sips.

Barefooted, she got up and carried the candle into the sitting room. Just to look at it again. There was a desk with a chair, and a shelf next to it with a place for books. An oil lamp on the table, and a wooden bowl for flowers, or maybe fruit. Her own window to open or close, just as she pleased, any time she liked. And a *fireplace*, with a soft chair, an upholstered chair, to sit in before it—those were the best things. No, the desk and the window were the best. Or was it the bowl for flowers? Something else she couldn't decide.

Deciding things was going to be a problem, she already knew that. The day they'd let her out of Dartmoor, she'd wished the wardress had come along to shout at her, "Walk to the station in Princetown, Forty-four! Watch out for your belongings! Buy your ticket! Get on the train, Forty-four, and no looking about you!" The simplest choices could still freeze her in place, petrify her with fear of the potentially drastic ramifications of every innocent act. In Ottery St. Mary, before the constable took her up, she had stayed for two nights at Mrs. Peavey's guest house. But she'd lurked outside in the wet street for hours first, uncertain of what to say to the landlady when she met her, how to get a room, how much to pay. And most of all, terrified that Mrs. Peavey would recognize her. She hadn't, of course; the name Rachel Wade meant nothing to her. She'd known a Rachel Crenshaw years ago, but that girl could never be the strange, furtive, haggard woman who couldn't even look her in the eye when she asked for a room.

She ought to try to sleep; tomorrow she'd have to be sharp and clever if she were to have any chance at all of keeping her new job. If Sebastian Verlaine had any notion of how profoundly unfit she was for the position he had inexplicably given her, he would . . . what? How could he *not* know? He must know. Then why had he hired her? Lord D'Aubrey was an enigma, as alien to her as a creature of another species; she understood nothing about him, could predict nothing he would say or do.

Except for one thing. But that was the strangest mystery of all. Why would he want her? A man like that, handsome and rich, powerful, a refined man with sophisticated tastes—why would he want *her* in his bed? Even for one night—one hour? Why?

Her head began to ache. She took the candle back into the bedroom, set it on the bedside table. She opened the shallow drawer, inside of which everything she owned fit easily, with room to spare: a hairbrush, a piece of flannel toweling, a few items of underclothing, a packet of hairpins, a spool of black thread, and a needle. She'd bought them in a shop in Princetown before boarding the train. They had depleted her finances alarmingly, but she hadn't seen any way to avoid making the purchases, since all that had been given to her on her release was the gray dress.

No, not quite all: they'd given back the one thing she had taken with her to prison ten years ago, in the naive belief that they would let her keep it with her in her cell. But they'd confiscated it, and over the years she'd forgotten it existed. She slipped her hand beneath the clothes in the drawer and drew out a small silver picture frame. The photograph in the frame had become, in the last few days, an object of grim fascination to her. It was a family portrait, taken only a few months before she'd met Randolph. Her parents sat side by side, stiff as staves in their straight-backed chairs, while she and her brother stood at attention behind them, Tom with his hand on his mother's shoulder. Mother had on her best dress, the one she stored away in the cedar chest except for special occasions; looking at it, Rachel could almost smell the camphor rising from the heavy black folds. Her father had on his new spectacles—"Maybe I won't go blind yet after all," he said when he got them, always surprised and a little irritated when life didn't go as badly as he expected. He looked like a schoolmaster in the photograph, which was what he was. She remembered standing behind him, wondering if she should put her hand on his shoulder, too. But she hadn't, because she didn't think he would like it.

And Tom—she'd forgotten how handsome he was, how much he looked like their mother. Everyone in the family had blue eyes, but Tom's were the bluest, his hair the blackest. She'd been tall at eighteen, but he towered over her, and he looked down his nose at the camera with all the arrogance of a healthy, handsome, twenty-year-old man with his future ahead of him.

Once, in the first year, they'd come to see her in prison. But it was too hard, the conditions for visiting too painful and barbaric; none of them could bear it. She'd asked them not to come again, and they hadn't argued with her.

Now they were all gone. Her parents had died eight years ago, first her father and then her mother, within four months of each other. Tom had emigrated to Canada, to escape the scandal and start a new life. She'd gotten prison-censored Christmas notes from him for the first few years, then nothing. The message that he wanted to forget her couldn't have been clearer.

Sometimes she put her finger over her own face when she

looked at the photograph, so she could see the others without being distracted. Distressed. Tonight, though, she wanted to look at herself. As always, her first impression of the small, sepia-colored image shocked her. *Not me; oh, no, she can't be me.* The girl, the stranger in the picture was a happy child on the brink of womanhood, smiling into the camera with artless self-confidence. An ingénue. She wore her hair in thick, shiny coils on top of her head in an elaborate, grown-up style that didn't really become her—but she'd been vain about her hair, her "crowning glory," as someone had once foolishly told her, and, of course, she'd never forgotten it. Her face, under the stiffness she'd had to maintain so the picture wouldn't blur, had a mesmerizing optimism bordering on complaisance. A pretty, blank, untried face. Rachel wanted to weep for that girl's innocence, her heartbreaking ignorance of what lay in store for her.

She replaced the photograph and closed the drawer. "I don't like your hair in this style," Lord D'Aubrey had said. "Don't cut it again." She touched the short, graceless locks, remembering the way he had touched them. (*Why* had he done that?) Of all the indignities she'd borne on entering prison, including the surrender of all her belongings, the assignment of a number, the degrading "medical examination"—the most horrible affront to the person of young Rachel Wade had been the cutting off of all her hair. All: the matron had laid the scissors flat on her head and cut away until there was nothing left. She'd managed not to cry until then, but when she'd put her hand to her head and felt the short, bristly fuzz on her cold scalp, she'd finally broken down. They hadn't scolded her for it—apparently it wasn't an uncommon reaction. Over the years, her prison crop had been allowed to lengthen a little, and six months before her scheduled release they'd stopped cutting it at all. Lord D'Aubrey might despise it, but to Rachel it truly was "luxuriant."

When she blew out her candle, the smoky smell of burnt wick

stung her nostrils. A good smell. She lay down, covering herself with sheet, blanket, and crochet coverlet. Three layers of warmth: what decadence. And her head lay on a real pillow, not her own folded clothes. No one was watching her through a sliding grate beside the door. No one would jolt her awake in the night with pitiful weeping or terrible screams.

But she would never fall asleep on this absurd mattress, which felt more like a cloud than a bed. It was ridiculous, really, a luxury carried to a foolish extreme.

The church bell began to toll the half hour. She was dreaming before the last note died away.

IV

SHE AWOKE AT five, as she always did, but today no clanging bell jarred her from her sleep. She simply woke up, gently and naturally, in the soft, silent pitch dark. What time did the D'Aubrey household rise? She should have asked last night. She listened for the sound of servants stirring, but there wasn't so much as a rustle; it was as if Lynton Hall lay under a thick blanket of snow.

When she woke up next, birds were chirping and bright light was streaming in through the gap in the blue curtains at her window. She jolted out of bed, electrified with panic. What time was it? She had no clock, no watch. She threw her clothes on with a pounding heart, dry-mouthed, hands fumbling and clumsy. She was late, they would—they would—

She rested her forehead against the doorpost, wiping her damp hands on her skirt. They wouldn't do anything. She wouldn't lose a mark on her record; no precious hour would be added to her sentence because of idling and sloth. She was all right. She was the new housekeeper.

Just then the church bell tolled, and she went limp with relief. Six; it was only six. Oh, thank God.

Her wing of the house was silent; no one else slept here. She walked along the stone floor of the hallway she'd barely noticed last night, peering through dark doorways at musty-smelling rooms whose functions weren't always discernible. In the L where her wing joined the main part of the house, there was a chapel, a small stone edifice, very cold, with dirty stained-glass windows. Next she passed an archway, beyond which steps led up and down from a stone landing. Servants' stairs; one set must lead to the basement. Was that where she would find the kitchen? No doubt. But she wanted to explore a little first, see what else was on this level.

When she turned the corner, the floor changed from stone to wood; this part of the house must be newer. She passed the dining room, and glanced in to see what it was like—last night she hadn't been able to take it in. It was large and formal, high-ceilinged, with chairs at the gleaming table for thirty or forty people. But in the harsh morning light the room looked tired and worn, a bit dingy. Right, then: one of her jobs would be to perk it up, give it some shine. She was good at that. Hadn't she polished the slate landing in front of her cell door on her hands and knees every morning for the last decade?

Reading room, sewing room, billiard room, morning room. And drawing rooms, drawing rooms—there must be half a dozen on this floor alone, including the one Lord D'Aubrey had taken her to last night. And a great hall, larger than her father's whole house, with high, smoky rafters and an enormous fireplace, stags' heads and antlers on the walls, muskets and rifles, swords, pikestaffs, shields, lances. That was in addition to the gun room, an oppressively masculine lair with more firearms and dead wildlife decorating the dark paneling. All the northwest-facing rooms, no matter how faded or old-fashioned, had a spectacular saving grace: their view of the little Wyck, sparkling in the sunshine, as lively and fresh as this spring morning.

Back in her own wing, descending the worn stone steps to the basement, she heard a voice coming from a door midway down the narrow corridor. Her steps slowed as she drew closer. She could hear several voices now, men's as well as women's, and the sound of cutlery. The servants' hall, then. They were having breakfast.

She stopped dead, clutching at her skirts. How could she

just—walk in? What would she say first? Maybe one of them would speak first. A knot in her stomach began to ache. She'd say her name, tell them she was the new housekeeper. *Hello*—no—*Good morning. I'm Rachel*—no—*I'm Mrs. Wade. I'm the new housekeeper.* After that . . . she couldn't imagine anything after that. Things would just happen, it would unfold naturally. Other people would talk, she would answer. She would look them in the eye and do what she had been forbidden to do for the last ten years: speak.

She brushed at her wrinkled skirts, smoothed her hair, straightened her spine. The knot had ascended to her throat, but she ignored it. Now or never. Taking a deep breath, she made herself march into the servants' hall.

There were too many of them. Someone's sentence broke off in the middle of a word and silence fell over the room. She took in a table, scrubbed oak, chairs all around it, only half occupied, but—*so many people.* And their faces staring, turning, gaping, eyes, eyes, looking her in the face, looking her up and down. She saw them all and kept looking, engaging all the eyes, because if she looked away, if she hunched her shoulders and made herself invisible, she would fail at this post and lose her only chance at saving herself. So she looked back at them, even though their wide, curious gazes felt like pinpricks all over her skin. But she could not, simply could not speak.

The silence lengthened, became absurd. And then someone laughed—a woman, with a high-pitched giggle, nervous and mean. Rachel made herself look at her. She was young, twenty or so, dark-haired, with small brown eyes in a pointed face. Beside her, a boy in the rough clothes of a stable lad began to snicker. Over the laughter, her voice quavered humiliatingly. "Good morning. I'm Rachel—I'm—Mrs. Wade. The new housekeeper."

The sharp-featured woman muffled more laughter into a glass of milk, like a schoolgirl, only the sound was nasty, not mischievous. Still no one spoke. At last, at last, the maid named Susan—the one who had taken her to her room last night, curtsied to her and said, "Yes, ma'am," and "Very good, ma'am,"—stood up at the table and blurted out, "Good morning, Mrs. Wade. I expect you'll want to sit here, since it's where Mrs. Fruit always sits. Used to sit, I mean. It's only porridge today, Cook's in a bad—um—not feeling too brave, he says. Clara, would you fetch Mrs. Wade a bowl an' spoon, an' a mug for 'er cocoa? Or there's tea, ma'am, if you'd rather." By now her freckled face was bright red, and her eyes were darting around the table, desperate for an ally. So: coming to the rescue of hapless, hopeless wretches was a risk for Susan, not an everyday thing.

Once, in prison, Rachel had been ill enough with bronchitis to be sent to the infirmary, and one of the matrons had patted her on the back and spoken softly to her during one long, bad night. The unheard-of kindness had devastated her; she'd broken down and sobbed into her pillow, overwhelmed with gratitude. She felt that way now, and had to grit her teeth to keep the emotion out of her face.

She took the seat Susan pointed to; it was at the head of the table. Clara, a plump, yellow-haired child no more than fourteen, brought her a bowl, and Susan plopped a great spoonful of porridge into it herself. Someone passed Rachel a pitcher of cocoa. She poured some into a mug and pretended to sip it; but her mouth was as dry as ashes, she was afraid she would gag if she swallowed anything.

Susan began to say the names of the people at the table. This one was Janet Barnet, she helped in the laundry; this was Bessie Slater, she was a kitchen maid; this was Jerny, he cleaned boots and ran errands. The words and faces blurred; Rachel couldn't have put the right name to a single soul afterward. Except Violet, the sharp-faced woman with the ugly laugh. Violet Cocker. She was a housemaid.

Somehow breakfast ended, and then the thing Rachel had been dreading happened: someone asked her what chores they should do today. She fingered her mug, twisting it in slow circles on the table. "What"—she had to clear her throat—"What do you usually do?"

Her voice came out absurdly tentative; she couldn't even blame Violet when she snickered and said, "Well, *you're* the housekeeper, don't you know?" Susan started to speak, but Violet interrupted. "Maybe you'd like us to pick some oakum, ma'am? Or take a turn on the treadmill?"

Someone gasped; someone stifled a giggle. "Violet!" cried Susan in a mortified whisper.

Rachel felt her face burning. No words came; she couldn't seem to move, react. She kept her blind eyes on the mug in her hand, turning it in small increments, round and round on the worn oak table.

"Go about your business, Violet," said a voice from behind her. Rachel turned to see a man in the doorway, a huge man, with shoulders so broad they nearly touched the posts on either side of the threshold. "Go on, get to yer chores. You know what they are right enough."

Smirking, Violet finished her milk, dawdling over it as long as she dared before getting up and flouncing out of the room. The others followed, nobody speaking, and in a few minutes the hall was empty except for Rachel and the man in the doorway.

She stood up. "Mr. Holyoake?" she guessed quietly.

"Aye, I'm William Holyoake. You're Mrs. Wade. Will you come wi' me, please?"

She followed him out into the corridor, past several open doors to a closed one. He opened it and stood back to let her go in before him, and she found herself in a small sitting room much like her own. "You can sit down," he invited awkwardly, and she took a seat in the straight chair beside his desk. He removed a

key from his coat pocket and opened the kneehole drawer in his
desk. "Expect you'll be needin' these," he said, putting a large set
of keys in the scoop of her cupped palms, scowling a little. He
had doubts about the wisdom of this transfer, the scowl said, but
he knew his place well enough not to mention them.

"Thank you." The keys were heavy, like the responsibility that
went with them. She could have told William Holyoake his misgivings were no graver than her own, and completely justified.
He sat on the edge of his desk and folded his arms, his powerful
legs stuck out before him and taking up most of the floor space.
He was dressed for outdoor work, and rather roughly, she
thought, for the agent of an estate as grand as Lynton. He wasn't
a handsome man; his broad, strong, fleshy face might even have
been called ugly. But something in his aspect was appealing, perhaps the intelligence in his mild blue eyes, or the bluff honesty
in his features. She listened as he took the keys back and told her
slowly and carefully what door each one opened. "Either me or
one o' the maids, Susan most like, will take you round the house
an' show you all the rooms an' what-not. I can't now, I've sommat
t' do away from here, but mayhap later in the day."

She thanked him again. They sat without speaking for a few
uncomfortable moments before she ventured to say, "Mr.
Holyoake, I am new at my post, which would be clear to anyone,
I'm sure, even if—even—" She stopped, tangled up in the sentence. "You must know how I've come to be here," she tried
again. "That is, how it came about that Lord D'Aubrey offered
me employment."

He nodded his big head slowly. "I've heard."

"Yes." She imagined the whole parish would hear soon
enough. "And so, it won't surprise you to know that I'm not—I
haven't the least—that is, I . . ."

"You don't know what to do."

She nodded, relieved that it was out. He didn't say anything more, though, so she struggled on. "I can guess what many of the tasks must be, the cleaning and tidying and so on, which would be common to any household. But I don't know quite where to begin, what's to be done first, what his lordship is particular about, and—so on." How *exhausting* this communicating coherent thoughts was.

Another long silence, while Mr. Holyoake seemed to be gathering his own thoughts. He rubbed the top of his head, which was covered with short, sandy curls, as if trying to stimulate his brain. Then he proceeded to tell her what to do.

She was right: most of it was common sense, the things one would do in any house, only on a much larger scale. But it helped just to hear the duties enumerated, learn what was most important in this house and what less so. Susan, Violet, and another girl called Tess were the housemaids, and they did most of the general cleaning. They traded off as parlormaid when there was a need for it, which there wasn't much, his lordship being new to the neighborhood and not having many callers yet. He had a valet, Mr. Preest, who took care of his clothes and personal effects, and also supervised the cleaning of his bedroom and bathroom, about which his lordship was very particular. After his room, the maids started on the first floor with their sweeping, polishing, and dusting. Mr. Holyoake screwed up his face, thinking hard; this wasn't really his bailiwick. The char girl laid the fires and cleaned the grates first thing every morning, he knew that. The cook, a Frenchy fellow called Monsieur Judelet, told the kitchen and scullery maids what to do, and if Mrs. Wade was smart she'd stay out of his way, him not having what you'd call an even temper.

"Is there a butler?"

"No, ma'am, and never has been, I can't say why. Mrs. Fruit ran things for as long as I've been alive, and she done a good enough job until she went deaf. After that, the house begun to run itself, you might say, leastwise after a fashion. That's why Violet was insolent before; she bain't used to taking orders. But she's a slothful, rude girl, and so are some o' the others. They need guidance," he summed up with force, looking at her dubiously.

She shared his skepticism. For reasons known only to Lord D'Aubrey, she had become the head of a large and complex domestic staff, and she was almost pathologically unfit for the post. Any one of her new charges was better qualified than she, including the footboy who cleaned the lamps and washed bottles.

And if she failed, she would lose much more than a job. She'd made a decision two nights ago in the Tavistock lockup, and nothing had happened since then to change her mind. If they tried to put her in prison again, she would find a way to take her life.

Sebastian spurred his sorrel stallion along the bias of a soft, fertile field, still unplowed, and listened to the meadow pipits and skylarks singing in the hedges, greeting the burgeoning spring all around. The beauty of the morning had tempted him almost to the edge of Dartmoor; he didn't turn back until he heard the croak of ravens in the tors, the gleaming rock summits dazzling bone-white in the sunny distance. It was the first time he'd been out riding on his own since before Lili's visit. She'd never let him out of her sight, not being the kind of person who got along well on her own resources. Come to think of it, Lili didn't have any resources.

The cattle had recently been freed from their winter cowsheds and let out to graze in the new green pastures, and the novelty hadn't worn off yet: full grown dairy cows cavorted like calves in the fragrant fields, with udders so milk-heavy they almost dragged the ground. Flocks of shaggy, raddle-daubed sheep followed along after them, cleaning up the meadows in their boisterous wake. In an expansive mood, Sebastian stopped on his way to speak to a passing shepherd or farm laborer, introducing himself and exchanging the time of day. To a man, his tenants were respectful but not obsequious, and definitely more curious about than awed by him. Beneath the courtesy, he sensed a reservation of judgment, a wait-and-see caution he attributed to the relative incompetence of his two predecessors, cousin Geoffrey and his father, Edward Verlaine—that and whatever reputation he himself came with, which was undoubtedly a cause of grave concern to these simple souls.

"Simple souls"—it had a patronizing ring, didn't it? It or something like it was how Sebastian and his friends usually spoke of the lower classes, particularly rural working folk. But the condescension in the phrase had never struck him until now.

South of Wyckerley, at the point where the village main street crossed the Tavistock road, he met his bailiff. Holyoake was mounted on a short-legged gray cob, as strong and honest-looking as he was. He said good morning, tipping his dented felt hat.

"Where are you bound for, William?"

"I'm for Swan's smithy, m'lord, to tell 'im o' the harrower we spoke of orderin'."

"Well, ride home with me a ways first, will you? I've something to ask you."

Holyoake nodded and turned his horse, and the two men began to tread the red, narrow, leafy lane to Lynton Hall at a comfortable pace. "Are you a Devon man, William?" Sebastian opened, reaching up to rub his stallion between the ears.

"I am, sir. My father was the bailey at Lynton before me."

"Was he? I didn't know that. So you've lived all your life in Wyckerley, have you?"

"Never been east of Exeter nor west o' the Tamar, and no farther south than Plymouth." He sounded proud of it, as if his insularity made him a better man than one who chose to go traipsing all over the globe. Which it may have done, for all Sebastian knew.

"William, I've hired a new housekeeper," he said after a pause.

"I made 'er acquaintance this morning, sir."

"Did you? And what did you make of her?"

"My lord?"

"How did she strike you? Will she do? Ought we to cover our backs when she's about?"

Holyoake looked unamused by his levity. "I should think she'll do all right after she gets 'er feet wet, so to say. At the present, she's very raw, m'lord."

He meant "new," but Sebastian thought she was raw in another way as well: she was tender, as unprotected as a fresh wound. "I've heard that she murdered her husband," he mentioned.

Holyoake grunted. "Aye, it's what they do say."

"Was Wade a local man?"

" 'E had a big house betwixt Wyckerley an' Tavistock, m'lord."

"How did he make his living?"

"I couldn't say as to the particulars o' that, except he had mining interests here and about, and I b'lieve he had other businesses as well. In general, 'e were a businessman. Him and the mayor might've had some dealings together."

Sebastian thought that over. "He must have been a good deal older than his wife when he married her."

"Hmm, ha," said William, signifying assent.

"Must've been quite a scandal when he was murdered."

William said nothing.

"How was he killed?"

" 'E were bludgeoned to death wi' a poker."

Sebastian swore softly, staring at Holyoake in shock.

"Aye, you could say that. It were a right panjamble, m'lord."

"Did she confess? Was there no question that she did it?"

"Oh, there were a question. And she never confessed." He was silent for a while, then added with obvious reluctance, "They'd've hung 'er if it hadn't of been fer the circumstances."

"What circumstances?"

Holyoake had a habit of pressing his lips together in a tight smile when he was thinking hard, or undecided, or uncomfortable. At the moment, he appeared to be all three. "They was only married about a week, as I recollect. He had a daughter who was Mrs. Wade's school chum. Lydia, her name is; she bides in Wyckerley now wi' her aunt, a widow lady named Mrs. Armstrong."

Bloody hell, thought Sebastian. Not only had he hired a convicted murderess, but her victim's family lived here in the village. Why hadn't Vanstone told him?

"At the trial," Holyoake resumed slowly, each word sounding more unwilling than the last, "it come out that Mr. Wade had certain, ah, peculiarities."

"Peculiarities?"

"Propensities. Of an unnatural nature. He weren't altogether normal-like in 'is sexual partialities, you might say. That and her being only eighteen is what made 'em let 'er off wi' penal servitude instead o' hanging. Or so it were said. And that's all I do know o't, m'lord."

And that's all he would say. At the river bridge, he turned his sturdy cob around and began to plod back toward the village. Sebastian had planned to ride to Tavistock this afternoon, to see what amusements the town had to offer. Instead he stayed home, and spent the rest of the day thinking about his new housekeeper.

V

THE LONDON SEASON began in earnest during the second week after Easter. By now, all of Sebastian's social acquaintance would be swept up in the annual storm of galas, court balls, concerts, and horse races. When he was in England, he never missed it, not because he found the frivolous whirl especially enjoyable anymore, but because there was nothing else to do.

This year, surprising himself, he didn't go. *I'll take the train up on Wednesday*, he would plan; and then, when the departure date came and went, *I'll go on Friday*. But something always came up, or he was too preoccupied, or he'd forget to tell Preest to pack. April turned into May, and without ever making a deliberate choice, Sebastian remained in the country.

For what? Sheep-dyeing and barley-sowing, orchard-pruning and field-manuring. No one who knew him would have credited it, but the process of farming was actually beginning to interest him. He wanted to observe the full cycle at least one time, witness causes and effects—planting and harvesting—maybe test his own resources against nature's. That was as close as he could come to defining the quality of his fascination with the lush Devonshire countryside in this spring of 1856. The novelty of landownership probably played a part, as well as the completely new experience of being the one to whom others looked for guidance, looked, in fact, for their very livelihoods. He could have been sitting on his bench in the House of Lords, looking at pictures in the Royal Academy, gambling at Strouds's, or taking his pleasure with the ladies at Ascot—or the girls at Mrs. Fielding's. Instead he rode his horse over his twenty thousand acres of field, pasture, orchard, and forest, meeting his tenants and measuring his hay crop; and at night he perused seed catalogs and books on wool marketing and ram sperm.

Captain Carnock was a gentleman farmer when he wasn't being a magistrate. Sebastian invited him to dinner and picked his brain on the minutiae of corn pricing, dairy improvements, and tenant cottage construction. But his true mentor was William Holyoake. There was very little about estate management the taciturn bailiff didn't know, and he was infinitely more willing to share that expertise than to gossip about ten-year-old neighborhood scandals. They spent hours in conversation together, and Sebastian couldn't deny that it was warming to see William's estimation of him go up a little, day by day. The bailiff hadn't thought much of him when they'd first met. Not that he'd ever said anything; no, he hadn't raised so much as a disrespectful eyebrow. But Sebastian knew. What he didn't know was why Holyoake's good opinion of him mattered one way or the other. But it did.

The other reason he stayed in the country was because he hadn't seduced Mrs. Wade yet. Hadn't had the chance. She glided around the house like a ghost, never seeming to speak—although she must, to *someone* if not to him, because his household was running smooth as a top with precious little help from him. Precisely the state of affairs he'd been hoping for when he'd hired her. But she was a slippery fish and she had a pure genius for avoiding him; he had to be quick just to catch a glimpse of her these days. So he'd recently contrived an ingenious ritual, ostensibly to keep up with domestic affairs: he made her come into his study every morning at nine o'clock and "report" to him on matters about which he couldn't have cared less—tradesmen's bills, menus, spring cleaning, the hiring of a new laundry maid.

At first he enjoyed making her stand while he lounged at ease behind his big desk. Why? Because that master-servant simulation had piquant sexual overtones he found stimulating. But after a day or two, he started inviting her to sit, because then he got to keep her longer, and their brief conversations could more naturally blend and merge into subjects unrelated to housekeeping.

She'd obeyed his command and bought a new dress. It was black, anything but stylish, obviously cheap; still, it was a huge improvement over the old one. Beauty wasn't what had attracted him to Mrs. Wade and made him hire her that day in the town hall, but here she was, looking . . . if not beautiful, then striking in her plain wool gown, high-necked and tight-sleeved, with a dainty white apron he'd have called coy on another kind of woman. After a few days of seeing her in her new dress, he'd told her he liked it but he didn't want to see it all the time. Get another one, get two more, he instructed, and this time defy housekeeper tradition and don't get black. Anything but black. The next day she appeared in his study wearing her second new dress: brown. Dark brown. But, strangely enough, it suited her, looked almost pretty on her, probably because it matched her hair, and so he hadn't complained.

She was by no means blooming, and yet she had come a long way from the silent, downcast spectre at the magistrates' hearing. She must be eating better; she'd lost her alarming pallor and even some of the angularity in her figure. She always wore her hair pinned up under a cap, and the shortest strands escaped and hung about her neck in a becoming way that came close to looking youthful. But she was still solemn as the grave, spoke only when spoken to, and never, ever smiled.

Holyoake's astonishing revelations had raised Sebastian's already keen curiosity about her to a new and salacious plane. He wanted very much to know what her one-week marriage had been like, and exactly what had been the late Mr. Wade's "ah, peculiarities." He entertained himself by imagining her in lewd sexual situations, but the man in his fantasies was always himself; when he tried to put a deviant or a pervert in them with her, someone who hurt her or degraded her—someone other than himself—the fantasies evaporated, leaving him with a bad taste in the mouth.

Whenever possible, he tried to shock her out of her brittle composure. One day, in the middle of a one-sided conversation about a chimney fire in the best drawing room, he interrupted her to inquire casually, "Tell me, Mrs. Wade, did you kill your husband?"

Annoyingly, her face didn't change. Her hands tightened on the accounts ledger she always brought with her, but otherwise she didn't react. After scarcely a pause, she said, "No, my lord. But everyone in Dartmoor Prison is there by some terrible mistake; certainly I never met a guilty inmate in all the years I was there. The English penal system was built to incarcerate innocent victims—were you not aware of that?"

He didn't know which was more discomfiting, her sarcasm or her indifference to whether he believed her or not. He sent her away with a curt word. This time the one who had been shocked was himself, and he didn't like it.

He wasn't sure why he tormented Mrs. Wade, why he had numerous new torments in mind for her in the future. It wasn't his usual style. But he'd seen a change coming in himself for a while now. Out of boredom and cynicism, he was starting to become nasty. He didn't approve of it, but in some ways he saw it as inevitable. Life, he'd decided years ago, was supremely, spectacularly pointless, and a wise man learned to deal resourcefully with that disappointing truth. Fortunately, Sebastian Verlaine had been born into wealth and comfort, two commodities that helped mitigate pointlessness no end.

But the older he got, the less fun he was having. It took more every day to divert him, and lately he'd begun moving gradually, with misgivings, into excess. There were no vices and few depravities he hadn't tasted, with differing degrees of satisfaction. He worried that when he ran out, he would choose a few favorites and indulge in them until they killed him.

In some ways, what he saw in Rachel Wade was what he couldn't see in himself anymore. She was like some raw, naked thing, stripped down to the basics, without illusions or hope, without vanity. The fire she'd been.through had burned her clean to the bone. She knew something now; she'd learned a secret maybe *the* secret—and he had some idea that if he could *possess* her, the essence of what he lacked and she had would be his. He would appropriate it.

It made no rational sense, but he told himself it was an instinct, and instincts were allowed to defy reason.

On a rainy Thursday morning, he sat at his desk in his first-floor study, paging through his correspondence while waiting for her to join him. She had a distinctive knock; he listened unconsciously for the soft *tap tap—tap* she always used to announce herself. But the appointed time came and went, and after only a few minutes he decided not to wait; he decided to go and find her.

He went to her room first. Cold gray light from the open doorway spilled onto the stone corridor, picking out every worn place and threadbare fiber in the thin carpet that ran down the center. He paused for the barest second, then entered without knocking. The sitting room was empty, but he heard a soft noise from the bedroom. Bad manners to walk in on a lady in her bedroom. Keeping his feet quiet on the meager rug, he moved toward the bedroom door.

She was coming out—they almost collided in the threshold. She started in surprise and backed up, begging his pardon. She had her white cap in one hand, the heavy accounts ledger in the other, clutching it to her chest. "I'm sorry I'm late, my lord. I was just on my way to come to you. There was a crisis in the kitchen just now, nothing terrible, but Clara burned her hand on the stove. It's not serious, but I stayed to see that she was all right and that Susan put the salve on—" She came to a sudden halt, flushing, gathering herself.

It never failed: the more agitated she became, the calmer he felt. "Relax, Mrs. Wade," he drawled. "Being late to our morning meeting is not grounds for dismissal."

She dropped her eyes, embarrassed. She had on her brown dress today; she must alternate: black, brown, black, brown. The bodice crossed modestly over her bosom and tied at the waist in two plain, practical bows. Such a demure dress. So easy to open. Yank, yank, and there she would be, clutching her corseted breasts, red-cheeked and wide-eyed. An enticing picture altogether.

He came farther into the room, and she had no choice but to back up. An invasion of her privacy. He did it deliberately, even as he wondered what in the world it was that made him want to test her, push her, see how far he could go before she broke.

"This is pleasant," he said, pleasantly, glancing around. It wasn't the austere nun's cell it had been a few weeks ago. She'd put jars of flowers in the window and on her small night table; a few actual possessions could be seen here and there. She had a yellow flannel nightgown, folded neatly at the foot of her bed. He thought of picking it up, shaking it out, bringing it to his nose to discover what it smelled like. He resisted the impulse, but imagining her reaction made him smile.

Something on the wall over her bed caught his eye. Pictures of some sort. He walked over to investigate, intensely aware of her standing, rigid with suppressed indignation, in the doorway behind him. There were two pictures tacked to the wall with pins, both on low-grade paper, neatly cut, as if from a magazine.

One was a pen-and-ink drawing of a small, ivy-covered house, much idealized; the other was a sentimental portrait of two children, one an infant in a carriage, the other older, wearing a woman's enormous bonnet and pushing the carriage, pretending to be the mama. Sebastian stared at them in growing discomfort, realizing what they were: Mrs. Wade's attempt to decorate her little room, embellish it, give it some human warmth with the only things she had at hand—cheap representations of other people's happiness.

He backed away, embarrassed, but before he could turn, his attention was caught by another picture on her bedside table. This one was a framed photograph. He sensed more than heard her soft, indrawn breath when he reached out and picked it up. It was a family portrait, and at first he thought it was another of her impersonal consolations. Then the face of the girl in the picture came into focus, and he realized it was she. Rachel.

She had heavy, black-silk hair, an oval face, a straight, willowy girl-figure, strongly provocative. Her light eyes stared straight into the camera, poised, winsomely confident, maybe secretly amused. The child and the self-possessed woman met and mingled in the startling image. She was a good, dutiful daughter, everything in the portrait proclaimed, a joy to her middle-class parents, the father stern-looking, the mother vapid but pretty. She was turned slightly toward her tall, handsome brother, and her smile was soft and unbearably sweet.

"What was your maiden name?" he asked, not looking up from the photograph. A moment passed. He lifted his head. She was staring at him, and in her face he saw everything that was in the portrait except hope. But that was everything.

"Crenshaw." Her intonation gave the two syllables a quiet, devastating bitterness.

"You were . . . lovely."

She made a dismissive gesture with her hand and looked

away, but not before he saw the sad mask of her face begin to crack, the crystal-colored eyes almost caressing in their melancholy. He put the picture down and crossed the small room to her in three strides.

She pressed her back against the door, thinking he was leaving, making room for him so their bodies wouldn't touch. When he stopped before her, she stiffened, realizing the truth. Her instantaneous understanding of what was going to happen helped him get over a bizarre urge to embrace her and hold her close, give her comfort. Comforting Mrs. Wade didn't figure in his plans.

Touching her did. He imagined caressing her breasts, holding them through her dress right now, with no preliminaries. Would she jerk away in fright? No. Oh, no, she would close her eyes and bear it, let him handle her as intimately as he liked, a martyr to the inevitable. There might be *nothing* he could do to her that she wouldn't bear. The thought excited him. Depressed him.

He lifted his hand to run his fingers along the line of her jaw. Fine white skin, virginal skin, smooth as warm glass. What had Wade done to her? The question was starting to obsess him. Wade the sodomite, Wade the flagellant. He pressed lightly against her opposite cheek, making her turn her head and look at him. Her eyes were downcast, and martyrdom had never been one of his aphrodisiacs. Leaning in, he ran his tongue along the prickly line of her lashes. She had stopped breathing. She waited for him to do the next thing, take the next conscienceless liberty with her body. Very well, he would. He gently inserted the tip of his middle finger between her lips. Her mouth moistened it, and he wet her lips with his finger, smoothing it back and forth, going back inside for more wetness when her lips went dry. He thought she might be trembling, and brought his other hand to the back of her neck to see. Yes. Soft, subtle quivers coursing through her, like a light breeze rustling the leaves of a small, slight tree. Her neck was so thin, so fragile. Had he ever had a woman more vulnerable than this one? His head was swimming.

He put his hands flat on her chest, feeling her heart thud, thud, as she drew a choking breath. She was going to the stake like St. Joan, brave and above it all. He slid one hand to her face, spreading her lips to the sides a little with his thumb and forefinger, parting them. She made a soft sound, helpless. He put his open mouth on hers, breathing on her, and tasted inside her lips with his tongue, circling them slowly.

Heat jerked through him, rough and willful, out of control. He stopped tonguing her, stood perfectly still, his mouth on hers but not moving.

Seconds passed. Control returned, but he was wary. A lesson had been learned. The seducer could be seduced.

Ruthless now, he used his teeth, biting her full lower lip until she whimpered, then soothed her with his slow, hot tongue. A taste of salt startled him. Blood? Impossible. He pulled back, and saw the long, lone tearstain on her pink cheek.

A good way to end this, tears, because he hadn't intended it to go this far. Not yet. And if they stood in this doorway much longer, the next step would be quite, quite inevitable. But what he wanted wasn't a fast, hot fuck in the housekeeper's narrow bed. What he wanted . . . he had no words for it yet. Possession. Appropriation. Whatever it was, it called for more finesse than this backstairs grope. He might not deserve more—although he didn't believe that—but she did. Rachel Crenshaw did.

He leaned in toward her and caressed her lips with his, just a soft, farewell brush. Her breath rippling over his skin excited him, invited him to linger, but he didn't. He could always master himself when he chose to, and he chose to now. But what was she thinking? Had he moved her at all? No way to tell; she kept her eyes down, and the pitiful little tear could mean anything.

"Have dinner with me tonight, Mrs. Wade. Since we've

missed our morning meeting." Not quite a command, but by no means a question. He stepped away so that they weren't touching, so she could entertain the illusion, if she wished, that she had a choice. "Six o'clock, you recall. I'll expect you, shall I?"

He was a patient man; he could wait forever. It seemed that long before she realized there really was no choice. "Yes, my lord." she answered, in a voice that started out steady and ended in a harsh whisper.

He couldn't ask for more. Not yet. He made her a slight bow and left her alone.

VI

"Putain! Imbeciles partout!" Monsieur Judelet smacked a wooden spoon against the side of a bowl of rennet with such force, the handle split and the spoon end went flying across the kitchen.

Rachel flinched, but held her ground. "I have said I will order the anchovies," she enunciated in her careful schoolgirl French. "They will arrive in time for you to make the fricassee of partridges, monsieur. Do not worry."

That didn't begin to appease him. *"Espece de vache,"* he snarled, brandishing a fork. "Idiot—get out!" Those were his three best English words; he spoke them so often, they came out virtually accent-free.

"Remettez-vous," Rachel dared to say—Calm yourself—but she didn't turn her back on him as she sidled out of the room. So far Monsieur Judelet had thrown everything except knives at anyone who came into his kitchen with bad news—that they were out of anchovies, for example, or Lord D'Aubrey had barely touched his woodcock in caper sauce—but there was a first time for everything. Out in the hall, she could still hear him shouting, words she was thankful she couldn't understand. "Temperamental" was too mild a term to describe the hotheaded chef, but his rages never truly upset her. He was evenhandedly vile to everyone, and he was the only member of the household staff who seemed completely indifferent to her personal situation, if he even knew what it was.

"Mrs. Wade?" She turned to see Tess coming toward her along the corridor from the servants' staircase. "Mrs. Wade, can you come an' look at the curtains in the yellow sitting room? Susan were beatin' 'em wi' a broom to get the dust out, like you said? An' all at onct they ripped something turrible an' come down on top of 'er 'ead. She were quite a object," she added, grinning at the memory. "Now we don't know what's best t' do, hang 'em up again or throw 'em away. So can you come an' have a look?"

The housemaids were cleaning and airing all the drawing rooms, one each day when everything went well. Next week they would start on the second floor, where, besides a cavernous picture gallery, there were eleven bedrooms and an uncounted number of dressing, sitting, and powder rooms. It was a task Rachel had set for them herself, on her own initiative, after the most perfunctory consultation with his lordship. The fact that she gave instructions to the servants and they actually carried them out still seemed like a miracle to her, akin to parting the Red Sea or walking on water. She could scarcely believe she still had her job at all, much less that she was performing it fairly well. Any day, any minute, everything could blow up; one egregious blunder would be all it would take. So she moved slowly, worried about everything, and kept out of sight as much as possible. She reminded herself of some slow, plodding animal, a night creature turned out of its lair, blinking in the scary daylight, hoping no one would notice it and bash its brains in with a shovel.

What a violent metaphor, she thought, following Tess upstairs. It would have disturbed her, except she was grateful for the fact that her mind was thinking in analogies at all. It hadn't in prison. Nothing was *like* anything there: everything was precisely, horribly, exactly what it was. Comparisons to anything better would have been pointless, to anything worse, impossible.

The yellow drawing room owed its name to the dingy, brocaded wallpaper, even though it had faded to a depressing shade of beige years ago. Before today, its best feature had been the blue velvet curtains covering the wide, west-facing windows. Rachel found Susan on her knees beside the fallen fabric, contemplating it with a jaundiced eye.

"They come down right in my hand, Mrs. Wade," she complained, blowing a damp lock of orange hair out of her eyes. "I promise you it weren't my fault."

"No, I'm sure it wasn't." She sank down beside Susan and ran her fingers over the stiff material, desiccated from age and dust, crumbling almost at a touch.

"What ought we to do, ma'am? The view's turrible without 'em, ain't it?"

It was. The bare window looked naked, and the unattractive vista was of the half-dead back of a boxwood hedge in need of trimming.

On the other side of the room, Violet Cocker squatted on the marble hearth, polishing a brass firescreen. She laid her blackened cloth aside and turned her full, malicious attention on Rachel. In a boldly taunting voice, she echoed, "Yes, ma'am, what ought we t' do?" Her spiteful eyes gleamed with anticipation; she was looking forward to witnessing the new housekeeper wrestle with this ridiculous dilemma, which to anyone else would be no dilemma at all. From the beginning, Violet had understood with devilish accuracy what Rachel's biggest fear was, the source of her deepest anxiety: making decisions.

"Should we throw 'em out, ma'am, or try to fix 'em back the way they was?" Susan asked innocently. "Dora's the handiest wi' a needle, but I'm thinking they're past that. Making new ones 'ud cost a fortune, I expect," she continued when Rachel didn't answer. "But the lookout through the window's that ugly, seems like it ought to get covered up *some* way. Don't it, ma'am?"

The ticking of the ormolu clock on the mantel sounded unnaturally loud and slow. What was best to do? Rachel's mind stayed nerve-wrackingly blank. She started when the clock chimed eleven. "See if you can hang them again," she managed at last. "Just—do the best you can. I'll have to speak to Lord D'Aubrey. He may want to replace them. Or repair them. I don't know. I'll speak to him," she repeated, feeling idiotic—and already dreading that encounter.

"All right, ma'am," Susan said, fingering the musty cloth doubtfully.

"I'd stay and help you, but I have an appointment in the village. I didn't realize it was so late. Leave them until I come back if you can't manage it."

"Aye, you'd best be hurryin' along," Violet spoke up from the hearth, "else we might get a visit from the high sheriff, wonderin' what's become o' you."

Rachel got to her feet stiffly, keeping her face still, making a show of dusting off her skirts. The proper retort eluded her, as usual. But Violet mustn't be allowed to belittle her in front of the others; some show of authority was called for. "They need guidance," Mr. Holyoake had warned her. Yes, yes—but when she raised her voice or spoke sharply to an insolent servant, it sounded in her own ears like lines read by an incompetent, insincere actress. She was the most transparent of impostors.

Still, she had to say something. But now too much time had passed. Her lame "Go about your business, Violet" came too late and did no good. The maid sent her a triumphant sideways smirk and went back to polishing the firescreen, smiling.

Hurrying along the corridor, Rachel tried to put the incident out of her mind. Easy—she'd worry about the constable instead. How could she have let the time slip away without noticing? Her appointment was at eleven-thirty; she would be late unless she ran most of the way. Not that being late would be a catastrophe. She knew that, and yet the thought of being reprimanded for tardiness or even questioned about it filled her with the same stupid, dark, shivery dread she'd lived with every day in Dartmoor. What if it never left her? What if she went to her grave terrified of the consequences of a raised voice or a frowning face? In a thousand ways she was like a child, the natural development of her emotions cut off at the age of eighteen. But in a thousand other ways, she felt like the oldest woman on earth.

She came to a sudden stop on the top stair leading down to the courtyard. For one cowardly second, she wanted to slide back behind the door and escape. But even as the craven wish formed in her mind, Sebastian Verlaine glanced up and saw her. Too late.

He was walking through the gatehouse arch, holding his hat in his hand, smacking it energetically against his thigh at every other step. He wore no coat or waistcoat, even though the May morning was brisk. His fine white cambric shirt had come halfway out of the waist of a pair of none-too-clean buckskin breeches, which he wore with scuffed leather riding boots. The rough clothes not only became him, they looked completely natural on him, and yet she couldn't help wondering if he wore them as an affectation, a personal ironic joke, because at other times it pleased him to dress in the height of languid, aristocratic chic. When he saw her, an unmistakable expression of surprised pleasure came over his hard, handsome features.

Helpless—that was how he could make her feel, as if a trap-door were opening under her feet or an irresistible wind were sucking her up into thin air. When she was with him, the careful, rigid walls she'd built, within which she barely knew how to exist as it was, disappeared and left her with nothing, no handholds and no rules to follow slavishly just to survive. He could cut through everything, see through everything, no matter how secure the barrier she tried to put between them.

"Mrs. Wade!" he called to her, in the faintly facetious tone he used when calling her by her married name. She suspected he thought of her in his mind as "Rachel," and the formality of saying "Mrs. Wade" to her amused him on some dry, sardonic level. "Ah, the black today." He stopped twelve feet away, hands on his hips, legs spread, waiting for her to come to him.

She closed the gap slowly but steadily, keeping her eyes wide on him so he couldn't chastise her for an indirect gaze. The way he watched her was not only unnerving, it was unfair—because she wanted to watch *him*, indulge in a long, uninterrupted scrutiny. He had a long, lean face, sharp-boned and intense, and wicked, heavy-lidded eyes the color of blue topaz. By contrast, his hair was practically boyish, brown and soft-looking, falling straight down from either side of an off-center part, with an impudent cowlick on one side. The combination in his features of youthfulness and jaded sophistication never failed to fascinate and unsettle her.

"Good morning, my lord," she greeted him levelly. And then, in an unwonted fit of extravagance, she added, "It's a beautiful morning."

His mobile, voluptuous lips quirked upward, signaling amazement. But it was his fault that she was so uncharacteristically forthcoming today: he looked different, not so suave, younger than usual, and unbearably handsome. "There's a new foal," he told her, his eyes crinkling at the corners. "It's a filly. Cadger's her sire, and she's a beauty. Come and see her." He held out his hand.

Heat radiated from his body with the earthy odors of stable and leather and healthy sweat. She stood stock-still. Did he think she would just—take his hand? "I can't," she said somewhat breathlessly.

"What do you mean, you can't?"

"I have an appointment in the village. I mustn't be late."

"What kind of appointment?" he demanded, in a tone that said he doubted she could have any engagement that couldn't be put off for his pleasure.

"Once a week, I am required to report to the parish constable's office, my lord. It's one of the conditions of my ticket of leave."

The good humor left his face; his black brows drew together in a scowl. She didn't think it was the loss of her company that irked him, but rather the news that someone besides himself had the power to control her life. He slapped his hat across his knee, making a sharp, impatient sound that inwardly jarred her. "What are the other conditions of your—what is it?"

"My ticket of leave. It's my release, the conditions of my release. I must also report once a month to the chief constable in Tavistock, and every week I have to pay a little on my fine."

"Your fine?"

"Yes, my lord."

He raised his haughty eyebrows, waiting for her to elaborate.

"I owe the Crown a fine," she said stiffly, determined for some reason to keep the amount to herself. "It's in retribution for my—crime, and represents as well the cost of the prosecution against me. I'm allowed to pay it off a little at a time." She closed her lips and returned his cool stare as boldly as she could.

"That's what you're spending your wages on, then? Paying off your fine?"

"In part."

His lips tightened; he wasn't used to evasion from his servants. "Why is it you never told me you would be taking time off in the middle of every week, Mrs. Wade, to tend to your personal business?"

Her heart stuttered in fear—foolishly; he was scaring her on purpose. But knowing it didn't make his tactic less successful. "My lord, I never intended to deceive you. Mrs. Fruit had a half day on Saturdays, and I made an assumption that I would be given the same liberty. It's at the constable's order that I visit him on Wednesdays, and it never takes more than two hours altogether, including the time going and—"

"Oh, very well," he snapped, and this time she couldn't comprehend the source of his irritation at all. "You'd best be on your way, then, hadn't you? The last thing we want is to have the constable descending on Lynton Hall, claiming we're harboring a fugitive."

His inexplicable coldness bruised her. She wanted to lash back, ask him, *Is that the royal "we," my lord?* But, of course, she said nothing at all. He brushed past her without another word and strode off toward the house.

She thought back over the encounter as she walked across the bridge and started up the winding lane that led to the village, replaying the words they'd said to each other over and over, until the futility of understanding him made her weary and she gave up trying. She'd dreamt of him this morning, but she couldn't remember the dream anymore. Except that it had left her feeling helpless. Nothing new in that: he must lie awake at night thinking of ways to make her do things she didn't want to do. Speak to him, for instance. His interest in her hadn't diminished in the weeks since she'd come to Lynton; if anything, it had only grown stronger. She didn't understand it, and she feared it. *What will he do to me?* was a question she asked herself daily. She'd thought she was impervious to everything now; short of locking her up in a cell again, what could anyone do to hurt her in any deep or lasting way? Nothing—and yet she feared Sebastian Verlaine.

He wanted to sleep with her, of course. She'd have to be made of stone not to know that. If that was all he wanted, she would count herself lucky. Her body was cheap; it had nothing to do with her; she never thought of it. But she was afraid he wanted more from her, or that he would *take* more from her if they ever became intimate. He was a patient man, languid and mesmerizing, predatory; he had complete power over her life, and she spent her days trying to please him, to save herself. But what if pleasing him brought down her ruin all the faster?

Stop thinking about him.

She hated going into the village, but she loved the solitary walk to it. Each time she went, the world seemed to have grown more beautiful. Devonshire lay in the green lap of May, and every bird, every wildflower, every fresh scent on the breeze was an unimaginable delight. Sometimes it was too much, the textures too rich, the shapes and colors too sweet, everything opulent, fertile, lavish. Sometimes she had to bend her head to the stolid ground and plod along without looking. She was used to gray and brown, metal and stone, the odors of public latrines and disinfectant, the sounds of cell doors slamming and angry voices shouting. Mercilessness and monotony and cold-hearted routine ruled her old world, and the new one bewildered her. She couldn't categorize it; it was infinite, unpredictable, and much too hazardous.

Ah, but the beauty, the beauty—it was nothing to find herself in tears, just looking at the pink petals of a marsh violet in her hand or watching the slow, undulating wings of a tortoiseshell butterfly on a branch. Today buttercups covered the unplowed meadows, and yellow cowslips bloomed on the roadsides with primrose and wild hyacinth, speedwell and wood sorrel. She saw a green woodpecker, she heard the first cuckoo, and she found a hedge sparrow's nest in a gorse bush, with four blue eggs. The sky through the leafing oak trees was blinding blue, adorned with cottony clouds the color of new snow. And the sun was a miracle. Her heart felt too big for her chest—she almost wished it would rain, so she could manage the loveliness, contain it better inside herself. Because this really was too much.

Trudging up the last hill before the crossroads, she started at the sound of hoofbeats. Before she could even compose her face, a man on horseback loomed over the hill in front of her. She stepped smartly sideways to let him pass, but he reined in his cantering chestnut as soon as he saw her and came to a shuffling halt by her side. She looked up in amazement, arrested by the suddenness of his appearance, the size of him and his horse, and his quite astonishing good looks. The certainty that she had seen him before confused her; how could that be? Then he took off his hat, and she remembered: he was Reverend Morrell, and she knew him because he'd come to Dartmoor half a dozen times in the last two years, as a guest chaplain for the Sunday services.

"Good morning," he greeted her, squinting into the sun that lit up his golden hair like a torch. He wore sedate black clothes, but no clerical collar. Even knowing he was a minister, Rachel could hardly credit it, because he looked too healthy and robust, too *physical* for a man of the cloth. "I'm Christian Morrell," he told her, holding his blowing horse in check with gentle hands; "I'm the vicar of All Saints Church."

"How do you do?" She dreaded telling anyone her name, but this man's directness left her no choice. "I'm Rachel Wade. I'm the housekeeper at Lynton Great Hall."

His face registered no surprise, so she suspected he'd heard of her. She was startled when he leaned down and offered his hand. Flustered, she touched it briefly, then stood back, so he could ride on. But he stayed where he was. "It's a pleasure to meet you, Mrs. Wade. I'm on my way to the Hall now, as it happens, to meet Lord D'Aubrey for the first time."

"You'll find him in, sir. I've just left him."

"Yes, I sent a note earlier; he's expecting me."

"Oh. Of course."

"I'd have come sooner, but I've been out of the country for more than a month. On my honeymoon," he said, smiling. "My wife and I only returned two days ago. We were in Italy."

She had no small talk, so she was surprised to hear herself respond, "I hope you enjoyed your trip?"

"Thank you, yes, we enjoyed it very much. It was—perfect."

The fact that speaking of a stranger's wedding trip in any but the most general terms might be indelicate was just beginning to dawn on her when she noticed the faint pink color seeping into Reverend Morrell's fair, handsome cheeks. It had just dawned on him, too. Somehow his embarrassment lessened hers. She relaxed, and said with more ease than she would have imagined possible, "I met your father once, Reverend. Briefly."

"Really?" He looked intrigued.

"Yes. He . . . married my husband and me."

He had the most extraordinary eyes, both gentle and penetrating, and she had the sensation that they saw a great deal more than she cared to reveal.

When he didn't say anything, she added hurriedly, "I hope he's well?"

"My father died about five years ago."

"I'm sorry. He seemed to be—a very kind man."

"Yes. He was."

What an odd conversation they were having. Or perhaps it wasn't; perhaps it only seemed odd to her because she so rarely had conversations. "Well, I won't keep you any longer. Good morning, sir."

He didn't look relieved; if anything, he looked surprised that she was ending the encounter so soon. Which made her wonder how much longer he'd have tarried in the middle of the road, passing the time of day with Lynton Hall's resident murderess-turned-housekeeper. Had he known Randolph? He must have. The thought disturbed her.

"My wife will be pleased to make your acquaintance," he said unexpectedly, and if he hadn't had one of the most open countenances she'd ever seen, she'd have dismissed that as a bald and not very kind social lie. "Her name is Anne. Her late husband was a cousin of Lord D'Aubrey's, you know."

Yes, she'd heard that bit of gossip already, from servants eager to share the news that the former Lady D'Aubrey was now plain

Anne Morrell, the vicar's wife. "I would be honored to meet her," Rachel said carefully—although the likelihood of it still seemed impossibly remote to her.

The vicar put his black hat back on. "It's been a pleasure," he said with every sign of sincerity, smiling down at her. "Perhaps I'll see you in church on Sunday, Mrs. Wade?" he asked, with just enough diffidence to make the question inoffensive.

Rachel had no great love of religion, or the bloodless, soulless clergymen who had harangued her and her sister-inmates in daily, sometimes twice-daily, sermons on what wicked sinners they were, how lucky to have been given such a humane chance at reformation, how grateful they ought to be for it. But to Reverend Morrell she heard herself say, "I look forward to it." And as she watched him out of sight, the singular thought struck her that she meant it.

Sebastian's peevish mood stayed with him as he stripped off his dirty work clothes, washed over the sink in his new bathroom, and pulled on clean shirt, trousers, waistcoat, and coat, Preest hovering over him all the while. He couldn't have said why he was still chafing over the idea of Mrs. Wade having to visit the blasted constable once a week; he seemed to be taking the whole thing personally. What was it to do with him? Still, it rankled. It was an imposition on her freedom, if nothing else. She'd paid for her supposed sins, hadn't she? Wasn't ten years enough? He felt riled up on her behalf, and angry with her for *not* being angry. Or not showing it, anyway. But then, there was precious little she did show. Her everlasting reserve was fascinating in its way, but he was getting bloody sick and tired of it.

Preest went to answer a knock at the bedroom door, returning a moment later to announce, "My lord, Reverend Morrell is here."

Sebastian swore under his breath, feeling mildly put upon. *So it's come to this, has it?* he taunted himself, peering into the glass at his clean, combed reflection. *A visit from the ruddy minister, for God's sake?* Respectability had been foisted on him by virtue of a title and a crumbling old manor house, and the onerous weight of it was getting on his nerves. When Preest started fidgeting around his shoulders with a lint brush, he shrugged away, muttering, "Oh, sod it," and stalked out of the room.

The maid had put the vicar in the rosewood drawing room. His broad back was in silhouette against the window, out of which he was gazing at the river bridge with such absorption, he didn't hear Sebastian until he said, "Reverend Morrell?"

He turned swiftly, as if jarred from a memory, and blinked a faraway look out of his eyes. They met in the middle of the room and shook hands. The minister had a vigorous grip. He was tall and good-looking, and about thirty years younger than the man Sebastian had for some reason been expecting. "Welcome to Wyckerley, my lord," he said warmly. "I'm sorry I wasn't here to say that to you when you arrived."

"I doubt that, Reverend, considering that if you had been, you'd have missed your honeymoon. But the sentiment's appreciated."

The vicar grinned, acknowledging the truth in that. "Mrs. Morrell asked me to give you her regards, and to say she looks forward to making your acquaintance very soon."

"That's kind of her. I feel as if I already know your wife, because of the correspondence we've shared in the months since my cousin died. You'll stay for lunch, won't you?" he asked, gesturing for the minister to take a seat on the sofa. One of the maids came in just then, with two glasses of wine on a tray.

"I'm afraid that's impossible today. Another time, I hope."

"Most certainly," Sebastian responded, with unexpected conviction. They said a few more conventional, socially correct things to each other, and then, almost imperceptibly, they both relaxed. They began to talk naturally and animatedly about the character of the village, its inhabitants, its potential for prosperity and advancement. Reverend Morrell showed himself to have an optimistic but unsentimental grasp on the economic realities of the neighborhood, and, thankfully, no unrealistic expectation of the new lord to perform miracles. Sebastian told him he was thinking of making a few investments in local enterprises, and the vicar made some intelligent-sounding recommendations, including a copper mine owned by Mayor Vanstone.

Eventually the conversation took a more personal turn, with the vicar confiding that he had grown up in Wyckerley with Geoffrey Verlaine for his best friend—Sebastian's cousin and the previous viscount. Reverend Morrell's marriage to the widowed viscountess had taken place barely a year after Geoffrey's death, Sebastian recalled. There was a story behind that intriguing fact, he was quite sure, but he wasn't going to hear it today, regardless of how swimmingly he and the vicar were getting along. In the same discreet spirit, he didn't burden the reverend with the news that Lynton Hall was only a stopping place for him, and when his father died and Steyne Court became his, he planned either to sell Lynton, lease it, or let William Holyoake run it for him in absentia.

Apart from all that, he was relieved to find that he liked Christian Morrell as a man. The circumstances of village politics and social custom would require them to deal closely together, at least for a time, so it was good to know that the vicar was sensible, not too pious, and evidently neither a saint nor a hypocrite.

The hour lengthened. "Stay for lunch," Sebastian urged again, more forcefully this time.

Reverend Morrell stood up. "I really can't, and I won't keep you any longer from yours."

They walked outside together. The stable lad brought the vicar's horse, a fine-looking chestnut gelding. The two men talked about horses for a while, and the minister surprised Sebastian again by being not only keen but uncommonly knowledgeable on the subject. He promised to come back and see the new foal when he had time, and gladly agreed to join Sebastian in a ride over the moors one morning soon.

With his hand on his horse's withers, Reverend Morrell mentioned casually, "I met Mrs. Wade this morning, my lord, on my way to the Hall."

"Oh, did you?" Sebastian knew he was imagining that his innocent tone of voice sounded disingenuous. It wasn't like him to indulge in a guilty conscience; something about the golden-haired minister just brought it out of him.

"I have a churchwarden who makes it his business to keep me apprised of more local gossip than I care to hear—and so I knew who she was before she told me. Knew her history, and how it came about that you employed her."

"Did you?" This time there was no innocence, only coolness in his voice. "Did you have some question about that, Reverend?"

Instead of answering, he said, "Miss Lydia Wade paid a call on me yesterday."

"And who might Lydia Wade be?" Sebastian asked, although he knew. Holyoake had told him.

"She's the daughter of Randolph Wade. She and Mrs. Wade were friends before the marriage—but perhaps you already know this."

He murmured noncommittally.

"It was news to me, frankly. I wasn't living in Wyckerley ten years ago, when my father was the vicar. As a matter of fact, he married Randolph and Rachel Wade—as Mrs. Wade was just reminding me."

"Indeed. And what was it Miss Wade came to see you about?"

The reverend's intelligent brow furrowed. "She was upset. She said she was in attendance at the magistrate's hearing when Mrs. Wade's case was heard."

Sebastian narrowed his eyes. "She wouldn't be a yellow-haired woman, would she?" he said slowly. "Rather pretty, a nervous manner, knits a lot?"

The reverend looked impressed. "That's Lydia to the life. She knits grave blankets, actually. Incessantly. Great black squares, one after another, more than the parish could ever—ah, well." He stopped, looking abashed, as if he'd almost said something uncharitable. "As I said, she was upset when she came to see me. May I speak bluntly?"

"Of course."

"She was more than upset, she was outraged, because—using her words—the woman who cold-bloodedly murdered her father and then lied under oath about his moral character is now abroad in the neighborhood, living the good life as a trusted member of our new viscount's household. Her words," he said again, apologetically.

Sebastian folded his arms combatively. "And what's this to do with me?"

"Lydia keeps very much to herself, but she's known to be somewhat high-strung. Unstable, frankly. She lives with her aunt, a Mrs. Armstrong, who is—forgive the cliché—a pillar of the community. But Mrs. Armstrong has been ill lately and not able to keep as close an eye on her niece as she would like." He ran his hand over the soft leather of his horse's saddle, frowning. When he looked up, his clear-eyed gaze defused Sebastian's vague, unsettled antagonism. "I'm afraid there may be trouble, my lord. And I wanted to pass on to you something that's . . . unpleasant, but which you have a right to know. A duty to know."

"What is it?"

"There's talk in the village that you haven't hired Mrs. Wade for a housekeeper, but for a mistress." He said it quietly and didn't look away; there was no accusation in his voice, only concern.

That made a sarcastic retort harder to muster. But Sebastian managed. "Forgive me, Reverend, if I make no reply to that except to say that village gossip has never been the guiding principle by which I live my life. In a word, I'm unimpressed." But anger was kindling inside him slowly, insidiously—from what source he couldn't imagine, since village gossip in this instance was dead on target. "No, 'unimpressed' doesn't quite cover it," he corrected with a sneer. "I'm contemptuous."

Reverend Morrell didn't turn a hair. "Then think of her."

"Think of whom?"

"Mrs.—"

"Mrs. Wade? Whom do you suppose I was thinking of when I hired her? Did your rumor-mongering churchwarden mention what they'd have done to her if I hadn't given her a post in my household?"

"He said—"

"They'd have sent her to gaol—for nothing, for being unemployed. Is that what Christian charity gets one in St. Giles' parish, Vicar?"

"I hope not, my lord."

"I hope not, too. Tell me, Vicar, can you save Mrs. Wade from the workhouse? What post have you got in mind for her?"

"I've thought about it. To tell you the truth, I haven't come up with anything."

Something eased inside; Sebastian felt an odd weakness, like a man girding himself for the fight of his life, only to learn that his opponent wasn't coming to the battlefield. "Then the point of this conversation escapes me," he said with finality.

Reverend Morrell's lucid blue gaze never faltered. "Understand, what I've said wasn't intended to offend you. I believe you're an honorable man. I also believe Mrs. Wade has paid for her crime and deserves to be treated with decency and compassion." He paused, looking as if he had more to say, but after a moment he only held out his hand. They shook and told each other good-bye.

Mounted on his horse, though, the vicar had parting words. "If you would like to continue this conversation, or"—he smiled with rather charming self-deprecation—"in the unlikely event that you would ever care to hear my counsel on the subject, I hope you won't hesitate to call on me."

"I'll keep that in mind," Sebastian said neutrally. Earlier, he'd written the vicar off as too unworldly a soul to understand the designs he had on Rachel Wade. Now he wasn't so sure.

VII

"AH, MRS. WADE, there you are. I'd like you to go to the village with me."

It was amusing to watch her lose her composure. She'd had her nose in an account book, making notations in it, while one of the maids, on her hands and knees just inside the cavernous linen cupboard, called out to her things like, "Sixteen muslin pillow slips, not embroidered. Twenty-one embroidered, all of 'em white."

"My lord," his housekeeper greeted him, flustered, "do you mean—now?"

"I thought now, yes, inasmuch as I'm meeting the mayor in half an hour or so. That is, if you can tear yourself away from this fascinating inventory-in-progress."

She colored, but whether from his sarcasm or the avid scrutiny of the maid, still kneeling in the closet—Violet, he thought her name was—Sebastian couldn't be sure.

"Yes, of course, my lord, I'll—this can wait. We'll finish later, Violet. You can . . . go and help Cora in the kitchen."

Violet scrambled to her feet. "Help *Cora*," she echoed in an aggrieved tone, and for a second Sebastian thought she was going to refuse the order. She was a parlormaid, he recalled; she must consider helping in the kitchen beneath her. She shifted her black-eyed glance in his direction, then back to Mrs. Wade. "Yes, ma'am," she muttered, half curtsied to him, and flounced off toward the servants' stairs.

"I hope you don't tolerate insolence among your charges, Mrs. Wade," he said seriously—as if it mattered to him.

"I'm still learning, my lord. And—I think I'm improving. Violet can be difficult sometimes, but the fault is mine as much as hers. Giving orders is not something I'm . . . particularly used to."

It was a long answer for her; she must be in a talkative mood. Side by side, they walked down the center staircase. In the foyer, she excused herself—"for two seconds, my lord"—while she went to get her hat, and she was almost as good as her word. That pleased him, if the hat did not. It was a poke bonnet of flat black straw, in the giddy height of fashion about fifteen years ago; its protruding sides, like giant blinders, almost hid her interesting profile. But she looked so enchanted with the bright morning when they stepped out into the courtyard, Sebastian lost interest in saying anything unkind to her about her hat.

"Shall we walk or ride?"

That brought her up. "Whichever you prefer, my lord," she replied dutifully.

"Of course. But in this case I'm asking you."

She looked worried; she feared a trap. "Are you in a hurry?"

"No, are you?"

"No, my lord." Was she smiling? He couldn't be sure because of the damned hat.

He waited.

"Shall we . . . walk, then?"

"Yes, if you like," he said agreeably, and they set off at a leisurely pace, rather like two friends out for a stroll. He thought of taking her arm, but decided against it. He wanted her company today, nothing more. This was a leisurely seduction; he was enjoying the preamble too much to rush the climax.

Knowing there would be no conversation unless he initiated it, he asked presently, "What did you particularly miss in prison, Mrs. Wade?"

After a surprised moment, she answered, "There wasn't one thing, my lord."

"Three things, then. And they needn't be the main things, if that paralyzes you. Just the three you think of first."

"Flowers," she said immediately, glancing at the steep sides of the hard-packed road, where milkwort sprawled in exuberant blue and white tangles. "And . . . light. Long views of the world in natural light."

He frowned. "You were not allowed to go outside at all?"

"On the contrary, we had daily exercise in the prison yard."

"What was daily exercise like?"

She glanced at him, assessing his interest. "We walked, my lord."

"Walked? Where?"

"Nowhere. In circles. Two circles, one inside the other. For an hour every day, immediately following chapel. That comes out," she added dryly, "to a distance of approximately two miles."

He mulled that. "You walked in silence?"

"Of course."

"Could you cheat? Whisper something to a neighbor as you passed?"

"Some did, yes. The art of ventriloquism flourishes in a prison yard, as you can imagine. But it's not easy; the guards are watchful, and one must always stay fifteen feet behind the prisoner next in the circle."

He tried to picture it. It seemed barbarous. "Was there no enjoyment in it, then, not even the pleasure of moving about?"

"We were a plodding procession, my lord. The pace was set by the slowest—old women or young children. The word 'exercise' doesn't really describe our little parade." He was still flinching mentally from the thought of children in a convict prison when she went on. "But, yes, there were compensations. The chance to see the sky, or the reflection of clouds in a rain puddle. The feel of wind, the smell of it. Sometimes there were birds to look at, rooks mostly, but occasionally a thrush or a lark. Once . . ." She broke off, making a sheepish face. He'd never heard her say so much at one go before.

"Once?" he urged, fascinated.

"Once . . . a dog bounded out of nowhere and tried to play with us. It was a yellow dog, very large and shaggy, very—excited. I never knew where he came from. I petted him." The bold, wistful way she said this last made him imagine her hoarding the thought of the yellow dog for months, even years, using the memories of soft fur and wet tongue to comfort herself in the long hours of her imprisonment. "But then," she finished softly, "the guards captured him and took him away."

A melancholy silence fell between them. "So," he said to break it. "Flowers and long views of the world in sunlight. One more, Mrs. Wade."

"It's . . . difficult. There are many things I could say."

"Say them, then."

She breathed a sigh. "Food with flavor. Warm water to wash in. Colors. One night of sound, peaceful sleep. But—all that—" She made a gesture with her hand, saying they weren't important. "The main thing . . ."

"What?"

She darted another glance at him. "People. Human contact, human warmth. Simple conversation. The lack of it made me sick. Not physically, but in my . . ."

"Soul," he murmured.

She made no answer. Evidently her soul was not a subject she was prepared to discuss with him.

"You were not permitted to speak at all?" he asked grimly. "To anyone?"

"We could speak to the warders, but only in answer to their questions. Never to each other."

"But surely—"

"Ways were got round it, yes, of course. But the punishment if one were caught made the risk . . . costly."

A chill of revulsion tamped down his unwholesome curiosity in the details of prison discipline. But not for long. "What kind of punishment—"

"My lord, do you come from Sussex? I believe someone told me that," she broke in, sounding almost shrill. He looked at her in surprise; she'd never dared to ask him a personal question before. Her features were set and stiff. It was clear that further inquiries about how order was kept at Dartmoor Prison would be futile.

"Yes, it's true," he answered equably. "I was born in Rye."

"Do you—is it—a large family?"

The simplest social discourse was still an obstacle course for her, around which she lumbered awkwardly, like a woman in shackles and leg irons. Then, too, he was a viscount and she was a domestic servant; no matter how politely or impersonally she phrased her diversionary questions, they were bound to sound forward, even impudent. He could sympathize with her dilemma, but he wasn't much keener to talk about his family than she was to talk about prison.

"No, not large," he said briefly. "Just my parents and a sister."

"Are your parents living?" she tried next.

"I suppose so. The last I heard."

She looked at him in surprise. "You aren't close?" she hazarded.

"Close? No, I wouldn't say we were close. My father is the Earl of Moreton," he thought to add. "He's dying; the doctors have given him half a year at the most."

"I'm very sorry. How terrible for you. You must . . ." She trailed off, seeing his expression, which he imagined was more amused than grief-stricken. "It must," she amended nervously, "be very hard on your family."

"No, not really. We don't care for one another much in my family."

She thought that over, gazing off through a patch of woods that flanked the road on her side. "I suppose you'll return to Rye, then, after your father's gone?"

"Yes, for a little while. Long enough to hear the will read, at any rate."

"And then you mean to return to Lynton for good?"

He laughed at that. "Lord, no. Why would I? I'll be rich, Mrs. Wade, and I'll be an earl. 'Why then, the world's mine oyster, which I with sword will open.' Or, more aptly in my case, with *purse*." She said nothing. "You're silent," he noted. "I think I hear disapproval in your silence."

"Not at all. Certainly not."

"Certainly not. You wouldn't presume."

"No, I would not."

"Ah. My mistake, then. But tell me, Mrs. Wade, if you were in my place, which would you choose: a life of absolute luxury and comfort, spent anywhere you liked, Paris, Rome, Constantinople, anywhere in the world, with time and the means to explore every earthly pleasure that man in his wicked ingenuity ever devised—that's on the one hand. Or a residence in what we might in charity term a backwater, populated by the salt of the earth, brave, honest souls who nevertheless lack a certain *je ne sais quoi*—sophistication, shall we say. A wholesome life, no question of that, lived close to God's good clean earth, but—forgive me—perhaps a trifle *too* close. Well?" he prompted. "Come, which would you choose? You might think of it as a choice between a fast Arab stallion and a big, sturdy Clydesdale."

Her lips quirked. "My lord, I can hardly decide which of my two dresses to put on in the morning. I'm afraid deciding between two completely different styles of life would be quite beyond me."

He'd suspected from the beginning that an arid sense of humor lurked somewhere beneath all the reserve. She showed him new facets of herself every day. What might it be like to have a normal conversation with her, both of them speaking naturally, unconstrained by status, or fear, or sexual politics? Diverting, perhaps—but that wasn't why he'd gone to the trouble of employing her. If he wanted normal conversation, there were any number of women with whom he could have it. Mrs. Wade was meant to serve an altogether different function.

He'd noticed her looking slightly less nunlike of late, and now he tried to guess why. It wasn't her clothes, which remained steadfastly black or brown and unrelievedly somber. It wasn't her face, which had more color but not much more animation than on the day they'd met. She still glided rather than walked, but he'd discovered that was natural, not learned, her usual, quite graceful way of moving. The difference was partly in her posture, the way she held herself—not stooped any longer, as if she expected the sky to fall in at any moment. She walked with her shoulders back and her chin up, meeting the world head-on. It was a small shift, but it changed everything. Her slender figure looked youthful because of it, not careful and pained, almost decrepit. It pleased him to see the change, and intrigued him to speculate on what other surprises she might have in store for him.

Oddly enough, as soon as the thought had fully formed in his mind, she changed again. Conversation on her end ceased. Her luminous eyes dimmed, and she stopped looking about her, training her gaze on the ground in front of her feet, holding onto her elbows.

Sebastian glanced around, trying to see what could have caused this abrupt withdrawal, but there was nothing. Except that they'd entered the village. Was that it? Cottages lined both sides of the High Street, a narrow, gently climbing thoroughfare whose hard-packed surface didn't give way to cobbles till the second bridge over the serpentine Wyck, almost at the village green. Passersby tipped their hats or bowed, hardly able to veil their surprise at seeing Lord D'Aubrey in the town, not only on foot but in the company of his infamous housekeeper. As he returned their greetings in kind, it struck him that Rachel might receive a much less hospitable welcome when she made her weekly visits to the constable's office. Did she ever meet open hostility? He thought of what the vicar had told him about Lydia Wade, her late husband's daughter. Did other people in Wyckerley feel the same violent antagonism toward her?

It was a disturbing thought. To counteract it—he didn't have time to worry about Mrs. Wade—he announced casually, "I've been thinking of having an entertainment at the Hall one day soon. Something for the locals, I think, a kind of open-house affair, nothing too formal, meet the new squire and all that. Does that sound like something you would care to organize for me, Mrs. Wade?"

Her steps slowed gradually until she stopped. They were in front of the mayor's unattractive Tudor home, two stories of half-timbers and whitewashed clay surrounded by a pretentious black iron fence. Rachel had turned pale as a sheet; she actually looked ill.

"It won't be much work," he said smoothly. "I'll give you a list of the people I wish to invite. Judelet can plan the menu, but I would want you to act as my hostess, greeting the guests and so on." She stared at his shirtfront, her straight mouth closed, the lips pressing together in intermittent nervous spasms. "What do you say, Mrs. Wade? May I count on you for that?"

"My lord," she finally got out.

"Hmm?"

Her glance flickered over him knowingly just for a second, telling him she fully comprehended the game he was playing with her now. "My lord, I would ask for a little more time."

He'd expected her to cave in, agree to his unkind plan without a whimper, and suffer the consequences with her usual hopeless stoicism. Was this tentative quibble progress? That depended on what the object was—his object, not hers—and as to that he wasn't sure; he alternated between wanting to save her and wanting to push her to her limit.

"You would ask for a little more time," he repeated, as if he didn't quite understand. "For what purpose?"

Her struggles with self-expression always fascinated him. "I'm not—I feel as if I couldn't—I'm afraid I wouldn't do justice to you or your friends at such an entertainment."

"Why not?"

She looked around for a distraction, but no one approached them, no one came to her rescue. "It's just—I'm not—fit . . ."

Uncharacteristically, he took pity on her. "You've spent the last ten years in a small room by yourself," he said softly. "You've lost the ability to converse easily with others, and you're still nearly incapable of making choices, even simple ones. The good people of Wyckerley believe you're a murderess, and you not unnaturally find dealing with them a trial and an embarrassment. You want to keep to yourself and attract the least amount of attention while you try to rebuild some semblance of a life. If it were up to you, you would rather not organize and play hostess at a party for a lot of hostile strangers."

Her astonishment—that he could have any idea of what her inner life was like—wasn't flattering, but it was intriguing to watch. The clear, nearly achromatic eyes widened; before self-consciousness overtook them, her features grew positively animated. Girlish—she looked like the girl in the stiff family photograph, young and fresh, still capable of amazement. She put her hands together in a fervent, almost prayerful gesture. Gratitude made her smile naturally, for once. "My lord, I'm very—"

"But, of course, it's not up to you, is it? It's up to me."

Ah, now it was dread he got to watch take over her mobile countenance, and—could it be?—a flash of righteous anger, quickly hidden before, God forbid, it could give offense. She was *too* easy to read, not enough of a challenge for him today. But what could account for anyone having a face that transparent? The absence of mirrors in her prison cell? Or had the ten-year prohibition against looking at others caused her to forget that people's faces gave away their emotions?

"Very well," he said solemnly, "I will grant you your wish—a little more time. But don't make the mistake of growing complacent," he cautioned in a lower voice, leaning toward her. "I'm not a hermit, and Lynton Hall is not a religious retreat. Sooner or later, you'll have to help me entertain my friends. Furthermore, when I engaged you, I had more duties in mind than merely seeing to it that my house is clean." He left it at that, not putting into words the other "duties" for which they both knew he'd engaged her. What was the need?

"Thank you, my lord," she said stiffly.

He made her a slight bow. They understood each other.

The clock in the tower of All Saints Church began to strike the noon hour. Time for his meeting with the mayor. But Rachel's bowed head distracted him, her face invisible beneath the unattractive bonnet. He had an idea.

"Come with me," he said abruptly, sliding his hand into the crook of her elbow to get her moving. Startled, she let him lead her along past the village inn, the alehouse, Swan's blacksmith shop. When he stopped and opened the door for her at Miss Carter's Frocks and Ready to Wear, she balked for a second, looking astonished and then bemused, and finally preceded him into the shop.

Sebastian had made Miss Carter's acquaintance over a month ago in the company of Lili, when his erstwhile mistress had insisted on going into the village for the express purpose of laughing, not very discreetly, at what passed for fashion in the local shops. Her performance hadn't endeared her—or him, by extension—to Miss Carter, a small, blond-haired woman whose welcoming smile didn't reach her eyes when she heard the bell and came out of a back room to greet her customers. And when she saw that the woman accompanying him this time was the notorious Rachel Wade, even the insincere smile waned, and he suspected that all that kept her from incivility was his title.

"Are you in mourning for anyone, Mrs. Wade?" he asked, lounging against the counter along the shop's rear wall.

"I beg your pardon?"

"Anybody die on you lately for whom you feel the need to wear black?"

"I—no, my lord."

"Or brown?"

"No, my lord."

"Splendid." With a flourish, he untied the ribbon bow at her throat and whipped the offending bonnet off her head. He couldn't have said which lady was more flabbergasted, the housekeeper or the shopkeeper. "You sell hats, don't you, Miss Carter?" he inquired of the latter. She nodded mutely. "I hope you have others besides that." He pointed to the one displayed on the counter, an extravagant leghorn affair suitable for the May Day procession and nothing else.

"Why, yes, my lord, I—that is, I have forms, you know, and—quite a large selection of trims to go with them, ribbons and such. Would you care to see them?"

"Very much."

"I'll only be a minute," she promised, and disappeared into the back of the shop.

"The poke bonnet had its heyday around 1842," he told Rachel while he waited, fingering a cheap pair of kid gloves on the counter. "Nowadays a lady of fashion wears a very small bonnet far back on the head, or, if she's quite dashing, a hat. With luck, that's what we're going to get you today, Mrs. Wade."

She had her head bowed, hands demurely folded; he couldn't tell what was going through her mind. Perhaps she was wondering about the propriety of receiving a personal gift from him, especially in a place as public as Miss Carter's. Well, she had better make peace with her scruples, because once she was his mistress—assuming she pleased him—he meant to buy her a dozen hats, and gowns to go with all of them.

Miss Carter returned with her "forms," which showed more promise than he'd dared to hope. "Do you fancy any of these?" he mused. "Try this one." He started to put it on for her, but she took it from him and settled it on her head herself. Miss Carter held the glass. After a few seconds, Sebastian and the shopkeeper said, "No," in unison, and the hat was rejected. Two others were tried and cast off just as quickly.

The fourth was of wine-colored plush, medium size, with a brim that curved rather rakishly on the side. It was pretty and it suited her, even flattered her, but Sebastian's attention wasn't on the hat anymore. It was on Rachel's face. A little while ago he'd wondered what other surprises she had in store for him, and it seemed he hadn't had to wait long for the next one. She was staring at her reflection as if she were looking at a complete stranger. An unexpectedly attractive one, if he was interpreting her look of fascination correctly. "Do you like it?" he asked softly, unnecessarily.

She gave a small nod, keeping her eyes on the glass.

"It's most becoming," Miss Carter piped up, "one of my very best, and only eighteen and six, which leaves plenty for . . ." She halted, coloring, realizing that economy probably wasn't high on Viscount D'Aubrey's list of criteria for hat-buying.

"Plenty for decorating," he finished for her kindly. "Show us your flowers, feathers, and furbelows, Miss Carter; we're squirming with impatience."

She went away again, returning in a moment with two boxes of hat-trimming possibilities. There were no ostrich feathers—too dear for the ladies of Wyckerley, apparently—and the other feathers, except for the gaudy peacocks, were dull or cheap-looking. They settled the matter of the ribbon expeditiously and unanimously—black velvet, the inch-and-a-half width. Veils and netting were rejected as too prissy for such a sleek, stylish hat, and that left only flowers. He was reaching for a handful of cloth violets when Rachel, who had been comparatively passive up to now, made a low sound of demurral and chose a bouqueted cluster of peonies.

"Ooh, that's cunning," Miss Carter said approvingly, holding the glass again. Her earlier reserve was wearing off as she got more into the millinery spirit. "I'd never've thought that pink would go, but it does, it most certainly does. Very fetching, madam, and it shows off your color very nicely."

An understatement, thought Sebastian. The peonies were large—too large, he had judged, but he'd been wrong—and their coral-pink shade matched exactly the pretty color blooming in his housekeeper's cheeks as she stared, entranced, at her own image. Again, it wasn't the hat that arrested him, or even how pretty she looked in it, but rather the subtle metamorphosis from age to youth, from caution to near-confidence in her expressive features. She couldn't take her eyes off herself, and neither could he.

He broke the spell when he touched her cheek, to smooth back a lock of her dark, silver-streaked hair. Self-consciousness replaced the fledgling approval in her eyes; she stepped away, out of his reach.

Just then the bell over the shop door tinkled and a woman came through. Tall, dark, expensively dressed, she looked vaguely familiar until she smirked at him in pleased surprise, and he remembered who she was: Honoria Vanstone, the mayor's tiresome spinster daughter.

"Lord D'Aubrey, what a fortuitous meeting," she exclaimed in an affected falsetto. "How do you do? I was telling my father only yesterday that it's been too long since we've seen you." She saw Mrs. Wade for the first time, looked between them, realized they were together, and said, "Oh," in a long, rising-and-falling intonation of delicate horror. It might have been amusing if it hadn't ruined the mood of tentative gaiety that, against all odds, had prevailed in the shop before her arrival.

Immediately Mrs. Wade's face and figure took on the familiar hooded, haunted look. If she'd been on her own, he was sure she'd have bolted. Had she encountered the Vanstone woman before in some unpleasant social connection? It would explain her abrupt regression to the downcast Rachel of old.

Impulsively he reached for her hand and drew her closer. The burgundy hat no longer suited her; the pink peonies looked garish next to her pallid complexion, and the jaunty, carefree style seemed to mock her. He felt her humiliation, and he was moved to help her.

What was it, then, that made him take the hat from her head slowly, almost caressingly—as if they were alone and he were undressing her? Her dark hair had grown enough by now to curl below the collar of her dress. He slid his fingers into it, ruffling it a little where the hat had flattened it. The attentive silence egged him on; now he felt as if he were on a stage, with one other player and a rapt audience of two. He brought his palms to the sides of Rachel's face, brushing her mouth with his thumbs. Behind him, Honoria Vanstone gasped.

"When can you have the hat ready?" he murmured. Miss Carter made some answer, but he didn't catch it. Rachel was holding perfectly still, eyes lowered, staring off somewhere to the side. He felt her breath flutter on his fingers, the helpless trembling of her lips. He could lean down and kiss her now if he wanted to. He could do anything. The tiny golden hairs on her cheeks beguiled him; he smoothed his fingers over them lightly, frowning at her. He wanted her to look at him, but she would not. At last he took his hands away and stepped back.

"I didn't hear you," he said, not taking his eyes from Rachel's face. "When did you say the hat would be ready?"

Miss Carter had to clear her throat. "By tomorrow, my lord, I expect. I should think. That is, unless—"

"Send it to the Hall with your bill, please. A pleasure, Miss Vanstone, as always," he murmured to the mayor's daughter, whose face had turned an unattractive shade of mauve. "Mrs. Wade?" Rachel still wouldn't look at him, but she had no choice but to take his arm when he offered it. Behind them, the affronted muttering started before they were even through the door.

Out on the cobbled street, he watched her jerk the ribbons of the old black bonnet under her chin in a turbulent, untidy bow. She was furious with him, but she would never say it. "You'll find your way home alone all right, will you?" he inquired facetiously.

Her eyes shot fire, but her mumbled, "Yes, my lord," was perfectly respectful. In her black dress, she looked alarmingly slight and somber against a riot of purple foxgloves blooming along the riverbank. He imagined her walking home through the village by herself, enduring the stares of the curious and the hostile; for all he knew, people even said things to her—insulted her. He wavered for a moment, actually considering going back with her, putting off his meeting with Vanstone on copper mine investments to another time.

Nonsense; he wasn't her guardian. And what a foolish precedent he would set by such an attention. *Begin as you mean to go on* was sound advice; he meant to go on using Mrs. Wade for his convenience, not the other way around. If her pariah status had increased today, it was by his own doing, and it was a little too late for guilt or second thoughts.

"Good day to you, then." He touched his hat and walked off toward the mayor's house, leaving her alone in the street.

Rachel watched him stride away, swinging his walking stick in the loose, arrogant way that seemed natural to him, not affected. He must be feeling quite satisfied with his morning's work: he had not only shocked two of Wyckerley's most respectable ladies, he'd also shamed her in front of them for his personal amusement. What she didn't understand was why. What perverse pleasure did he take in tormenting her? It wasn't anything as simple as cruelty, she was sure of that, because his mind was too subtle, his depravities too complex. Whatever his motive, she told herself it didn't matter, that the joke was on him because she had no pride or public honor left to humiliate. But even as she thought it, she could feel the icy stares of Miss Vanstone and Miss Carter, like a cold breeze on the back of her neck. When she turned around, she saw them in the window, eyes narrowed, mouths moving, contempt and dislike distorting their faces. Now they had two things to hate her for: she was a murderess, and she was Lord D'Aubrey's whore.

She started up the street, moving blindly in the opposite direction from the route he had taken. The sun was high, the air mild and gentle, but the pleasure she'd taken in the day only an hour ago was gone. The street made a sharp turn at the top of the square, adjacent to the vicarage and the blocky Norman edifice that was All Saints Church. She didn't know if it was fatigue or a reluctance to brave the gauntlet of staring townsfolk again so soon—or something else entirely—but instead of turning around and starting for Lynton Hall, she walked through the arch of two enormous sycamore trees and passed into the shadowy church-yard.

As soon as the rusty lych-gate clicked shut behind her, she knew why she'd come here. She had almost come last Sunday, after the church service, but too many people had been milling about and she hadn't wanted anyone to see her. Now she was alone, and she could accomplish her mission without witnesses.

They'd arrested her early on the morning after Randolph's murder, and later she hadn't been allowed out of gaol to attend his funeral. As a consequence, she'd never seen his grave. But she found it easily enough today, because his stone was taller than anyone else's, and grander, and an enormous wreath of fresh flowers lay at its base. She read his name, *Randolph Charles Wade*, and the dates of his birth and death, but when she started to go closer to read the smaller, ornately lettered inscription, she found she couldn't move. She stood twelve feet away, her back pressed against the rough granite of a neighboring monument, rooted to the spot and unable to go a step closer.

What was this fear, and why would it come over her now? Randolph was dead, he couldn't hurt her again. But even his marker upset her, the stony straightness of it, the cold, phallic implacability. All at once, memories she thought she'd buried years ago burst in violent pictures before her tightly closed eyes. She had to turn away and drop her face in her hands. But it wouldn't stop, and she could still see herself as if from a distance—exactly as she had seen herself when it was happening to her—and suddenly she was his victim again. She knew the same bewilderment, and then the same enveloping horror. The precise design of the floral carpet in his bedchamber filled her mind's eye, giant cabbage roses on a sky-blue background. She saw herself kneeling on it, in front of the low, broad, obscene ottoman, her hands behind her back. Waiting. She heard his quiet voice, always patient, always merciless, instructing and explaining, never angry, not even when he hurt her, not even when—

She broke away, pressing her fists against her mouth. Opening her eyes, she saw the ash-colored bark of a copper beech, and she put her hands on it, pressed her forehead against it and held on, feeling the cool, hard reality of it under her palms. God! Why had she come here? What if the dreams started again, and the sleeplessness and the paralyzing fear? She'd thought she was strong enough to come and look at his grave, bear the sordid memories, acknowledge all the ugliness, but she wasn't. Maybe he would always, always win.

No. No. No. She let go of the tree, but she couldn't turn around. To the thin gray bark of the copper beech she said out loud, "You can't touch me. I'm not afraid of you. You're rotting in the ground, you can't hurt me. Somebody . . . killed you and you got—you got—what you deserve. Dead, you're dead, Randolph. If you're burning in hell, I don't care. I hope you are."

Her heart was racing. It took a minute to overcome a superstitious dread that he would rise up and punish her somehow for that profane exorcism. But nothing happened. The birds overhead kept singing; the wind continued to flutter the new leaves in the beech tree. Nothing happened. She put her hands on her cheeks, taking slow, deep breaths to calm herself, and she thought, *It's over. I'm glad I came, because now it's really finished.*

But she was even gladder to leave. She wiped her damp palms on her skirt and hurried toward the gate. She almost collided with someone coming through it.

It was a woman. "Oh!" she exclaimed. "Sorry, I didn't see you." That was no wonder; a huge armload of cut flowers almost obscured her face. Lowering them, she came to a full stop and regarded Rachel curiously.

She felt called upon to identify herself, explain her presence, especially since the woman appeared to belong here; she wore no hat or coat, not even a shawl, and even though she was young, she had an air of proprietariness about her. "Excuse me," Rachel faltered. "I've been—I was looking at the graves." She made a mental face; what else would she be doing in the churchyard?

"Oh, yes, it's beautiful this time of the year, isn't it? I'm quite fond of graveyards myself." When Rachel didn't respond, she said, "I'm Anne Morrell. My husband's the vicar, you know."

No help for it. "I'm Rachel Wade," she said, and waited to see what that would bring.

The woman's interesting face showed no disapproval, but her attention narrowed subtly, focused on Rachel more closely. "How do you do, Mrs. Wade. Christy told me he'd made your acquaintance, and I've been looking forward to meeting you."

Rachel very much doubted that, but she returned Mrs. Morrell's friendly smile as best she could.

"These are altar flowers," she went on, explaining the burden of lilies and sweet peas in her arms. "We have ladies in the village who replace them from their gardens twice a week. I can't bear to throw the old ones out, because they're never really *dead* enough, you know, and so I end up putting them on the graves."

Rachel nodded politely.

"Do you know the Weedies?"

"I beg your pardon?"

"Mrs. and Miss Weedie, two parish ladies who do most of the flowers for the church—well, Miss Weedie mostly, now that her mother's so ill."

"No, I—I don't know them. I don't really know anyone."

Mrs. Morrell's astute gray eyes were examining her, sizing her up in a way that, for some reason, didn't give offense. "Well," she said lightly, "you really ought to make Miss Weedie's acquaintance, because she knows everything there is to know about flowers. And unless a miracle has occurred at Lynton since last fall, when I lived there, I expect the terraced gardens behind the house are still a shambles. It's quite a shameful ruin, I could never persuade the gardener to do a thing about it."

"I had forgotten that you used to live there." Rachel said.

Mrs. Morrell's wry smile widened. "What a terrible house-keeper you must think I am."

"Oh, not at—"

"But it simply defeated me, Mrs. Wade. All those rooms, the drafts, the leaks, everything crumbling—I found it much easier to hide away in a little sitting room in the attic and ignore every-thing that was falling apart on the two floors below me."

Rachel couldn't help smiling back, in sympathy with that sen-timent. "It is a lot of work," she admitted. "We're trying to tackle one room at a time, beginning on the first floor with the drawing rooms. But it's a struggle, even with four of us working every day."

"How wonderfully enterprising of you." She used the back of her wrist to push a strand of reddish hair out of her eyes. "Tell me, is Violet Cocker still at Lynton? I see Susan and some of the others in church, but never Violet."

"Yes," Rachel answered neutrally, "Violet's there."

"Then I admire you for more than your enterprise. Also your tolerance and saintly patience."

Rachel almost laughed. Something close to delight welled up in her; she hadn't spoken to another woman in this easy, good-humored way since her school days.

They continued to talk about Lynton Hall and its eccentrici-ties and compensations, agreeing with each other on everything, until the church bell in the tower behind them chimed a quarter to one. "Oh, heavens, I'd forgotten the time," Mrs. Morrell fret-ted with sincere-sounding regret. "I've got the churchwarden's wife coming for lunch in fifteen minutes, and I'm not even dressed yet."

Rachel thought she looked beautiful in a gauzy, loose-fitting gown of flowered blue gingham, but perhaps it wasn't formal enough for the churchwarden's wife. "Please don't let me keep you any longer," she said hurriedly, moving around her to the gate. "I'm—I'm very glad we met, Mrs. Morrell."

"I am, too," she answered, and this time Rachel believed her. "I expect we'll see each other all the time now, so won't you call me Anne?"

She paused, her hand on the gate latch. "Thank you," she managed to say in a normal voice, but her emotions were dangerously close to the surface. "I'm Rachel."

Anne smiled. With a little nod instead of a wave—her arms were still full of flowers—she went off to lay her offerings on the graves.

All the way home, Rachel felt breathless. She might have met a friend, and the possibility thrilled her. But uncertainty still plagued her, and she worried that Mrs. Morrell didn't really know who she was. What if, out of charity or discretion, Reverend Morrell had neglected to tell his wife about her past? And what if, through some bizarre oversight, village gossip hadn't reached her yet?

But no—when Rachel had said her name, there had been something in Anne's eyes that indicated she knew exactly who Mrs. Wade was. But, incredibly, she hadn't been any more censorious than her husband had the day Rachel had met him in the lane. The Christian virtues of tolerance and forgiveness hadn't been much in evidence at Dartmoor Prison, even among the chaplains who had preached daily sermons on sin, guilt, and redemption. But apparently those virtues did exist in Wyckerley, at least in the persons of the vicar and his wife. A *friend*. Her euphoria lasted all the way home.

She was taking her bonnet off, still smiling to herself, when she noticed Susan bustling down the hall toward her. "Mrs. Wade," she announced with a worried frown, "you've got a visitor."

She was certain she'd misheard. "*I* have a visitor?"

"Yes, ma'am. I wasn't sure where to put 'er, in yer room or one o' the drawing rooms, so I put 'er in the green parlor. I hope that was right—I didn't know what else t' do."

"Who is it, Susan?"

"Why, ma'am, it's Miss Lydia Wade."

VIII

Through the gap in the sliding doors to the drawing room, Rachel saw her. She was seated on the couch with her head bowed, hands busily knitting on a black square of cloth, so large it covered her lap and half the sofa. She'd grown stout. Her pretty yellow hair had darkened, but she wore it in the same long, careful side-ringlets that had been the envy of every girl at Mrs. Merton's Academy. In spite of her almost total ignorance of modern fashions, Rachel knew Lydia's flowered pink and white frock was outdated; in fact, it looked exactly like the kind of dress she'd worn at school eleven years ago.

The unlikely thought crossed her mind that she and Lydia might have something in common—that the aftermath of Randolph's death might have had the same stunting effect on his daughter's emotional growth as it had on his widow's. If so, was there a chance for any kind of rapprochement between them now? Probably not; it was probably folly even to speculate on such a thing. Still, something in Lydia's posture, the angle of her bent head, so strange and at the same time so familiar, reminded Rachel of herself.

At the murder trial, Lydia had stood in the witness box and testified that her father was a kind, gentle man, that Rachel has seduced him, that on the last night of his life he'd confided to his daughter that his new wife wasn't the sweet-natured, biddable girl he thought he had married. If it were so, if he had really said that, then he'd been speaking no more than the truth—for by the end of that hellish first and final week of their marriage, Rachel had indeed changed. But Lydia must have changed as well, because in a way she, too, had had her innocence stolen. Wasn't that a beginning, something on which they could try to build a semblance of understanding?

Sliding the heavy doors apart, Rachel said in a quiet voice, "Hello, Lydia."

The fast-moving hands stilled. She lifted her head—and Rachel saw at once that her hopes for a reconciliation were pathetic, absurd. In Lydia's round brown eyes there was only one emotion, and it was hatred.

She stood up slowly. "I've heard cats always land on their feet," she said in an unsteady voice, eyes wide, measuring her from head to toe. "Now I know snakes do, too."

Rachel released a long, hopeless breath. "What do you want?"

"Look at you. Oh, my God, look at you." Her peeling laugh sounded horribly false. She came nearer, still scrutinizing her. "Did you really think you could disguise yourself?"

"What do you—"

"Did you think that black gown could fool anyone? That there's a soul here who doesn't know exactly what you are?"

"Lydia, what's the point of this?" she asked tiredly. "Why did you come here?"

"Why did *you* come here?" she snapped back, voice rising, eyes flashing. "*Here* of all places?"

"You know why I came—it wasn't my choice. I was sent away from Dorset when I couldn't find work."

"You should have been transported. A woman like you, you should have been put on a ship and sent to hell."

She closed her eyes. "There's no point to this conversation."

"Did you see me at the trial? I was praying every minute that they would hang you. Did you see me?"

"I saw you."

"When the sentence came down and it was penal servitude, I lost my faith in a righteous God. But then I changed my mind! Because hanging wouldn't have been enough!"

"Lydia, for God's sake." She had to step back, away from the loathing that seemed to come from her old friend in hot waves.

"You were always the one with the chums, all of them hanging on you, fawning over you—'Rachel's so pretty, oh, Rachel's so smart.' " Her voice and the curl of her lips were ugly and disturbing. "Do you know what's made me happy all these years? Thinking about you being locked up in a cell. Day in and day out, month after month and year after year. *All by yourself.*"

"I want you to go now." She moved away from the door.

"I fell asleep every night picturing you in your little cell. Sometimes I'd pretend I was you, lying on a cot instead of in my bed. I found out what it's like at Dartmoor—I know everything about the silence and the punishments. I even know what you wore, what you ate."

Although she understood the utter futility of a denial, she heard herself say, *"Listen to me,"* in a low, intense voice, *"I did not kill your father."*

Lydia bared her teeth and came closer. "You murdered him in cold blood."

"No, I found his body—that morning—we were to go away that day on our honeymoon, but he was *dead,* he was already *dead*—"

"Don't you touch me!" She smacked at the hand Rachel had lifted toward her. "First you enticed him, corrupted him, and then you killed him!" Her shrill voice broke. "And he was a good man, kind and gentle, and because of you—"

"No, he was—*not* kind, he—"

"Liar!" She drew her hand back; before Rachel could dodge, she slapped her across the face.

She held her stinging cheek, blinking one watering eye and trying not to tremble. "You don't know what you're saying."

"I know! I know! You slandered him once—I'll see you dead before I'll let you do it again!"

Over Lydia's shoulder, Rachel saw Sebastian in the doorway. For a second he stood still, transfixed. Then Lydia lunged, shoving her hard in the chest with the heels of both hands. She stumbled backward, threw her arms up for a shield. With a desperate cry, Lydia came at her again, her fingers curled into claws.

Before she could strike, Sebastian's forearm streaked around her waist and jerked her completely off her feet. She fought him, cursing, shrieking like a furious child, twisting from side to side. But his grip was unbreakable, and suddenly she went limp, hanging over his arm like a cloth doll.

He set her on her feet warily. Rachel couldn't talk; when he looked at her, she shook her head, to tell him she wasn't hurt.

A commotion sounded from the hallway, raised voices and running feet. Susan, looking flustered, skidded to a halt in the doorway. A woman darted around her and rushed into the room. "Lydia!" Ten years ago her hair had been brown, not gray, but Rachel knew who she was. "Oh, gracious, oh, my heavens—what's happened?"

Sebastian glared at her. "Who the devil are you?"

"Lord D'Aubrey, I sincerely beg your pardon! I'm Margaret Armstrong—Lydia is my niece." She put her arm around Lydia's waist, mumbling, "Oh dear, oh dear." Lydia was still breathing hard, still glaring at Rachel with loathing.

Sebastian moved between them, blocking Rachel's view. "I'd advise you to take your niece home, Mrs. Armstrong. At once."

"Yes, of course. I'm most terribly sorry, my lord, but—Lydia hasn't been well. Please forgive this intrusion and this unfortunate—incident—"

"It isn't my pardon you should be asking," he cut in coldly. "It's Mrs. Wade's."

Lydia had begun to move toward the door, but she stopped at that and twisted around. "Beg *her* pardon? Beg that murdering whore's pardon?" Nothing but Sebastian's hard body prevented her from renewing the assault. When he advanced on her, she snarled at him but gave ground, muttering something low and vicious.

"Lydia, come with me, for pity's sake," Mrs. Armstrong pleaded softly, pulling on her hand. Finally Lydia went.

Sebastian followed them out into the hall, pausing in the doorway to throw a glance back at Rachel. She pushed away from the curtained window, against which she had all but collapsed, to show him she was all right. He sent her an indecipherable look, then went after Lydia and her aunt.

Her knees wouldn't stop shaking. She crept to the sofa, holding onto it like an old lady while she sidled around and lowered herself to the cushion. Her cheek still smarted and her chest ached, as if the muscles were bruised. It would have been a comfort to press her face into the padded arm of the sofa and burst into tears. She conquered the urge by squeezing her eyes shut and gritting her teeth.

She'd forgotten about Susan. The maid appeared at her side, hands fluttering, her kind face pinched from shock. "Ooh, ma'am, how horrible. I never, I swear I just never in my life. Are you all right?"

"Yes."

"Can I get you some water or anything? Something like brandy, maybe, or—"

"No, nothing. Thank you."

"Are you sure?"

"Yes. I would just like to sit here a moment. By myself. Thank you," she said again.

Susan dithered for another frustrated minute, sighed, and said, "Well, all right, then, ma'am," and left her alone.

She felt as if she'd been in an accident. No, worse; an accident was impersonal, a mere catastrophe, while this—this was an encounter with hate so intense, she could still feel its blistering heat. The dreadful isolation of prison had had a compensation: it had kept her safe from all but the most generalized contempt, expressed in a hundred small ways every day by guards and warders, even other prisoners, until it numbed and deadened the senses. But she wasn't inside gaol's protective egg any longer. She was an orphaned fledgling, limping through the tall, dangerous grass of the real world. And she had a powerful enemy.

At a sound, she lifted her head from the back of the sofa to see Sebastian across the room, watching her. Wordless, he crossed to the side table, which served as a liquor cabinet, and poured wine into a glass. She was surprised when he brought it to her rather than drinking it himself.

Out of politeness, she took a small sip. "If you don't need me right now," she said, handing the glass back, "I would like to go to my room."

Ignoring that, he sat down beside her, frowning. "What was that all about?" She flinched when he lifted his hand to her face. His eyes darkened. "Did she hurt you?"

"No. I'm fine now." But he touched her anyway, gently, his palm cool on her stinging cheek. She held perfectly still.

"What did she say to you?"

She took a shuddery breath. "What you would expect her to say. She thinks I killed her father. Excuse me," she mumbled, standing up. She couldn't stay here any longer; his hovering concern confused her, made her feel worse, not better. "I would like to go to my room, my lord. May I?"

He sat back, dragging his hands from his knees to his thighs, his long legs spread. "Yes, go," he said, sounding angry.

They stared at each other. What was he looking for, she wondered, what did he expect? Did he think she would *confide* in him now? Trust him—let him comfort her? She had no intention of showing him anything.

"Thank you," she said, barely courteous, and hurried from the room. She couldn't wait to be alone.

She stayed in her sitting room for the rest of the day, brooding profitlessly, languishing. Susan came with a tray at dinnertime, but she sent her away, unable to eat anything. After that, no one bothered her.

The house grew quiet. Around ten o'clock, the solitude she'd craved earlier began to oppress her, and the night to come yawned empty and endless, probably sleepless. Pictures from the long day floated past her mind's eye as she lay in bed, drifting in and out of half dreams . . . Lord D'Aubrey's ebony walking stick swinging in a wide, arrogant arc ahead of his fine leather boots . . . banks of wildflowers on either side of the red clay lane that dipped and rose, shaded by oak branches . . . her own face in the mirror in Miss Carter's shop, looking pretty and almost young . . . Sebastian's expression of appreciation, almost . . . admiration, and then a surprised sort of gentleness. . . .

Honoria Vanstone's high, strident voice, the accent artificially genteel, disturbed the dream; she came fully awake, remembering the last time she'd seen the mayor's daughter—a week ago, when she and another lady had crossed to the other side of the narrow High Street in a pointed and deliberate snub.

To soothe herself, she thought of Anne Morrell. An image of her kind gray eyes came on the fancied odor of lilies and fresh moss, turned earth and clean wind. *Won't you call me Anne?* Rachel's heart fluttered, as it had this afternoon, with hope and gratefulness. Then her thoughts tapered off and her mind began to float again, the events of the day gliding farther and farther away beyond a thickening blanket of drowsiness.

Without a warning, not even a second's uneasiness, the blackness shattered in a burst of light, and a vision of a grave marker's sharp marble point stabbed into her brain like a thrusting sword. She shot up in bed, eyes wide and darting, scouring the room for a glimpse of something real, something solid to dispel the violent image. Scrambling out of bed, she rushed to the window and threw back the curtains. Starshine glowed on the flags of the empty courtyard. She pressed her forehead to the glass, shuddering, whispering, "No, no, no," to break the silence and lessen the horror, to reclaim herself.

She lit a candle and carried it into her sitting room. Gradually its comfortable ordinariness calmed her: she touched the objects on her desk, her pens and her ink blotter, the pretty quartz stone she used for a paperweight. She opened her accounts ledger, and the neat, orderly lines of figures soothed her. Everything was up to date; she had no bills to pay, no letters to write. And no book to read. She didn't want to sleep—didn't want to dream; if she were going to get through this night, she would have to have a book.

The library was in her wing, across the stone corridor from the chapel. It wasn't cold, but she pulled her wrapper tighter around her shoulders anyway, shivering a little because of the quiet, and the lateness of the hour, and the shadow-corners her candle couldn't penetrate. A week ago she'd made another midnight visit to the library, but Lord D'Aubrey had been there; she'd seen the yellow light from his lamp spilling out into the hallway. She'd spun around in a panicky half circle and hurried back to her room, unnoticed.

Thank God, tonight the high-ceilinged, musty-smelling room was deserted. She reshelved her old book and began searching for a new one—never an easy task in this disappointing library, and one best approached with low expectations. She found all five volumes of *Dwight's Theology*, and mentally cringed at the realization that she'd actually read two of them, Dwight being considered a very improving author at Dartmoor Prison. She'd read Horseley's *Biblical Fragments*, too, and Bingley's *Animal Biography*, and most of *The British Essayist*.

Eureka, she thought wryly—a book published during her own lifetime, although just barely: *Swallow Barn*, by John P. Kennedy. "Sketches of Plantation Life in the American South," the title page promised. Sighing, she carried it to the window seat, where there was an overhead niche for her candle, and began to read.

Sleep was a wily enemy. After ten minutes, she had to get up and walk around the room to wake herself up. Drowsiness returned the second she sat down and reopened *Swallow Barn*, whose lifeless, turgid prose killed any interest she might have had in the author's subject. By concentrating fiercely, she fought her way to Chapter 3. Two pages later, sleep crept up from behind and swallowed her.

As always, the dream's approach was slow, insidious, deceptively innocent. She was standing in the middle of a room she didn't recognize, waiting for something. The dread only began when she realized she *had* to wait, that she wasn't allowed to move. Then she wasn't standing anymore, she was sitting on the edge of a high bed, her legs dangling over the side. She was naked, and the sight of her own white thighs terrified her. Now she recognized the room; it was her husband's bedroom, and everything in it was sharp-edged and nauseatingly familiar. She wanted to bolt up from the bed and run, but she wasn't allowed to move. She had to sit and wait for him, sit with her legs apart, just so, and her hands clasped behind her neck. It was the "first position," the least degrading, but already she was trembling, the breath backing up in her lungs.

She heard a noise outside the door, and she began to cry—silently; if he heard her weeping, he would punish her. A dark shape appeared in the doorway. She knew it was he, but the real terror didn't begin until he stepped into the light. Then her fear rose higher and higher in layers until she was full, she couldn't hold anymore. His wine-colored dressing gown sickened her, but she couldn't look away from its silky, shiny surface. It was cold to the skin, she knew that, and when he moved it made a rustling sound that brought bile up in her throat.

He was holding something in his hand.

Helpless, heart-pounding panic engulfed her. She started to sob, feeling like a child when she begged him not to—*please, oh, please, please!*—but he never stopped moving toward her, gliding toward her in the obscene dressing gown, endlessly nearing, his face stern and patient, his arm outstretched to show her what he had in his hand. The moment stretched into madness and just beyond, and then her courage failed and she began to scream.

Sebastian saw the pale glow of a candle above the window seat, flickering in the air currents, barely illuminating something dark and slumped against the paneled wall. He didn't know it was a person until he heard a choked-off cry, a sudden, guttural *huff* that made the hairs on his neck rise, and he didn't know it was Rachel until he went closer and saw her fall forward over her knees, curling up tight, pushing her hands into her dark hair.

Alarmed, he set his candle next to hers. He said her name, but she was crying and she didn't hear. There was a raw, bottomless agony in the sound of her weeping that he literally could not bear. He touched her lightly, and she lifted her head. When he saw her face, he had to turn away. He went to his desk and got a handkerchief from the drawer.

Sitting down next to her on the padded window seat, he pushed the cloth into her hand, and she buried her nose in it. Her narrow shoulders were shaking; he stroked her softly, feeling her intermittent shudders. "Why are you crying?" No answer. "Why?" She muttered something he couldn't understand. Taking her by the shoulders, he made her face him. "Tell me why you're crying."

"Dream," she got out, clearly this time.

"A nightmare?" She nodded. "What did you dream?"

She shook her head and kept on shaking it. She wouldn't tell.

"You're all right now." He had wanted to hold her today, give her some kind of comfort after Lydia Wade had abused her, and he'd been angry when she wouldn't let him. He circled her with his arms now, pulling her against him. She allowed the intimacy, but she didn't relax, wouldn't lean on him. He could smell her clean hair; he could see the candlelight glittering on the silver streaks, turning them golden. Her tears kept coming, but the helpless sobbing seemed to be over. She was wearing a cheap cotton robe of indeterminate color, the material stiff, not soft yet from wear or washing. It only reached to her knees, but under it she had on the long yellow nightgown he'd once seen folded at the bottom of her bed. How slender she was. How compelling her sadness and her brittle vulnerability. How incredible that he'd kept his hands off her this long.

She dropped her head, and he could see the white nape of her neck, the little bump that was the first vertebra of her spine. He brought his lips to her temple, letting strands of her hair tickle his mouth. Soft. Through the arm he had around her, he felt a new awareness slowly seep into her body. She didn't move, but the softness retreated; he could almost hear her hoping against hope that she was mistaken, that this wasn't the inevitable moment she must know it was. He thought of prolonging her uncertainty, keeping her on this exquisite edge a little longer. But either sympathy or impatience made him end the suspense by drawing her closer. "Mrs. Wade," he said quietly. "Mrs. Wade, I think it's time."

"Time." The word came out on a wispy breath. He saw deep resignation in her wet-silver eyes. Which wasn't quite the same as acquiescence, but for now he deemed them close enough. If there was dread there as well, he chose not to notice it.

"Past time." He tipped her chin up, so she couldn't look away while he slipped his other hand inside her nightgown and caressed her soft round breast.

How like her not to give him the satisfaction of reacting. Her lips flattened slightly; the slow slide of his thumb across her nipple elicited a tiny gasp, nothing more. But she was twisting his wet handkerchief in her lap with both hands. She tried to dip her head, but he kept his hand under her chin. Searching her lovely, tear-streaked face, he asked, genuinely curious, "What is it you hope for, Mrs. Wade?"

"I hope . . ." She licked her salty lips. "I hope to be able to bear it."

She didn't mean only this. She meant her whole life. Her fatalism had the usual effect of making him want to take her, and making him want to set her free. His baser side won, as it had been doing regularly of late. He bent and kissed her, scraping her bottom lip into his mouth with his teeth.

Her eyes glazed. She made a low-pitched sound in her throat that set him on fire. "I don't want this."

Did he hear her right? Any resistance, even this weak, whispered one, warred with his image of her as a hopeless stoic. Before anything as subversive as his conscience could surface, he said, "Do you think I could let you go now? I'm afraid it's not possible." And it wasn't.

Her lips curled in faint but unmistakable derision. "A condition of employment?" she asked, with a sneer in her low voice, her face turned away.

The phrase nettled him; he thought they understood each other well enough by now that such labels weren't necessary. But he answered without hesitation, "Precisely." And then for some reason he added, "There's no need to be afraid." He slid his hand under her knees and rose from the window seat, holding her in his arms.

He didn't go far, only to the leather couch in front of his desk. She was disturbingly light, and as stiff in his arms as a sack of sticks. He set her on her feet, because it was easier to undress a woman when she was standing. The candlelight was dim here; he could barely see her. That must seem like a blessing to her. To him it didn't much matter; he would see her soon enough, and often enough, in as much light as he wanted.

Her silence and her manner—completely withdrawn—suggested that their first time together was not going to be particularly transcendent, and that his best course would be simply to get it over with. That was one way. Another would be to exploit her provocative unwillingness, use it to heighten his pleasure—and hers, too, if she would let it. For the hundredth time he wondered what her husband had done to her. Since he didn't know and she wouldn't tell him, it seemed he had no choice but to enjoy her in any way he liked.

A cold-blooded resolve, but he didn't stick to it for long. Because what he would have liked at that moment would have been to say, "Take off your clothes," and then watch her—himself fully dressed, of course—while she stripped for him. She would tremble and blanch, she might even refuse, and he would find her resistance a potent aphrodisiac. But even as the libidinous image took shape in his mind, his hands went to the collar of her modest night robe, and he began to undo the buttons himself.

But he couldn't deny himself the pleasure of watching her face while he undressed her, even though it would've been kinder to hold her close, let her bury her head against his chest, eyes shut tight to deny what was happening. She was unique among his current female acquaintance in that her mind fascinated him every bit as much as her body. He felt a compulsion to know what she was thinking while he seduced her.

But it wasn't to be. Except for anxiety, her colorless eyes gave away nothing, not even when he pushed the robe over her shoulders and began to unfasten her flannel nightgown. The buttons stopped at her navel; he opened the gown slowly, baring her breasts a little at a time. He thought she was blushing, but in the pale light he couldn't be certain. "Very pretty," he murmured, meaning everything about her. She shut her eyes; his appreciation meant nothing to her. He put his fingers on her nipples and pinched—lightly; enough to startle, not enough to hurt. He gave her credit for her sangfroid: she never moved. He increased the pressure playfully, then not quite so playfully. Her lips trembled.

That was all he'd wanted, a reaction. He used his palms to soothe her, stroking back and forth slowly, softly. Her skin beguiled him, the sleekness of it, the coolness; it was tempting to imagine that no one had touched her like this before.

But someone had.

"What did he do to you?" he asked as he pulled her arms, one at a time, out of the sleeves of her nightgown. Of course she didn't answer. The gown slid down her hips and pooled on the floor at her feet, and he forgot the question.

Voluptuous, full-bodied women were his usual passion—if that was the word for the soulless, heartless couplings that had been his lot for the last few years. This woman was anything but voluptuous, and yet her lithe body pleased him. It was shapely, healthy, surprisingly youthful, not quite what he'd been expecting. More than ever, she made him think of a virgin.

She was staring straight ahead, but he didn't think she was seeing him; she'd erected a kind of visual wall to keep him away from her. To test the wall's thickness, he began to take his clothes off, boots first, then shirt, then trousers. Before he finished she turned her face away, gazing off toward the flickering candle flame. So much for her visual wall.

He put his hand on her shoulders, drawing her closer until her breasts touched his chest. Her skin was slightly damp; beneath his fingers he felt her start to shake. The charms of martyrdom were beginning to dim for him. He kissed her, opening her mouth wide with his, using his tongue roughly to force a response. He liked her taste, the sleekness of her mouth. She held still and bore it without a whimper.

"Relax, Mrs. Wade," he whispered. "Don't make it a rape." He opened one of her closed hands and pressed it against his chest, slid it across his nipple.

"If I . . ."

It came out the barest sigh, possibly not words at all. "If you . . . ?" he prompted, brushing her hair with his lips. How could he ever have disliked her hair?

"If I begged you . . ."

"If you begged me to what?"

"*Stop,*" she gasped, at the moment he slid her rigid palm down to his stomach.

He soothed her by holding still, not moving her hand lower, where he wanted it. "There are many things I look forward to hearing you beg me for," he murmured against her forehead. "But do you know, stopping isn't one of them."

He didn't want her flat on her back on the leather sofa, because she would lie there like a corpse. Necrophilia wasn't one of his depravities yet; he wanted her active, not passive. He urged her closer to the couch with a hand on the small of her back, and she went, stiff-kneed and full of trepidation. "I'm not going to hurt you," he promised, but she gave no sign of hearing.

Keeping her hands, he sat down on the sofa's edge. He put his knees together and pulled her toward him, making her open her legs around his. Her eyes went wide with shock; she pulled back with her hands, but he held them firmly. The sight of her pale, wide-apart thighs excited him. There was no point in telling her again to relax. "Lean forward. Put your hands on my shoulders." Rather than touch him, she put them on the high sofa back. But he didn't quibble; the movement brought her breasts closer to his mouth. He took advantage of it immediately, dipping his head and suckling her strongly. The high-pitched gasp she made sounded surprised, not pained. But when he slipped his hands between her legs to push them farther apart, she moaned.

"Don't be afraid."

Useless advice; the tendons in her thighs were vibrating like harp strings. Gently, gently, he cupped her soft mound, fluttering his fingers against her delicate flesh, fondling her. He licked her between her breasts, tasting the salt tang of her sweat. She couldn't stop the trembling in her legs, so he pulled on her knees from behind until she was kneeling on the cushion, straddling his lap. He tongued her shallow navel while he kneaded the backs of her thighs, drawing her up hard against him, opening his mouth wide and using his teeth on the sleek skin over her ribs. She was panting now, but whether from fear or the beginnings of desire, he didn't know. Fear, probably, but he was very nearly past caring. She cried out when he slipped his smallest finger inside her.

Best to get it over with; erotic preliminaries only tortured her more. He considered stopping everything and letting her go, but only for a split second, before the thought flew off to wherever bad ideas go. After that, there was nothing left but the need to possess her.

Murmuring soft, specious comfort, he coaxed her down, guiding himself into her gently, slowly, and when she stiffened and balked he let her pause, allowing her the illusion of control.

But not for long. He wanted all of her, now, and he wanted it quite badly. His own control was slipping, which was new. He made himself hold still inside her, embracing her with all the tenderness of a real lover, and she quieted, as if she had given up. She let him hold her, let him feel the pounding of her pulse deep inside.

Even now her husband obsessed him. He lifted his face from the hot hollow between her neck and shoulder to ask, "Did he hurt you, always? Was there never any pleasure for you?"

She wouldn't answer.

He studied her tense face, so close to his. The wall was back, but as ineffective as before. She had the look of a saint enduring unspeakable tortures rather than betray her religious faith. He cupped the sides of her face and pressed slow kisses to her lovely, lovely mouth. She wouldn't close her eyes. He thought her lips began to soften, but just then she turned her head aside; her hands, which had been resting on his shoulders, fisted against his chest.

"A martyr to the end," he murmured in her ear, making her quiver. "I think you would find a way to hate this no matter who your lover was."

"Let me go, then," she whispered unexpectedly, into the air over his shoulder.

"Don't be childish," he admonished her gently. "Now I would like you to rise up on your, knees, like this. And down now. Again, and don't stop." But she wouldn't continue unless he made her, his hands holding her hips steady, guiding her. He reached out and patted the fat round arm of the couch. "Would you rather I bent you over the sofa, Mrs. Wade, and took you from behind?"

No response; he might as well have made his intriguing threat to a mannequin.

"Very well. It's immaterial to me, and we have all night."

She brought her hands to her face as if to hide it, but she kept pushing her fingers back into her hair, folding in on herself, hunching over, trying to wrap her body up in a ball. It was worse than weeping, worse than screaming. She was grinding the top of her head into his breastbone, growing smaller, tighter, doing her best to disappear, and still not making a sound.

"Don't do that," he whispered, aghast. "Stop it. Stop now." He lifted her off his lap and turned her, made her unwind and lie flat on the sofa. She didn't even try to close her legs, and he covered her and slipped back inside her with an unexplainable sense of relief. Not possession—relief. Her eyes were shut tight, but she wasn't crying. "Now you're all right," he murmured. "Shh, Rachel, you're all right." He kissed her until she sighed, until he couldn't take any more, and he slid his hands underneath her body and began to move in her.

She was so hot, so tight, and there was no sense in trying to make her like it but he did anyway, courting her with his body, harking to the soft clues of her breathing. Hopeless—he would only end up hurting her if he continued. "Hold on to me," he told her, and she did that at least, clutching his sides with stiff, love-less fingers. He took her as gently as he could, and until the last second it was a cool, controlled act of sexual release. Then he lost his head. He saw the light around him dim and recede, objects disappear. In absolute blackness, he drove and drove into her, conscious of nothing but pure sensation, impossible pleasure, storming and raging in him, until he surrendered and let it take him over the blinding white edge.

IX

Lord D'Aubrey had lit a fire in his bedroom, even though it wasn't cold. "Come here, please," he said. *"Come."*

Rachel moved toward the marble hearth and stood in front of the sparking grate, careful not to let any part of her touch him, not even her clothes. She felt his eyes on her as he went to a side table and poured something into a glass. She hated his peremptory tone, the same one he'd used a few minutes ago in the library. Only then he'd asked, "Where are you going?" while he lounged, still nude on the floor, his back against the sofa where they'd lain when he . . . raped her? Not exactly. Seduced her? Not that either, although she thought that had probably been his intent. "To my room," she'd answered in a careful monotone. But she hadn't been able to keep the gruff edge from her voice when she'd added, "You've finished with me, haven't you?"

He'd stared at her while he rose to his feet, slowly, gracefully, unembarrassed by his nakedness. He'd smiled at her. "By no means." And while she watched, he'd begun to dress.

"How do you feel, Mrs. Wade?" he asked her now.

She had to force herself to look at him. His boyish hair, tousled from his recent exertions, looked incongruous with his big, dangerous body. He hadn't bothered to button his shirt; she could see his chest and the flat ridges of muscle across his belly. Before she could shut out the thought, she remembered exactly how the hair on his thighs had felt, that rough-soft brush against her legs when he'd pressed them apart. Her stomach fluttered—

but she wasn't sure what she was feeling. Randolph's cruelties were hopelessly mixed up in her memory with the things this man had done to her. Need and revulsion, pleasure and pain, desire and disgust—neither her mind nor her body could be relied on tonight to sort them out accurately.

He was holding out a glass to her. She thought of refusing it. It looked like brandy, though; maybe it would steady her nerves. She took it and answered his question. "What difference does it make to you?"

His eyes narrowed; his lips thinned. Once that look would have daunted her, but she didn't care about his anger anymore. The worst was over, and this false concern came too late. She wouldn't salve his conscience by giving his spurious question a second's thought.

And yet, here she was, intact, not hurt, sipping brandy and conversing with him with only a little more stiffness than was usual between them. It was probably too soon to say that her fear of him was over—and besides, she wasn't naive enough to believe he was through with her—but her physical terror of him, of what his body could do to hers, seemed to be gone. At least for now. In a way it was a relief that the thing she'd been dreading for weeks had finally happened, was now finished. And she had lived through it. She had one odd regret: that she could never be Anne Morrell's friend. Because now she truly was Lord D'Aubrey's whore.

He came closer. "I asked you a question. I expect you to answer me."

They had a brief staring contest while she noticed something new about him: his eyes were blue at the tops of his irises and green at the bottom, below the dark pupils. "How do I feel?" She pretended to think about it. "I feel used."

He frowned. "Did I hurt you? Answer me."

He had the lapel of her robe pinched between his fingers to

keep her from moving away. "You want to know if you hurt me," she said in a disbelieving whisper.

"Your body," he specified, and for a moment she saw doubt in his eyes. Self-doubt, guilt's unsavory neighbor.

"My body survived, my lord, and seems to be functioning normally. If you were worried, you can set your mind at rest on that score."

When he smiled unpleasantly, she felt a prickle of the fear she'd just told herself she'd conquered. "I'm much relieved," he said softly. "Take off your clothes, Mrs. Wade, and get in my bed."

Hot blood rushed to her cheeks. "I don't want to," she said, aghast.

"Yes, I know. It adds a certain piquancy to the situation that I find I can't resist."

"Monster."

"I think we can dispense with name-calling." He turned away to light two more candles from the single low taper he'd brought up from the library. He folded his arms. "I'm waiting."

"Damn you. You can't hurt me."

"I sincerely hope not."

"Why do you want me?" she burst out in desperation.

He seemed to ponder. "I've been asking myself that question since the day we met. I'm still not sure of the answer. Come, undress for me, Mrs. Wade. I want to look at you. Surely you and I are beyond coyness now."

How she hated the sound of "Mrs. Wade" on his lips. It made the things he did to her crueler, colder. She stood still, in an agony of indecision. Everything in her rebelled against doing what he wanted, but the consequences of refusing would probably be just as unpleasant.

"Tell me this—did your husband make you strip for him?"

She stared back, unable to answer.

"Tell me. If he did, I won't ask it of you. Did he?"

She couldn't even nod, and it took all her willpower not to look away in shame.

Instead he was the one who looked away. He ran a hand through his hair, taking a sudden breath. His savoir faire slipped for an instant; she caught a glimpse of the man beneath the veneer of coolness and sophistication. But only for a second. He swung back to her with a determined air and said, "Turn around." When she hesitated, he turned her himself, by the shoulders.

Reaching around her, he untied the belt of her wrapper with quick, efficient movements, pulled the robe off and threw it across a chair. Immediately he returned to her and began to unfasten the buttons of her nightgown. This was meant to be a kindness, she supposed, him doing the undressing for her, with her back turned to him. And it was, after a fashion. But if he expected gratitude for it, she couldn't oblige him. She bowed her head to watch his long, nimble fingers, remembering the way they had touched her before. A feeling in the pit of her stomach couldn't be explained. It was like dizziness, like anticipation.

The slow slide of the gown over her shoulders and down her back made her tremble in spite of herself. She covered her breasts with her crossed arms, but for once no memories from the past surged up and tried to drown her. She stood still, feeling Sebastian's eyes on her back, and now his fingers, tracing down the bones of her spine. He caressed her buttocks, and she could feel her skin quiver under his hand, feel goose bumps erupt everywhere he touched her.

Then the lightness disappeared; he tightened his grip, holding her by her hips. She tried to turn, but he prevented it by force. She looked at him over her shoulder. His face was strange. "Don't move," he commanded, and reached behind him for one of the candles. She felt its heat on her back, then her thighs. When he swore in a violent undertone, she knew what he'd seen.

It surprised her; she thought he'd noticed the scars before, in the library. It must have been too dark there, and somehow he'd missed the faint ridge of flesh at the top of her left thigh, the only one that could still be felt with the fingers.

"Who did this to you?"

She almost laughed. How could he not know who?

"The prison guards," he guessed grimly. He turned her to face him. He'd gone pale; he looked dangerous.

"Men are flogged in prison, not women. It's against the rules. They found other ways to discipline us."

"My God." Now he knew. He searched her face, looking for something. "I'm sorry. I'm sorry this happened to you."

"I'm not. My scars saved my life. No one would have believed me without them. The things he did, the—things you want to hear me say—they were too beastly for the judges to credit. Not without proof."

He couldn't seem to speak. There was a new expression in his eyes, and if she didn't know better she'd have called it compassion. What a nerve-wracking thought: pity from the Viscount D'Aubrey. It confounded her so thoroughly, she turned her back on him again.

She heard him blow out the candles he'd just lit. Carrying only one, he took her arm with his other hand, his clasp unwontedly gentle, and led her to the bed. He even pulled back the counterpane, the blanket, and the sheet for her. She was cynically amused. All the solicitousness in the world couldn't mitigate the baseness of his motives, and the gentlest manner couldn't transform ravishment into something more palatable.

But she didn't resist him this time. She was weary, and she wanted it over with.

The sheets were silk—of course. She pulled the top one up to her collarbone, resting her shoulders against a soft mound of pillows. He sat beside her, and watched her in silence for a minute or two before he began taking off his shirt. There was no cruelty or teasing in his thoughtful face while he did it; in fact, he didn't look at her at all. So she looked at him. Because his physical manner was nearly always languid and effortless, it was a surprise to find that his body was muscular and fit. Powerful-looking, the opposite of decadent. She could find no fault with his form; with all the objectivity she could muster, she had to admit that he was handsome. Very handsome. Odd; Randolph had been comely, had had an attractive physique for a man his age. And yet the sight of his body after their first night together had made her sick. Literally, ill.

Sebastian stood up to remove his trousers, and then she did look away. A second later the mattress dipped as he got in bed beside her. He hadn't spoken in a long time; she found she was curious about what he was thinking. Why did he still interest her at all? Why didn't she loathe him more for what he'd done, what he was going to do again?

No answer to that question. She understood why her fear of him had diminished, though. It was because she'd discovered from the most intimate experience that, unlike her husband, he was not thoroughly corrupt. He spoke of the "piquancy" of her unwillingness, and she didn't doubt that he found it so, but he had never hurt her, not really, and she knew with a bone-deep certainty that he never would. His methods of coercion were subtler, and maybe it was sophistry to say that therefore they were kinder. But she had been used by men in both ways now, brutally and gently, and she could say without equivocation that she much preferred Sebastian's.

He was watching her again, lying on his side, the sheet bunched around his lean hips. He took her hand and examined it by the light of the candle on the table, stroking her calloused palm, frowning. His hair fell straight down on either side of his long, fine-boned face. He raised his gaze and looked at her speculatively. "Have you ever once experienced pleasure with a man?"

His voice was low, mild; he might have been asking if she'd ever been to Wales in the summertime. But the question was hardly idle, and the quick gleam in his hooded eyes gave away the full extent of his avidity.

"Why do you think you can ask me such a question?" Her own voice, too high and too loud, gave away her agitation. But how silly she was being, how pathetically demure. They were lying naked beside each other in his bed, and she was worrying about the propriety of the conversation.

His hard mouth pulled into a slight smile. "It's rude of me," he acknowledged dryly. "Answer it anyway. I want to know if you've ever enjoyed yourself in bed with a man."

"Why?"

"Ah, you're under a misapprehension. The rules of this game say that you have to answer my questions but I don't have to answer yours."

"The rules—"

"Aren't fair. Very true. That's because I invented them."

She turned her face to the wall. "I don't have to tell you anything."

When he didn't speak, she began to hear the echo of what she'd said in a new light: it began to sound like famous last words.

At last she heard the rustle of the sheet, soft and decadent-sounding, but she kept her gaze resolutely turned away. He had a grouping of miniatures on the wall, tasteful oils by an artist whose signature was too small for her to read. Landscapes. Not quite what she'd have expected on the walls of a rake's bedroom. But perhaps satyrs and naked bawds were passé; she wouldn't really know. She focused on a pastoral scene and tried to ignore the sounds of movement behind her.

Impossible. A drawer opened, and suddenly dread began to creep across her skin like a viper. *Oh, no.* What was he doing, what was he—getting? A sharp sound, and then the drawer closed. The sour taste in her mouth became nausea; she bit down on her lips, feeling sweat break out on her body.

The mattress shifted. Sebastian sat beside her, facing her, one of his thighs pressed lightly against her hip. He said her name in a question, but she couldn't move. When he touched her, she jumped.

"What is it?" he asked, sounding puzzled. "You've gone pale as the sheet."

His fingers on her cheek made her shudder. "For pity's sake . . ." It came out a faint, horrified whisper.

He looked down at something in his hand. She couldn't look at it; her stomach lurched. "This?" he said.

Before her fluttering eyelashes, she saw a little jar. That was all. Just a little jar. Her heart slowed its staccato pounding. "What"—she had to clear her throat—"What is it?"

He had the wickedest smile, slow and one-sided, infinitely suggestive. He opened the jar and brought it to his nose, breathing in with closed eyes. "Try it," he murmured, holding it out to her.

She sniffed warily. The clear contents of the jar, some kind of ointment, smelled like . . . she couldn't identify the scent. Flowery, but really sweet; musky, heavy, disturbing somehow. "What is it?" she said again.

Instead of answering, he smiled the wicked smile and pulled the sheet away from her bare breasts. She gave a little squeal. When she tried to cover herself, he pulled her hands away and forced them down to her sides. "Don't move. Not a muscle."

As soon as he let go, she disobeyed, crossing her forearms over her chest and staring up at him, glassy-eyed, trying not to look as scared as she felt.

He observed her for a few seconds, seeming more bemused than angry. "Something I'd enjoy very much," he said thoughtfully, "is tying your hands to the bedposts, Mrs. Wade. One day I expect I'll do it. In the meantime, since you won't speak of your late husband's atrocities, I'm left to conclude that bondage was one of the items on his varied plate. And that, being the son of a bitch that by all accounts he was, he didn't take the time or the trouble to make that particular delicacy palatable to his young bride. Blink your eyes if I'm on the right track here."

She looked away, flushing.

He dropped the ironic tone. "Take your hands away," he said almost kindly. "I'll tie you if I have to, but I'd much rather not. Not just now."

You bastard, she thought. But she didn't say it, and after a few hot, furious seconds, she dragged her hands down to her sides.

"That's it. Now don't move—as I was saying." He reached for the jar without looking away from her; he seemed to be spellbound. "You have very lovely breasts, Mrs. Wade. Very, very beautiful."

"What are you going to do?"

"Shhh." He was dipping his fingers in the jar, coating them with the pungent salve, his eyes looked dreamy, but his mouth was hard. "What do you think I'm going to do?" he mocked her softly.

She honestly didn't know for sure until he brought his slippery fingers to her nipple and began to spread the unguent over it. She gasped—jumped—almost sat up straight in the bed. But something kept her where she was.

"Good," he murmured. "Lie still for me. Don't move again."

Panic flickered along every nerve ending. But she could not lock him out the way she'd learned at the end to lock Randolph out—a trick of the mind, a last-ditch gambit of the truly desperate that involved not breathing and pulling down a mental curtain between herself and everything around her. She tried it now, and it worked perfectly until the first outlaw spark of sensation zigzagged past the mind-barrier, and she realized Sebastian wasn't hurting her. He wasn't hurting her.

The salve liquified the moment her skin warmed it, and the indescribable fragrance grew so potent and heady she felt dizzy. He went back to the jar for more and, as he had before, he brought it to his nostrils and inhaled. "Eucalyptus," he said in a low voice, deceptively casual; she could see a vein in his throat pulsing strongly, quickly. "And laurel, and lemon. In sandalwood oil, I think. Do you like it?" He brought his fingers to the same breast again and smoothed the ointment around the aureole of her nipple in maddening circles, apparently fascinated by the changes she could feel in her treacherous bosom, and now fascinated by her face, which she wanted to bury in the pillow, out of his sight.

When he straightened, she entertained, extremely briefly, the foolish hope that he was through with her. Of course he wasn't. He slicked his hand into the jar again, and this time he took a taste of the ointment on his tongue. The wicked smile flashed. "I like it," he announced, and began to soothe her other breast with the same slow, careful, painstaking enjoyment. Her toes curled. She could not possibly like this. She hated sex, which was violent, brutal, and degrading. She could endure it, but she could not enjoy it. No matter, completely irrelevant, that some people claimed to take pleasure in it—she knew what she knew. And yet, when Sebastian leaned over her and put his mouth on her, put his lips on the nipple he'd warmed and stimulated with his hands and his devilish unguent, a stab of such exquisite pleasure shot through her that she groaned, and the longer he teased and tongued and bit, the more excruciating it became.

"Stop it," she cried out, and to her intense astonishment, he did.

He bent to her, blue eyes snapping like fires in a wind, his mouth shining wet, lips ruddy from suckling her. "Try not to be so frightened," he whispered, his own excitement visible, barely leashed. "Let yourself feel." While he stared unblinkingly into her eyes, his face a breath away, he trailed one long, slippery finger down to her belly, taking the silk sheet with it. Her body went rigid, tried to merge into the mattress. He covered her stomach with his hand and caressed her, kneaded the tense muscles to relax her. The gentle massage wouldn't stop. *Oh, do it, just do it,* she wanted to shout. But part of his plan was to make her insane before he debauched her, and he went on and on with his nerve-wracking fondling. When at last he pulled the sheet away, baring everything, she was wound up tight; one more twist would break her.

But she didn't know what she could bear until she had to bear it. Sebastian moved down in the bed until they were thigh to thigh, taking his jar of ointment with him. Her legs were pressed together so tightly, the muscles were quivering. "You know what I want," he said quietly, and if she hadn't known, the direction of his gaze would have enlightened her. "We don't need to have another conversation about tying you, do we?"

She didn't move, except to twist her head on the pillow.

"I'll only add that, as much as I'd enjoy lashing your hands to the posts, I'd like tying your ankles even more." The blue of his eyes glittered like jewels. "I'd like tying them wide apart. Stretching your legs wide apart. Opening you." Her next breath was a rough hiccup—a ludicrous sound, but he didn't laugh at her. "Part your legs," he commanded softly. "Come, open them. Don't make me do it."

But she couldn't. And she wanted to. But she couldn't.

He sighed. He slid his hands down to her ankles and seized them, holding tight. She knew everything about helplessness and immobility, everything about sexual submission. There was nothing he could do to her that hadn't been done. Then why was this worse? Why was this painless seduction breaking her up, annihilating something deep, deep inside?

In a clear voice she said, "Don't do this to me."

He looked up, eyes alert, interested. Paused for so long, she thought he would stop now, stop everything. "What difference does it make? We've done this before. What does it matter now?"

She passed her tongue over her dry lips. *Because I might like it,* she thought frantically. "You know," she said aloud.

He weighed that, and finally acknowledged it with a nod. "Yes. I do." He dropped his head and contemplated his hands, still clasped around her ankles, then let his gaze travel upward. She held her breath, fingers clawing the sheet on either side of her hips. He looked into her eyes. And then he pulled her legs wide apart and crawled between them to keep them open.

She started to cry. She stared at the ceiling while tears trickled down her temples and into her hair. He had his knees pressing against hers, pressing them out, and she felt his breath on her abdomen, the cool swish of his hair on her thigh. Unhurried fingers parted her pubic hair, pulled her labia apart by the hairs, gently, and she felt his breath again, and then the quick flick of his tongue. She couldn't understand the words he was saying. He used one hand to hold her open and the other to smear the slippery cream on her, into her, deep inside, lavishing it, coating her with it, not stopping, on and on. She couldn't get her breath and she couldn't get away. She called out, "No," and "Stop," but he wouldn't stop. He said, "Look at me," and he had his fingers in her while he slathered the ointment on his own stiff sex. Stiff and thick, jutting, her worst enemy, she wanted to kill him—she wanted him inside her. She said, "Do it, then," and he lay over her, coming into her on a long, smooth glide, sailing right into her. He pulled her hands up and made her curl her fingers around the bed rails over her head, squeezing her fingers shut tight while he glided inside her, thick and sleek, stretching her, stroking her. She didn't know his face; he was lost, unrecognizable, and her fear of him wavered because if he lost control, he couldn't control her.

He drove her higher, pushed her against the rails, cold wood hard against her shoulders, driving, driving. Sweat glistened on his face and chest, his straining arms; sweat dripped from his damp hair and fell on her breasts. He kissed her, opening her mouth wide, thrusting into it with his tongue in rhythm with the steady plunging of his sex inside her. She knew what he wanted, knew he wouldn't stop until she gave it to him. She wanted it, too—but it was out of reach, impossible. She let him pull her legs around him, tight around his waist, and she moved her own body to his fevered rhythm.

"Let go," he panted against her neck, grazing his teeth across her throat. "Give in." He pushed his hand under her, dragged it down her back and between her buttocks. She felt his slick finger slide against the tight walls of her other opening, and she yelled out a curse and tried to squirm away. But he had her in a perfect position; there was no escape. His finger slid in easily, not far, but enough to madden her. She bucked again and again, jerking against him. He wouldn't stop, he wouldn't stop, and then a hoarse groan tore from his throat and he went still, clutching at her for an endless moment before his body convulsed. She held him while he poured into her, bearing his full weight and the violence of his driving release. He began to curse before it was over, and she didn't know or care if he was swearing at her or himself.

Relief that it was over warred with hurt and anger and a wrenching, bottomless dissatisfaction—a brand new legacy, and something else she could hate him for. She wriggled out from under his wet, spent, panting body and rolled away from him as far as she could go.

She left him in the gray hour before dawn. He felt her silently rise and slip from the bed, thinking he was asleep. Heard the soft glide of cotton as she put on the gown and robe he'd taken from her hours ago and thrown over a chair. He lay on his stomach with his head turned toward the wall, and although they hadn't been touching, his skin felt cool in her absence and his body felt more than twice as alone. But he didn't move, even though he could see her in his mind's eye, watching him. He knew how her face looked, the way she was clutching her hands at her waist, maybe worrying at the tie of her cotton dressing gown. Twice before she'd tried to leave him, and both times he'd pulled her back down, murmuring to her that she wasn't to go, then taking his hands off her. He could feel her crystal-colored gaze on him now; his mind's-eye picture was clear and complete, but he had no idea what she was thinking. Not the slightest clue.

He didn't hear her slippered feet on the carpet; it wasn't until the door hinges rasped and the latch clicked that he knew she was gone. He lay motionless a little longer, trying to capture a last trace of her elusive scent. Not the eucalyptus smell, but the smell of Rachel. He watched his hand in the half-light, sweeping the sheet where she'd lain, halting to touch the cooling shadow of her heat. Regret was a bitter taste on the back of the tongue, a sick prodding in the belly. He closed his eyes. For the first time in the course of the long, unruly night, his body obeyed him. He went to sleep.

X

DAYS PASSED. HE caught glimpses of her going about her chores, exactly the same, no change, or none visible to the eye. At first he didn't send for her; her gliding, dark-garbed figure was an effective silent reproach, whether she intended it to be or not. He went about his own affairs not exactly as if nothing had happened, but almost. The only difference was that he was aware of her at all times, knew precisely where she was and what she was doing, with an unfailing accuracy that he resented.

One morning he sent for her. She came into his study promptly, carrying her ledger; her ring of keys, the noisy badge of her profession, rattled from a chain pinned to her waist. He looked up from his own accounts book, which he'd been pretending to read so he could keep her waiting, and saw that she was wearing a cap. An old-fashioned mobcap, white, voluminous, and indescribably ugly. She wore it to mock him, he hadn't a doubt. "Take that off and never let me see it on your head again," he said in a harsh voice. It was a shock to realize how angry he was.

"Yes, my lord." She removed the cap and stood with her naked head bowed, forearms crossed over the ledger at her breast. For all that it was a clever disguise, she looked nothing like the cowed prisoner behind the bar at the magistrates' hearing. Was it she who had changed, or his perception of her? Either way, her submissive bearing had been real once and now it was a fraud. Fine. Even better. Much more entertaining to persecute the strong than the weak.

But that amoral resolve rang rather hollow. Nothing had changed. He still didn't know what he wanted to do more, bedevil her or save her.

"Sit down, Mrs. Wade."

"Yes, my lord."

He smiled thinly. As far as formal address as subtle insults went, the score was roughly tied. He leaned back and folded his hands over his stomach. It occurred to him that he should have arranged this meeting in the library; then he could have made her sit on the sofa, and she'd have to remember the last time she'd had occasion to sit on it—no, recline on it. He felt like reminding her of it now; but, of course, such a thing would be too crude. Anyway, it was he who needed the reminder, for he was finding it almost impossible to reconcile the small, sober, blank-faced woman in front of him with the one who had wept in his arms three nights ago, cursed him and enflamed him, squirmed under him, and finally suffered the full brunt of his passionate attentions with all the enthusiasm of a crucified saint.

"Why hasn't this bill been paid?" He tapped the end of his pen on a yellow slip of paper on his desk.

"My lord?" She got up uncertainly and took a few steps toward him. "What bill?"

"This one. For copper pots, twelve guineas' worth. Judelet says he knows nothing of it. This is the second request, and the smith's added eight shillings' interest."

She couldn't believe it. She wanted to see the bill, but she didn't want to go anywhere near him. "I can't account for it, my lord. I never saw the original bill, which should have come to me in the normal course."

"So Judelet's lying?"

Her eyes flashed, then dropped to the desk. "No, of course not. There's been a mistake; the first bill was lost, or the smith never sent it."

"How did these pots come to be ordered in the first place?"

"I don't know."

"You didn't commission them?"

"No, my lord."

"Well, if you didn't and Judelet didn't, who the hell did?"

"I don't know, my lord."

He couldn't rattle her today. "Who's going to pay the eight-shilling fee for a lot of pots nobody will admit to ordering?" he demanded, trying hard to sound as if he gave a damn.

She looked at him steadily. "I will, my lord. If you think it's fair."

He stared at her until he felt foolish. "Sit down," he snapped. "Why are you standing over me?" She went back to her chair and sat.

He picked up another paper from his desk, this one a letter on thick vellum stationery. The effeminate scrawl in light blue ink annoyed him, but he schooled his features into affability and said, "Some friends of mine are coming down from London on Friday, Mrs. Wade. Three or four, I think, possibly five, and almost certainly a lady or two with the gentlemen. You may know one of them—Claude Sully. Your late husband's nephew, I believe. And heir, if I'm not mistaken. Do you know him?"

"No, my lord. I don't know him." But she'd gone a little pale.

"Never met him?"

"No. I think he was—at the trial."

"The trial?"

Her lips tightened. "My trial."

"Was he? How interesting. I hope that won't cause any awkwardness between you. Because of the circumstances. Sully's more of an acquaintance of mine than a friend," he expanded, for no particular reason. "He knew my cousin Geoffrey—the late Lord D'Aubrey, you know."

She said nothing.

"I recall that you were reluctant to help me entertain the natives, so to speak. I hope that squeamishness doesn't extend to my London acquaintance."

"No, my lord."

"Good, excellent," he said, although he knew she was lying. In fact, he was counting on it. "They arrive on Friday, as I say, probably in time for dinner. You'll have rooms readied. I think we can expect a valet or two in the company, perhaps a lady's maid as well, so you'll want to make accommodations for them, too. I'm not sure how long they'll stay. Let's plan for three nights and then see where we are. None of this is beyond you, is it, Mrs. Wade?"

"No, my lord."

"Judelet can organize the menus without your help; indeed, I doubt he'd have it any other way. Things should go smoothly, I can't think why they wouldn't. Oh, one last thing. I'd like you to join in the party as much as possible, take your meals with us and so on. Act as my hostess, in other words." She was watching him through narrowed lids; if looks could kill, he'd be slumped over his desk, stone dead. He smiled at her. "Will that be a problem for you, Mrs. Wade?"

"No, my lord."

"Oh, good. Then I won't detain you. You must have a million things to do."

Claude Sully and the others arrived a little after noon on Friday, much earlier than expected. Mrs. Wade, who had to report to the chief constable in Tavistock every month under the conditions of her release, was not at home when the hired coach from Plymouth rumbled over the flagstones, upsetting the rooks and sending the house cat scurrying. Sebastian greeted his friends alone.

There were four of them: Claude Sully, Sir Anthony Bingham, Mrs. Wilson, and Bertram Flohr. He knew them all except Flohr, a fat, morose, sullen-looking fellow with a midcountry accent. While Kitty—Mrs. Wilson—threw her arms around him for a greeting, Sebastian tried to remember if he'd ever slept with her. She looked flushed and disheveled, as if she'd just finished servicing all three of her traveling companions in the coach. He wouldn't have put it past any of them.

But he was glad they'd come. They were among the most dissolute of his friends, and he looked forward to being amused by their brittle, acerbic wit. The pastoral charms of Devon had begun to seduce him, incredible as it seemed, and he deemed that Sully and the others were just the antidote he needed for all this cloying rusticity.

As usual, Bingham was drunk. "I remember this place," he exclaimed, wheeling around unsteadily, gaping up at the granite walls of Lynton Hall and the crenelated gatehouse. "*Been* here, by God. With *you*, Sully, remember?"

"Of course, you sod, that's what I've been telling you. Two years ago, when Geoffrey was still alive. Oh, say, sorry about your cousin, Sebastian. Hunting accident, wasn't it?"

Sebastian returned Sully's smiling, insincere sympathy in kind. "That's what they say," he said casually, and led the party into his house.

They laughed at it. Kitty was the least inhibited in her raillery, and in spite of himself Sebastian couldn't help seeing through her mocking eyes all the flaws and eccentricities he'd learned to overlook. "Bastian, what on *earth?*" she cried, dancing down the central hall with the men in her wake, throwing open the doors to one drawing room after another, laughing with exaggerated astonishment at their worn and outdated furnishings. She wore her straight black hair loose and nearly down to her waist, and she liked to fling it back from her shoulders by lifting her chin and giving her head a dramatic shake. That reminded him: they *had* been lovers, for about a month back in '52 or '53.

And she'd found uses for that black hair that had awed and bedazzled him.

They settled in the rosewood drawing room, stretching out on sofas and loveseats, making themselves at home. Soon the serious drinking began. "Where's that deaf housekeeper?" Sully wanted to know, unbuttoning his yellow waistcoat and loosening his cravat. "Mrs. Apple, Mrs. Pear—"

"Mrs. Fruit," Bingham said unexpectedly from the floor, where he lay with a glass of claret balanced on his chest. "Stone deaf, couldn't hear a word unless you roared it in her ear."

"She retired," Sebastian said.

"Bugger it," said Bingham.

"Bugger it," Sully agreed. "We said things to her when she wasn't looking," he explained to the others.

"Right," said Bingham. "Dirty words, you know, rude suggestions, right in the old girl's ear. Geoffrey started it. Bloody good fun." He snickered, splashing wine on his shirt.

Sully got up from his chair and came over to sit beside Kitty on the couch. He was combing his curly blond hair forward these days, Brutus-fashion, to hide his balding crown. Maybe it was the contrast with the ruddier, healthier stock Sebastian was growing used to in Wyckerley, but Sully looked wan to him, soft and almost effete. He had shifting blue eyes and a thin mouth that turned down when he smiled, not up. His expensive clothes were in the height of fashion; he looked as out of place in the seedy drawing room as a courtier in a convent. He had his arm draped across the back of the sofa, resting his hand on Kitty's neck. "Why the devil are you still down here, D'Aubrey?" he demanded. "What's the draw? Come, tell us, we want to know what strange allure the place has for you."

"Yes, tell," Kitty seconded. "Tony says it's a woman."

"Must be a woman," Bingham affirmed, nodding. "And if it ain't a woman, it's a sheep. God knows there's enough of 'em around here for a bleeding battalion. Of Irishmen," he added with a coarse laugh, and Kitty giggled with him.

Sully smiled across at Sebastian while he pulled on the low collar of her dress, uncovering her shoulder. From the window seat, Flohr leaned forward, elbows on his plump thighs, eyes slitted and staring. Observing him, Sebastian rearranged his conclusions about Kitty. If she'd bestowed her favors on anyone in the coach up from Plymouth, it hadn't been on Flohr. Because Flohr, he would bet his last sovereign, was a watcher.

"Well?" Sully prodded. "What's Lynton Hall got that London in the Season hasn't?"

He pretended to consider. "Peace and quiet. Healthy air, regular hours. Birds that aren't pigeons."

Bingham snorted. "It's a woman," he said positively, and turned over on his stomach.

Sebastian was sitting on the arm of the sofa, next to Kitty. She smiled up at him and began to stroke his thigh. Her wedding ring was a band of bloodstones in a gold setting. He watched her soft, small hand move lazily across his leg and listened to the sound her nails made on the smooth tweed of his trousers. He took a sip of his drink. Got up and walked across the room to the piano.

It had arrived a week ago from the London house. As soon as he'd begun to play, he'd wondered why he'd waited so long before ordering it sent down. It felt like an old friend. It made Lynton Hall seem almost like a home.

He began to play chords at random, a quiet accompaniment to his guests' desultory chatter. Once in a while a bit of scabrous gossip arrested him, but for the most part he didn't pay attention to their talk. He was waiting for something. He wasn't sure what it was until Rachel came. Then he knew.

She arrived silently, as usual; he didn't know she was standing in the doorway until he heard the room go quiet. Bingham was the one who broke the stillness, by saying softly, "What did I tell you."

She advanced a little way in from the threshold, pink-cheeked, trying to smile, trying to look back into all the eyes that scrutinized and examined her. He tried to see her as they did in her plain black gown and cheap shoes, her unfashionable hair, the wary look in her silvery eyes. Had he thought she was pretty when he'd first seen her? He couldn't remember now, and the question didn't interest him any longer. She was Rachel, she was here. For now, nothing else mattered.

Standing up, he said quietly, "Mrs. Wade, these are my friends. Mrs. Wilson; that's Tony on the floor, Sir Anthony Bingham; Mr. Flohr—sorry, I've forgotten your first name."

"Bertram."

"Right. And this is Claude Sully. I'd like you all to meet Mrs. Rachel Wade. My new housekeeper."

They greeted her facetiously. "Well, well, well," Bingham said slowly, snickering, and Kitty smiled and said, "Oh, the *house-keeper*," in a knowing tone. Sully was the only one who bothered to get up. "Mrs. Wade?" he repeated, studying her with acute interest, coming closer. "Would that be . . . oh, surely not. Could it possibly be Mrs. *Randolph* Wade?"

Her features tightened with dread, but she only said, "Yes."

"My God." He was quietly, odiously delighted. "My dear lady," he breathed. "You murdered my uncle."

Like hounds scenting a fox, the others came to attention. Bingham struggled to his feet; Kitty put her drink down and stared. Even Flohr got up from the window seat, his round face turning florid.

Why didn't she deny it? But she said nothing, just stared back at Sully with wide, expressionless eyes. He reached for her hand and began to pull her toward the sofa. She resisted, and in her agitation she threw a veiled glance at Sebastian. He almost spoke before he caught himself. Shoving his hands in his pockets, he leaned against the piano.

Sully put her between himself and Kitty, who was eyeing her with open fascination. "You went to prison," he said wonderingly. "In Exeter for a few years, as I recall, before they opened Dartmoor. Am I right?"

"Yes."

"When did they let you out?"

She glanced up at Bingham and Flohr, across at Kitty. Cornered. "On the thirteenth of April," she answered, almost inaudibly, kneading her skirt over her knees with both hands.

"Gor," said Bingham playfully, but he was as mesmerized as the others.

"Bloody hell, Claude, you inherited all his money, didn't you?" Kitty said, figuring it out as she spoke. "I remember now. After the uncle died, you got it all—a *fortune*."

"I did," he smiled, showing pointed teeth. "Do you know, I think this calls for a toast." He lifted his wineglass. "To you, Mrs. Wade, with gratitude and admiration. Thank you for hastening my inheritance, something I confess I'd often thought of doing myself. You saved me the trouble. Bless you. Oh—but you haven't got a glass! Shocking oversight. Please, allow me to—"

She withered away from his outstretched hand and managed to stand up without touching him. "You must excuse me, I have—things I should see to before dinner." Backing toward the door, she dared another quick glance at Sebastian. "My lord?"

"Thank you, Mrs. Wade," he said dismissively. The gratitude in her eyes recalled him to his purpose. "But you'll dine with us, of course," he added pointedly. She made him a short, cold bow and withdrew.

"Lydia's my cousin, you know," Sully confided, angling his body closer, resting his hand on the back of Rachel's chair. She couldn't move away any farther; Bingham sat on her other side, and he was craning toward her to hear Sully's soft-voiced conversation. "I haven't seen her in years. You must have, though, living in the same quaint little village, eh?" Rachel nodded once and kept her eyes on her plate. "What was that like? Hmm? Bloody awkward, I should think."

She murmured something; Sebastian couldn't hear the words. He wondered how much longer she could push the same piece of trout around on her plate without taking a bite.

"Lydia's got no use for me. Makes no sense, but she blames *me* for the fact that she's practically penniless. As if I had anything to do with the terms of dear Uncle Randolph's will." Sully swirled wine in his glass. "Woman's logic," he said with the turned-down smile, and Bingham muttered, "Drink to that."

On Sebastian's right, Kitty took time off from massaging his calf with her stockinged foot to ask, "How long were you locked up altogether, Mrs. Wade?"

She lifted her head. "Ten years."

"Good Lord! Wasn't it awful?"

"Yes."

Her low, fervent agreement stopped Kitty, but only for a second. "What was it like? Tell us everything."

She stared back as if the question made no sense.

"I . . ." She put her fork down. "What do you—particularly want to know?"

"Well!" Kitty shrugged her shoulders animatedly. "What was the food like?" she asked, laughing, as if a lighthearted game were beginning. "Did you sit in a dining hall with the other prisoners?"

Rachel sagged slowly against the back of her chair. "No. We took our meals in our cells."

"Did you have a roommate? A cellmate, I suppose it's called."

"No."

"No? You had to eat all by yourself?"

She nodded slowly.

"What sort of food did you get?" asked Bingham.

Every question was like a knife prick to her skin. Sebastian wondered if they could tell. Not the extent of it, he didn't think. They knew they were wounding her, but they couldn't know how much. But she was a novice and they were experts; it wouldn't be long before they found her out.

"The food . . . was shoved through a trapdoor in the wall. It was always the same."

"What was it?"

"Bread and stirabout. Potatoes—"

"Stirabout?"

"A kind of gruel. Meat sometimes. Soup. And cocoa. Six things."

Sebastian watched them all look down at their plates, smiling self-consciously, mentally contrasting the delicacy and variety of Judelet's repast with Mrs. Wade's stirabout and potatoes.

"Well," Kitty decided, "at least it was filling. At least you had enough."

Rachel stared at her until Kitty had to look away. Sebastian pushed away a memory of how she'd looked at the magistrates' hearing. Half starved. A week ago, when he'd taken her clothes off, he could see her ribs.

Sully put his hand on her shoulder; she controlled a start and began to turn a spoon over and over on the tablecloth. "What was your cell like? Hmm? How big?"

It was starting. Sebastian signaled the footman for more wine, and when his glass was full he drank half of it down without pausing.

"It was . . . eight feet by five feet. A seven-foot ceiling of stone. An iron door. Corrugated iron walls."

"No window?"

"A window. High in the wall. Thick glass. It looked out onto the interior of the prison."

"Was it cold?"

"Yes."

"I once had a groom who spent nine months in Millbank," Bingham put in. "Said the bed was a wooden board. Said you woke up feeling as if you'd been flogged in the night with planks."

They stared at Rachel, Flohr openly, the rest in secret glances; they were avid now, their curiosity whetted.

"What did you wear?" Kitty wanted to know.

She was growing smaller before their eyes. If they kept at her long enough, would she disappear?

"A dress. Brown, made of serge. A white cap."

"I've heard they pay the prisoners to work."

"At Dartmoor. Not at Exeter."

"What did you do?"

"I worked in the prison laundry at first. Then the library. The tailor's shop."

"What did you do all day at Exeter?" Kitty again.

It took a moment before she was able to say, "I picked oakum in my cell."

Oakum. Filthy, tar-covered rope, used for caulking. Sebastian looked at her clean, short-nailed fingers, remembered her calloused palms.

"How do you mean? What's 'picking,' exactly?"

She took a deep breath. "The ration was three pounds a day. Raw rope, thrown in through the trapdoor. We had to pick it— separate all the strands until it was a pile of soft flax. In the evening they weighed it, to make certain we'd finished our quota."

"How very . . . tedious. There's no real purpose to it, is there, no reason for it. Wasn't it tedious?"

Rachel lifted one eyebrow in a way that finally made Kitty flush. "Yes," she agreed. "You could say it was tedious."

The muted show of spirit caused Kitty to narrow her eyes, then smile. "How interesting. Now tell us about discipline, Mrs.

Wade," she said in a soft, silky tone. "What did they do to you when you were a bad prisoner?"

Sully leaned in closer. She must be able to feel his breath on her cheek. But she didn't move, trapped between him and Bingham. Kitty's smile turned crafty. Flohr licked his thick lips. Sebastian had a sudden, rabid desire to get drunk.

Her pale face slowly suffused with blood. "One was sent to the refractory cell." They waited, poised like cats over something still twitching, still trying to get away. "I must see to—"

"Were you sent there? What had you done?"

In spite of Sully's arm, she managed to push her chair back and stand up. "I must go and help—excuse me, I'm needed downstairs now. Pardon me. I'll—" She looked at Sebastian, but only for a second. No help from that quarter, she knew by now. "I'll come back," she said hopelessly, and fled.

But she didn't come back. He had to send for her, after they'd reassembled in the drawing room. He didn't wait for Sully or one of the others to ask him to do it; he did it on his own, deliberately, cold-bloodedly, because baiting Rachel was to be the evening's entertainment. Everyone knew it. The fact that he'd lost the stomach for it himself didn't signify; on the contrary, it pointed to a new and dangerous weakness in himself he didn't like and was determined to snuff out. Sully and the rest could be his proxies while he regrouped, reminded himself of who he was and of what his purpose in life had always been—the pursuit of selfish pleasure.

Sully called for cards. The sharp-faced maid named Violet brought them, and stayed by the door afterward until Sebastian noticed her and told her to go.

"A little game?" Sully proposed with cunning in his eyes. He began to go through the two decks, culling out the crown cards and laying the others aside. "It's called Truth. Know it?"

No one did. Kitty, on the floor, inched closer to him until she was sitting at his feet. She laid her hand over the instep of his shoe and asked, "How do you play?" Her long hair gleamed blue-black in the lamplight; she pulled it over one shoulder and stroked it lovingly over her bosom with her open hand.

"Nothing to it. I'm the dealer. Since we're six, we'll have two cards apiece. Ladies are queens, gents are knaves and kings. Mrs. Wilson, you'll be the black queen, spade and club."

"I like that," Kitty cooed, squeezing his foot.

"Mrs. Wade, you're the red queen, if you please. Heart and diamond."

Rachel nodded. She sat straight and stiff in a ladder-back chair she'd pulled as far from the group as she could and still pretend she was part of it.

"Bertie, you be king and knave of diamonds; Tony, you're king, knave of hearts. Sebastian, king, knave of clubs. *Et pour moi,* king and knave of spades. Do we all know who we are?"

"Yes, yes. What's the object?" Bingham demanded. His dinner had made him sleepy; he lay backward on the chaise longue, supine, with his knees cocked over the top.

"It's quite simple. What can I use for a table? This." He found an old issue of *The Field* in a basket by the sofa and put it on his lap. "Two stacks of cards, notice, twelve each. I pick one from the left—king of hearts. That's you, Tony."

"Right-ho."

"And one from the right. Ah, the black queen."

"Me," smiled Kitty. "Now what?"

"Now the king gets to ask the queen a question, any question, to which she's bound to respond with the truth and nothing but. Hence the name."

"Any question?" Bingham asked, turning on his side.

"I have said so."

"Gor blimey."

"Your slang is becoming tiresome, Tony," Kitty complained. "Amusing for the first year or two, you know, but not anymore."

"Oh, do you think so?" Bingham's vapid face formed a sneer. "Answer this, then. Who was the first man you cuckolded Wilson with?"

She didn't even blush. "George Thomason-Cawles," she answered readily. "We met him in Athens on our honeymoon."

Everyone laughed, even Flohr. Sully shuffled all the cards again and drew two more from each pile. "Queen of clubs may ask queen of diamonds anything she likes."

Kitty took her hand off his knee and sat up straight. "Oh, lovely. Mrs. Wade, I want to know what a refractory cell is and what you did to be sent there."

"That's two questions," Bingham pointed out.

Sully said, "The dealer, whose word is law, will allow it."

Sebastian had been playing a one-fingered melody on the piano. He stopped suddenly, and the room fell quiet.

Rachel sent him one last glance, but this time it was more of an acknowledgment of his complicity than a plea for help. She was drowning, but the look said she knew for certain that there would be no lifeline flung to her from him.

She directed the answer to her knees. "The refractory cell is a room. It has no window. No furniture, no bed. No light—the walls are painted black. Two doors, to make sure the silence is . . . complete. It's a dungeon."

He couldn't bear it. He looked down to see his hand clenched around the stem of his empty brandy goblet so tightly, his fingers ached when he released it. He got up and went to the drinks table for a refill.

"Second part of the question," Sully reminded her. "Why were you sent there?"

"The first time, for looking about in chapel."

"Looking about?"

"It's forbidden in prison to look at anyone."

"My God. How long did you have to stay?"

"Ah, ah," Sully corrected Kitty. "That's too many; you'll have to wait for another turn."

He shuffled the cards again. "Knave of spades—that's I—demands the truth from king of clubs. You, D'Aubrey. Hmm." He scratched his head, pretending to ponder. Kitty giggled, pulled on his trouser cuff. He bent down and she whispered something in his ear. He smiled when he straightened. "What I would like to know, Sebastian, is whether or not you've bedded Mrs. Wade yet."

He said, "Yes, of course," as quickly and casually as possible. It worked: except for the inevitable laughter, they let the subject drop, sensing no tension, no undercurrent. Like sharks, they smelled no blood and swam on.

Rachel, of course, said nothing; he didn't look at her, but from the corner of his eye he saw that she remained motionless, expressionless, not moving a muscle.

The questions and answers continued. Sex was usually the topic, who had slept with whom, who wished he was sleeping with whom, what sleeping with so-and-so had been like. The sameness of it began to numb; nothing sounded coarse or shocking anymore, only dull. The unimaginativeness of his friends' preoccupations ought not to have surprised him, but it did. Had they always been this shallow and insipid? This vicious? What made him think he was any different from them?

Rachel was the target of the questions too often for Sully not to be engineering it on purpose, but no one called him on it. Indeed, the conspiracy against her became more obvious as the evening wore on, until no one even snickered when every second or third question was directed to her. Whether they could admit it consciously or not, she was the only interesting one among them, and now they wanted to know all about her.

Sebastian drank steadily and heavily, but he couldn't get drunk. Kitty came and sat on his lap, pushed her hand inside his waistcoat, squirmed on his thighs. When his turn came to ask a question, he asked her how old she was. It cooled her ardor for a while. Her perfume was lilac, powdery and more than cloying; suffocating. Her long hair repelled him. He thought of Rachel's shorter hair, the way the silver in it shone like speckled jewels in candlelight. He remembered the precise shape of her skull when he'd molded it in his hands.

Horror after horror she enumerated for his jaded friends, forced admissions of constant hunger, petrifying monotony, despair. Bingham asked her about the "dry bath," a degrading, dehumanizing strip search she'd endured once every month for ten years. So: in prison they'd even robbed her of the freedom of her own body. So had her husband. So had he.

How long would she let it go on? For as long as he'd known her, she'd never surrendered to anything, not really, no matter how callously he'd treated her. But this was different. This was worse. He was letting it happen, watching it grow more beastly by the minute, because he wasn't testing her anymore. He was testing himself.

Sully was the smartest, and the most dangerous. While the others kept asking Rachel their lewd questions about prison— had a guard ever touched her? did the women prisoners ever seek each other out for amorous comfort?—Sully asked her about her husband. She tried to be circumspect, but eventually they caught on. Randolph Wade, they began to realize, had been a pervert. Bingham vaguely remembered the story in the newspapers; Kitty went on blind instinct, uncannily accurate in her guesses; Flohr followed it all with his dark, ophthalmic eyes, obscenely fascinated.

Sully had been saving the best for last. Once more he turned over his own card and Rachel's worn queen. "Ah, back to you and me, Mrs. Wade. I hope this won't embarrass you. You've been so wonderfully forthcoming."

The worst for Sebastian was recognizing his own soft, mocking tone in Sully's despicable cadence. He felt physically sick.

"I'm recalling something you said at the trial. Something that must have helped you enormously at the sentencing, assuming it's true. It's rather dreadful; one hardly knows whether to believe it or not."

She hadn't moved in ages. But she looked up at that, as if she knew what was coming. Her eyes took on a haggard cast.

"Can it really be true, Mrs. Wade, that on the last night of his life your husband tied you over a chair and used a riding crop on you? A special sort of crop, one whose—wait now, I haven't finished—"

She'd stood up. The horror in her ashen face riveted their attention, and Sebastian thought of slavering wolves moving in for the kill. She moved toward the door, her legs stiff and jerky.

"I haven't finished the question." Sully's voice, although he didn't raise it, grew shrill with suppressed excitement. "Is it true, Mrs. Wade—" She began to run, awkward and uncoordinated, the necessity for flight robbing her of grace. "I say!" Sully jumped up. "Is it true," he called to the empty doorway, "that the handle of the riding crop was a phallus?"

The thud of her running footsteps died away quickly.

No one spoke for a moment, then they all spoke at once, in low voices full of lewd enjoyment and manufactured shock. Sebastian couldn't hear the words over the soft buzzing in his ears. Something was tearing inside. Something was coming completely apart.

Sully was still on his feet. He came into Sebastian's line of vision, mouthing something, the words barely audible over the buzzing. "I said, where's her room?"

He blinked at him. "What?"

"Where's your housekeeper's room?"

Kitty laughed low in her throat and her breath, soured by wine, fluttered against his cheek. He separated the question from its implications and considered it in the abstract. "Her room is in the chapel wing," he said in a strange, offhand tone. "Near the library."

Sully's face was flushed. "Last question. Is she yours?"

"Is she mine?" he repeated blankly. "No. Of course she's not mine." It sounded foolish. What an absurd question.

"Good. Then she's mine." He gave Bingham a playful kick, snatched up the wine bottle from the table, and strolled out of the room.

Sebastian kept his gaze on the empty doorway. *They're gone,* he thought. *He's gone and she's gone, and they've gone together. It's out of my hands.* Brandy stung the back of his throat; he grimaced, and Kitty put her hands on the sides of his face. He couldn't hear what she was saying to him because the buzzing was louder and more raucous now. He felt the tear down the middle of himself widening, and that was wrong; it should have been narrowing. He'd just done a thing to make himself whole again. He poured more brandy, knocking Kitty's arm away to get to the bottle, and he muttered, "Excuse me." She spoke; her breathy voice rose at the end, so she must have asked a question, but he couldn't make out the meaning. He pulled her closer and kissed her.

Something happened then. He wasn't on the piano bench with Kitty on his lap. He was halfway across the room. He heard a snap in his head, exactly like a bone breaking, and at once the eerie fugue state evaporated. His past and his future had broken cleanly in two. This, now, was the present, a violent limbo he had to smash his way out of to survive.

He began to run. His legs pumped blood to his brain; clean air filled his lungs, clearing his head. He ran as fast as he could, his shoes sounding hollow on the wood floor, sharp on the stones when he turned the corner to the chapel wing. No lights here; he ran in the dark, heart pounding, his breath coming hard. He saw faint candlelight spilling out on the stones thirty feet away—Rachel's room. He'd opened his mouth to shout when he heard her, then saw her. She was beside him, nearly invisible in the blackness, and Sully was behind her with an arm across her throat and one around her waist. The sound she'd made was a strangled, "No."

He pounded past them before he could stop. Whirling, he said, "Let her go," his voice ringing out clear and metallic in the stone corridor, echoing off the walls. Sully pivoted, taking her with him, then pushed her away. Turning back, he blocked her with his body. Blood from a scratch on the side of his neck spattered his shirt collar. He bared his teeth. "No fair," he said in the horrible mocking voice that was too familiar, too much like Sebastian's. "Second thoughts don't count. You distinctly said—"

Sebastian grabbed his jacket, cursed in his face, and jerked him out of the way.

She had her arms wrapped around her waist and she was pressing back against the wall, trying to push through it, merge into it. Fear was like a film over her eyes, like smoke. She couldn't see him. He couldn't touch her—he'd lost the right. He said her name, standing close, outlining the shape of her shoulders in the air with his hands.

Sully grabbed his arm and yanked him around. "I said no fair." Mild words, but his face was contorted with rage. "Out of the way now, D'Aubrey. You don't want to fight with me."

Sebastian shoved him in the chest, sending him flying.

"Rachel." This time he couldn't keep his hands off her. Miraculously, she didn't shrink away when he touched her arm. "Rachel," he said, and the mist of fear in her eyes began to clear.

Then she screamed.

He didn't turn in time. A stabbing, ice-cold pain streaked down his side and turned fiery hot in an instant. Before he could dodge, Sully slashed him with his knife again, sideways, missing his throat by inches.

Sebastian whirled. The knife gleamed sharp as a razor in the dull light. Holding it out at arm's length, Sully began to back away, eyes darting. Sebastian followed without care, without caution. He waited until Sully reached the splash of light from Rachel's room, and then he sprang, feinting right, coming in low on the left, under the blade. He caught Sully's wrist in both hands and thrust it up and back in a high, overhead arc. Flesh and steel met stone in a bone-crushing *smash,* and Sully shrieked. The knife dropped to the floor from his battered hand.

Sebastian was upon him. They stumbled in jerky, ungainly circles, grappling, until Sully lost his footing and thudded backward onto the hard floor. Sebastian couldn't see his face, he could only see Rachel's, pale and lifeless, done in, finished. Red rage consumed him, and a deep, scorching shame. Sully was the blind target of his fury. He beat him with his fists even when someone pounded on his back and someone else dragged at his shoulders, his coat. He only stopped when he realized the voice crying, "Stop it! Stop! Stop!" was Rachel's.

His whole body was shaking so violently, he could hardly stand. Strong hands helped him; he looked up to see William Holyoake standing by his side, looking big and competent and worried. "Right, then," he said hopefully. "That's all right then. Here, lad, have done. You can leave some for the crows, ay?"

The shaking worsened. He was bleeding like a pig onto the stone. He watched Sully flip over, struggle to his knees, and eventually stand. They faced each other. Sully looked sideways, and Sebastian noticed Bingham, Kitty, Flohr, all of them hovering, curious as cows. But enjoying it. Kitty especially; she probably liked the smell of blood, the taste of it, for all he knew. "Get out," he said, not wasting much breath on them. "All of you."

Sully's lips were already swollen and his eyes would be in a minute. Blood ran from his nose in a black stream. He blew a bubble of blood out of his mouth and made his threat. "You're going to be sorry."

Before Holyoake could stop it, Sebastian hit him again. Just a gut-punch, weak and one-handed, but it felt good. Sully's breath came out in a ludicrous whoosh that made his threat sound laughable. "Get the hell out of my house," Sebastian told him, and it was good, it was sweet to have the last word.

XI

DR. HESSELIUS WAS completely bald, with gentle, wide-spaced brown eyes behind the thick lenses of his spectacles. The bowl of a pipe stuck out of the top of his waistcoat pocket, and the odor of tobacco smoke floated around him. "Any wound is serious," he was saying, in answer to William Holyoake's question. "This one is fortunately not deep—although it is long; it took sixteen stitches to close it—but there's always a danger of infection. Who's going to be nursing him?"

Rachel glanced blankly at William, who glanced blankly back.

"Someone's got to change the bandage," the doctor explained, "and keep an eye on the wound for signs of infection."

"Mrs. Fruit used t' do it, nurse the maids when they took sick and whatnot," William said. "Since she left, we haven't had anybody. Haven't had the need o't."

There was a pause.

"I would do it."

Dr. Hesselius turned to Rachel with relief; he'd been waiting for her to speak up, she knew. She was the housekeeper—she was the logical one. "Have you any experience in this sort of thing, Mrs. Wade?" he asked kindly.

"Only from books." He looked skeptical. She had no wish to convince him, no wish to be Sebastian's nurse. But for some reason—pride?—she added, "Burton's *Pathology; Fever Nursing* by Campion."

His spaniel eyes widened. "Do you tell me so? Well, very

good, then you'll know what to look for, won't you? Yes, yes, excellent."

Excellent.

What in God's name was she doing?

She found him in his study, not his bedroom. In spite of the prodigious quantities of alcohol he'd consumed tonight, he'd never been drunk. But he was now.

He was leaning against the glass doors to the terrace, holding his right arm against his side. When he heard her, he swung around too quickly and staggered, almost lost his balance. Brownish liquid sloshed on the rug from the glass in his hand. He wore a black velvet dressing gown, untied, over his trousers; she could see the white of a cotton bandage across his bare middle.

"I would like you to leave," he said very slowly, very carefully. But his eyes were burning; despite what he'd said, they seemed to hold her where she stood. She couldn't move. "Go away," he enunciated—firmly, politely. Then he blinked to clear his head, and she was released from the odd, penetrating stare.

"Dr. Hesselius has asked me to . . . look after you."

He showed his teeth in a quick grimace—an acknowledgment of the absurdity of the situation. She agreed with him completely. "Dr. Hes . . . Hesselius has . . ." He had to stop; he couldn't say it. Seconds ticked past. "Asked you to look after me," he finally finished. "Ha." He was back to staring at her again. Examining her blearily, studying her, scrutinizing her.

She gripped her hands together, unnerved. "How do you feel?"

He rubbed the back of his wrist over his eyes. His hair was standing on end, wild. She thought his left hand shook when he brought the glass to his lips and finished whatever was in it. His body jerked, and he thudded against the door behind him, striking his shoulders. He looked surprised, then grateful for the support. He regarded his empty glass for a second, then stuck it in the pocket of his dressing gown. "Mrs. Wade."

When he didn't continue, she said, "My lord?"

"Mrs. Wade. Am I not the owner of Lynton Hall?"

"Yes, my lord."

"Am I not the . . . the . . ." He shut his eyes tight, then opened them. "Do I not employ you?"

"Yes, my lord."

"Then—don't you have to do what I say? Yes," he answered himself with finality, nodding.

"You want me to go?"

"Immediately. Do not return. Thank you."

"Fine."

But she stayed where she was, watching him push off from the door and move gingerly to his desk, where a cut-glass brandy decanter rested on a silver plate. He unstoppered it and picked it up, then just stood there and looked at it. A ridiculous amount of time passed.

"It's in your pocket," she snapped. Of all the emotions she could have felt at this moment, aggravation because he wouldn't let her take care of him was surely the maddest.

It went on for days. "Who's changing his bandage?" she demanded of Preest after Sebastian sent her away for the half-dozenth time. "He is," the valet told her. "Banned me from the room, won't have me anywhere about."

All he did was drink, the servants informed her. Trays of food went untouched, visitors unseen, correspondence unopened. When Dr. Hesselius came again, Sebastian sent him away, too. He wouldn't even talk to Holyoake. Late at night she could hear him playing the piano, nothing but baleful chords and dissonant melodies that jangled her nerves and made sleep impossible. Occasionally she saw him from a distance, and each time he looked worse than before. He hadn't shaved; his fierce black beard made him look criminal, like a degenerate pirate. Once she tried to speak to him, but it was exactly as before: first he stared at her, virtually devoured her with his eyes, and then, with precise, drunken courtesy, he told her to please leave him alone.

Even her irritation, mild as it was, finally drifted away. When she thought about the night Sully and the others had tormented her, she found that there were large chunks of the evening she could barely remember. Because she didn't want to remember them—yes, of course—but the whole experience was not nearly as painful to recall as it ought to have been. It was as if her mind had wrapped the memory in a layer of gauze to cushion her from the worst of it.

What she could not forget was that Sebastian had saved her. He'd saved her. Not out of selfless kindness, she didn't think— she hadn't completely lost her mind—but she couldn't believe he'd done it out of pure possessiveness, either. Something in between, then.

She felt restless and on edge as time went by; something was pending, unfinished, hanging in the balance. She ought to be *glad* he wouldn't see her—how absurd to think about him or care at all what happened to him. But she was at loose ends without him. He'd been the center of her life for too long. It was as if, without him, there wasn't anything else compelling enough to hold her interest.

On the fifth day, he fell. She learned of it from Holyoake when she returned from her weekly visit to the constable. " 'E were comin' down the stairs when 'e slipped. Must've missed four in a row at least, and fetched up at the bottom all in a heap. Susan heard him and run for me, and between us we got him up to 'is room."

"My God. Is he hurt?"

"How the blazes would I know?" He ducked his head. "Beg pardon, but I'm that vexed, and I don't know what else t' do for 'im. 'E won't have the surgeon, o' course," he went on, fuming. "Preest fluttered round 'im for a time, cleaning 'im up and what-not, but he sent 'im away, and now he says he wants *you* t' come and no one else."

"What?"

"Aye." He nodded heavily, as amazed as she. "Says 'e wants you t' come as quick as you can."

She looked at the floor. "He's drunk, isn't he?"

"No, 'e ain't."

"No?"

"No. I thought sure he would be, but he weren't."

"Then—why did he fall?"

William shook his head and shrugged. "So. Will you go to 'im, then?"

She glanced at him sharply. What must he be thinking? Impossible to tell; there was no one more discreet than Mr. Holyoake, and at the moment his kind face was expressionless. "Yes, I'll go," she said levelly. "Since he's sent for me."

"Mph. Preest says he's neglected 'is wound."

"Has it festered?"

"Preest says not, but it needs tending to. I've told Jerny to take up hot water."

"Good."

"Do you want me to come wi' you?"

She almost smiled. "Do you think I'll need protection?"

"No, no," he said too quickly, abashed. "Help; I were thinkin' o' help."

No, he wasn't. "Thank you, William. I think," she said, with much more confidence than she felt, "I'll be able to manage on my own."

The bedchamber was empty; his lordship must be in his bathroom. She took a moment to gather herself; even ordinary encounters with Sebastian were unsettling, and this one was bound to be beyond that.

His bedroom always surprised her: it wasn't the exotic lair she'd have expected a man like him—a sensualist, a voluptuary— to inhabit. In fact, it was uncommonly plain. It had once been Anne Morrell's, when she'd lived here as Lady D'Aubrey, but since then all traces of femininity had been eradicated. There wasn't even a mirror. The furniture was good but sparse. The bed . . . the bed looked strange from here; her memories of it were acute, but the perspective from a distance was off, almost disorienting. Like one's first sight from shore of the ship on which one has taken a long sea voyage.

She whirled at a sound from behind her—but it was only Jerny, carrying a brass can full of steaming hot water. "For the master," he said needlessly, and she gestured for him to precede her into the lavatory.

Sebastian sat on a stool in front of the enormous marble sink, shirtless, holding a towel against his right side with the flat of his arm. The room was dim because the curtains had been drawn across the windows, but even in the feeble light of only one candle she could see that his face was too pale. But Holyoake was right: he wasn't drunk.

"Bring a lamp, Jerny," she murmured, after the boy had poured hot water into the stoppered basin. "There's one in the bedroom; light it and bring it here."

During the two minutes he was gone, she stood with her arms folded and looked around at everything except the room's other occupant, whose quiet stare she could feel but wasn't prepared to acknowledge. If his bedroom was spartan, the master's bathroom epitomized—at least to Rachel, who was used to different amenities—the ultimate in luxury and extravagance. Besides the marble sink, there was a bathtub the likes of which she'd never even seen in pictures, never even dreamed existed. Gleaming bronze with gold handles and spouts, long and sleek, Greek or Roman, possibly Byzantine for all she knew, it personified decadence; a full-grown man could lie down flat in it—and if Violet Cocker's gossiping tongue was accurate, Lord D'Aubrey had done exactly that on any number of occasions in the company of full-grown women.

The walls were tiled in gorgeous pink marble. Ivy hung from pots before the two windows flanking the sink, and between them the biggest mirror she'd ever seen soared to the ceiling. Another graced the wall at the foot of the bathtub, and an elegant, man-size cheval glass stood beside the door. Surprisingly, the effect wasn't garish or even particularly sybaritic; rather, candle-light in the mirrors' multiple reflections mellowed the hard, shining surfaces of bronze and marble, making the room seem glamorous, unearthly, almost magical.

Jerny brought the lamp then, and the mystical quality dissipated somewhat in the brighter light. Rachel remembered the basket in her hands and set it down beside the sink. "I've brought linens for bandages, my lord, and some basilica powder. But I must tell you that I agree with Mr. Holyoake. I think the doctor should—"

He'd dismissed Jerny with a nod, and now he cut her off by reaching for her hand. She didn't fear him now, but the strong grip of his fingers startled her. She thought he would pull her toward him, take some liberty with her person. Instead he drew her toward the padded stool beside his, and urged her with a gentle pressure to sit down. She returned his narrow, enveloping gaze as well as she could. In truth, she was glad to see him, glad to look at him. Preest had shaved him; she could smell the bay soap on his skin and the clean scent of his hair, still wet, slicked back from his fine, high forehead.

"I can't tell what you're thinking," he said after a curious pause. "Usually your face is as transparent as glass in a window, but not now." She stared at their still-clasped hands and didn't speak. "Possibly I should have kept on drinking. Left you alone even longer. Forever. It's not as if I know now what to say to you," he said harshly, releasing her hand all at once. "It's not as if I've—come to any rational conclusion about you, or myself, or anything else under the sun."

"My lord, did you hurt yourself?" He looked blank. "When you fell. Mr. Preest told—"

"This is nothing," he interrupted almost angrily. "Less than nothing." But when he lifted his arm from the towel clamped to his side, she saw bloodstains. "Rachel," he said before she could move, "are you all right?"

He'd never called her by her given name before. The uncertainty in his face was new as well, and even more disturbing. "I don't know what you want me to say. I'm well. I'm fine. And—I'm not the one with a stab wound in the side."

"You're fine?" he repeated slowly. His voice had gone hoarse. "Yes. I'm—"

"You're fine? You're well?" He was holding a half-full glass of water. "Being baited and ridiculed and brutalized by a gang of villainous, contemptible, barely human derelicts is an everyday occurrence for you, something easily recovered from, easily—shoved behind the wall of your infernal, everlasting self-control—!" He smacked the glass down on top of the marble vanity; only a miracle kept it from shattering. She jumped, but she still wasn't frightened, only startled—because the anger bottled inside of him wasn't directed at her.

"Don't mistake me," he went on, in a tone that was quieter but no less intense. "I don't exclude myself from their number. By no means. And I have no reason, no motive to offer to you that could possibly explain my behavior, much less excuse it."

She almost said, *You were drunk,* but a second's thought reminded her that that wasn't really true. Besides, why would she want to help him name an excuse for what he'd done, even one as deplorable as drunkenness? "The water is cooling," she said evasively. "Let me clean your wound, my lord."

"I want you to do something," he said, and his eyes shone with a self-directed bitterness she'd never seen and didn't understand.

"What is it?" she asked warily.

"I want you never to call me your 'lord' again. Never again, alone or with others. My name is Sebastian. What you and I have been to each other . . . I wouldn't presume to name it. But I think even you will admit that we are something, and whatever it is has been . . . intimate enough to warrant dispensing with titles and—other verbal formalities. Oh, hell," he muttered, and dropped his forehead down on the arm he had stretched out along the sink top.

She reached for him, afraid he was fainting. She held his shoulders, and his cold skin went clammy under her hands. "My lord, you're *ill*. Please let me send for the doctor."

He turned his head to look at her, and a pained smile pulled at one corner of his mouth. "I'm not ill. All that talking did me in. And it hasn't even helped—you're still my-lording me. Say my name, Rachel. Say it once, for practice."

"I don't—What difference does it make? Please, let me—"

"It makes a difference. Say it."

She took her hands away to say it. "Sebastian."

"You see?" he asked softly, alertly. "It makes a difference. Do you feel it?"

She felt it, the facile, instantaneous razing of one of the barriers between them. Too facile; she didn't trust it. No matter. There were a hundred other barriers to keep them apart.

"If you're comfortable in that position, then don't move," she said, trying to sound brisk; "I can clean the wound like this." He only grunted. "Lift your arm a little." He winced when she took the towel away; no wonder—it had already begun to adhere to his wound. But there was very little fresh blood, and the black stitches Dr. Hesselius had sewn in the long, uneven gash that ran from the bottom of his rib cage to his hipbone were still intact. "I have no experience at this, my . . . I have no experience at this."

"Does it sicken you?"

"No."

"Then do it. Please. I don't want anyone but you to touch me."

Immediately she flushed. Her throat hurt; the most foolish desire to weep welled up in her without warning. She wanted to whisper, *Why?* but she held her tongue. She would not regard what he said, she would not regard the way he was treating her. It was an anomaly. It meant nothing.

The water in the sink was still hot, so she cooled it by turning on the tap for a few seconds. The fact that cold water actually flowed through pipes all the way to the second floor of Lynton Great Hall was a source of much wonder in the household, probably in the village at large. Hot water still had to be carried up from the kitchen by hand, but rumors were rife that his lordship had plans for a boiler that would heat water and pump it through new pipes all the way up to his bathroom. A miracle if it was true, which most people doubted.

She bathed his wound as gently as she could, then dabbed basilica powder on it. She couldn't look at him, touch his naked skin, or smell his sweat without remembering the night he'd taken her to bed. The same man who meekly submitted to her ministrations, whose demands on her now were tentative, even courteous, was the same patient, methodical, remorseless lover who had made it a crusade to steal every last shred of her pride. She told herself that if she forgot that or ignored it, she would deserve all the consequences.

"Sit up if you can," she said. He did, and she began to wind a strip of clean cloth around his middle. She had to touch him with her body, no help for it, her chin, her breasts, brushing against his bare skin as she passed the bandage from hand to hand behind his back. He made it easier by not looking at her, but the quiet between them only underscored the tension. She broke it to say, "Mrs. Oldham gave me the bandages and the powder. She had them in her room. She knows a little about nursing and herbs and such things." Something she wished she had known before she'd volunteered to be his nurse. Or did she?

"Who," he asked tightly, "is Mrs. Oldham?"

"She was the cook before Monsieur Judelet came. Now she's a sort of assistant."

"A sort of assistant. The poor woman. Judelet's an unholy terror; she must be a saint to stay on." Rachel didn't answer. "You must think it callous of me not to know the names of my own servants."

"No, of course not."

"Don't lie. I've never heard of anyone called Mrs. Oldham; I doubt if I'd recognize her if I rode my horse over her. It's not the way a good country squire ought to conduct himself. It's appalling, in fact." She kept her head down, frowning at the knot she was trying to tie over his stomach. He ducked his head— making a joke of trying to see her face. "Come, agree with me. I'm sure it's what you think. Don't you? Lord D'Aubrey's an arrogant, conscienceless libertine with too much money and time on his hands. You won't admit it? Well, I can't blame you. Who knows what the consequences might be?" He sighed—then flinched at the pain sighing had caused him.

"I'm finished," she said. "I think you should lie down."

"Only if you'll lie with me."

Maybe he *was* drunk. A slight smile played about his lips, but she couldn't tell if he was joking or not. As if he hadn't spoken, she stood up and began to rinse out the bloody linens in the lavatory.

"Leave that," he said. "Come, Rachel, help me to bed." He

held out his left arm, and she had no choice but to come to him and let him drape it over her shoulders. He had a half-healed wound in his side, and when he'd fallen on the stairs he hadn't hurt himself. There was no reason why he couldn't walk the twenty-some feet from his bathroom to his bedchamber unassisted. But she didn't point that out. Taking up the lamp, she moved with him in a slow, intimate procession, letting him lean on her, and when they reached the bed she turned back the covers for him and tried to pretend that the cool silkiness of the cream-colored sheet brought back no memories.

She wasn't surprised when he held onto her hand as she started to leave. "Don't go." Remarkably, it sounded like a request, not command. "Stay and talk to me for a little while."

"You should sleep now."

"I should, but I don't want you to go. I don't want to be alone." He looked down at their hands, hers in both of his. "It's not fair to say that to you. But I'm asking this favor of you anyway."

"All right," she said faintly. "I'll stay for a little while."

"Thank you." He brought her hand to his mouth and held it there for a long moment. Again his gentleness confounded her. "Will you lie down with me, Rachel?"

"What?"

"Just that. I won't touch you. I have something to tell you." She began to shake her head. "Please. I have to lie down, and I don't want to be in this bed and you in that chair." He smiled. "I'm very weak, you know. Voice can't carry. Might faint if I have to shout at you."

She looked away. "When will it end? When will it—be enough?"

"What do you mean?" He touched her cheek, making her look at him. "Don't be sad. It's changing, I swear it. Nothing will be the same. You can't believe that and you can't trust me, so I have to take advantage of your helplessness one more time. To show you."

She whispered, "I don't understand you."

"I know. Lie down with me."

So she did. Self-deception wasn't one of her failings, so she didn't tell herself that she was obeying him again because she had no choice, that her compliance was one more "condition of employment." In truth, he wasn't the only one who couldn't bear solitude right now. She needed the comfort of another human being, and although it was the height of irony, the only person to whom she could turn was the very one who had put her in need of comfort.

Ah, well. It wasn't an uncommon phenomenon; she'd seen it in Dartmoor often enough—the prisoner so desperate for sympathy and companionship that she grew dependent on, even attached to, her gaoler. Was it twisted? A corruption of reality? In the end it didn't matter, because the deadliest enemy was still loneliness. It put all the others to shame.

She took off her shoes, helped him take off his. They half lay, half sat in the bed, their backs against the pillows. At the instant she began to think that it seemed strange to lie together but not to touch, he picked up her hand and laid it palm-down on his upraised thigh. Stranger still—because they were enemies, weren't they?—such an intimacy from him no longer alarmed her. Maidenly shyness was a condition she hadn't been able to claim since her school days. But was Sebastian her enemy? Why did he sometimes seem like her only ally?

"Sully's not a friend of mine," he said carefully. "I have my share of shallow, profligate friends, but Sully's not among them. Our paths cross often enough in London and elsewhere, because we're both idle and aimless. But we are not friends."

He laughed humorlessly. "I'm telling you this to justify myself, but of course, it's too late for that. When I received his letter saying he and his friends were coming, my first reaction was relief. I wanted him here. I wanted his cynicism and vulgarity, his contempt for anything simple or decent. I wanted him to remind me of my roots, you might say. Because for some time I had felt myself moving in a slightly different direction and it . . . and it . . ." He stared at her fingers, absently pressing them apart one by one. "It frightened me."

She listened to the echo of that extraordinary admission, and could think of nothing to say.

"As soon as I saw them, I knew I'd made a mistake. But I didn't understand the enormity of it until you came. Then it was . . ." He put his head back and closed his eyes. "Biblical analogies," he said with another mirthless laugh; "lamb to the slaughter, all that. Painful. Excruciating to watch, almost unbearable. But I managed. Perhaps you thought I was enjoying myself. You might take a little comfort from knowing that I suffered. Not as you did—I couldn't claim that. But I suffered."

"Why did you do it?"

"I don't know." He kept his eyes shut, so she watched him closely. "I honestly don't know."

She didn't believe him. She even thought she knew the answer, but she didn't offer it. Not because he would deny it, but because saying it out loud would upset this odd, new, peculiarly enjoyable peace they were sharing.

"I thought you would ask me why I hated it," he said after a moment, looking at her. "Why I finally stopped it. I'll tell you, even though you won't ask. It's because I saw myself when I looked at Sully and the others. Heard my voice in their voices. What they did was despicable, indefensible, and they were the mirror of me. I could see it clearly, and it revolted me. I was glad when Sully drew the knife, because that gave me permission to kill him. I wanted to kill him, wring his neck, stop his heart. You won't believe it, but I know that it was the vileness in myself I really wanted to kill."

Face to face at last, she thought. They looked at each other through nothing but the air, no veils of deception between them, no pride, no determined cruelty, no trumped-up impassivity. Even so, she drew back; as much as she welcomed this openness, she also feared it with her woman's discretion, her natural armor.

He sensed it—changed tacks. "Why aren't you angry?" he asked in the gentle voice, the devastating one. "Why are you here? How could you tie a bandage around me and then lie down with me in my bed?" To make it worse, he caressed her forearm, beneath the tight sleeve of her dress—he'd unbuttoned it a minute ago and she, silly woman, had barely noticed. "Are you mad?" he murmured. "Or that compassionate? That foolhardy?"

The last guess was the best one. "I found out about anger in prison," she said slowly. "In the first year, it ruled me. I couldn't control myself. I'd never been treated rudely in my life, and I didn't know how to cope with such callousness. The refractory cell I described that night—do you remember?" He didn't answer; his expression said she had just asked a very stupid question. She blushed, but for a second she felt airy inside, almost breathless. "I spent . . . quite a lot of time there in the early days. Because of my anger. They call it 'breaking out'—smashing everything in your cell, screaming, shredding your clothes. It keeps you from going mad for a little while, but the consequences are . . . dire."

"What was it like?"

"I can't describe it. They never beat me. Once they hobbled me—tied my hands and feet together behind my back. Left me in the dark cell."

"How long?"

"Days. Two or three, I don't know. That was the worst time. After that, I changed. I became a model prisoner."

He was watching her carefully, really seeing her; she had his complete attention, and it made her nervous. But under the nervousness lay a quiet, secret excitement. *It's only the novelty,* she assured herself. The newness of being listened to by someone, by anyone. But the effect, she couldn't deny, was elating.

She continued in a low, tentative voice—so he could stop her whenever he chose, whenever he tired of this. "But it wasn't really the solitary cell or the shackles or the denial of food or privileges that made me change. After that first year, I came to understand that the anger and fury, the terrible sense of injustice I felt—they were eating me alive, and keeping me in a prison every bit as vicious and confining as Exeter. But I could free myself at least from *that* prison if I could let all the rage and hurt go, just— let it go. And so I did."

"How?"

"I stopped caring."

He nodded, but she saw his skepticism.

"It doesn't seem possible," she conceded. "I think, to understand it, you would have to have experienced life in a convict prison. To survive, one becomes like an animal. No memories, no hopes. Dulled senses. I can't explain it, it's—not like anything. There are no words. You cannot imagine it." She sighed, hopeless again. Words, or the futility of them, depressed her.

A silence. Sebastian shifted uncomfortably, holding his side. "Have to lie down," he mumbled, moving down in the bed until he was flat on his back, only his head on the pillow.

"You're tired," she said, embarrassed, starting to get up. "I'll—"

"No, don't go. I'm not tired anymore. Stay, Rachel—come down here beside me."

She didn't even argue with him this time. This was where she wanted to be. She might be losing her sense of proportion, of propriety, of self-preservation, she might even be losing her mind— but it was lovely to lie here in the semidark and murmur a few of her deepest secrets to this man who held her fate in his hands. A few nights ago he'd seduced her body, taken everything a man can take from a woman. What would he think if he knew that a truer, more devastating seduction was the one going on here, this minute?

"I'm sorry about Sully," he said quietly, his eyes on the ceiling. "I couldn't say the words before. I wanted to imply it—much easier than saying it. Now I'm saying it. I apologize to you."

She kept the ridiculous tears in by squeezing her eyes closed. "It's all right."

"No, don't say that. Keep your anger—it's completely justified. I didn't apologize to you so that you would forgive me." She doubted that, and a second later he smiled and added sheepishly, "Although I was very much hoping you would."

She smiled, too. "I'll tell you something curious." He turned onto his good side, facing her. "I hated the things they said to me, the way they treated me, all of that. They made me feel like an object, not a person, something pitiful and despicable. They made me feel dirty. But—here is *my* confession—when they started playing the 'truth' game and I had to answer their questions, I felt—of course I hated it, but—deep down, something in me was *glad* to answer. Glad because I was being made to speak, finally, even in that awful way, of the things that happened to me in gaol. Can you understand this? It's . . . hard for me to talk—of course, you know that; it's obvious. But they *made* me talk, and I was . . . relieved. That sounds pitiful."

"No."

"Crazy."

"*No.* I felt something like it, too. What happened was absolutely hellish, a nightmare, but at the same time I was glad to find out some of your secrets at last. It wasn't lewd curiosity, I promise you." He pushed his hand through his hair. "Why should you believe me?" he asked softly, rhetorically. "But if I were to ask you now to tell me what it was like in prison, would you believe that something more than prurience motivated the question?"

She thought, but not for long. Probably not long enough. "Yes. Now. I would now."

They were both quiet for a time, holding hands under the covers. She couldn't measure the risk she had just taken because it was too big, incalculable. But she felt alive for the first time in a long time, and the extraordinariness of that couldn't be measured either.

And then it started. With the gentle encouragement of his thoughtful, judicious questions, she began to speak of the last ten years of her life. It wasn't an orderly recital; she let her thoughts wander in time, forward or back, over events and milestones and states of mind. She told him of the bitter indignities she'd suffered at the hands of ignorant, underpaid, casually vicious warders, the constant bullying and hectoring, the battering of the mind and soul that never stopped, never, not for four thousand days. The deadly monotony, the barren, brutal months, the unspeakable loneliness. The flies and spiders she'd befriended; the mouse she'd kept for a pet for one whole winter. The SILENCE signs on the walls of every cell, every corridor. The time they'd given her two days' bread and water for smiling at a fellow inmate on Christmas Eve. Loneliness could become so real, it took on a life of its own, became a kind of company. She told him her number—forty-four—and that she hadn't heard the sound of her own name in more than nine years.

He asked about her family, and she told him about the one and only time they'd come to see her. She'd been locked up in a large wooden box with wire netting for a window; four feet away her father, mother, and brother were locked inside an identical box. Two warders stood between the boxes, listening to the conversation, such as it was. Her mother had never stopped crying, and after the first shocked greeting, her father couldn't speak. It lasted ten minutes, and when it was over she asked them not to come back. She never saw any of them again.

She told him about the library, the only light in the long darkness of her prison term. It had four hundred books, and she'd eventually read all of them, some many times.

At first, she'd feared dying in prison. That had seemed the ultimate horror, being nailed up in a prison coffin and thrown into an unmourned grave. But after her family was gone, she stopped caring, and soon she began to pray for death. She hated, hated, hated everything, especially a world where such an unspeakable travesty of justice had been allowed to occur. But even the hatred had waned as year followed empty year. "You erased yourself," Sebastian said, and she said, "Yes. That's it, exactly. I killed myself without dying."

She rested, exhausted from the telling. The lamp by the bedside had long since sputtered out; they lay in the dark, she listening to his breathing. She'd told him terrible things, painful, degrading truths she'd thought she would take to her grave. By rights, she ought to be frightened, but all she could feel was tired and relieved. Unburdened.

Extraordinary.

He still had her hand, but she thought he'd fallen asleep. She was surprised when he said, "Rachel."

"Hmm?"

"Who do you think killed Wade?"

She blinked, trying to see his face. "What?"

"Who killed him? You must have thought about it in prison. Who do you think it was?"

She tried to speak, but only a wheezing sound came out before her throat closed up. She realized she was squeezing his hand too tight, using all her strength. She let go and sat up in bed, hugging her knees.

He sat up, too, and put his hand in the middle of her back. "What's wrong? Are you crying?"

She shook her head. A pitiful lie—her eyes were swimming,

face dripping; only by swallowing repeatedly did she keep back embarrassing sobs. Emotions she couldn't blame on weariness or tension hammered for release, threatening to burst out of their careful bounds. Sebastian had his arm around her shoulders, his hand on her wet cheek, trying to make her look at him. She knew him by now: he would keep at her, he wouldn't stand for evasions.

"I'm just—grateful," she got out, voice strangled. "Because no one believed me. You can't know—" She gave up, couldn't talk.

"What do you mean? That you were innocent? What rot. Don't cry, I can't stand it," he whispered, holding her against him, both arms around her now, and she was soaking his skin with tears.

She put her hand on her aching throat and told him the worst. "No one believed me. *No one.*"

"You mean . . ."

"*My family.*"

There, it was out, the worst thing, the most grievous hurt. As soon as she said it, she calmed. The emotional storm passed, and she was left trembling in reaction.

"Impossible," he said lightly, stroking her hair like a father, rocking her a little. "I always knew it. I doubt if you could kill an insect. You're the gentlest person I know. And the saddest."

"Stop." Or she wouldn't be able to stop crying.

He knew the surest way to banish tears. He kissed her. Not like a father. He kissed her like a lover, slow and hot, their mouths wet, clinging, salty from her crying. As soon as she stiffened, he stopped. In unison, they lay back down on their separate pillows. "You're tired," he whispered. "Go to sleep, Rachel."

She was tired. She covered a yawn with her hand. "I could never sleep in prison." A minute later, she was dreaming.

She dreamt she was in her prison cell, lying on her hard cot in the dark. Even though her eyes were closed, she could see everything. Someone was watching her through the spy hole beside the door. She feigned sleep, not moving, trying not to breathe. A key scraped in the lock. The door opened an inch, two inches, and cold, paralyzing dread congealed in her stomach. The eye in the spy hole was still watching her, and she knew who it was. Then her blanket was gone and her legs were bare. She wanted to push her dress down, cover herself, but if she moved he would know she was awake. The door widened.

She whimpered in fear . . . and the dream faded, grew vague. A low voice told her she was safe; someone touched her and called her by her name. She calmed, slept deeply, and drifted into a different dream.

She was in a flower meadow, lying on a bed of grass. There was no horizon; in any direction, the flowers stretched forever, soft and waving, every color imaginable. A man lay beside her, a different man, not the one in the doorway. This was the empty-handed man, the one who never hurt her.

They lay without touching until she put her hand on his shoulder. Afterward she knew it had been the signal—that he couldn't touch her until she touched him, because that was their rule. *Why didn't I do this sooner?* she thought, or said, and the empty-handed man smiled just before he kissed her.

She could see their mouths, like two other people's mouths coming together. Delicious, how sweet, how luscious the kiss was. She changed the dream by an act of her will so that it could be her mouth under the man's, tasting and being tasted. Lips and then teeth, soft and then hard, and tongues gliding together with such serious playfulness, the perfect mouth caress. Drowning, she was drowning in sensation, and everything was allowed, everything was permitted. *Don't make me wait,* she thought, or said, and the dream changed again and they were rolling and turning over the crushed sweet grass, and the empty-handed man's hands glided on her skin, leaving color wherever he touched, blue-green over the white of her belly, bright yellow on her breasts, purple and crimson on her thighs. His body floated over hers and she had him, yes, and it was what she wanted, but—it wasn't enough, she couldn't *feel* him, and everything was just out of reach. Half awake now, she knew it wasn't real, and she wanted to weep from the frustration, the maddening inadequacy of this dream.

When she opened her eyes, she found herself staring up into Sebastian's. Was it nighttime? He'd lit a candle; she could see the shadows flickering on the wall behind his bare shoulder. He watched her with his head propped on his hand, his brown hair tousled. She thought she would smooth her fingers back over the boyish cowlick—and realized she was resting her hand on his chest.

Then and now mingled as fragments of the dream floated back in disorienting patches. Had she touched him in her sleep? Was he the one who had soothed her with his voice? She opened her mouth, but she couldn't think of anything to say. Her scattered thoughts came together, and finally she knew who the empty-handed man was. The connection slid into her brain smoothly, hardly causing a ripple, but afterward nothing was the same.

Why didn't I do this sooner? the dreaming woman had wondered. Touching the man had been the key, the beginning. But Rachel couldn't speak, couldn't move. Some things never changed, and her fear was one of them. She couldn't move.

How would she have answered if Sebastian had asked her then if he could touch her? Too late; she'd never know now. And all she felt when he finally lowered his head and put his mouth on hers was gladness.

She lay quiet and passive, drifting between dreamer and actor, reluctant to decide, putting off thinking of anything. This was like the dream and not at all like the dream. Sebastian never hesitated, and all his movements were fluid and smooth, like a dancer's, and the way he loosened and pulled and peeled away her clothing was like a dance, a seamless ballet for bare arms and shy, naked legs. She could hardly wait to feel their stomachs touch, and for a little while that was enough, just the slide and press of their skin, his with a downy fleece of hair to rub against hers. The center of herself seemed to be in her belly, and she thought that heavy, intimate pressure would be enough. But it wasn't. She felt the dream-frustration, the identical emptiness at the real center, and she embraced him with her legs, and closed her eyes when he penetrated her.

Gentle and soft, sweet, unrushed, the quietest lovemaking, like a dance still, real but not real. The music was their breathing, and the slide of fingers on warming skin, and the whispery sound of kisses. *It's you,* she began to chant to herself at odd intervals. What did it mean? *It's you.* What did it matter?

She couldn't touch the goal he was urging her toward so gently, could not let go of herself to reach out for it. Did he know? Could he tell that this tender striving was futile? Oh, but it was lovely, the touching and the closeness, she wanted it to go on and on. He murmured something, a most intimate question, and she answered it with the truth—"No, I can't." He kissed her with a desperate sweetness that moved her and made her heart ache. "Sweetheart," he called her. Then he buried his face in her hair and set himself free, his body trembling a little in the effort not to hurt her. Holding to him tightly, she knew a moment's envy, because he could surrender his self-control as easily as hold onto it.

"I broke my word," he said when it was over, curling on his side behind her, pressing her back against him.

"Are you in pain?" she whispered. "Your side—"

" 'I won't touch you,' I said. Now I could tell you I'm sorry. Would you believe me?"

"I don't know. I'm not sure."

She felt his breath on the nape of her neck. He was laughing. "Sweet Rachel," he murmured, "it would be a lie."

Arrogant as always. She did something she'd never done before: she initiated a kiss. On his fingers, which were entwined with hers. She felt his lips on her shoulder, then his teeth, his lips again.

After he fell asleep, she pretended they were married, an ordinary husband and wife taking their rest together, their arms and legs tangled unconsciously because they trusted each other. Loved each other. Since this was as close as she would ever come to that domestic ideal, she allowed herself to enjoy it. Just for the moment.

Sleep crept closer. Before it overtook her, she heard the echo of the whisper in her head again—*It's you. Please, God, don't let it be true*. But she was afraid it was true. If it was, she was lost.

XII

"MRS. WADE? YOU in there?" His arms were full of a big, bulky box; Sebastian had to knock on Rachel's door by kicking it with the toe of his boot. "Open up, Mrs. Wade!"

He heard rushing footsteps just before she threw open the door. Her surprised face was damp and she still had a towel in her hand; she'd been freshening up before she went down to see about getting the evening meal started—he knew her house-keeperly schedule almost as well as his own now.

"What's wrong?" she asked worriedly, staring at him, staring at the box.

"Nothing's wrong. Close the door, then come and open your present." He went past her and set the wooden crate in the center of her sitting-room rug. "Hurry, this present won't wait."

Her cheeks flushed pink. She sidled closer, holding her hands together under her chin. "Is it really a present?"

"Yes. It's a gigantic hat; Miss Carter and Miss Vanstone and I have been working on it for days." He laughed when her eyes went wide as saucers: she'd actually believed him for a second. Well, why not? He'd never told her a joke before. "No, it's not, you goose. Hurry and open it, will you?" *Before it opens itself.*

She came closer. "What could it be?" she wondered, running her hand along the top of the box. Just then a snuffling sound came from within. "Oh," she said, and snatched her hand away. "It's alive!" Sebastian made a face, as if to say, *Who knows?*

A small hook around a nail head was all that was keeping the lid down. She flicked it open with her finger and lifted the hinged top carefully, half an inch at a time. Before the dark gap was two inches wide, a nose and then a head poked through, then two yellow paws, and finally the writhing, wriggling body of the whole excited puppy, leaping out with a graceless but effective bound and landing on the floor at her feet.

"Oh, it's a dog," she cried softly, and immediately sat down on the floor beside it.

Sebastian knelt beside her. "I thought you might like to have it."

"Ohh," was all she could say as she stroked the animal's soft sides and let it sniff at her and lick her cheek.

"I told Holyoake to ask among the tenants and see if he could find one. I told him there was only one criterion—it had to be a yellow dog."

She lifted her head from the puppy's to look at him. He'd had reservations about the wisdom of this gift, but the expression on her face told him his idea was perfect. Inspired. "Oh, Sebastian." She shook her head at him, at a loss. He wanted to kiss her, but the dog got in the way and kissed her first. "What's his name? Is it a he? Where will I keep him? Oh, it's a *beautiful* dog."

It was hardly that. Halfway between a puppy and an adult, it was a gawky adolescent dog, vaguely retriever-ish, with something else thrown in, something too immature yet for precise identification. Hound? Terrier? Only time would tell. "Yes, it's a male. He may have a name, but William didn't catch it. He's yours now, Rachel, if you want him."

"Oh, yes, I want him. My brother had a dog when we were little," she confided. "They gave me a cat, but I always liked the dog better."

They sat on the floor together while the puppy began to explore the room. Sebastian watched her while she watched the dog, and her delight was his dazzling reward for a moment's thoughtfulness. She was beautiful. She had on her black dress today, and even though he'd grown fond of it in a way, as one grows fond of anything one associates with a lover, a sweetheart, he had hopes that he was seeing it for the last time. He'd ordered new gowns for her from a dressmaker in Exeter, and with any luck they'd begin to arrive this week.

"A name," she said consideringly, following the dog's antic explorations with her shining eyes. She leaned her shoulder against his. "Since he's a yellow dog, we could call him Amber. Is that too feminine?"

"Definitely."

"Mmm. What about Apricot?"

Sebastian snorted and made a face.

"I know—Buttercup."

Now she was teasing *him*, and the novelty was enchanting. "If you name this dog Buttercup, I swear I'll take him back from whence he came."

The puppy found its way back to them and began to play a game of tug with the handkerchief Rachel whipped out of her pocket. "I've got it. *Dandelion*. No, listen," she insisted when he started to quibble, "he could be 'Dandelion,' but we'd call him 'Dandy.' That's all right, isn't it? Dandy!" The pup's ears went up at that, no question about it, and Rachel sent Sebastian a look of triumph.

He was besotted. "He's your dog; name him Powder Puff for all I care. You can keep him here if you like, although you'd have to house-train him. Or he could sleep in the stables with Collie and the lads. No telling how big he's going to get. Shall we take him for a walk?"

"Now?"

"Why not?"

She took some persuading; she still had work to do, she said, and a meeting with Judelet later to discuss the kitchen staff's shortcomings. Sebastian overruled her halfhearted objections, and a few minutes later they were strolling through the gatehouse arch, with Dandy at their heels.

They stopped on the bridge to watch the sun sparkle on the chattering river and to look at the house. "Do you think Lynton Hall is ugly?" Sebastian asked conversationally. He could hardly remember his own first impression of it anymore; it was simply Lynton to him now, the house where he lived.

"Oh, no, I think it's very handsome. It has a few flaws, but I think it carries them with great dignity. And it doesn't take itself too seriously, does it?"

He smiled, thinking of the ridicule Sully and the others had heaped on it. Rachel was right and they were wrong, because she was a better person. She saw more clearly, not only with her shrewd eyes but with her tolerant heart.

"I thought I'd have that chimney fixed," he mentioned, pointing. "And new slates put on the eaves where the rain's been washing in. Holyoake says it's been washing in for about a hundred years."

She looked at him quizzically. She was probably thinking it was odd that he was the one breaking a hundred-year-old tradition of neglect. He couldn't account for it himself. "What's your house like in Rye?" she asked as they started to walk again.

"It's called Steyne Court. It's huge, colossal, a great beast of a house. I've always hated it."

"Why?"

"Don't know. It swallowed me up when I was a child. It has all the warmth of a memorial to the war dead."

"But you'll go to live there, won't you, once you inherit your father's title?"

"Yes, I suppose, for a primary residence. Most of the time I expect to be in London. What else? It's what one does." Frowning, he picked up a stick and flung it into the path ahead of them for the dog to chase. They went along for a while without speaking. "Do you ride?"

She smiled and shook her head.

"I'll teach you. I know the horse who would suit, a mare called Molly, gentle as a lamb. Are you game?" The prospect intrigued him.

"I don't think so."

"Are you afraid of horses?"

"No, it's not that."

"What, then? I promise you'd enjoy yourself."

She shook her head again, smiling, keeping her eyes down.

He let it pass. For the first time it dawned on him that she might not want their affair carried on in public. Of course; that must be it. He felt like slapping his forehead. For a man who prided himself on his understanding of women, he'd been remarkably slow where this one was concerned. But he would do better. When all his faculties were engaged, there was no sharper student of the feminine mind than Sebastian Verlaine. He really believed it.

They'd come to the far reaches of an abandoned canal, a tributary of the Plym, used ten or twenty years ago for transporting goods up from Devonport and Plymouth to the moorland towns. "Is this your land?" Rachel asked, and he nodded. "And your cows?" She pointed to a lazy huddle of fawn-colored Jerseys, idling under a tree in the near field. While they watched, the cows began to lumber toward them, curious, phlegmatically craving a diversion. The low stone wall forty feet away kept them at a respectful distance. Dandy, who had been snuffling in the weed-choked canal water, jumped a foot in the air when he saw them. After one brave yip, clearly counterfeit, he made a dash for Rachel and dived behind her skirts.

"I knew we should've named him Buttercup," she joked, petting the excited dog to calm him.

"Ingrate. He's known me longer—ten minutes at least—but he comes to *you* for protection."

"If you wore skirts," she said consolingly, "I'm sure he would come to you. And don't forget, you put him in a box and I let him out of it. He's a very smart dog; he knows who his friends are."

They sat down on a fallen beech tree not far from the river and contemplated the stagnant water, the piercing blue of the sky, the wildflowers blooming along the riverbank. "I used to dream of flowers," Rachel told him presently. "Sometimes I could close my eyes and pretend that my cell was a greenhouse." She smiled wryly. "Quite an imaginative feat, but I had a lot of time to practice. I'd picture myself watering and pruning with the hot sun streaming through the glass. Pulling up weeds. Digging with my hands in the clean soil."

He took one of her hands from her lap and kissed it. She smiled and shook her head slightly, telling him not to feel sorry for her. But pity wasn't the emotion he felt. "That's over. All that bleakness—it's finished."

She bowed her head. "Yes, of course. I know that."

"No, I don't think you do. But you will." He smiled, to lessen the solemnity; that had almost sounded like a threat, and he'd meant it as a vow. "They sent you to an early grave, Rachel, but I'm going to dig you out of it and resurrect you. Revive you."

She looked at him strangely. "I'm not sure anyone can do that."

"I can."

She lowered her eyes, hiding her skepticism. "I'm not un-happy now."

He noted the double negative, but he didn't worry about it. He had two immediate goals: to make her laugh and to make her come. He thought of telling her, but decided it would make her too self-conscious. Might even inhibit her, slow down the inevitable. But that both goals would eventually be realized, he hadn't the slightest doubt.

The summer sun dipped behind the oak trees at their back; a fresh breeze had sprung up from the south, bearing the faint, barely noticeable odor of the sea. Rachel stood up and began to pick the moon daisies that grew in patches alongside the canal. He watched her for a while, admiring her slow, effortless grace. Dandy brought him a stick. He threw it over and over, at lengthening distances, until the puppy began to flag and finally collapsed, with only enough strength left to chew the stick.

Rachel wandered back, resuming her place beside him on the log. She was easy with silence, easier than he was; certainly she was more used to it. He could make her smile now, but her eyes were always sad. He put his arm around her, and she relaxed against him, taking back one of the flowers from the bouquet she'd given him and holding it to her nose.

"How did it begin?" he heard himself ask. "Why did you marry your husband? Tell me about the girl in the photograph."

"Oh," she murmured. "That girl." She took two more flowers from him and began to plait the long stems together. "I look at her sometimes and wonder who she was, what became of her. As if she were an old acquaintance I can barely remember."

"Tell me about your life before you went to prison."

"What would you like to know?"

Everything, he thought. "Were you happy when you were a child?"

"Yes," she answered, but not very forcefully. "But I was very shy. And spoiled, I'm sure. My mother always told me I was beautiful, that I was destined for great things. Great things," she repeated, her voice full of melancholy. "She had such high hopes for me. I never felt I was doing enough to live up to her expectations."

"What about your father?"

"My father didn't expect anything of me. We weren't very close."

"And now they're both dead?"

"They died when I was in gaol, within months of each other."

"It must have been painful," he said, conscious of the inadequacy of the word. "And your brother?"

"Tom. He lives in Canada now with his own family. We don't correspond anymore."

"Why not?"

She lifted a hand and let it drop. "We did for a while; but letters in prison are so thoroughly censored, it's almost better not to have any."

"You could write to him now."

"Yes. But he has a new life. He went to Canada to get away from what happened. I don't think he would welcome being reminded of it now."

He thought of her grief when she'd told him her family believed she was guilty of murdering Wade. Of all the heartaches and indignities, that must have been the hardest one to bear. He imagined her as a child, shy, obedient, anxious to please a mother with "high hopes" and a father who ignored her. "How did you meet Wade?" He had to know it all now, but he was beginning to wonder about the wisdom of opening this sorrowful subject.

"Lydia and I—My parents sent me—My father was—" She stopped, blowing a frustrated puff of air. "I keep having to start further back."

"Start anywhere. Tell it any way you like."

"I want you to understand, though. I want . . . I need to justify myself."

"Not to me."

Her hands went still and she looked at him for a moment, her eyes arrested, face alert. "To myself, then. In some ways, I ruined my own life. I try to forget it, but the truth always comes back."

He couldn't believe it; some too-fine sensibility was at work here, he was certain. If anything good could come from making her tell the story, maybe it would be that she could see she was blameless.

"My father was a schoolmaster," she began again. "He had his own boys' school in Exeter until his health began to fail. Then he moved the family to Ottery St. Mary and did private tutoring, preparing students for university. I was about twelve at the time. It was a comedown in the world, but I wouldn't have minded it, none of us would, I don't think, if my mother hadn't taken on so about it. She missed the city, despised village life, hated what we'd 'come to,' as she always put it. My brother's future was secure by then—he was reading law with a judge in Torbay. He would be solid and steady, we all knew, even if his career would never be spectacular."

"And your mother," Sebastian guessed, his mind skipping ahead, "wanted one of you to be *spectacular*."

"Yes."

"And that left you. And you were beautiful." Already he could see where the story was heading.

"I *wasn't*," she denied, smiling—and he could tell she believed it. "But I was all right, not ugly. Tall for my age. I had pretty . . ." She touched the side of her head, then gave an impatient shrug and dropped the subject. "Anyway, as you've guessed, my mother had marriage plans for me. I didn't understand it until much later. I knew they couldn't afford it, but when they sent me to an expensive girls' school in Exeter when I was fifteen, I honestly thought they wanted me to go there for an education. Not so I could become some wealthy family's governess, either, but so I could be a *scholar*. Like my father. I really believed it." She shook her head, and beyond the amused self-mockery he could see the remnants of a still-deep personal hurt.

"I had underestimated my mother's ambition, but eventually I understood. A coming-out in London was out of the question for me, but she was working early on the next best thing—cultivating friends of the right sort who *would* come out. And these friends would have beaus, or brothers or cousins or friends, one of whom I—I—"

"Would snag."

She nodded. "Once I understood the conspiracy, I entered into it willingly enough. You see, I was a shallow thing after all. I wanted to please my parents. I wanted them to be proud of me."

"That's not such a sin."

"Isn't it? I think it depends on the consequences. In this case, I think you'll agree that a sin of sorts was committed."

"No," he said, "I won't. But even if you're right, I think you'll agree that the sinner has paid a penance far out of proportion to her sin."

"I won't—"

"Let's argue the fine moral points later," he suggested. "What happened next? You met Lydia, I suppose."

"Yes. Under . . . memorable circumstances. I walked into the lavatory one night and found her trying to cut her wrists with a letter opener."

"Good God."

"She hadn't really been in my set before, my circle of friends, but after that night I felt responsible for her, I suppose. She was so very unhappy."

"Why?"

"Oh . . ." She lifted her shoulders, as if the task of explaining that was beyond her. "She was troubled, she had changeable moods, highs and lows one could never anticipate. A mercurial temperament, I suppose it's called."

He could think of other things to call it. "Yes, but why?"

"Why was she unhappy? Her mother had died when she was eleven. She—oh, Sebastian, I don't know. Why, under the same circumstances, are some people all right and some people completely destroyed? Lydia wasn't a strong person. She hated herself, she was morbidly sensitive, couldn't keep friends, she was rude to everyone, nobody liked her." She gave a short laugh. "How could I *not* be her friend?

"But she was loyal and she could be very kind, and funny in a dark way that I found interesting. And I didn't for a moment believe she'd truly meant to kill herself. She swore me to secrecy that night, and I never felt the least temptation to betray her. She was showing off, trying to get somebody's attention."

"And it happened to be yours." What a ludicrous, circumstantial mash life could be. If someone else had walked into the lavatory that night at her fancy boarding school, Rachel might never have befriended the friendless Lydia Wade, never met or married her father, never stood trial for his murder. How often must she have had the same futile thought? How could she be anything but bitter? "What do you hope for?" he'd asked her once, and he understood her answer perfectly now: "I hope to be able to bear it."

She stood up. The sky had turned opal-white overhead, coral in the west. The cows were gone; he hadn't noticed their silent decampment. The dog got up from beside the log, waddled over to Rachel, and flopped down at her feet. She knelt, and while she petted him she said, "In my last year at school, Lydia invited me to her home in Tavistock for the spring holiday. I didn't particularly want to go, but my mother was set on it—time was running out, you see. And the Wades were wealthy, definitely the 'right sort.' Who knew what might come of it?" She shook her head at the unpleasant irony.

"You'd never met Wade before?"

"No, but I'd heard about him from Lydia, what a wonderful man he was, the world's best father. I was prepared to like him."

"And you did."

She looked up. "No. Actually, I didn't. Not at first."

"Why?"

"I'm not sure. I didn't know then, either. Something about him made me uncomfortable, something more than the fact that he was interested in me as a woman, not as his daughter's school chum. He made that clear almost from the beginning, and that was unsettling enough—but there was something more. I couldn't put my finger on it. And then it went away."

"What do you mean, it went away?"

"He became charming. Perfectly agreeable, attentive to me in a kind, flattering way. I forgot my first impression, or convinced myself I'd been mistaken."

"And then?"

"And then . . . I knew he liked me, but I was flabbergasted when he wrote to my father and asked if he could court me. Permission was granted, you may be sure, and that summer he visited us in Ottery on three occasions. Then he proposed—through my father again—and eventually I was persuaded to accept."

"Persuaded to accept."

They had come to the heart of it. She kept her gaze on her hands as she played with the dog's ears, scratched his neck, ruffled his coat. "I capitulated. In spite of all my girlish ideas about love and romance, and in spite of the reservations I'd forgotten or hidden from myself, I accepted a man I didn't love or completely trust. I let other people decide my life. In other words, I sold myself."

"Oh, come now." He got up and went to her, squatted down beside her, the dog between them. "How old were you?"

"I'd just turned eighteen."

"You were a child."

"No, I wasn't a child."

"Was Wade ugly?"

"What? No, he was really quite handsome, he—"

"Was he old?"

"I thought so then. Now, of course—"

"How old? Forty, fifty?"

"Thirty-eight."

"Young, then. Young, handsome, rich, charming, and the world's best father. And you say you 'sold' yourself to him."

"I—"

"If he'd turned out to be a model husband, would you still use that term?"

"No, perhaps not, but . . ."

"What were your parents' arguments? How did they persuade you to accept him?"

"They said . . . I'd be happy, that he was a perfect catch. My father's eyes had been deteriorating; they said he could retire and maybe not lose his sight, or not as quickly. I wouldn't be that far from home, we would still see one another often. My mother could have a few comforts in her old age. I'd have servants, beautiful clothes, I could travel . . ."

"So," Sebastian said softly. "Let's see. You would be wealthy, you'd live with a paragon who adored you, and you'd save your father from blindness. Sounds like pure selfishness to me."

"But I didn't love him," she countered heatedly. "And if I'd refused, they would never have forced me. It was my choice, I've never blamed them for it."

"You should have."

"No. No, you don't understand. If I'd said no, I could have saved myself. I should have listened to the instinct that told me all along to stay away from him. Instead I let some mistaken notion of duty and—and—"

"Kindheartedness."

"*Weak*heartedness. And guilt, stupidity—"

"Gentleness. A sweet nature."

"Insipidity, spinelessness—"

He took her hands and pulled her to her feet. He had to step over the dog to embrace her. Foolish to think he could erase her guilty conscience by holding her, but he needed to give her comfort somehow, and words weren't working. "Shut up for a minute," he said gruffly, and wrapped her up in his arms. They stood still, and after a while her stiff body began to soften. "I never thought I'd ever have to tell you to stop talking," he mused.

"I'm all right. Really. It's not easy to tell you these things, but it's—not nearly as difficult as I thought it would be. And I never thought it would be you . . ."

"No," he agreed, rueful. But he was all she had, even though he'd abused that power more times than either of them could count. He supposed it was a measure of her aloneness that he was still the one in whom she confided.

"What did Lydia think of the marriage?" he asked presently.

"What you would expect her to think. She was appalled. She didn't fancy me as a stepmother, and I couldn't blame her. But she made the best of it, no scene at the wedding or anything like that. She was stone-faced and speechless, obviously suffering, but she never said anything harsh to me.

"We were married in Wyckerley by the old vicar, Reverend Morrell's father. That's where I met your friend, Sully. And Mayor Vanstone, although he wasn't the mayor then. There was a reception at Randolph's house afterward. A modest affair. My mother wanted something bigger, showier, a more public exhibition of this social coup she believed she'd pulled off, but Randolph wanted it small, in deference to Lydia's feelings. Or so he said. And so we were married. A week later he was dead."

She stepped away and turned her back on him, gazing across the stagnant canal at the empty pasture. He watched her, a tall, straight-bodied woman with silver-streaked hair, somber-looking in her dark dress. "How did it happen?" he asked quietly.

"He was beaten to death with a fireplace poker. In his study. It wasn't a burglary; nothing was taken. Lydia had been staying with her aunt that week, to give us—" She hugged her arms and looked up at the sky. "To give us privacy. Except for the servants, we were alone."

"Did you find him?"

She shook her head. "One of the maids, early in the morning. We were to leave for France on our wedding trip that day."

"Why did they think you'd done it?"

"We'd argued the night before and the servants heard it, heard him shouting, me—weeping. No one had broken in. And then, of course, after he was dead and the police made me tell them what our marriage had been like, they thought I had good reason to kill him. Sometimes . . . sometimes I used to think I *did* do it. In my sleep, or in some sort of trance. I wanted him dead, and then he was dead."

"No, you didn't kill him. You know that."

She glanced back at him, acknowledged it with a grim smile.

"Why didn't you tell anyone what was happening? Your parents or—"

"I did. I wrote them a letter. But I was deplorably ignorant about what was normal between husbands and wives and what was not. My mother had told me almost nothing, except that I probably wouldn't like it. And I had couched the problem in such delicate language that my letter didn't alarm them."

Sebastian thought of the time, not very long ago, when he'd wanted to know everything Wade had done to her, all the lurid details, the more shocking the better. There were few things in his sin-ridden life that made him more ashamed than that. Now he wanted to know *nothing*, wanted the subject closed, off-limits between them, shut away and forbidden. But it was too late. Rachel wasn't his plaything or his possession anymore, she was his lover. She could tell him anything she liked and he would have to listen, no matter how much it distressed him.

He went to her, put his hands on her shoulders from behind. A strange tenderness welled up in him as soon as he touched her—strange because its gentleness was wedded so evenly with sexual desire. It was an uncommon mingling for him, for he was used to women he wanted only to bed, or to look at because they were beautiful, or to keep around him because their admiration and their easiness flattered his pride. Had he ever been in love, really in love? Had a woman's needs ever come before his for very long, or for any motive other than seduction? He thought of the handful of lovers who had ever meant anything to him. They were pitifully few, and there had been none at all in a very long time.

Rachel rested her cheek on his hand. "I'm all right," she said again. "It's late. Maybe we should start for home."

"We can do that. Or you can tell me what your marriage was like." She couldn't know it, but his atonement for all the injustices he'd done to her began at that moment, with that question. He waited for her decision, patient, open to anything.

She dropped her head. "No," she said very softly. He had to bend closer to hear her. "Not now."

"All right." He said it with cowardly haste.

"Sometime. I want to tell you sometime, but not now, and not all at once. It's too hurtful, even though I'm sure you—it's nothing that you—couldn't—imagine. Maybe nothing you haven't . . ." She came to a full stop.

The implication jarred him. "Nothing what? Nothing I haven't *done*?" She didn't answer. "Rachel, I've never hurt a woman with sex in my life unless she wanted it, and even then—"

"Unless she wanted it?" She spun around. Her quicksilver eyes were crackling with ire. "What woman would want a man to hurt her?"

"It doesn't sound—If you've never experienced it, it's hard to imagine, I'll grant you. But there are such women. You can take my word for it."

Apparently she couldn't. "I don't believe you. I believe there are cruel, conscienceless men who want to *think* it's true, because then they can beat and degrade women and not feel any remorse. But you will never convince me—that a woman—that *anyone* could derive enjoyment from pain and torture and humiliation. It's a *lie*."

She pushed him away and began to walk off, arms swinging, legs striding. Dandy popped up from a sound sleep and took off after her. She had to slow down when he scampered ahead and turned around, intent on a new game of trying to jump up in her arms. "Down," she admonished him, as sternly as it was in her to admonish anyone. Her angry but dignified retreat was ruined. Tongue lolling, tail wagging, Dandy wouldn't let her pass.

Although she'd just called him cruel and conscienceless, Sebastian reveled in her anger and took hope from it. A universe of powerful emotions lay under the hard surface of her reserve, he was sure of it, even though the strongest ones she'd shown him so far were only endurance and resignation. He couldn't even picture it, but he wanted to see her mad enough to throw things, stamp her feet and shout ladylike swear words at him. It would probably never happen, but he thought the miniature tirade she'd just delivered was an excellent beginning.

"So. You think I'm cruel and conscienceless." He snatched the puppy up and started to walk backward, talking all the while, until she had no choice but to follow. "I don't blame you. How could I? I'll even agree that I've treated you *as if* I have no conscience, but I must take issue with 'cruel.' I wasn't intentionally cruel to you, if that's worth anything. Selfish, yes—"

"I never said you were cruel or conscienceless," she snapped. "Don't twist my words, please."

"Sorry," he said meekly. The dog came to his rescue by licking him in the face, a silly sight which made it hard for Rachel to hold on to her pique. He set Dandy on the ground and reached for her hand. When she didn't pull away, he knew she'd forgiven him. She was much too forgiving. Much, much too good for him.

At the river bridge, she hung back. She didn't say it, but she wanted him to go home first, her to follow, in another gesture toward discretion. A useless one, probably, but by now he'd have done anything she asked of him, short of letting her go. He was at her command, if she only knew it. Best that she didn't.

"Thank you for this dog," she told him, coloring prettily. "He's lovely. I don't know how you knew that I would want him so much. He makes me smile just to look at him."

"I was hoping for that," he said softly. "He'll be a handful, though. What do you think of telling Jerny or one of the other lads to feed him and take him out and so forth for *me*, because he's *my* dog? He wouldn't be, but only you and I would know it."

When her face filled with relief, it came to him that the logistics of dog ownership, at least in her special circumstances, had been keeping her from fully enjoying his gift. He'd just solved several problems at once, including the awkward one of how to give his mistress a present without embarrassing her.

"That would be fine," she said. "I love him, Sebastian. Truly. Thank you, for him—and for remembering. About the yellow dog."

Nothing but the fact that they could be seen by anyone looking out a window kept him from kissing her. It had taken him an unconscionably long time to figure out that it was gentleness that devastated Rachel, not ruthlessness. Now he wondered if there was an ancillary lesson to be learned as well: that gentleness could disarm the seducer as thoroughly as the seduced.

"Come to my room tonight," he murmured, bending close but not touching her. "Just come, Rachel. Not to thank me. Because you want to."

He loved her lack of hesitation almost as much as her answer. "Yes," she said. "I'll come."

XIII

Rachel had never been to the post office before. It was located in the first-floor sitting room of Mr. and Mrs. Brakey Pitt's thatched-roof cottage at the top of the High Street, directly across from the church. Mrs. Pitt was the postmistress. Today was Wednesday, Rachel's day for visiting the constable; when Susan mentioned she had to go to the village this afternoon to post Lord D'Aubrey's letters, Rachel had offered to do it for her. It wasn't like her; in the past she'd limited her business in Wyckerley to matters that couldn't possibly be avoided. A trip to the post office was fraught with uncertainties and potential disaster. But she was feeling brave these days, actually fearless sometimes, and she wanted to test the mettle of this interesting but embryonic self-confidence.

Mrs. Pitt was cross-eyed. Rachel handed her Sebastian's letters and gave her money for stamps, all the while wondering if the postmistress's natural expression was irritation, or if Rachel had done something to annoy her. Waiting for her change, she tried to think of a way to tell Sebastian a joke about Mrs. Pitt; something like, "You know, I'm so sensitive, I fell apart when she looked at me cross-eyed." No, that didn't quite work—but it felt good to be thinking up jokes at all, even bad ones.

"You're Mrs. Wade, aren't you?" Mrs. Pitt said unexpectedly, counting four pennies into her hand. Rachel admitted it. "You've got a package. Came this morning. Want it here or delivered up to the Hall?"

"*I* have a package," she repeated, certain she'd misheard.

The postmistress reached under her counter and produced a small, paper-wrapped bundle. " 'Mrs. R. Wade,' " she read, " 'in care of Lynton Great Hall, Wyckerley.' Want it now?"

"I—yes, I'll take it. Thank you. Thank you very much." She was so rattled, she didn't even look at the package, just shoved it into her reticule and hurried out of the post office. It wasn't until she looked at it again, under an alder tree at the edge of the green, that she realized her agitation was unwarranted—the package had a Tavistock postal return but no sender's address. Of course it must be from Sebastian—who else?—but thank goodness he'd been discreet enough not to put his name on it.

Her appointment with Constable Burdy was ten minutes away. Plenty of time to open her present. Should she? Probably not; she should take it home and open it in private. Or with Sebastian—that would be even better.

Impossible. Her curiosity might be childish, but it was also irresistible. Pressing down a smile, she walked out to a bench in the full sun and sat down.

Under the brown paper and string, the small paper-board box weighed almost nothing. With a little thrill of excitement, she pried open the lid. Tissue paper covered something soft. A scarf? Handkerchief? She peeled the tissue away and uncovered her gift.

She sat frozen on her bench for a full minute, staring at a cheap square of gray towcloth. The figure coarsely sewn on it in black thread looked like a crow's foot—that's what they had called it in prison. But it wasn't. It was the Broad Arrow.

Anger and despair coiled in her stomach, and a sick dread that made no sense. She'd served her sentence, they couldn't send her back to gaol—but just the sight of the hated emblem filled her with superstitious fear, the waking counterpart of her worst nightmare: that she was back in her prison cell, and the horror was beginning all over again.

She stood up, clutching the wretched cloth in her hand. Her heart was pounding. Could her enemy be watching her right now? She scanned the peaceful street, distrusting its ordinariness, the innocent look of the people strolling in the noonday sun. She wanted to run away, she wanted to weep with fury and humiliation—

"Rachel? I thought that was you!" Anne Morrell was coming down the walk from the vicarage, smiling a greeting already. "I saw you from the window," she called, and kept talking all the way across the green. "How are you? I haven't seen you in ages. To speak to, I mean. I've seen you in church, but Christy's got me singing in the choir now, if you can believe that, so I'm among the last getting out after the service. How are you?" she asked again, finally stopping in front of her, slightly breathless.

"Fine." The fluttery smile she attempted was a pathetic failure.

She could tell that Anne was trying to decide whether or not to pretend she didn't notice anything amiss. In the end, she didn't. "What's wrong?" she asked, as all the gaiety in her manner changed to concern.

"Nothing, really. Someone has played a little joke on me," she said lightly, determined to minimize it. She looked down at her fisted hand and opened it.

"What's that?"

"It's the Broad Arrow." She pointed to the embroidered emblem. "The crow's foot, we called it. It's stamped or sewn on everything in prison."

"I recognize it," Anne said slowly. "I've seen it on military ordnance. It means it's the property of Her Majesty."

She nodded. "It was everywhere at Dartmoor, on the blankets, the towels, every piece of clothing, even the tinware. It's—a symbol one grows to despise."

"Oh, Rachel." Compassion and anger mingled in Anne's face; her reaction, like Rachel's, was to search the street with her eyes, as if the sender might be standing somewhere nearby, watching them. *"Damn it,"* she swore, shaking her head in hopeless sympathy. "Come home with me. Come inside and we'll talk."

"I can't. But thank you."

"You can. We'll have tea—no, we'll have a *drink,* that's what—and we'll talk, and after a while it won't all seem so beastly. Come—"

"No, really I can't. I wish I could, but I'm late now." She steeled herself. "Once a week, I must pay a visit to the constable. It's one of the conditions of my release." She could feel her cheeks heating, and she waited in dread, half-expecting Anne to recoil from her now, because her life was so irredeemably sordid.

"I'll walk with you to Mr. Burdy's office, then. For the company."

For a minute, Rachel was too moved to speak. "Thank you," she whispered.

"Throw that away," Anne advised, nodding at the cloth Rachel was still squeezing between her fingers.

She considered it, then changed her mind. "No," she said slowly, "I think I'll keep it." And she put it in her pocket.

The short walk to Constable Burdy's office in the moot hall was one of those brief, unremarkable, but utterly indelible moments in time she knew, even as it was happening, that she would never forget. She wanted it to go on forever. There weren't many people on the street today—she wished there were more. The few passersby looked at the two women curiously, interested but apparently not horrified to see them together. When they greeted the minister's wife, they had no choice but to greet Rachel, too. Unquestionably, Anne's company lent her existence legitimacy, rendered her automatically respectable. And even though she knew full well the condition wasn't permanent, she reveled in it.

That was a bit of a revelation. She liked her temporary respectability so much, she was forced to acknowledge how much she'd secretly yearned for it. But she'd kept the wish unexamined because the likelihood of it coming true had seemed so pathetically remote.

Anne made small talk as they went, idle chatter about parish events, her husband's comings and goings, village gossip. Rachel listened in fascination, wondering if the vicar's wife had any idea how blessed her quiet, ordinary life was. Much too soon, they arrived at the courthouse.

"Thank you for—" Rachel started to say, but Anne waved her hands and wouldn't let her finish.

"Come to see me sometime," she invited. "Christy's away so much, I get lonely."

What a generous-hearted lie. Rachel murmured thanks.

"And be sure to give my regards to Mr. Burdy. Tell him . . ." She thought for a second. "Tell him not to forget the vestry meeting next Thursday."

She was lending Rachel her good name again—protecting her with her most valuable possession: association with her own impeccable social standing. "I don't know why you're so kind to me," Rachel told her softly. "You won't let me thank you. But you must let me tell you that whatever becomes of me, I'll never forget you."

They squeezed each other's hands tightly. For once Anne, always so glib, was speechless. Rachel smiled and told her goodbye, and went inside to make her report to the constable.

Afterward, she hurried home, anxious to see Sebastian and tell him about her unpleasant surprise package. She looked for him in his study first. Wrapped up in her own thoughts, she knocked only once on the closed door and opened it without waiting for an answer.

"Oh—I beg your pardon—I didn't realize you had a guest, my lord. I'll come—"

"No, come in," Sebastian called to her, getting up from behind his desk. Reverend Morrell, who was with him, rose, too. "Christy, you've met my housekeeper, Mrs. Wade, haven't you?"

"Yes, I've had the pleasure," said the vicar, smiling at her.

"Good afternoon," she said, distracted. "I've—I saw your wife today. Anne. We—she was very—" She mentally shook herself. "I met her in the village. We spoke."

"Did you? Aha." Meaningless words; something in the way he spoke them, his voice or his manner, the compassion in his eyes, made them seem uncannily sympathetic.

Sebastian was watching her closely. "Is anything the matter?"

"Oh, no," she assured him, crushing the piece of towcloth between her hands. "Only a question, and it can easily wait. I'll come back later."

"No, sit down with us," Sebastian urged, and Reverend Morrell gestured for her to take his chair. "I've sent for Holyoake, and I'd like you to hear this, too. The vicar's been telling me about a situation with one of my tenants, and I want—ah, here's William."

Holyoake, dressed in his work clothes, looked surprised to find Reverend Morrell—not to mention Rachel—waiting for him in his lordship's study. He shook hands with the minister, whom he seemed to know well, and they all sat down.

"William, you know Marcus Timms, don't you?" the vicar began.

"Aye, o' course. Farms corn on a hundred acres over to Wyckham Cleave for the Hall Farm. Been a tenant all's life, and 'is father before him."

"Have you ever known him to be a violent man?"

"Marcus?" Holyoake squinted his eyes and rubbed the bridge of his nose with his index finger. "No, not as I can recollect. I'd say he were a quiet man in general. Lost his wife a few years ago; 'tis only him and 'is daughter now, and one hired boy who works for 'em at haying. Has Marcus done something wicked, Vicar?"

"I'm afraid that he has. His daughter limped into the village yesterday, beaten and lame, and fainted on Dr. Hesselius's porch step."

"Merciful Jesus," breathed Holyoake, his cheeks reddening. "And it truly were Timms who beat 'er?"

"Yes. And she says it wasn't the first time. Her name is Sidony," the reverend said for Rachel's benefit. "She's seventeen, shy and a bit awkward, but a very sweet child. Hesselius says she'll be all right, although she may never walk normally again. She stayed with us at the vicarage last night, and my wife got out of her that Timms knocked her down more than a year ago. That's when she injured her hip."

Rachel jumped when Holyoake suddenly banged one huge fist down on the arm of his chair and exclaimed, "Damnation!" without apology. "I should've knowed it, I should ought to've figured it out. I recollect now a time I seen her and she were hurt. Last autumn, around Michaelmas time. I went out to speak to Marcus about sommat or other, and Sidony had a bad bruise on 'er face. 'What happened to you?' I asked 'er. 'Oh,' she said, 'I were haulin' the bucket up from the well and it whacked me on the jaw.' And damn me for a fool, I believed her!"

"It's not your fault, William. You couldn't have known."

"No, Christy, I ought to've seen it." He shook his head, miserable. "Poor little mite, wi' no mother and no one to tell about her trouble. Well, what's to do? Have you told the constable?"

"Dr. Hesselius reported it, and Burdy went out to Timms's place yesterday. Marcus admitted he struck her. He showed no remorse at all, and said he couldn't understand why everyone was making a fuss about it."

Holyoake swore again under his breath, then mumbled, "Beg pardon," glancing at Rachel.

"He said it was his right as her father to punish her when she was disrespectful and disobedient. Now the girl's afraid to go home. Since Timms is completely unrepentant, I don't blame her. I'm not sure what ought to be done. I've come to ask you and Lord D'Aubrey for advice."

"Can't a place be found for her somewhere else, William?" Sebastian asked his bailiff. "With another tenant family who could use the girl's help, either for board or a wage, until she's eighteen and can look for something on her own? I suppose this is all assuming Timms doesn't decide to dig in his heels and insist she must stay with him. That would complicate matters."

"I don't think it will come to that. If it does," the vicar said, with quite a fierce gleam in his normally mild blue eyes, "I'll see to it that he's arrested for assault."

"I'm a magistrate," Sebastian said—as if he were just remembering it. "I'll see to it that he goes to gaol."

"I barely know the girl, so I can't say what she's handy at besides general housework. And I can't call to mind anyone who'd be needin' help just now. But mayhap sommat will turn up in the course o' things."

"Yes, but what's to be done for her in the meantime?"

Rachel broke the thoughtful silence to say hesitantly, "One of the kitchen maids gave notice two days ago. Katie Munn—she's leaving at the end of the week."

"Good Lord, another one gone?" Sebastian asked, incredulous. "My chef," he informed the vicar, "is as intolerant as he is intolerable. We go through kitchen help faster than Palmerston goes through deputies. Well, what do you think? Does that sound like a post the girl could handle?"

"Yes, I'm sure of it," Reverend Morrell answered, looking relieved. "She's a bit backward and she hasn't much to say, but she's a bright girl and very willing to work. Thank you very much indeed, my lord—and thank you, Mrs. Wade, for the suggestion."

Rachel said, "You're welcome," with a pleased smile.

They decided that Holyoake would go with the vicar and bring Sidony Timms back with him in the pony gig. Dr. Hesselius had said she was all right, but it would be Rachel's job to decide when she would be well enough to start working—probably only a matter of a few days, everyone agreed. Until then, she could recover more easily at the Hall than the vicarage, if only because there were more people here to look after her.

"My wife asked me to send you her regards," Reverend Morrell told Sebastian at the study door. "And to say we'd both be very pleased if you would dine with us again one night soon."

"Thank you, I'd enjoy that," he answered, sounding as if he meant it. "And then I hope you'll allow me to reciprocate, if only so you'll understand why I keep my insufferable French cook."

"Delighted," the vicar smiled.

"I've been wanting to ask your advice about a couple of local investments I'm considering," Sebastian went on, and Rachel immediately moved away to the window to give the two men privacy. But she heard him add, "The mayor's invited me to purchase shares in his copper mine, but I'm not convinced that's the best use of my capital right now."

The brief exchange surprised her. She'd taken Sebastian at his word when he'd said Wyckerley was only a stopping place for him while he waited for his real inheritance. Why invest in local enterprises, then? Just because he was a businessman and that was the practical thing to do? Probably. No doubt. To speculate that he meant to stay any longer than he absolutely had to was self-deluding. It would also violate the two strategies for survival to which she was adhering with iron determination: live only for the moment, and hope for nothing.

The minister and William left together. "Wait for me," Sebastian said softly from the doorway, leaving her in the study while he went to show them out.

She'd almost forgotten about the Broad Arrow. The dread and the irrational fear she'd felt before had diminished to manageable dimensions. After all, it was only a piece of cloth. And now she could even guess who had sent it.

Sebastian returned. He paused in the doorway to look at her, and she had time to reflect on the ways in which he'd changed from the bored, sophisticated, impeccably dressed gentleman who had rescued her at the magistrates' hearing. He seemed bigger, for one thing, a perception not altogether in her mind, since lately he'd taken to joining his estate laborers in pursuits as ungenteel as haymaking and fence mending. What the parish thought of such eccentric behavior in their new viscount she could hardly imagine. He might be doing it for a lark, but the end result was that he looked handsomer than ever. The summer sun had ruddied his skin and lightened his soft brown hair, which had grown unfashionably but becomingly long. More subtly, his blasé, unsurprised and unsurprisable manner was gone, replaced by a new alertness. He radiated energy. He no longer looked like someone who not only knew everything but was also tired of it. He looked like a man who was finding it an agreeable surprise to learn that his life wasn't going quite as predictably as he'd thought it would.

Right now he looked worried. "What's the matter?" he asked, closing the study door and coming toward her. "I could tell something was wrong as soon as you came in. What is it?"

It almost seemed silly now. She pulled the square of coarse linen out of her pocket and held it out to him. "This was at the post office today, in a package addressed to me."

He frowned. "What is it?"

She told him.

His face hardened. "Who sent it?"

"There was no note, no sender's address. Just this. It upset me at first, but—"

"Yes, of course, you—"

"But I'm fine now, truly. It was only a prank, and there's no harm done. I'm surprised something like it hasn't happened before. It's really—"

He made an impatient sound, interrupting her. He grabbed the cloth from her hand, flung it to the floor, and reached for her, forcibly pulling her into a close embrace. At once all the pain and mortification resurfaced, and she was amazed to find herself fighting back tears. "Bastards," he muttered against her hair. "Ruddy sodding bastards. If I could prove they did this, I'd make them pay."

"Who?"

"Sully, who else? Him and his worthless mates."

"Sully!" She pulled back to look at him. That possibility had never occurred to her. "I thought . . ."

"What?"

"Perhaps I'm mistaken. I shouldn't say."

"Rachel, tell me whom you suspect."

"But if I'm wrong—"

"Tell me."

"All right. I thought it might be Lydia. She despises me—I couldn't tell you the things she said to me that day. She could have done this. Easily. I think it was she."

He slipped his fingers into the hair at the back of her neck, soothing her. "If it was she, she won't do it again, I promise you that."

"What will you do?"

"Speak to her. Threaten her if I have to."

"Oh, no. Please don't do that."

"Why not?"

"Because she's not well, not responsible. I think her hatred of me has affected her mind. If you talk to her about this—she might grow worse. She might do something more."

He considered that. "Very well, but I will speak to her aunt. Don't worry, I won't eat her; I'll tell her what we suspect and advise her to keep a sharper eye on her niece, nothing more." He stroked her cheek with his thumb. "Is that all right?"

The novelty of being asked for her approval kept her silent for a few seconds. "Yes. But, of course, it might not be Lydia at all."

"True. Another reason why I'll be gentle."

He was gentle now, brushing her damp lashes with his fingertips. He stroked her lips with his tear-wet fingers and then kissed her, tasting her with the tip of his tongue. She was helpless when he touched her like this, in thrall to his erotic tenderness. "Come to me tonight," he murmured, nuzzling her lips, finding the most sensitive places to kiss. "I have something to give you."

"But you mustn't give me any more gifts."

"You'll like this one."

"No, Sebastian, I mean it, I don't want anything."

"This isn't a gift. Or not a *thing,* I should say." A devilish glint in his eyes made her stomach flutter. "You're blushing. God, how pretty you are."

"I'm not blushing." She wasn't pretty either, but when he looked at her like this, she felt as if she were. "I have to go, have to get . . . a bed ready in the servants' quarters for the new maid, tell the others . . ." She sighed and let him go on kissing her, because he was just too hard to resist. He could melt her with the simplest touch, sometimes with only a look. She thought of the brittle, ice-cold woman she'd been, dreading the thought of a man's touch, because she'd only known one kind of touching and it had been horrific.

Ironic that the man who could bring her body to life was exactly like her late husband in one way—interested in her sexually to the point of obsession. But the comparison ended there, because Sebastian only wanted to give her pleasure, and Randolph could only find pleasure in giving her pain. Sebastian insisted the two extremes were a little closer than she thought, to some even indistinguishable. The key, he said, was consent, and she had never consented to Randolph's cruelties. She'd never consented to Sebastian's softer ravishment either, and yet she'd taken a secret, incipient pleasure in it.

It was all so confusing. What he knew and she didn't know about sex could fill half the library in the British Museum.

"Come at ten o'clock," he instructed in a warm whisper, breathing in her ear. "The time is important, so be punctual. But don't be early or it'll spoil the surprise. Will you come?"

Once more he hadn't ordered, he'd asked. But did it really matter? His eyes held such a sweet, tantalizing promise, it was hard to think of any circumstances under which she'd have refused him.

"Everything is in readiness, my lord."

"Good. Right on time, too. Preest, you're a treasure."

"Thank you, my lord." The valet inclined his totally bald head in dignified acknowledgment.

"And you were discreet about the arrangements, were you?"

He looked hurt. "Of course, my lord."

"Of course." Preest relied on years of experience in arranging romantic assignations; discretion, after reticence, was his finest quality.

"Will there be anything else, my lord?"

Sebastian thought of asking him about the status of belowstairs gossip concerning Mrs. Wade and Lord D'Aubrey. The answer would tell him not only what was being said at the Hall but in the village as well, one being so intimately connected with the other. But he couldn't bring himself to mention her name, not even to Preest. Remarkable, considering how freely he used to discuss with friends and acquaintances the most private details of his amorous liaisons. It was expected; it was part of the sport. Now the shallowness of that behavior embarrassed him. He would as willingly speak of Rachel in public as strip her, or himself, naked in a roomful of strangers. Unthinkable. She was private. She was his.

"No, there's nothing. Good night, Preest."

"Good night, my lord."

Exactly four minutes later, a soft knock sounded at the door. Sebastian smiled to himself, came off the bed, and padded barefoot across the room to the door. "Perfect," he greeted her, taking her hand and pulling her inside.

"You said ten."

"I don't mean the timing. You."

She gave a little shake of her head, which was how she dismissed most of his compliments. He was wearing nothing but a pair of black trousers, and her light-eyed gaze traveled from his face to his feet and back again with frank interest. He felt his body tighten. *Steady on*, he told himself, *the night is young. The night is a mere infant.*

He brushed his lips across the backs of her fingers. "You look beautiful, Rachel."

"The dress is beautiful. Thank you."

It had arrived from the dressmaker's last week; tonight was the first time she'd worn it. "It suits you." It was lovely, relying on simplicity and the rich, understated garnet color for its graceful effect. "If you would let me . . . ah, well." Useless, he knew, to try to persuade her to take everything he wanted to give her—more beautiful dresses, soft, feminine underclothes, shoes and boots, kid gloves and saucy hats, parasols, embroidered handkerchiefs, fans, reticules—all the pretty, frivolous, beguiling items in a fashionable lady's wardrobe. She wasn't a fashionable lady, she argued, she was a housekeeper. He would press the point again, but not tonight. Tonight they would have no disagreements.

"Your gift is in the bathroom."

She looked dismayed. "But you said it wasn't a gift."

"I said it wasn't a *thing*."

"What is it, then?"

"Come and see."

Preest had done well, he saw at a glance. Candles warmed the room's marble surfaces with a mellow, rose-colored light, repeated in mirrored reflections everywhere. There was a new rug—white bear fur; it felt wickedly soft under his bare toes. Fresh peonies crowded a glass bowl on the edge of the sink, perfuming the air. Next to them, champagne cooled in a silver bucket. A stack of thick, fleecy towels, a basket of scents and soaps, a platter of fresh fruit—verily, the stage was set for the softest seduction he'd ever attempted.

Rachel was looking puzzled, eyeing the sudsy, steaming tub. "Are you going to bathe?"

He smiled at her, enchanted. "No, darling, you are. My gift to you is a bath."

"Oh." Delicate pink color stole into her cheeks. Her lips curved up at the corners. "But I'm . . . already clean." The blush deepened.

He laughed softly. "Cleanliness isn't the only object in bathing."

"It isn't?"

"No, indeed. Now, you have a choice of undressing yourself or letting me do it for you. Either way, we mustn't dawdle or the water will get cold. Which would you like?"

She couldn't meet his eyes, but she couldn't stop smiling. "I'm a little embarrassed," she confessed.

He drew her close and put his cheek next to hers. "Don't be—that would ruin everything. I want to spoil you tonight, Rachel, pamper you and make you sigh. But I can't if you're ashamed. I've seen you without your clothes before. I love your body. It's perfect." She started to say something, but he stopped her with a lingering kiss. Under his hands, she went soft and pliant, swaying against him. "I've forgotten how this opens," he said after a moment of deeply pleasurable fumbling.

"In the back," she breathed with her eyes closed.

"Turn around, then."

She did, and together they watched in the steamy cheval glass as her clothes fell away and slipped to the floor. He kept her still with his hands on her stomach. "You see? Perfect." She didn't know what he would do next, where he might touch her, and it was exciting to watch her lips part and her nostrils flare a little while she waited, taking quick, silent breaths. Their eyes met in the mirror. "Hop in the tub," he said huskily. "Before it gets cold." He took his hands away, but he couldn't resist a slow kiss on top of her shoulder.

She moved away, and he leaned back against the lavatory to watch her sleek, graceful, fascinating entry into his bathtub. She tested the water with her hand first, then turned her back to him to step over the edge of the tub, first her right leg and then her left. Crouched in half, she lowered her pretty backside into the water, giving little hiccuping gasps with every inch of new flesh she submerged.

"Too hot?" he inquired, and she shook her head and made a low, ecstatic moan he took to mean no. When she was seated in the tub with water up to her rib cage, he brought her the basket of soaps and oils. "Which do you like?" He handed her the soaps, one by one, and uncorked all the little glass vials for her to sniff—oil of roses, oil of orange peels, sweet almond, lavender, lily of the valley.

"How can I choose?" she wondered, but eventually she decided on bayberry soap and oil of bergamot.

"Excellent choice," he approved, like a wine steward, pouring the oil for her and swirling it in the water. "Sweet, feminine, and substantial. Subtle. Like you. Now lie back and relax."

She smiled dreamily and obeyed. "This is a sin, isn't it?"

"If it isn't, we're not doing it right. Here, take this."

She opened her eyes. "Oh, my," she said when she saw the glass in his hand. "I've never drunk champagne before. It is champagne, isn't it?"

"Drink it slowly or it'll go straight to your head."

She took a minuscule sip and wrinkled her nose. "Tickles," was her initial pronouncement. Her second was more favorable: "Ooh, la."

"Like it?"

"Mmm. Sebastian?"

"Here."

"Am I in heaven?"

"Not yet." He took the soap and a rough-textured sponge and moved to the end of the tub, drawing up a stool. "Foot, please." She didn't move; she looked blank. "*Foot*, please. Thank you." He hooked her heel over the rim of the tub and began to rub soap between her toes.

It made her squeal, then suck in her breath through her teeth. But she didn't try to escape; she slid farther down, keeping her elbows on the edges of the tub to stay afloat, and balanced the wineglass on her chest. "*Now* I'm in heaven," she declared on a long, satisfied sigh.

"You're not even halfway there." Ah, but what a sight she was with her long leg cocked up at that wanton angle, her breasts bobbing in the warm water, just the nipples breaking the surface. Her dark hair curled on the ends in the humid air, and her eyes were closed, her face relaxed, almost slack from pure pleasure.

She opened her eyes when she heard him chuckle. "Why are you laughing?"

"I'm thinking there should be a medal for the kind of willpower it's taking for me to keep my hands off you. Except for your feet."

"The Order of the Bath?"

He looked at her in surprise. "That's funny."

"What?"

"What you just said. You made a joke."

"Did you think I was incapable of it?"

"You never have before."

She thought that over. "Maybe someone has to be washing my feet to bring it out of me."

He chuckled again. That was joke number two. He remembered that one-half of his goal was to make her laugh, but it had never occurred to him that her making *him* laugh might be just as good. "You're wonderful," he told her, reaching for her other foot. She only smiled, and shifted her long body to accommodate him. Progress was being made before his eyes. If his patience held out, part two of the goal would be, as William Holyoake would say, a lead pipe cinch.

When he finished washing her feet, he added more hot water to the tub from one of the copper ewers Preest had thoughtfully left. "Sit up," he instructed Rachel, moving his stool to the head of the tub. She sat up, and he set about the pleasurable task of washing her back and shoulders.

"Oh, I can do it," she protested halfheartedly.

"I'm sure. But isn't this better?"

She agreed on another soft, drawn out moan.

"Your skin feels like wet silk." He soaped her breasts, leaning over her from behind, holding their soft weight in his palms and slicking his thumbs across the perky nipples. Her head came back, and he stole a kiss from her parted lips while he slid his soapy hands down to her abdomen, and finally, under water, to the soft hair between her legs. Stroking her there, just for a moment, he listened to her gasp, and felt the springy tendons in her inner thighs begin to quiver. She turned her head and pressed her lips to his neck. He took his hands away with deep reluctance. "Time for a shampoo," he decided, and this time she acquiesced without a murmur.

He liked the small, neat feel of her skull under the lather. Her long neck looked fragile, vulnerable, almost too slender to support the weight of her soapy head. She had her eyes closed, forearms dangling limply over her bent knees. She looked half asleep, but she said in a soft, clear voice, "I know why you're doing this. All of it, the bath, the soaps. The delicacies you tell Judelet to make for me. Dandy. I understand why you give me these gifts."

After a moment he said slowly, "If you understand, then there's no need for us to talk about it. Do you agree?"

She thought for a second, then said, "No. I need to thank you."

"Ah, now there you're wrong. Thanks is the last thing I want from you."

"What do you want from me?"

"Nothing."

She gave a small shake of her head. She disagreed.

"What I want is for you to be happy. As happy with me as you were unhappy in prison. If that's possible. I want . . ." *I want to heal you,* he almost said, but it would have sounded too arrogant, even for him. How could he explain the compulsion he felt to purge all her memories of loneliness and cruelty? His methods were crude: he gave her scents and perfumes to eradicate the stench of prison, sweets and trifles and breads made from white flour, pretty, soft-textured clothes, a silly yellow dog for a boon companion. The elaborate scene he'd set tonight in this voluptuous bathroom wasn't even a seduction, not in the usual sense.

He wanted to introduce her body to the ultimate pleasure—yes, of course, but even more, he wanted to ravish her mind, erase the past from it so that nothing existed but here and now. He wanted her to start over. He wanted her reborn.

But, of course, he couldn't say any of that to her.

"Put your head back and close your eyes." She obeyed, pliant as a child, and he poured the last of the warm water over her hair to rinse it. "I'm finished. Pretty mermaid, do you want to get out now?"

"Yes, please," she answered, smiling beatifically. "Otherwise I might slide down the drain with the bath water."

He helped her out of the tub, folded her into a gigantic bath towel, and blotted her dry. He found a smaller towel and wrapped it around her head for a turban.

Unexpectedly, she lifted her arms and embraced him. He held her close, a warm bundle of damp terry. "Thank you," she said. "That was a perfect gift. I would like to give it to you someday."

"What a stimulating thought. But your gift isn't over yet." When he began to peel the towel away, her eyes lost the dreamy look and sharpened attentively. He smiled, because what she thought would happen now wasn't going to happen for a little while longer.

But it was hard to wait. In the glow of the candles, her skin looked warm and inviting, flushed pink from her bath. And she was smiling at him in a way she never had before—knowingly, eagerly, wanting exactly what he wanted. Her slender, fine-boned body was perfect, just as he'd said, and she was infinitely more desirable than any woman he'd ever known.

He unfurled a dry towel and spread it over the rug, knelt on it and pulled her down beside him. "I want you to lie down," he said gently. "No—on your stomach." Something flickered in her eyes before she could look away. He touched her cheek with his fingers. "It'll be all right. I promise." She hesitated another second, then stretched out beside him, facedown on the soft towel.

Trailing his fingertips down the long, graceful line of her backbone, it came to him that he'd been wrong all along about what he really wanted from Rachel. Power, he'd thought; the ability to control her. But that wasn't it at all. What he wanted was trust, and the thing she'd just done told him he finally had it.

He pressed his lips to her shoulder blade. "Thank you," he whispered, conscious of the inadequacy of the words. "You are lovely. So very beautiful." Her lips curved in an indulgent smile. She didn't believe him. But she would.

He chose a small glass bottle from the basket, uncorked it, and poured a few drops into the shallow, enticing hollow at the base of her spine. She made a low, indescribable sound, squirming her hips, then lay still. "This is a special oil, Rachel. It has unique properties."

"What does it do?"

"It eradicates all of one's inhibitions."

She pillowed her cheek on her folded arms. Her smile was slow, sly, self-conscious, and it went straight to his heart. "I think you've washed all mine away already."

"There may be a few left." He began to fan the oil out from her spine with his thumbs, pressing gently at each vertebra, smoothing the balm into her skin. She went softer, limper by the minute, her body like warm wax he could shape and mold in his hands. She loved having her shoulders rubbed, and she told him so with low, heartfelt groans that only increased his arousal. He used the heels of his hands on her long, strong thighs, gliding them up and over the slope of her buttocks. There he lingered, beguiled, lavishing all his care and creativity, and his reward was another squeal of pleasure and the stimulating feel of her muscles bunching and relaxing under his palms.

If he could, he'd have ignored the small white ridge of scar tissue at the top of her left thigh. Each time he saw it or touched it, helpless anger came boiling up, and deep, hot sympathy. A nightmare picture would flash in his mind before he could censor it, and he would see it happening, the unspeakable violation of the pretty, sweet-faced girl in the family photograph. *Eighteen years old.*

"Sebastian?"

She'd risen on one elbow and twisted around to look at him, wondering why he'd stopped the massage. He made himself smile. "Sorry. I was distracted," he told her, pretending nothing was wrong. This was no time for ugly memories.

"By what?"

"Hmm? By this very fetching behind." He smoothed his hands over her bottom, and soon she was purring again like a warm kitten.

"Turn over now."

She rolled onto her back, slowly, languidly, keeping her arms over her head. Her face was fascinating. She watched him, speechless, lax, all eyes and slack muscles, waiting. He slipped a white satin pillow under her head and fed her a grape from the fruit basket. "More?" he asked innocently, and when she nodded he held the bunch of grapes an inch from her mouth. She captured one with her lips and pulled it off with a succulent *pop*, then chewed and swallowed it with slow relish. She was smiling, but he doubted she had any idea what she was doing to him.

He lay down beside her and propped his head on his hand. Watching her eyes, he tilted the vial and poured a drop of oil on the nipple of her right breast. She caught her breath. "Don't close your eyes. Look at me." Their gazes locked while he plucked and rolled the tight, crinkling bud between his fingers. She moaned softly. "If you knew what you look like. Your mouth . . . you have the most delicious mouth."

"Kiss me . . ."

"I will." He trailed his hand in lazy circles down her belly, inserting a gentle finger in her navel. "No, don't look away," he murmured, his mouth a breath from hers. "This is where I'm going to kiss you," and he made a comb with his fingers and feathered it through her curly pubic hair. He was losing himself in the lucid wanting in her eyes, wide on his, incandescent with hope and fear and excitement. "May I kiss you here?" She couldn't speak. He slipped his fingers inside her very slowly, and when she closed her eyes he glided his tongue between her parted lips. Sweet. Warm and wet, ah, tight and sleek, her muscles pursing, her tongue circling. She clutched at him, squeezing her legs together while her body writhed and stretched and lengthened on the damp towel. He took a last bite of her full lips and sat up.

Now her eyes were like smoky mirrors, and he watched them darken as he gently pressed her thighs apart. Her legs were shaking. He bent to her, sleeking his tongue up the soft fruit of her sex, splitting her. She jumped slightly, made a whimpering sound. He penetrated her, stroking her with his stiff tongue, making her gasp. She cried out, "No," when he found her little nub—"*No.*" But he softened his mouth and tasted her again—because he wanted her this way, had to have her like this.

"Stop," she begged, twisting under him. "Please, I can't bear it. Sebastian, don't, oh, don't. Stop, *please.*"

Finally it was impossible to go on. "God, Rachel," he grated, rubbing his mouth on her taut abdomen, leaning over her. She was distraught, almost weeping. She really couldn't stand it. "You're afraid," he accused in a hoarse whisper.

"Yes!"

"Afraid to let go."

"Yes."

"Why?"

"I don't know! Just don't—do that to me."

"Shhh," he soothed her, kissing her cheeks, smoothing the

damp hair back from her forehead. "It's all right, I won't do anything you don't want me to do."

She calmed quickly—but then she was embarrassed. "I'm sorry. Oh, God, I've ruined it all, haven't I?"

"Don't say that." He kissed her again. "Don't be an idiot."

"You, though—you . . . I want you to . . ." She stopped, inarticulate.

"Say it. It's just you and I, Rachel. It's just our bodies. What do you want?"

"I want," she whispered, eyes downcast, "you to—have me. Come inside me. I want to give myself to you."

If he were a strong man, he would resist this sweet, halting invitation, swear her off, renounce her body until she could find pleasure in his. That way they could suffer together.

But he wasn't that strong. He was aching for her, but even that throbbing, localized agony was bearable compared to the need he felt to be intimate with her; not to "have" her, but to join selves, to mate with her.

She touched his throat with shy fingers, trailed them down to his chest. "Make love to me," she murmured. "That's what I want. Right now. You want it, too, don't you?"

What a question. He took her hand and dragged it down the length of his stomach—slowly, so she could pull away whenever she liked—to show her exactly how much he wanted it. Instead of pulling away, she squeezed him softly, experimentally, molding the hard flesh under his trousers in her palm. He pressed his forehead against her shoulder.

She whispered his name. "Shall we get in bed?"

"Sorry," he answered, breathless, coming up on his knees to unbutton his fly. "I can't wait that long." He shucked off his trousers and lay over her, taking his weight on his forearms. When he came into her, they sighed together, and kissed, holding still to savor the sensation.

"I'm sorry," she said presently, her breath warm on his skin.

"Why, sweetheart?"

"Because I couldn't do what you wanted. But I . . . it was just . . . too much."

"I don't want you to be sorry about anything. Have you learned nothing tonight?"

That made her smile. "I've learned a great deal. You have no idea."

"Everything you do, Rachel, everything about you pleases me. It's just that I wanted you with me," he tried to explain.

"I am with you. Right now." She cupped the sides of his face and brought his mouth down to hers in the lightest of kisses. "Love me," she murmured.

Holding her hands, he began to move in her. She met him thrust for thrust, her eyes wide on his, her face open and giving. He didn't hold back, did not restrain himself, and in the end it was the cleanest, strongest act of love he'd ever committed. And the most revealing. Always he hid himself at the last moment, afraid or embarrassed, wary of his dignity, fearful of losing control—but now, for once, he felt no self-consciousness, only Rachel's acceptance, her absolute acceptance of him. Love? She'd never said the word. How could she love him? It didn't matter. He let her see his naked soul, needy and trusting, yearning for her, and at the end he gave her all of himself.

Afterward, he felt lost in the tenderness of her touch as she stroked him and soothed him, the sweetness of her kisses on his damp face. "Darling," he called her. "I wish . . ."

"Yes," she sighed with him. "But it's all right. I loved your gift, Sebastian. Thank you for the loveliest night."

She had it all backward. He rolled to his side, taking her with him. Most of the candles had sputtered out; through the open window, he could see the half moon rising, like a luminous profile watching them. "I'm falling in love with you." The words came with no premeditation, no warning; they surprised him as much as they astounded her. "It's true," he said, in case she doubted it.

She didn't say anything. He waited, but the moment when she could have answered came and went, and afterward the silence sounded strange, unnatural. He kissed her to lessen the strain of self-consciousness. "Sleepy?" he whispered, and she nodded. He sat up, gathered her in his arms, and carried her to bed.

XIV

IT WAS HIGH summer, the beginning of July. No breeze blew in Rachel's open window, and moonlight made the hot room too bright. She kicked off the damp sheet and got out of bed. Remnants of a dream—the usual one, that she was back in her cell because her prison release had been a mistake—clung to the walls of her mind, depressing her. She decided to get up and go outside, walk along the river until she was tired enough to sleep again.

She never had the nightmare when she slept with Sebastian. Her unconscious mind must know she was safe then, even in sleep, if she could feel his warm body wrapped around hers, feel the beat of his heart under her hand, the weight of his arm across her waist. But tonight she was alone in her own small bed, for the first time in many nights. Sebastian had gone to Plymouth to see his solicitors, one of whom was a family friend who had invited him to have dinner and stay the night. He wouldn't return until tomorrow.

She dressed in the dark, quickly, forgoing a candle; even though no one else slept in her wing, she went quietly down the shadowy corridor, in deference to the quiet night. Passing the arched entrance to the chapel, she heard a soft *thump, thump,* and froze for a startled second before she realized what it was: Dandy's tail, smacking the floor just behind the last pew. He liked to sleep in the chapel on hot nights because the stones were cool.

"You," she said softly, and he rolled over on his back, sleepily delighted to see her. "Some watchdog you've turned out to be." She crouched beside him and rubbed his chest, combing her fingers through his soft fur. He had old, kind, knowing eyes, and they seemed to smile up at her now in a stray beam of moonlight. She scratched him under his rope collar, and he grinned at her and heaved a deep, ecstatic sigh. Luckily he was a patient, affectionate dog, because she never tired of petting him, never seemed to get enough of *touching* him. He was a funny, happy companion, and the unlikeliest gift she'd ever received. Of all people to give an unruly puppy to, she was surely the most improbable; it was like giving a book to a blind woman, or sending a clown to entertain a recluse. That Sebastian had somehow known that Dandy was exactly right, the *perfect* gift for someone like her—starved for laughter and silliness, hungry for touching—moved and delighted her almost as much as the gift itself.

"Want to go for a walk?"

He scrambled up in a flurry of scraping, slipping toenails, energized by the word "walk," his favorite. Watching him scamper ahead of her toward the courtyard door, she realized her vague loneliness was gone, and the dregs of the prison nightmare with it. Could anyone be cheered so thoroughly by a dog, she wondered, or did you have to be a particularly pathetic case?

The night was hot and still, airless, no wind stirring in the alders that arched over the river's steep-sided banks. Dandy bounded down for a drink in the trickle of water that was all the Wyck could manage in July, then raced after her, snuffling at exciting scents in the weedy grass along the path sides.

The moon in any phase was still a private, special joy, because she'd gone for so long without seeing it. She gazed up at the gauzy platinum disk and thought of her family, her home, the parents she'd lost. If there was a heaven, could they see her now, look down on her like the moon's smug, knowing face seemed to

226

be doing? And if so, what did they think of the life their bright, obedient, sweet-tempered daughter had come to? They would be dismayed, of course, and deeply mortified. She wondered sometimes why *she* wasn't ashamed of what she had become—a kept woman, for all intents and purposes. It was an identity that flew in the face of every ethical principle she'd ever been taught. But she wasn't shocked and she felt no shame.

Prison had done more than make her cynical about the criminal justice system; it had also demolished most of her conventional moral assumptions. Now she was the ultimate pragmatist, she supposed. Life wasn't simple. For the sake of "morality," she could leave Lynton tomorrow, walk into Wyckerley—or Mare's Head, or Tavistock—and search for employment. She would find none, and sooner or later she would end up where she'd begun three months ago: in a hearing room where men in robes and wigs would deliberate for a few minutes before deciding what the rest of her life would be like. She could do that—but what purpose would it serve? Better to live in the unprincipled moment a little longer, renewing herself, gathering strength and preparing for the next trial. She could feel herself changing, getting stronger. She might be a kept woman, but she also had a job she found satisfying. And she was good at it: incredible as it seemed, she'd turned into an efficient housekeeper. How long could her new life last? Since there was no answer to that question, why waste her scarce emotional resources worrying about what she couldn't change? Best, she'd learned a long time ago, to ask for nothing.

Easier said than done. Weeks had passed since the night Sebastian had told her he was falling in love with her. He hadn't repeated that implausible declaration, and she knew he'd spoken it in the heat of the moment, passion-words that were true for that instant, but weren't any longer because their meaning had burned up in the heat of sexual desire. She was trying to forget she'd heard them, to go back to the compliant, unexpectant woman she'd been before he'd said them. He was offering her a different gift, a great gift—not love, but the renewal of the body and the senses. She'd been buried alive, and it was because of him that she wanted to squirm up and out of the earth and into the light. If only she could keep her hopes limited to the flesh, be the pure sensualist that he was! But it was too hard—she couldn't separate body and spirit like that; for her, they always mingled.

The visit of his London friends had changed him. He was a complicated man; she hadn't understood him before, and she didn't completely understand him now. She wasn't so naive as to think his about-face was completely unselfish, but she was needy enough to welcome it on any terms. Affection, warmth, kindness—she couldn't have rejected those gifts if an ogre had offered them. Under other circumstances, she might withhold trust from a man who had done to her the things Sebastian had done. But these were her circumstances, and pride and prudence were luxuries her bankrupt emotions couldn't pay for. At least not yet.

Was she in love with him? God help her if she was—but how could it have happened? She'd thought she was dead inside, that the last emotion she would ever feel was passion for a man. She thought of him constantly; when they were apart she felt lonely, and when they were together she was happy. More than happy— her world made sense and she was contented.

She thought of the day, a week ago, when she'd paid her obligatory visit to Mr. Burdy in the village. It had been fair all morning, but as soon as she left the constable's office and started for home, it began to rain. She hadn't even brought her shawl; she was soaking wet in ten minutes. Slogging through the puddles in the lane, holding her sodden skirts, she hadn't heard hoofbeats until Sebastian's sorrel stallion was nearly upon her. Horse and rider were wetter than she was, and a lot muddier. "Sebastian," she'd greeted him in amazement—"I thought you were buying a ram from Mr. Murdock!" He'd grinned at her, rainwater streaming down his face. "I told him I'd just remembered something important, and left him with Holyoake."

She was the "something important"—he'd galloped halfway to Wyckerley to save her from drowning in the downpour. She was so happy and so moved, she couldn't speak. He'd pulled her onto the stallion's back and surrounded her with his wet arms. Before they'd gone twenty yards, the rain stopped. They'd laughed all the way home.

She thought of the lightheartedness of that damp, bumpy ride, the pure joy in her heart while he'd teased her and held her close, stealing kisses and making jokes about her ruined hat. How could she not love him? He was everything to her—as perfect a lover now as he'd been a perfect tormenter, before Sully and the others had come and changed everything. But for how long? She was a housekeeper; Sebastian was a viscount. She was a felon; he would be an earl. How long would he want her for a mistress? How long before she needed more?

It was useless to wonder. She was living in the unprincipled moment, she reminded herself. And the quiet night was lovely. She wasn't hungry, thirsty, or cold, and she could see the moon. She had a dog. Really, how much more did one woman deserve?

A soothing thought. She kept it as she turned away from the river and went along the path that led to the park. Watching Dandy, she didn't see the figure on the path ahead of her until the dog stopped suddenly, ears and tail lifting to attention. She knew a second of fright before she recognized the tall, broad-shouldered form of William Holyoake. He raised his hand as soon as he saw her, and said her name in a quiet voice so she would know who he was and not be startled.

"Good evening, Mr. Holyoake."

"Good evening to you, Mrs. Wade."

"You're up and about late tonight."

"And you."

"I found it too hot to sleep."

"Aye." He stooped to pet Dandy, who was butting at his knees. "He's growing fast. Looks like 'e means to be a big un. You can always tell by the feet."

His enormous hands touched the puppy with great gentleness, and she remembered what Susan had told her—that William's own dog, a black and tan sheepdog called Bob, had died a few months ago.

He straightened and touched his forehead, as if he meant to leave her. "Will you walk with me for a little, Mr. Holyoake?" she asked. "Or perhaps you're tired now. It's late, I was just—"

"Aye, I'll take a turn wi' you. Thank you," he said solemnly, and something in his heavy, courteous manner told her she had done exactly the right thing. That William might be a lonely man was a possibility that had simply never occurred to her. Tonight, maybe because of her own pensive mood, it seemed self-evident.

They went down the sandy walk that skirted the slope of terraced gardens behind the house. The fragrance of moss roses and eglantine was a subtle cologne in the heavy, humid air. For a while they walked along in easy silence, and it occurred to her that she and William had many things in common, one of which was their reserve. That must be why she always felt comfortable with him. Eventually he broke the stillness to inquire, "The girl Sidony, how is she getting along wi' her work in the kitchen, Mrs. Wade?"

"Not very well, I'm afraid, William."

"Aye, I heard sommat o' that." He sighed heavily.

"She's a sweet-natured girl, and bright, I believe. And it isn't that she's unwilling to work."

"Mayhap the Frenchman is too hard on 'er?" he guessed hopefully. Monsieur Judelet was known below-stairs as "the French-man" only when one was being polite; at all other times, the names he was called would blister the ears of a sailor.

"No, I don't think it's that. She says not, anyway. And Mary Barry tells me Judelet has been surprisingly gentle with her." Mary Barry was the scullery maid. "I don't know what the matter is," Rachel admitted, "but I'm afraid she's not working out. She's never where she's supposed to be, never finishes the tasks she's assigned. Mary says she spends most of the day in the kitchen garden, whether she's been sent there for something or not. And she looks a fright most of the time, as if she sleeps in her clothes."

William grunted and stuck his hands in his pockets, shaking his head. " 'Twould be a shame to send 'er away. She's only a girl, wi' no family but 'er father, and I wouldn't wish the likes o' him on a dog."

"No."

They fell silent for a time, then began to speak of other things, exchanging the daily news of their respective bailiwicks, house and farm. The moon was sinking; it was very late. Dandy had run ahead, and they were passing below the pavilion, a small, derelict, stone building that had once been used as a summer house, when the dog suddenly broke into a frenzy of barking. They halted, gazing up the slight, grassy rise. "Shush, Dandy!" Rachel called softly. "Lord, he'll wake the whole house." At that moment something small and dark darted out the door, halted against the white stone facade for a second, then dashed back inside.

William immediately reached for Rachel's arm and put her behind him. "A prowler, and he's trapped now. Stay right here."

She felt grateful for his solicitousness, but she wasn't afraid; she thought it more likely that Dandy had surprised a pair of trysting lovers than a prowler. She stood obediently still and watched the bailiff stride up the mount to the pavilion, his manner cautious and fearless at the same time. Dandy had stopped barking; in fact, he was whining a welcome. Either he really was the world's worst watchdog or the intruder in the pavilion was a friend. She heard William call out, "Who goes there?" exactly like a Roman sentry in a play. A low voice said something in reply. A woman's voice. Unable to stand the suspense, Rachel gathered her skirts and started up the hill.

William stood in the low, arched doorway, his broad frame obscuring the view, having a soft, one-sided conversation. Rachel stood on her toes to peer over his shoulder. At first she couldn't see anything but shadows in the damp, musty, not very clean enclosure, but as her eyes adjusted to the dark, she made out a slight figure at the back, pressed against the wall. It was Sidony Timms.

"You did ought to come out now," William was saying in a soothing voice. "Nobody means to harm you. Come out, it's all right. Mrs. Wade is wi' me; we was out havin' a walk. Why'nt you come out so we can talk? That's it, that's a girl."

He stepped back, and Rachel backed up behind him, making way for Sidony. She crept out of the archway, darting glances at them through the curtain of her long, rather wild black hair. She was barefooted; her shoes were lined up neatly on the doorstep, and beside them were a tattered shawl and a pillow.

"What are you doing here, Sidony?" Rachel asked, taking Holyoake's cue and speaking gently. "Were you sleeping?"

She stared down at her feet and said, "Yes, ma'am. I wasn't hurting anything, I promise. I was just sleeping."

"But why? Because of the heat?"

She didn't answer; she glanced up at William, who towered over her like a giant, and then at Rachel. After a long, odd moment, she finally murmured, "No," and looked back down at the ground.

Perplexed, Rachel said, "What, then? Why would you want to sleep here, Sidony? Is there something wrong with your room?" Tess was Sidony's third-floor roommate, a mild, good-tempered girl—surely Tess couldn't be the problem.

"Oh, no, ma'am, my room's lovely, I never stayed anywhere so nice."

"Then what?"

She traced the edge of the concrete step with her big toe and nervously plaited her skirt with her fingers. "It's just that I can't stay in there, not for long at a time. I can't bear it. It's crazy-sounding, but I can't stand the walls." She glanced between them, pleading for understanding, then gave a hopeless shrug and looked away.

Rachel felt a quick frisson of recognition. Impulsively, she touched Sidony's shoulder. She herself hadn't suffered that particular torment in prison—the irrational terror of enclosed spaces—but others had, and their miserable cries and useless protests still rang in her ears, because she'd heard them almost daily for ten years.

"Why?" William asked kindly. "What harm can walls do to you?"

Rachel was about to answer for her—that the fear might be groundless but it was still real, still horrible—when Sidony spoke for herself, and the answer made Rachel gasp. "None, I know, but it makes me think on all the times my pa locked me up in a box, and then I feel like I've got to start screaming or I might die."

Holyoake's honest face blackened with emotion. But his voice was deep and calm when he said, "Let's set down here for a minute, shall we? Myself, I can always think better when I'm setting."

So they sat down on the top step of the little porch in front of the summer pavilion, Rachel and William on either side, Sidony in the middle. The moon was gone; the chimneys of Lynton Hall were etched in sharp black against the hazier black of the sky. Filled with pity and shock, Rachel could think of nothing to say. She was grateful when William said quietly, conversationally, "So. Yer pa shut you up in a box, and that's why you can't keep long to yer work in the kitchen. Because o' the walls." Sidony nodded faintly. "Why would the man do such a low and heartless thing?"

"He said because I was wicked. But . . . 'twould be for small things, leaving the churn out in the rain or not polishing the tin-ware to 'is liking. I didn't mind the hitting so much as the box. 'Twas a cupboard for blankets and such. He'd empty it out an' make me get in." She wrapped her arms around her knees—a frighteningly revealing posture. "Just for a night usually, but once for the whole day, too." Her voice broke at the end; she hid her face in her skirt.

Chilled, Rachel put her arm around the girl's thin shoulders and hugged her. William looked miserable; his big hand hovered over the curve of Sidony's spine for a moment, but then he dropped it back to his side. Rachel sent him a commiserating look. She was a woman, so she could comfort Sidony by touch-ing her; William was a man, so he could not.

Sidony wiped her face with her hands, her hands on her skirt. "I'm all right now, ma'am," she said softly, and her wobbly, grate-ful smile went straight to Rachel's heart.

"Mrs. Wade," Holyoake said ponderously.

"Yes?"

"I was just now thinking. Esther Pole, you know, she's not as young as she used t' be."

"That's true. Esther's been slowing down; I've heard others say it." She knew exactly where he was leading, and wondered why she hadn't thought of the solution herself.

"She could do wi' some help, and no mistake."

Sidony's dark-lashed eyes widened on him. "Miss Pole, the dairy woman?"

"Aye. She's slowed to a crawl," he avowed—a shameless exaggeration. "Now you, Sidony, what do you think o' dairy work? 'Twould be harder'n kitchen work in many ways, not least of all the regularity of it, so to say, plus it takes some muscle, and you being sommat of a puny thing—"

"Oh, I could do it, Mr. Holyoake, I know I could," she said excitedly. "I'm the one who always milked Baby, our cow at home, and I helped her birth the calf, too, and 'twas a hard labor, with no one about but me. I'm sure I could work in the dairy for Miss Pole if you'd try me. And I think"—she smiled suddenly, with a charming, adult wryness—"I think 'twould be a great kindness to the Frenchman, for I've tried his patience sorely."

William looked over her shoulder at Rachel, lifting his eyebrows to ask her opinion. She gave a nod of approval and he said, "You could start tomorrow, then. Meet me in the dairy barn at six o'clock, and we'll tell Esther together. Now," he continued before Sidony could speak, "there's still the matter o' yer room. You can't be sleeping out here on the grounds anymore. 'Tisn't seemly for a young girl."

She dipped her head and nodded. "I know. I'll try—"

"The lads sleep in the stable wi' the horses. Rough quarters they are, naught but straw beds on planks and a place for a few clothes, wood partitions between them and the animals. Still, they're snug and warm, and I've never heard complaining. What if I was to rig up sommat o' the sort in the dairy barn? You'd be all alone, but I could make a wee bit of a room, nothing fancy, wi' a door and a lock so you could be private. The thing is, it'd be open on top, like; 'twouldn't feel enclosed. And—the animals would be there for company." He said that self-consciously, as if his sensitivity to Sidony's plight embarrassed him slightly. "Do you think that would be all right, Mrs. Wade? Think 'is lordship would object for any reason?"

"I can't imagine that he would, Mr. Holyoake."

Sidony's small, pixyish face was a study. Rachel felt in sympathy with her when her hand stole over to Holyoake's sleeve and touched it shyly. "Thank you," she said in a small voice. "How kind you are. I don't know what to say to you, sir."

William was smiling warmly until she said the word "sir." Then he gave her hand a brisk, fatherly pat and got to his feet. "'Tis late. Six o'clock'll come in no time, so you'd best be going off to bed, girl. Your *own* bed, I think."

She nodded, resigned to it.

"I know another place," Rachel said suddenly, and they looked at her in surprise. "It's cool and spacious, very airy, and it has a nice high ceiling. A little hard, maybe, but you've got your pillow. And you'd have Dandy for company."

Sidony's face was all eyes and open mouth. "Where is it, ma'am?"

She smiled. "Come along and I'll show you."

XV

A YOUNG LADY was coming out of Sebastian's study just as Rachel entered it. She was blond, attractive, smartly dressed, with a proud, confident carriage that made her seem taller than she really was. Sebastian, who was behind her, evidently on his way to see her to the front door, halted in the threshold. "Ah, Mrs. Wade," he said, smiling—a smile that went a long way toward banishing an emotion Rachel recognized with dull surprise as jealousy. "Have you met Miss Deene? Miss Deene, this is my housekeeper, Mrs. Wade."

The two women bowed to each other and said how-do-you-do. Rachel had seen Sophie Deene in church and knew who she was; indeed, in a village as small as Wyckerley, a woman with her self-assured manner and radiant looks couldn't go unnoticed for long. Close up, Rachel was struck by the girlish freshness in her features, which seemed slightly at odds with the poised, mature air she projected.

"I'm happy to meet you, Mrs. Wade," she said with a clear, blue-eyed gaze that appeared guileless, but it was impossible to tell if she meant that or not. "Anne—Mrs. Morrell—told me she'd made your acquaintance; I've been hoping you and I would meet."

"How is Mrs. Morrell?" Rachel asked. "I haven't seen her in church lately."

"She's been a little under the weather. The doctor's had her keeping to her room these last few weeks."

"Oh, no. Oh, I'm very sorry to hear that."

"She's not really *ill*, only a little, um . . . just not quite herself, you know. And now she's *much* better."

"I'm so glad," Rachel said warmly. Something in Miss Deene's manner told her as clearly as words could have that Anne Morrell was pregnant. "Please give her my best regards when you see her."

"Yes, I will."

They said good-bye. Sebastian told Rachel he would be back in a moment, and went out of the room with Miss Deene.

While she waited, Rachel tried to come to terms with the bleak mood seeing him with the lovely Sophie Deene had cast over her. It wasn't the lady herself, it was the fact of him being with, speaking to, admiring, being charming to *any* woman that made her feel cold and miserable. But what an imprudent reaction; she'd thought she had her emotions in better order. Jealousy implied prior possession, some degree of ownership, and all she owned of Sebastian was his transient attention. She was currently an object of interest to him, a sort of experiment, really. That he would move on to other women when the interest waned was so obvious it didn't merit a second thought.

But she was making him her best friend. Even knowing she couldn't have him, she was opening herself up to him a little more each day. She was sinking deeper and deeper, not into despondency but trust. Once she'd wondered if the reason she couldn't find satisfaction in bed with him was because she was afraid he wouldn't want her afterward—that the challenge she represented would then be met, and discarded as no longer interesting. But she knew now that the real reason was because she wasn't brave enough to bear the consequences of ceding to him so much trust.

She heard his footsteps and turned toward the door. When she saw him she started to speak, but he crossed the room quickly, purposefully, and before she could say a word he caught her up in a lavish embrace and kissed her.

Breathless, she pulled away. "What was that for?" He kissed her again, slowly and thoroughly, and when he was finished she had the answer to her question.

They broke away, both remembering at the same moment that the door was open. Smiling the same secret smile, they took up places on either side of the mantel, a discreet six feet apart, Sebastian with his hands in his pockets and rocking on his toes a little, the conscientious country squire having a word of business with his housekeeper.

Rachel heard herself blurt out, "Miss Deene is very attractive, isn't she?" She could have bitten her tongue.

"Yes, she is," he agreed, a little too heartily. "Bright, too. I like the way her mind works. I like her enthusiasm." Rachel nodded glumly. "As a woman, what's your impression of her?"

"My impression?"

"Yes. Would you trust her? Does she seem competent to you? Levelheaded, honest?"

"Yes, all of those, I suppose. But of course," she couldn't help adding, "I hardly know her."

"No, but I value your opinion. And I'm inclined to agree with you. Which is why I've decided to invest in Sophie's mine and not her uncle's. It won't endear me to Mayor Vanstone, but that can't be helped. What are you smiling about?"

"Nothing." She resolutely wiped the grin from her face. But she couldn't help feeling relieved that he was interested in the beautiful Miss Deene as a business associate, not as a woman.

"I've got a surprise for you," he said softly. She blushed; he laughed. "Not that kind of surprise, nothing you have to take your clothes off for. Unless, of course, you want to."

She had a fleeting vision of it, herself naked for him right now, right here. The blush deepened; she actually felt weak in the knees. She fiddled with a candlestick on the mantel, pretending nonchalance, but Sebastian's alert look told her she wasn't succeeding. "What is the surprise?" she asked carelessly, and he laughed again.

"Come and see." And he took her hand and pulled her out of the room.

They passed down the corridor toward the east wing of the house. He was taking her either to the library, the chapel, or her own room, and it said something for the deplorable state of her mind that she hoped it was the latter. But it wasn't; it was the library. Most of the floor space was taken up by three enormous wooden packing crates and half a dozen smaller ones.

"Guess what's in them," Sebastian challenged, sitting down on one of the big crates and folding his arms.

The only guess was the best guess. "Books," she said hopefully.

"No. Dogs. All different sizes, males and females, purebreds and mongrels, furry ones, sleek ones—"

"They're not, they're books! Oh, *lovely*. They are books, aren't they?" When he said yes, she clapped her hands in delight. "Can we open them? Oh, Sebastian, how wonderful. But where will you put them? There must be a *hundred* here."

"Over three hundred, actually. Handpicked by a London bookseller I know and trust. I told him I wanted *new* books, nothing more than twenty years old, because I have a peevish housekeeper too smart for her own good who keeps grousing about the shortcomings of my library."

She laughed gaily. "But there's no room—you'll have to add an annex!"

"Well, what I thought we could do—*you* could do, since the books belong to you—I thought you might go through the old ones and weed out the wheat from the chaff, the chaff being the ones you've already read. Keep whatever you think is worthwhile,

I leave it entirely up to you. For the rest, I thought we might give them to the subscription library Christy Morrell is trying to start for the parish."

"Oh, that's a wonderful plan." Of course the books didn't belong to her; the very idea was too outlandish to contemplate. But he'd ordered them with her in mind as the primary reader, and the thoughtfulness of that added another snarl to her already tangled emotional state. How could she accept more things from him, even nominally, even when she had no intention of keeping them?

"Look." He'd prized open one of the smaller crates and was lifting books out by the handful. "Turgenev, Trollope, Thackeray, Tennyson—this must be the T box. No, it's not, because here's Stowe, *Uncle Tom's Cabin*, and here's Browning and Balzac. Have you read them all, my little bluestocking? You couldn't have read this—*Little Dorrit*, Dickens—because it's only just come out. Do you like plays? Poetry? We have Ibsen, we have Dostoevsky, Charlotte Brontë, Mrs. Gaskell. I know you think I'm an illiterate, but here's one I've actually read myself—*La Dame aux Camelias*. Great pathos; reduced me to tears, I don't mind admitting."

She would be reduced to tears herself in another minute. Each new volume was a wonder, a miracle. In prison, reading had saved her life—literally, she truly believed—and even though her new life was rich and full, sensually and intellectually alive, stimulating, *dazzling* in comparison to her old one, she'd missed the pleasure of new books, new voices. "If you had given me jewels," she said haltingly, "if you had given me paintings on—*gold*—you couldn't have made me any happier. Thank you. Thank you. That's inadequate, I know, but there aren't any words to tell you what I'm feeling."

His eyes softened with tenderness. He threw down the book in his hand and came to her. She thought he meant to embrace her, but he only took her hand. "There's more."

She started shaking her head. "What do you mean? How could there be?"

"I've had a letter from my mother, Rachel. She says my father's worse."

"Oh, no."

"She's said it before, but this time it might really be true. In any event, it looks as if I'll have to go to Rye."

"Oh, Sebastian. I'm so sorry."

He sent her a quizzical look. "It's all right. Thank you for your sympathy, darling, but it's not necessary. I've told you before, there's no love lost in my family. When my father dies, I'll go through the proper forms for decency's sake, but I won't pretend that his passing means anything to me."

He seemed to mean it. He said it without bitterness or irony, simply as a statement of fact. "I'm sorry," she said again, because it was sad.

He made a dismissive gesture. "The point is, I've got to leave for Steyne Court tomorrow. I wanted this to be a surprise, but I can't see how to manage it without barring you from the entire west side of the house."

She frowned. "What?"

His eyes twinkled with suppressed excitement. He waited, watching her, prolonging the suspense. "I wish I had a picture to show you. Well, I do, actually, come to think of it, but it's not— you won't really be able to *see* the thing, at least I can't, it looks like a lot of squiggles to me—"

"*What?*"

He waited another excruciating minute. "All right, I'll tell you. I'm having a glass conservatory built on the west wing, oening off the great hall. That day I was in Plymouth, I hired a fellow to design it, a landscape architect, supposed to know what he's doing. He sent me these drawings"—he opened a drawer in the big library table and pulled out a sheaf of papers—"but I can't make much out of them." He put the papers in her hand.

"Anyway, it'll be big and it'll overlook the river. He's built in all sorts of things I told him you wanted—a shed for your tools, a separate place for a table and a bench where you can sit and have tea or read a book, whatever you like, plus it's heated in winter—your sitting place, I mean—with a stove that's shielded from the plants so they don't get too hot. Which doesn't seem like something you'd have to worry about in wintertime, but apparently it's a danger. This here, this taller part, he calls that the orangery. Pretty, isn't it? Can you picture it? Think of it as a tower on a house; I think it'll be quite graceful-looking as you approach the house from the bridge. It's for orange trees, of course, or lemon trees, although you'd have to call it a lemonary then, I suppose. The architect fellow says you could do camellias there, too, since apparently they can grow very tall in the Devon climate. He suggested a *fernery* as well, but I thought that was a bit much. I mean, where does it end, where does one draw the line? A rosary, a gladiolary, a petuniary. But of course if you *want* a fernery, that would be an entirely different thing. I suppose it might be all right, damp and close, aquatic, somewhat fetal, really, but—"

He stopped, finally realizing she was crying. She'd turned her back to him, pretending to be absorbed in the architect's diagrams, but she couldn't see anything because her eyes were blurry with tears.

"Ah, Rachel." He sighed, stroking her shoulders. He didn't ask why she was weeping, and she was glad. "Don't be afraid to be happy, darling. Open yourself up. Take what I want to give you."

She let him hold her, press her back into his arms, squeezing her tight against his chest. A rather bleak insight came to her, warring with the fledgling joy that wanted to burst out and take over: it wasn't that she was afraid of happiness, not anymore;

what she feared was losing everything. And everything had come to mean Sebastian.

"I'll miss you," she told him, turning in his arms. "I wish . . ." But she didn't finish the thought. It wasn't in her yet to wish for things.

He rested his cheek against hers. "I wish you could come with me. I would take you, but you'd hate it, and I wouldn't inflict my family on anyone. Least of all you." He let his fingers drift over her cheek. "Smile for me, Rachel. How beautiful you are, even though your eyes are sad. Do you like your gift?"

She couldn't speak, only nod. She thought of the day she'd told him of her prison daydream—that her cell was a greenhouse filled with flowers and damp, sweet-smelling earth. Her heart ached, and she knew that what she felt for him was love, not gratitude. A complicated love, born out of need and helplessness at first, but moving away from them as time went by, moving into a cleaner, clearer place as she grew stronger, less dependent on him for survival. Where would it end? Maybe, without knowing it, he was helping her to prepare for the day when she'd have to live without him. Maybe—but why not be happy now anyway? Why not seize the chance for it that he held out to her time after time, disregarding his motives, accepting his gifts not just with thanks but with gladness? Why not?

"I love it," she answered, holding his face between her hands. *I love you,* she thought, and kissed his lips before he could see it in her eyes. "God keep you safe, Sebastian. I hope you find some peace with your family."

"It won't happen. The only thing I hope is to come back to you soon." He kissed her, with a mixture of passion and tenderness that devastated her. She clung to him, shameless. As long as he held her, she could pretend that his home was here, with her.

"Tell me again that you'll miss me," he said.

"I will miss you." But she was thinking of the future.

* * *

Three days after Sebastian left for Rye, a letter arrived, addressed to Rachel, from the Home Secretary in Whitehall. She opened it fearfully, as she did any official document that came her way, never able to shake off a baseless fear that the gates of prison were reopening to take her back. What she found was a letter, signed by the Secretary, ordering an immediate remittal of her ticket of leave. She stared at the one-paragraph message for a full minute, reading it again and again, unable to believe her eyes. The Secretary gave no reason for this astonishing piece of news; he simply stated that Her Majesty was pleased to set aside the remaining conditions of release of Rachel Wade's license to be at large; Mrs. Wade was no longer subject to such conditions and was now and henceforth free of all parole obligations.

No more weekly visits to the parish constable—no more monthly visits to the chief constable's office in Tavistock. No more payments toward her fine. *She was free.*

She couldn't contain herself. Happiness and frustration made her feel manic—how could she wait until Sebastian came home to tell him? She was bursting with the news, dying to share it with someone. Who? There wasn't anyone—so she did a little dance on her sitting-room rug with Dandy, and only stopped when his excited barking threatened to bring the servants knocking at her door.

The next day was Sunday. She dressed with special care, even donning the stylish flowered hat Sebastian had bought for her that long-ago day at Miss Carter's. Declining a ride in the carriage with the other servants, she walked to church because the day was perfect, and she sat in a back pew and stared at her neighbors through new eyes. Could it be true that her presence disgusted no one, scandalized no one? Certainly the looks she intercepted were bland, sometimes courteous, sometimes even— imagine it—friendly. The inevitable inference was that she herself had been responsible—partly—for her own isolation: she'd turned herself into a pariah by assuming she was one. Could it be true? Lydia Wade was nowhere in sight; if she had been, a very different perception of the atmosphere in All Saints Church this morning would surely have colored her conclusion. But in the absence of the one person in the world who truly hated her, Rachel was free for once to feel *normal*. A resident of a village, a parishioner of a church, an employee of a household—a citizen of the Empire. What power, what an undervalued privilege; what rich contentment ordinariness conveyed. For the first time in many years, she gave thanks to God for a blessing and meant it.

Reverend Christian Morrell delivered one of his fine, rather long sermons, this one on the virtue of tolerance, and afterward he asked the congregation to pray for the repose of the soul of Mrs. Eleanor Weedie, an elderly parishioner who, he said, had died peacefully in her sleep on Thursday evening. Rachel stole a glance through her lashes at Miss Weedie, the deceased's middle-aged daughter, who stood with her head bowed a few pews closer to the chancel. Beside her, hovering over her solicitously, stood Captain Carnock, one of the magistrates at Rachel's hearing. He was a gentleman farmer when he wasn't administering justice. At the hearing, she'd thought him thick-witted and heartless, but now she saw him in a different light. His face, even his posture looked benign and protective; he cared for the grieving daughter of Mrs. Weedie, and he seemed to be feeling the same pain she felt.

How many other people had Rachel misjudged?

Outside on the church steps, she shook Reverend Morrell's hand and told him she'd enjoyed his sermon. His handsome face looked skeptical, but he only thanked her, and invited her to attend a "penny reading" in the vicarage meeting room on Friday evening next, when his wife was set to begin reading *Villette* in weekly installments to as many parishioners who cared to come and hear it. "It's a pleasant way to meet people," he added, smiling his rather beatific smile. She murmured noncommittally, but the idea intrigued her.

Just then Anne waved to her from the bottom of the steps, and Rachel bade farewell to the vicar and went to greet his wife. She looked young, fresh, and uncommonly pretty in a tartan skirt and crimson blouse—an ensemble Rachel would not have expected the wife of a minister to wear to church, but which looked charming on her nonetheless. It also failed to even try to hide the interesting fact that she was at least four months pregnant. The two women greeted each other amiably, Rachel mentioning that she'd heard from Miss Deene that Anne had been unwell, and she was happy to find her completely recovered.

"Oh, did Sophie say 'unwell'? How delicate of her," Anne said with warm, laughing eyes. She had a lovely way, Rachel thought, of puncturing social conventions without wounding individuals. "No, as you can see, I'm in the very *pink* of health. Dr. Hesselius is a little old-fashioned; if he and Christy had their way, I'd be in bed till Christmas." Rachel took that to be *her* delicate way of confiding her baby's due date. "But *you*," she exclaimed, standing back and making a show of looking Rachel up and down. "You look wonderful! I think our little village agrees with you."

Rachel thanked her, coloring a little, but privately delighted with the compliment.

"I understand Lord D'Aubrey's gone to Sussex to visit his father."

"Yes, the earl is very ill. But there's been no word yet, and we don't know how much longer he intends to stay away."

They spoke of casual things for another moment, before Anne hesitated and then said in a low, apologetic voice, "Wyckerley is so tiny, we all know one another's business; and of course it isn't only the servants who gossip, as much as we like to pretend we're above such things." Rachel felt her face tighten, and wondered exactly what bit of gossip had reached Anne's ears. "You may already have heard this, but if not, I thought it would interest you to know that Claude Sully has been seen in the neighborhood."

"Oh," Rachel said, taken aback. It wasn't the news she'd been expecting.

"He's a thoroughly unpleasant person," she went on, nodding as if agreeing with Rachel—who must have given her thoughts away by her expression.

"I wasn't aware that you knew him."

"Yes, I know him. He was a friend of my late husband. I detest him," Anne added with surprising vehemence. "I'm sure he's harmless—cowards usually are—but I thought you should know that he's here."

Rachel remembered the threat Sully had made before Sebastian had thrown him out of the house. It ought not to surprise her that others had heard of it; half the Lynton Hall domestic staff had witnessed the late-night brawl. "Thank you for telling me," she said faintly.

Anne nodded. "You mustn't worry. He's here on business, I believe. Evidently he has some financial interests he inherited from . . ."

"From *my* late husband," Rachel finished for her. There was a short, awkward pause.

"Now that I'm all well again, why don't you come and visit me one day soon?" Anne suggested. "Come for tea—I'd love that."

"I will. I'd like it very much."

"Good. Oh—there's Honoria Vanstone." Rachel turned slightly, to watch Anne bow and smile formally as Miss Vanstone drew near. "Good morning," she said without much enthusiasm. "Nice to see you."

"Good morning, Mrs. Morrell. You're looking . . . colorful." Miss Vanstone laughed artificially; she kept her shoulders turned away from Rachel and didn't look at her. "My father and I were wondering if you and the vicar would be free to come to Wyck House for dinner on Wednesday evening."

"How kind. I'll ask Christy about his schedule and let you know, shall I? Thank you so much." There was a pause. "I'm sorry—do you know Mrs. Wade?" She touched Rachel's arm lightly. "This is—"

"No, I do not," Miss Vanstone announced in cool, firm tones. "Do let us know about Wednesday. Good day to you, Mrs. Morrell." Still without looking in Rachel's direction, she nodded once, pivoted, and walked off.

Anne looked mortified. "Oh," she exclaimed in a low voice. "Oh, I'm so sorry! Rachel, forgive me—I had no idea. That was *unconscionably* rude."

"It's nothing, nothing at all."

"No, but she's an insufferable woman! I've never been able to stand her."

A second passed, and then Rachel said, "Neither have I."

They stared at each other with relief and new interest—and frank admiration. Rachel was amazed, in addition, to discover how much better pure, uncomplicated anger felt than humiliation or embarrassment.

"Wyck House," Anne muttered disgustedly, gray eyes twinkling. "That's another thing—I *hate* it when people name their houses. Not very English of me, I suppose, but it's pretentious, don't you think?"

"I don't know." She laughed almost gaily. "Is it?"

"Let's get to the bottom of it tomorrow. Come to tea then, won't you? If we leave our date indefinite, it could be weeks before either of us does anything about it. Can you come tomorrow?"

"I would love to."

"Shall we say three o'clock?"

"Yes, three. It sounds perfect."

*   *   *

At home, another novel trial awaited her.

In Sebastian's absence, she'd begun sorting and shelving his new books and trying to decide what to do with the old ones. It was dusty work. After lunch, she changed out of her Sunday best and set to work with Susan, pulling down musty-smelling volumes, dusting them, then reshelving them or putting them in boxes for the parish library. Violet, who had the morning off, had been told last night that she would be expected to help in this fairly pleasant task, but by two o'clock she hadn't appeared. According to Susan, she had a new beau; she claimed he gave her expensive presents, but no one had ever seen him.

At two forty-five, Rachel looked up and saw her leaning in the library doorway, looking vacant, nibbling on a slice of bread.

"You're late."

Violet shrugged.

"Almost three hours late."

Violet chewed her bread and stared back, impudence in every line of her body.

Rachel sighed inwardly. Pointing, she said, "You can begin by taking the books down from those shelves, please, and putting them in boxes. Dust the shelves, and if there's mildew, wash it off with soap and water. There's the bucket."

The maid didn't move. She swallowed the last bite of bread and brushed crumbs from the bosom of her dress. Even from this distance, Rachel could smell the odor of her cheap perfume. "I don't want to get my gown dirty," she protested languidly, pulling the flounced skirt out to the side to show it off. "It's my best."

"Then go up and change," Rachel said shortly.

"Anyway, it's the Sabbath. I shouldn't ought t' be doing any work a'tall."

Susan, motionless on the floor beside a stack of books, turned her wide-eyed gaze back and forth between them, as if watching a particularly engrossing badminton match.

Rachel spoke quietly. "Violet. I'd like you to go upstairs and change your dress, quickly, then come down and help us with these books. Do you understand?"

"No."

"What is it you—"

"I understand. I'm not doing it."

Silence followed this pronouncement, a tense, dangerous hush that unnerved Susan so much, she went back to her dusting, head down and cheeks flaming. Rachel wondered why it didn't unnerve her as well. But it wasn't intimidating, she realized; in fact, in a strange way, it was exhilarating.

"Susan," she said slowly, "would you mind leaving Violet and me alone?"

"Yes, ma'am. I mean, no, ma'am." She scrambled up and was gone in seconds.

Rachel dropped her dusty rag on the floor and moved closer to Violet. She was still slouching in the doorway, although her indolent posture looked forced now, contradicted by the nervous glitter in her small black eyes. "I've given you an instruction," Rachel told her in a steady voice. "Are you going to do what I've asked?"

"I don't have to." She had a nasty, derisive smile. "What are you going to do about it?"

She took a deep breath. "I'm going to discharge you."

Violet's face registered shock for a split second; then hostility. "You can't do that."

"What makes you think I can't?"

"Because. Who do you think you are? You're nobody. You're a *convict*."

"Yes. But I'm also your superior. I'll give you two weeks' wages but no reference, and I want you gone by dinnertime."

Violet couldn't speak for a full minute. She had family in the neighborhood—Rachel wasn't casting her out into the cold. But she was almost past caring about it one way or the other. If the girl had backed down now, apologized and asked for another chance, she'd have given it to her. Reluctantly.

But she didn't. She found her voice and said scathingly, "Keep yer bloody two weeks' pay, I don't need it. And I'm glad to be shut o' you, you stuck-up, murdering slut."

"Get out. Pack your things and leave now."

"I'll leave, all right, but you hear this." She sighted down a long, pointing finger and vowed, *"You're going to be sorry."*

Then she was gone, and Rachel found herself shivering with nerves and triumph. But her shaky elation didn't last long. Only until she remembered that Violet's unpleasant last words to her were exactly the same as Claude Sully's had been to Sebastian.

XVI

BETWEEN DANDY'S WILD barking and the clatter of carriage wheels in the flagstone courtyard, Sebastian didn't see how Rachel could miss his arrival. He jumped down from his rented coach, Preest behind him, and glanced toward her open window. Impossible to see inside, but he imagined her springing up from her desk, patting at her hair, shaking her skirts. The thought made him smile. But after five minutes, while he paid the driver and told Preest to take him down to the kitchen for a bite and a nip before he started the trip back to Plymouth, only a couple of lads had appeared in the courtyard, to carry his luggage into the house. Where was she?

Holyoake came through the archway from the direction of the stables. "How was your journey, m'lord?" he asked, shaking hands.

"Tedious, William. And hot."

"And your father?"

"Ah, well. I'm not an earl yet."

Holyoake's jaws clamped shut and his heavy brows came down: his disapproving look.

Sebastian bowed his head contritely: "My father's gravely ill. I don't think he can live much longer."

"I'm that sorry, m'lord."

"Thank you. Well, what's the news?"

"Not so much. We've had fine, dry days, and 'tis been quiet-like, all in all. The harvest's set to begin next week. Been gather-

253

ing the teams o' hands and readying the machines and wagons and such. All's in order there, I b'lieve."

" I'm sure of it."

"There's a thing or two we might discuss about corn market prices, strategies and whatnot. But I expect you'll be tired from yer trip just now; mayhap we can talk later."

"Right you are, William. Tonight, perhaps, or better yet, first thing in the morning. Where's Mrs. Wade?" he asked casually.

"Why, she walked to the village, m'lord. Said she were going fer tea wi' the vicar's wife."

"Did she?" They exchanged tactful looks of surprise and, Sebastian thought, satisfaction. "I'll see her later, then," he said in the nonchalant tone, and Holyoake nodded blandly.

Just as well, thought Sebastian as he took the stairs two at a time to his room. He was hot from his trip, and not all that clean. He'd have a chance now to smarten himself up for her.

Judelet even made good lemonade. Sebastian sipped from a tall, cool glass while he surveyed what the workmen had accomplished on Rachel's greenhouse in his absence. There wasn't much to see yet, just a hole in the ground for the stone foundation and a lot of piled-up equipment. The conservatory would have painted wood framing on the outside, brass on the inside, the rest glass, with a brick floor and a drain, running water from a hidden cistern, adjustable shades for regulating the light. She would like it. He imagined coming upon her here in the late afternoons, watching her putter about with soil and watering cans, maybe humming a song to herself as she tended her flowers. They could sit in chairs and tell each other what their day had been like, sipping tea, watching the sun go down. He could hardly wait.

Four-thirty now; she'd be home soon. He gazed past the river bridge to the lane that disappeared in the trees at the top of the rise. No sign of her yet. He decided to stretch his legs, take a walk around his house.

Calling Lynton Hall eccentric was a generous-hearted indulgence; the place was downright odd. But he liked its peculiarities and appreciated its amusing, architectural flaws. He was fond of it, in a way he could never be fond of Steyne Court. Strolling through the terraced gardens at the back, he spoke briefly to McCurdy, his gardener. Besides a rake and a hoe under his arm, the taciturn Scotsman carried two small pails of strawberries. "Give me one of those, will you?" Sebastian asked, and McCurdy grunted and obliged. "Thanks." He hadn't had time to buy Rachel anything; he'd give her strawberries.

Wandering farther, he went down the steep gravel path to the edge of the park. The woods were filling with shadows as the sun began its slow decline, but lazy bees still droned in the shrubbery. The smell of acacia blossoms sweetened the air, and McCurdy's perennial garden blazed with color in a long slant of afternoon light. Leggy, a little overgrown, the garden looked neglected; McCurdy put his energies into the one above it, this one being remote from the house and seldom seen, probably hard to water. Beside it, a peeling wood gazebo was decaying—like so many other things on the estate. Sebastian sat down on the splintery bench to contemplate his domain.

Silence; peace. What a pleasant spot. He wanted Rachel to enjoy it with him. Where was she?

There—topping the rise, hurrying, skirts bunched in her hands. She stopped when she saw him, and her face lit up in a smile so genuine and unrestrained, he felt a twist in his heart. Then she was running down the hill and he was striding out to meet her. By the time he swept her up in his arms, they were both laughing.

Laughing. He swung her around in a circle, euphoric. Half the goal had been realized.

When they stopped kissing, they stood back to look at each other. "What's happened?" he demanded. "Do you *thrive* when I'm away?" She looked different—confident, womanly, radiant.

"No," she denied. "I pine."

"No, you *blossom*. Has something happened?"

"Yes—but I'll tell you later. How was your trip? How is your father?"

"Alive, but only barely."

She took his hand. "Are *you* all right?"

"I'm fine. My trip—it's not important." He could hardly remember it. He turned with her, and they walked slowly back to the shady gazebo. "I want to know what's happened to you, Rachel. Tell me now."

They sat in the dappled shadows with their arms around each other, ignoring the glorious sunset. He'd never seen her so lovely. Her hair had lengthened in the months since she'd come here; it curled at the tops of her shoulders now, dark and mysterious, and he'd grown to love the silver strands that brightened it, like stars winking in a black sky. They were unique; they were Rachel.

"Sebastian," she said in a reverent voice, "my ticket of leave has been canceled. All the conditions of my release were dismissed, withdrawn. It was in a letter that came from the Home Secretary four days ago."

"And this makes you happy." He touched her cheek. "I can see that it does."

"Yes. Oh, yes. It's exactly as if a weight's been lifted—I'm truly not the same person I was."

"Had you petitioned for this, written to the Home Office?"

"No, and I don't know why they've done it. It's unusual for a remittal to come this soon—I've only been observing my conditional release for five months. You didn't write to them, did you?"

"No, I didn't. Why didn't you ask me to? It never even occurred to me." Her happiness was contagious. He kissed her on the temple. "So you're through with visits to Tavistock and the constable in Wyckerley?"

"Yes, that's all finished. I'm free now, truly free."

She looked free. Fresh and youthful, full of hope. He was fascinated by this newest change in her.

"You'll never guess what I did yesterday."

He shook his head. "You went dancing on the village green?"

"I sacked Violet Cocker."

"Violet Cocker . . ."

"She's a housemaid. If you had been here, of course I'd have asked you first—but you did say that all the hiring and firing would be my responsibility, you said that in the very beginning, and so I—"

"Quite right. Out with the wench."

"Sebastian, she was insufferable—rude, lazy, insulting—"

"Is she that black-haired girl with the ferret face?"

She laughed with guilty delight. "Yes! I gave her two weeks' pay out of the housekeeping money, and this morning she was gone. And I feel—*powerful.*"

"Do you?" He smiled, enchanted.

"What do you think it means? Do you think I'm vindictive?"

"Oh, come now."

"No, but what if it turns out I'm a mean sort of person once I've got any power at all, the kind who takes pleasure in besting the Violets of this world?"

"What's wrong with that?"

"Well, it—"

"Nothing. The Violets of this world deserve besting, and a lot worse. But you're not like that and you know it. You got rid of a woman who's been a thorn in your side from the beginning. I'm proud of you."

She looked down, smiling. "I am, too," she confessed. "Violet ought to have been let go. She really did deserve it."

"Absolutely."

"The point is, I couldn't have done it a week ago. I feel as if a new life is starting for me. This morning, another Broad Arrow came in the mail, and I didn't—" He cut her off with an angry oath, and she put a calming hand on his sleeve. "It was exactly the same as the first one, no note, no sender's address. It didn't *prostrate* me the way the first one did, though—that's what I'm trying to tell you. I think it's starting: I think I'm finally beginning to put the past behind me."

"Darling. I'm very glad. That's the best news you could give me." He gave her shoulders a squeeze before he said seriously, "But I'll have to have another word with Mrs. Armstrong. This can't go on."

"I wish you wouldn't speak to her. She's very ill—Anne Morrell told me so this afternoon. There's no harm done. Honestly, it's nothing."

"Well, we won't argue about it now." To change the subject, he said, "So you're friends with Christy Morrell's wife, are you?"

"Not friends exactly," she said carefully. "Not yet, but I think we could be. I like her very much. And—she likes me."

"Of course she does. She's an intelligent woman."

"She makes the most irreverent jokes. And she's easy to talk to. So easy that today I screwed up my courage and asked her a question."

"What?"

"I asked why she's gone to the trouble and the risk of seeking out my acquaintance when, for all she knows, I might have killed a man."

He touched her cheek. "That took courage. What did she say?"

"She said she's never believed from the moment we met that I could have murdered anyone. And she said her husband told her all about the trial and conviction, and then she didn't much care if she was right or not, because Randolph was a beast and deserved what he got." She gave a laugh. "She's very outspoken for a minister's wife."

"How nice that you have such a wise friend."

"She told me something else—I almost forgot. Claude Sully is in the neighborhood, Sebastian. On some kind of business, she thought."

"Is he?" He searched her face, which had suddenly grown tense. "You're not afraid, are you?"

"No, not for myself. It was you he threatened."

He felt the old antagonism stir inside. "I wish he would try something. By God, I do." The things Sully had done to her—the things Sebastian had let him do—they still had the power to sicken him.

"That's all over," she said quickly, reading his mind.

"Yes. It is over. In a way, you know, I owe Sully a debt. Thanks to him, I saw myself clearly for the first time in—I don't know how long. Years." He still had a long way to go to change that mirror image Sully had shown him, but he thought he'd mad a good beginning. He laid his palm on the side of Rachel's face, stroking her cheek with his thumb. A very good beginning.

Her lashes fluttered closed; smiling, she pressed his fingers to her lips one by one. "I missed you. I thought you'd never come home."

They shared a soft kiss, slow and welcoming, and he thought about how lucky he was. Because this woman was his, and she had been waiting for him. He let his hand drift down the silky skin of her throat to the collar of her dress. "How does this unfasten?"

Her eyes flew open. They widened in surprise, then warmed with excitement, and her smile cast a spell over him. "It . . . hooks. In the back." And she bent her head to make it easy for him.

"Pretty dress," he murmured, undoing the little hooks at the nape of her neck. "Pretty lady." Truly he had come home.

"I thought of you all the time," she confided in a whisper. "Of this. Sometimes . . . I feel as if my body doesn't belong to me anymore. It belongs to you."

"Then I must be careful to take very, very good care of it." It wasn't a sexual overture; he meant it literally, a kind of vow. His hands were almost reverent as he slipped the bodice of her gown over her shoulders and gently pulled her arms out of the tight sleeves. "Look at you," he breathed, beguiled by the smooth swell of her bosom under her dainty white chemise. He ran his fingers along the ribbon at the frilly top, listening to her slow breathing. A stray sunbeam gilded her shoulder. He put his lips there, and murmured, "How lovely to touch you like this. Do you like the way the sun feels on your skin?"

"Yes."

"And the breeze."

"Yes."

"And my mouth . . ."

"Yes . . ."

She smelled like the lilac soap he'd given her for a present. He eased the shift over her shoulders so he could look at her breasts. Ah, so pretty. He told her so, kissing them softly, circling the nipples with his palms.

She whispered, "I'm drowning," pink-cheeked, her head angled to the side, languid as a heavy flower.

He took a kiss from her parted lips. "Mmm, sweet," he said, "like a sip of honey," and she sighed, smiling, stroking his chest. "Rachel."

"Hmmm?"

"Make love with me now."

She straighted her neck. "You don't mean *here*."

"Yes. Here, now."

"But what if someone sees?"

"No one ever comes here except McCurdy, and he's gone for

the day. There, on the grass beside those tall lilies. Wouldn't you like to lie there with me?"

She looked at the spot he was pointing to, her fingertips on her lips, thinking it over. He was in love with her serious profile, the heavy sweep of black lashes and the strong nose, the contrast in her pretty skin of ivory and faint pink. She turned back to him and smiled. "Yes. All right," she said, and her low voice thrummed with eagerness.

They knelt together in the cool grass, the lilies nodding at their shoulders, yellow and coral, half closed now. The odor of flowers was everywhere and the air was as soft as a whisper, as soft as Rachel's skin. Swallows cut through the sky over their heads; in the park, crows called from bough to bough. Sebastian unbuttoned his shirt and stripped it off along with his coat, all in one fast movement, smiling at his own excitement. Rachel was slower, more deliberate. Intentionally provocative? The possibility mesmerized him.

"Shouldn't we leave something on?" she mused, fingering her silky chemise.

"Leave something on?"

"In case someone comes."

The idea had merit, but he wasn't sure she'd see the point in leaving on only her stockings, or only her shoes. They'd save that erotic refinement for another time. "In for a penny, in for a pound," he challenged, holding her gaze while he unfastened his trousers. The glimmer of amusement in her eyes told him she'd caught the double entendre.

They came together, still on their knees, clasping each other with glad, impatient hands. He tent her back, kissing her deeply, wanting the thrust of her breasts against him, the round, sleek swell of her buttocks under his hands. They fell to the grass, rolling, both of them avid and intent, locked in a possessive embrace. Her hands were everywhere on him, touching him with a new freedom, an unabashed giving and taking of pleasure that was the essence of seduction. He savored her eagerness—her gift to him; it made all of his to her seem paltry in comparison.

She pulled him down, urging him with her body, inviting him without shyness. "Now I'm home," he said when he came into her at last, and she said, "Welcome," and neither of them smiled at the sentimentality of that, because they felt it too deeply, meant it too literally.

Wordless, they moved together. The pleasure was raw and shocking, and she was with him, so close, they could've been one. Deep kisses, slow, passionate touching. *This time,* he promised her, holding her tight, giving her the best of himself. *This time, darling.*

But she couldn't let go. Her body was striving, straining for the release she couldn't allow it. "Give in," he coaxed, stroking her shallowly, listening to her sighs for clues to her pleasure. She couldn't quite bring herself to tell him, so he had to ask—"Do you like this? And this?"

At length he rested, his muscles taut, trembling a little. He kissed her damp, tragic face. "I'm sorry," she mourned, holding on to him. Smiling, he rolled to his side. "Sorry," she said again.

He sat up, eyeing her, thoughtfully stroking her stomach. She looked miserable, sheepish and disappointed. "You trust me, don't you?" he asked her, and she nodded immediately. "Sure?"

"Yes, I'm sure."

He found his trousers where he'd flung them and reached into the pocket for his knife. When he opened it, her eyes went wide, not with fear but puzzlement. He grinned. "No, I'm not going to stab you. Sexual inhibition isn't a capital offense."

"Is that what's wrong with me? Sexual inhibition?"

He bent to kiss her navel. "Nothing's wrong with you."

The edge of the perennial garden bordered their grassy trysting place. Leaning, Sebastian cut one white lily off at the base of its long, thin stalk, then two of its neighbors. Snipping off the tips, he laid the flowers on her breasts, and a whimsical one pointing up between her thighs. She smiled, embarrassed but amused, and he laughed for the sheer pleasure of seeing her smile. Throwing his knife aside, he began to bend the stems all along their crisp stalks, top to bottom, snapping them in half-inch segments until he had three long, whippy branches.

"Give me your wrist."

She waited a beat, then slowly extended her right hand. Circling her wrist with the end of one of the stalks, he tied a loop and knotted it.

"The other one." Her hesitation was longer this time. Her eyes clouded with doubt. "You trust me," he reminded her.

She gave him her other hand.

He made another loop, another knot, and with the third lily stalk he bound the two wrist-cuffs together.

"Why are you doing this?"

"To make you helpless. You have too much self-control, and I'm taking it away from you."

He sat back on his heels, scanning what was available nearby. To his left, a thin wooden stake was holding up some tall, droopy flower, possibly a dahlia. The stake came out of the soft earth easily; he had more trouble pressing it back into the porous soil beyond Rachel's head. But he managed, because where there was a will, there was a way.

She watched him in rapt silence all the while, missing nothing.

"Sit up for a second." He took her tied wrists from her lap and kissed them, then lifted her arms over her head and slipped the juncture of her bound hands over the stake.

"Lie down." She obeyed, and he said, "You're caught now. You can't move." Of course she could; a couple of strong yanks, and her stalk-shackles would shred to pieces. It was the symbol that counted—which was why he stopped smiling then, and why he used a quiet, dangerously patient voice to tell her, "Don't think of trying to get away from me, Rachel, because you can't. You're completely helpless. And you're mine."

Her dilating pupils darkened her luminous eyes; either she believed him or she was learning very quickly to play this game. Either way, his own excitement was mounting higher with every heartbeat.

He made himself comfortable beside her. He took note of her breathing—fast, uneven. When she licked her dry lips, he reached out and began to stroke them with his thumb, caressing the slippery insides, pressing lightly against her teeth. He found her tongue and rubbed it, just the tip, enjoying its nervous quiver.

He'd forgotten McCurdy's strawberries; the little pail was under his coat. He found a fat one and took a bite out of it, letting the juice spurt into his mouth. He brought the rest of the berry to Rachel's mouth and rubbed it against her parted lips until they were the same color as the juice. "Bite," he commanded, and her white teeth closed around the succulent fruit. Their eyes met in a frank, erotic glance. He took a sticky, juicy kiss from her mouth while he dragged the wet berry over her chin and down her throat. She stopped breathing when he circled her breast with it and then the aureole of her nipple, not touching the peak until she groaned in frustration. "What do you want?" he whispered.

"You know . . ."

He took pity on her and sleeked the fruit across the turgid tip of her bosom, slowly, playing an intent, luxurious game, dyeing her nipple with the purple juice. She was trying to be quiet, trying not to moan. "That's very nice. Very tasty-looking," he said in the detached voice—a sham, since he was anything but detached. "What do you want, Rachel?"

"You know."

"You must say it."

She couldn't—so he ate the strawberry and picked another, leisurely nibbled the tip, and went back to rubbing her with the slick, juicy rest of it. "What do you want?"

"Damn it," she burst out with a short, helpless laugh. "I want—you—to kiss me."

"Where?"

She squeezed her eyes shut. Her arm muscles tensed and her fists clenched; she looked as impotent and incapable of escaping as he'd told her she was.

"Where?"

"Oh, *God*," she said to the sky.

"Where?"

"My—breast!"

Good thing she'd capitulated, because he couldn't have held out much longer—he had to taste her. Bending, he tongued the sticky liquid off her hot skin, taking long, slow licks, skirting her nipple, gradually narrowing the circle. He took it suddenly, suckled it strongly, and she gave a low, hoarse cry, her body stretching, straining. He sucked harder, until she couldn't stand any more. When he touched her between her legs, she bucked in surprise and then pressed upward with her hips, wanting more.

He moved down over her, fluffing her soft hair with his palm, but giving her nothing, tantalizing her. He picked another berry from the pail. There were so many things he could do to her now. She was panting, her eyes slightly glazed, watching him intently. She jerked whenever he touched her.

"What would you like now?" She rolled her head from side to side. "Tell me," he said with manufactured menace, "or I swear I'll tie your legs apart."

She gave a tortured whimper, biting her lips. "I want you."

"You want me to what?"

"Please . . ."

"Please what?"

But she couldn't say any of the words he'd taught her for what she wanted now.

"I'll tell you what I want," he said threateningly, leaning over her until they were mouth to mouth. While he spoke, he skimmed his finger down the moist crease of her sex, making her suck in her breath through her teeth. "I want to put my cock inside you very slowly. Feel your heat. Feel you stretch and tighten around me. I want to feel the beat of your pulse deep inside. I want to see your face when you lose control—and you will lose control. And when you come, Rachel, I want to hear you cry out my name."

Two spots of bright pink color stained her cheeks. She couldn't catch her breath. He rested his finger over the tight, swollen nub of her sex just to let her know he knew where it was. "What do you want?"

"I want you to touch me," she ground out through her teeth. "There. Now. Do it."

He smiled. "Yes," he said, and began to make gentle, insistent circles around her little kernel, listening to her choked-off cries. "Don't move. Don't think of moving. You're at my mercy, and I don't have any mercy. And I'm not going to stop."

His gruff threats changed gradually until he was grating love words in her ear and saying, "Now. Now. Now," as desperate for her release as she was. They were striving together, both panting, straining. He took her fruit-stained mouth in a rough, hungry kiss, and when he pulled away she followed, arching up with her neck and shoulders for more, trying to bite his lips. He kissed her again, again, plunging with his tongue in time with the remorseless caress of his fingers. All at once she drew in a harsh breath and went rigid.

He could feel the edge nearing for her as surely as if it were his edge, too. Her eyes went wide with surprise for an instant before she shut them tight, grimacing, jaws clenching to hold back a high, ragged cry. Gentling his touch, he dipped into her and felt the warm, slow pursing of her secret flesh. He had to kiss her, even though her mouth was distorted in a grimace of pure, shocking pleasure.

His chest ached. He pressed his cheek next to hers and called her his love, his dear. By slow degrees, her body softened. He calmed her with his hand while a strange and altogether new peace stole over him. His own body throbbed with wanting her, but he lay still and watched a tear squeeze past her closed eyelashes and glide down her flushed temple into her hair. Another one followed, and he traced its path with his finger. He could smell her skin, and the crushed grass under her body, and the dying scent of flowers. He found his knife, and used it to cut her flower-stalk bonds. Her arms went limp, collapsing on the ground over her head.

He kissed the side of her breast, her armpit, the warm skin inside her elbow. Her breathing had become deep and even; she'd stopped crying, but she wouldn't look at him and he couldn't quite fathom her mood. "Darling," he said, molding her breast in his hand.

"So . . ." she breathed. But then she said no more, and he began to think she'd only sighed.

"What are you thinking? Talk to me."

She heaved another deep sigh. Of satisfaction, he hoped, but he was afraid he heard sadness in it, too. At last she turned her face to his. "Thank you," she said.

He smiled, trying to make her smile back. "The pleasure was mine." The expression in her eyes troubled him. "Are you sad? I didn't hurt you, did I?"

"Hurt me?" She shook her head slowly.

"What, then?"

"I'm not sad. How could I be?"

She was lying, he knew it. "What do you think I've taken from you?"

"Nothing. You've given me a beautiful gift. The most generous gift."

"Rachel." He felt confused, disappointed. "I would do anything not to hurt you."

"But you haven't."

"Then what is it?"

"Nothing." She turned, reaching for him. "Nothing."

He closed his eyes, needing her to touch him. He felt her lips brush his cheek, the warm fan of her breath. "Tell me you're happy."

"I am." She lifted her arms and slipped them around his neck.

"Tell me . . ." *Tell me you love me,* he thought, but he didn't say that. Too many lovers had said it to him, at this precise moment. He knew how cheap it was, and how easy the answer. "I wish you could talk to me," he said instead. "I know why it's hard for you, but I wish you could. It's something we shall have to work on."

Her straight, sweet mouth softened at the corners. "Will we work on it?"

"Yes," he said positively. "We will."

She touched his shoulder, the hollow of his throat. "I wonder for how long," he thought she murmured. Before he could answer, she drew him down, embracing him. "I would like to tell you what that felt like—what you did to me. But I don't have any words. I don't think anyone could describe it."

"Many have tried," he said, smiling determinedly.

"No—hopeless—there aren't any words. But I could show you. I'd like to show you."

An inkling of the cause of her wistfulness glimmered at the corners of his consciousness, but when he tried, he couldn't catch it; like a faint, faraway star, he couldn't see it when he looked at it directly. Her warm lips were enticing him, her hands stroking him to life. She kissed her own tears from his lips, and his mind began to shred at the edges. He would think about it later, he told himself, turning and turning with her in the sweet-smelling grass.

XVII

PLYMOUTH SOUND WAS alive with boats, so many that the dark blue water served as a mere backdrop, a recessive frame for the colorful tapestry of white sails, black masts, and bright red chimney stacks. Rachel and Sebastian were peering at the ships through side-by-side telescopes mounted on a stone wall at the end of the Hoe, a popular promenade on a headland overlooking the bay.

"Look at that one," Sebastian told her, pointing. "Beautiful, isn't it?"

"Which?"

"Just behind the second blue buoy, almost—"

"The barkentine?"

"Barkentine? Is that what it is?"

"The one with three masts? Yes, I think so. If it had two, it would be a brigantine." Straightening, she glanced at him. He was staring at her as if she'd just said something remarkable, like the names of all the constellations in alphabetical order. She smiled, shrugged. "I read an encyclopedia once. Abridged," she added when he looked amazed. "It's left me with a peculiar expertise in any number of obscure subjects."

"Has it?"

"Yes, it has." She didn't say so, but as a matter of fact she *could* name the constellations, although not in alphabetical order.

A burst of the bracing wind pushed at her, stinging her cheeks and making her eyes water; she grabbed her hat to keep it from blowing off. Gulls swooped, screaming, for the bits of bread an elderly couple nearby was tossing over the low stone wall. Beyond the ships, beyond the green slopes of Mt. Edgcumbe, a cloudless sky met the endless blue line of the Channel at the knife-edge of the horizon. It was a perfect day, the kind Rachel had often dreamt of in prison, a day so achingly beautiful it gave her a hurtful, too-full feeling in the chest, and had her more than once on the brink of tears.

Sebastian turned back toward the Sound, shading his eyes with his hand. The sea breeze blew his hair straight back from his forehead and whipped the two ends of his wine-colored necktie over his shoulder. His profile against the stark azure sky was sharp, hard, and indescribably handsome. She loved the haughty angle of his aristocratic nose, the clean line of his jaw, the way his voluptuous mouth could curve in a smile of unbearable sweetness just for her. He turned his head and looked at her then, and for the instant their gazes held, she saw softness in his sea-colored eyes, then awareness, then a flare of pure sensual anticipation.

She looked away first, flushing. He slipped his hand under her arm and pressed her to his side, oblivious to bystanders. She felt the back of his hand against her breast for a half second before he let her go. "Shall we find a place to have lunch?" he asked lightly. In a softer voice he added, "Or shall we go back to the Octagon?"

"Lunch," she answered, but not very forcefully. Returning to their hotel room at one o'clock in the afternoon would be for only one purpose. Tempting as it was, she couldn't get past a notion that she ought to be opposed to such daytime dalliances. She was a fallen woman with that most onerous of burdens, at least according to her lover: a middle-class conscience.

"Lunch," he said, with mock wistfulness, and they began to amble up the grassy hill, away from the sea. The Hoe was Plymouth's finest amenity, a spacious promontory overlooking the Sound, with flower-lined walks and delightful gardens, and views of the estuary reaching from Mill Bay to Sutton Pool. To see the sky and the ocean like this, great gulps of the wide world in vistas that stretched literally for miles—it was almost too much. It was another of Sebastian's gifts, this clandestine three-day escape from Lynton and everyone who knew them, but sometimes Rachel felt she needed his hand to anchor her to the ground. The opportunity to stare at dozens, *hundreds* of people was wonderful, too, but even more dizzying. She'd been doing it for the better part of two days, and the novelty hadn't worn off. Children in particular fascinated her; for nearly an hour this morning she'd watched, engrossed, while a ragtag group of boys sailed toy boats and played fox-and-geese around a fish pond in the Hoe. What Sebastian thought of her preoccupation she couldn't tell, but he'd indulged her in it without impatience or complaint. A most generous gift.

They found a pretty eating house in Alfred Street, from whose second-story window they could see the people on the promenade and smell the sea. Sebastian ordered prawns and mussels with lemon and butter, a creamy chowder made with clams and succulent oysters, two salads, one with tomatoes and the other with watercress and endive, a whole loaf of bread and a crock of Devon butter, fresh blueberry tarts still hot from the oven, a platter of cut melons and fruit with a dish of whipped cream in the center—

"Stop!" Rachel protested. "There's no more room on the table." Much less in her stomach.

Unperturbed, Sebastian refilled her glass from a bottle of Bordeaux wine and clinked glasses in a silent toast. "We might be hungry again later. We're not in a hurry, are we? Unless you want to go now—there's a band concert in the Esplanade at three o'clock; we could go and hear it if you like."

"I might have said yes half an hour ago, but now I can't move. Anyway, this is lovely, isn't it?" She gestured toward their open window, and the dim, cool, nearly empty restaurant at their backs. "I think I could sit here all day."

"Then that's what we'll do."

"No, they close at two-thirty," she reminded him.

He sent her a bland look. "We won't worry about that."

"Oh." He must have given money to the proprietor. It was something she'd expect of Lord D'Aubrey, but for the last two days he'd been Mr. James Hammond, and she was Mrs. Hammond. "Why Hammond?" she'd whispered when he'd registered at the Octagon. Because his name was Sebastian James Ostley Selborne-Hammond Verlaine. Did she like any of those better? Hammond was fine, she'd said from the corner of her mouth, and he'd smiled back conspiratorially.

But privately, the need to lie distressed her, even though she knew the subterfuge was for her protection, not his. And although it was foolish, she couldn't help wondering how many times, in how many other hotels, he'd signed the registry for "Mr. and Mrs. Hammond."

"Would you like to go on a picnic tomorrow?" he asked, interrupting her reverie. "There's a beach at Stonehouse Pool. Or we could take the ferry to Cremill. We might even go for a swim if it's fair."

"But we have no bathing costumes."

"We'll buy them."

"Not on Sunday."

"Ah, Sunday. Well, then, we'll go tonight. In the nude."

She laughed at him—although she considered it highly likely that he wasn't joking. "I've never swum in the sea before. Once when I was a child my family went to Lyme on a holiday, but it rained every day and we never bathed. It was a bitter disappointment." He touched her hand in sympathy. "Tell me about your travels," she urged, gazing out at the ships in the bay. "I've been to London once, but I was twelve and my memories are very childish. Have you been everywhere?"

"Not everywhere."

"To Europe, though."

"Yes."

"Tell me about it."

"I'll take you there."

She only smiled.

He leaned back in his chair, holding his wineglass to the light and squinting at it, and began to speak of the places he'd been and the sights he'd seen. As he talked, she had the sense that he was answering just to please her, not because the subject held any interest for him at this moment. And when, after a few minutes, he tapered off and stared rather distractedly out at the gulls wheeling in the blue over the headland, she didn't prompt him with more questions. She let the silence lengthen until he noticed it, sent her a wry look, and began to speak of what they would do tonight.

Last night they'd gone to the Royal Theater to see a play called *Petticoats*, a silly, mildly risqué revue, very tame for him but deliciously shocking to her. She'd never dreamed women were allowed to appear in public with so little on—outside Paris, that is, or possibly Bora Bora. Which showed what she knew, and how provincial she truly was for all her encyclopedic knowledge.

When Sebastian trailed off again and frowned down abstractedly at a spoon he was turning over and over on the tablecloth, she had to ask, "Is something wrong?"

"No."

"Would you like to go home today instead of tomorrow? This is the day they're delivering your new horse," she remembered suddenly. "If you want to—"

"No, I don't want to go home. Do you?" She shook her head. "I wasn't thinking about the mare."

"What, then?"

He looked at her speculatively. She began to think he wouldn't answer when he said, "I'm thirty years old, Rachel. As of yesterday."

"Yesterday was your birthday? I didn't know—I'm sorry. Happy birthday, Sebastian." She touched his sleeve, trying to gauge his mood; he patted her hand absently. "I wish I'd known."

"It doesn't matter."

"Does it make you sad?"

"No, not sad. Thoughtful. It's a time to be thoughtful, don't you think? Especially if one hasn't been particularly reflective before. Some would say thirty's a little late to begin, but better late than never, I suppose." He sipped his wine. "Needless to say, I haven't come to any conclusions yet about my life. Except that I'm not very proud of it—but that's hardly a new insight."

She stared at his stern profile, feeling close to him and shut out at the same time. "I believe self-discovery is a process," she said slowly. "It has no end."

"Yes." He looked up. "But I think you're a bit ahead of me in the process."

"It's possible. Certainly I've had more opportunities." She knew they were both thinking that being locked up alone in a small room left opportunities for little else. "Do you know, it's not as painful for me to think about prison as it used to be. Or even to speak of it. At least to you."

"I'm glad." He sat back in his chair, taking her hand and lacing their fingers together.

"You've helped me to heal. Thank you," she said simply. It seemed strange that she'd never said it to him before.

He gave a quick, dismissive shake of his head. "But you're still sad sometimes. I can see it in your eyes."

"Oh, no. I'm not, truly, I'm happy, I promise you." To the extent that it was true, it was because of him. Freedom, employment, friends—of course they had all contributed to her metamorphosis from the wan, speechless ghost behind the prisoner's bar, but the primary agent of the change was Sebastian. She'd stopped asking herself if he could have been any man, if she'd been so needy and helpless that *anyone* who held her future in his hands could have made her love him. It wasn't true. She loved him, Sebastian Verlaine, because there was a softness in him he couldn't even see himself, and a decency, and a clean, hard-edged integrity that was no less real for being, until lately, somewhat . . . underutilized. He was on a journey of his own, his life riddled with questions and dilemmas he'd never faced before. It was himself he was testing, his philosophy he was trying to understand when he pushed against the boundaries of convention and morality. She loved his energy and tirelessness, his constancy. How different they were: her answer to the catastrophe that had wrecked her life had been to withdraw from life; to die, in effect, in every way she could while her heart still beat and her blood still circulated. Their plights were nothing alike, although something had scarred him, too—the coldness of his family, the absolute lovelessness of his childhood—but he'd confronted his handicap by *embracing* life in all its uncouth, sensuous, too-human varieties.

But that was all in the head, her intellectual motives for loving him. Just as deeply, she was simply infatuated. Everything about him was beautiful to her. Her body reacted to the sight of him before her mind had time to register his presence. She was like a compass, always turning back to him as her focal point, her body's natural center. She loved his hands, the set of his shoulders, the deep timbre of his voice. He liked to tease her, and that was such a sweet, rare treat. He talked to her, listened intently to everything she said. They lay in bed at night for hours, sometimes until dawn, talking, talking, talking. And laughing. And making love.

"I'm restless," he said suddenly. "Do you mind if we go?"

"No, I don't mind." She studied him surreptitiously while he paid the bill. He looked preoccupied again.

But he smiled when he caught her eye. "It's nothing—I just feel like walking."

"Really?"

"Yes. I'm still a beginner, you know; a little self-discovery goes a long way with me."

They left the restaurant holding hands.

They strolled along the shady streets of the town, looking in shop windows, watching the other pedestrians. By mutual agreement, they decided against visiting the Maritime Museum, and browsed for an hour instead in a musty old bookstore called The Silverfish. Rachel had a pound and four shillings in her purse, and castigated herself for leaving the rest of her fortune—two pounds, four pence—in her case at the Octagon. Wandering away from Sebastian, she found the section, very small, where the proprietor kept books about music. There were biographies of composers, volumes on music theory, dozens of old hymnals, a few collections of sheet music. Nothing struck her particularly until she came upon a libretto for the opera *La Traviata*, new-looking and in perfect condition. Tamping down her excitement, she carried it to the tiny counter, behind which the shopkeeper sat on a high stool, making marks in a notebook with a pencil.

They had a whispered consultation. He wanted two pounds for the libretto. The art of bargaining was one Rachel knew, like so many other things, only from books. With manufactured indifference, she offered him a pound. "One and six," he countered. "Twenty-two shillings," she said—carelessly, almost wearily. The bookseller looked disgusted. "One and four," he snapped, "and that's as low as I'll go." Her heart was pounding.

She waited one more second, said, "Oh, very well," with great nonchalance, and gave him all her money.

That night, in a crowded, lamplit eating house called Selby's, she gave Sebastian his birthday present. She'd known he would like it, but she wasn't prepared for his unqualified delight. "Rachel, this is *wonderful*," he exclaimed, avidly riffling the pages, as thrilled as a boy on Christmas morning. "When did you buy it? How did you know I wanted it?"

"You told—"

"Did you know I saw *Traviata* performed in Venice in fifty-three? And again in Covent Garden just last spring?"

"Yes, you told—"

"It's magnificent, I wish you could hear it. Verdi's a genius. *Traviata*'s from Dumas's story of *The Lady of the Camellias*, you know. Look, here's the finale to Act Two—'*Alfredo, di questo core.*' I'll play it for you when we get home. Try to, anyway. What a perfect gift, darling. Thank you." And in front of all the diners at Selby's, he leaned over and kissed her on the mouth.

She blushed furiously, not from embarrassment but from feeling. The depth of her pleasure because she'd pleased him with her simple gift was profound, and anything but simple. Her emotions were raw; she'd been teary off and on all day. An hour ago, when they'd stood on the headland to watch the sun drop through bands of orchid and gold clouds and sink into the sea, such a storm of melancholy had seized her, she couldn't keep from weeping. "It's so beautiful," she'd explained when Sebastian had asked, with tender amusement, what ailed her. But that wasn't it. The hours they spent together were too perfect—she loved him too much. It couldn't last, and she couldn't bear it.

Sebastian ordered more wine. The waiter made small talk while he poured it, referring to Rachel as "your wife, sir." Their eyes met, Sebastian's amused, hers sheepish. After the waiter left, he leaned toward her and murmured, "The man needs glasses. We don't look anything like a married couple."

"We don't?"

"Not in the least. We're talking, for one thing. Enjoying each other's company. We look as though we *like* each other."

She smiled, but his facile cynicism oppressed her. She tried to echo his light tone. "Do we look like lovers?"

"Definitely."

"Then I suppose I'll have to give up my hopes of tricking anyone in Wyckerly into thinking I'm a lady. Perhaps I would do better as your London mistress. There at least I'd have a chance at anonymity, if not respectability."

"Oh, no," he said easily, "then I'd have to spend all my time in the city, and I much prefer it here."

She couldn't look at him. She made a business of breaking off a piece of bread and spreading it with butter. But when she tried to eat it, it stuck in her throat like sand.

That night, she told him about Randolph.

She hadn't meant to, hadn't thought she could. But Sebastian made love to her with such gentleness, such soft, deliberate tenderness, that when it was over she found herself in tears again. This time he wouldn't accept her inarticulate explanation. While he held her close, caressed her, and murmured to her, the terrible confession came out. It shocked both of them; she was as dismayed as he was to hear herself speaking the unspeakable, telling, in jerky, whispered rushes, the awful things Randolph had done. Once she started, she couldn't stop; she was compelled to describe the very worst, every lewd, despicable act. She knew she was horrifying him, but she couldn't stop. In the back of her mind, she had a sick certainty that time was running out—that if she didn't tell him now, she never would. Would never tell anyone. This was her last chance.

When she finished, they tried to console each other. "My dear," he called her. "Oh, my dear."

"But I'm all right now," she said urgently when he cursed Wade and admitted the violence he'd have done to him if he could.

They held each other for a long time, and slowly, surely, the bittersweet knowledge came to Rachel that the worst had happened: she had opened herself up completely, and Sebastian was going to hurt her. They had never spoken of it, but she thought he must know it, too. How could he not? She'd come to him with her eyes open, had never asked for promises, never hoped for a future. He couldn't help being who he was; she couldn't claim she didn't understand him. Today she'd lied and told him she was happy. But for all that her life had turned into a spectacular dream, she couldn't be content, not in any deep, true way, any more than an actress could be truly, deeply happy because her play was a great success. One day the play would close—and one day Rachel's time with Sebastian would end.

But she had him now. The things she'd told him were ugly, and she could feel the lingering distress in his body where it touched hers in the bed. The candle burned low, casting slow-dancing shadows on the dark walls and the pale ceiling. It was very late; the city slept without a sound, and the thick silence deepened and sharpened the intimacy between them in their rented room. She stroked his arm, the smooth curve of his shoulder; she put her lips on his chest where his heart beat. In the garden at Lynton he'd taught her passion's rise and fall, its question and the sweet, explosive answer. Another gift, another addiction she would have to overcome.

But she had him now. And his skin was warm, and the sound of his sigh when she touched him was full of longing. Randolph's depravities mustn't be allowed to linger or to poison what was between them. But he wouldn't reach for her first—the brutality of the story she'd told had appalled him and made him careful, wary of touching her. So she touched him. The silky skin over his hipbone. The hardness of his thigh. And she tasted him. The salty-sweet hollow in the base of his throat. His mouth. The palm of his hand and his long, sensitive fingers.

Gasping, he tried to pull her down, but she slipped out of his grasp. She needed him this way, receiving instead of giving. She couldn't speak the words, but she had to show him what she felt. She had to make love.

"He made me do this to him," she whispered, letting her hair graze his stomach.

"Rachel—"

"I hated it. It made me gag." His strong, narrow hips were beautiful; she rested her hands on the sides and stroked the tops of his thighs with her thumbs. Dark hair grew in a line from his navel to his groin. She brushed the length of it with her tongue.

"Rachel. God, Rachel."

"He said it was good. He said it gave him pleasure. Do you like it?"

He had his fist on his forehead, grinding it between his eyebrows. All he could say was her name.

She took him in her mouth. "I can taste both of us," she murmured after a moment, and he brought his fist down on the sheet beside them with helpless violence. She knew everything, all the refinements that would please him, but she listened, listened, watched and felt, alert to the subtlest nuance of his pleasure. When he couldn't stand any more, he reached for her—but she shifted away again, wouldn't let him take her. "Let go," she whispered—exactly as he'd whispered it to her. She smiled into his startled face. If he had eyes to see, he must know that she loved him. "Don't hold back. Give yourself to me, Sebastian. Because I want you."

She let him keep her hand when he grabbed for it. He

squeezed it tight, so tight he was hurting her—but then his punishing grip slackened and a groan tore from his throat. Panting, he lifted his head from the pillow and dropped it back heavily, twice, too stunned to speak. She could feel him trembling, feel the tension in his muscles and the light sheen of sweat everywhere she touched him. His fingers tangled in her hair. "Rachel," he said on a sigh, and he sounded sated, resigned, almost hopeless. "Too much. Oh God, Rachel."

She rested beside him, her arm across his waist, thinking, *Ah, then you know how it feels.* It was good that he knew. When she left him, they could feel, at least for a time, the same loss.

XVIII

RACHEL WAS LEANING over the arch of the stone bridge, tossing sprigs of pimpernel into the river and watching the sluggish current carry them away, when she heard a light footstep on the dusty stones. Looking up, she saw Sidony Timms, smiling shyly, coming toward her from the direction of the house.

"Saw you from out the window," she greeted Rachel, taking a place beside her. "Thought I'd come out and say good afternoon t' you. I don't get to talk to you as much now that I'm workin' in the dairy."

"Mr. Holyoake tells me you're doing very well, Sidony. Do you like it?"

"Yes, ma'am, I like it fine. I can never say thank you enough for thinking of it for me."

"But I didn't think of it, William did.".

Sidony ducked her head, acknowledging that. "He did, didn't 'e? He's been ever so kind to me, Mrs. Wade. You ought to see the place he fixed up in the barn for me to sleep in. It's nicer'n my room at home! These last weeks, I don't think I've ever been so happy."

She looked happy. Healthier, too, and there was a new confidence in the way she moved. Her limp was improving, but Dr. Hesselius had examined her again recently, and his judgment was that she would always be lame.

"I'm glad you like your new job," Rachel told her. "It was kind of Mr. Holyoake to fix the place in the barn for you."

"It was," she agreed.

Rachel hesitated, then asked, "Do you ever see your father?"

"I saw 'im in church last Sunday. He wouldn't look at me, so I didn't speak to 'im. It's hard on him, I think, me being gone from home. Not just the work. I expect he's lonely on his own."

Rachel tried to dredge up some sympathy for Marcus Timms, but found she had none to spare.

"I could never go back, though. Even though I forgive him, I can't be his daughter anymore. Sometimes . . ." She sighed, resting her forearms on the ledge and leaning over to look at the water. "Sometimes I feel like I'm an old, old lady. Mrs. Wade?"

"Yes?"

"I was wanting to ask you about something." She sent her a quick glance from under her lashes. "It's kind of personal. It's about me, not you," she clarified hastily, and Rachel relaxed, smiling to think Sidony could read her so easily.

"Go ahead," she invited. "Ask me anything you like."

"Well, ma'am, it's about Mr. Holyodke. He's been ever so nice to me, as I said, what wi' the place in the cow barn, and talkin' to me in the evenings when I can't sleep and he can't either. He's probably the best man I've ever known. He's not a real gentleman, I know that, not like 'is lordship or anything—but to me he is, you know, because he's good. And strong, and he would never tell a lie nor do a dishonest deed."

"William has been kind to me as well, Sidony. He is a gentleman. In the truest sense."

"There, ma'am, I knew you would understand. I don't know why I can talk to you, you being educated and a lady and all. But I can."

Rachel knew why, but she didn't tell Sidony the reason. She was ready to receive the girl's confidences, but not, regardless of how much their unhappy pasts had in common, ready to share any of her own. Not with anyone but Sebastian.

So she only smiled and said, "I'm glad you feel you can trust me. Is something troubling you about William?"

"Well . . . 'troubling' bain't the word, exactly," she said slowly. "Here's how it is. I talk a lot to 'im at night, sometimes in the barn, other times walkin' on the grounds, and I been telling him things about myself. Things about my father, but not just that. Once I told him what I wished would happen to me—that I'd find somebody who could love me, and we'd get married and have a family. And I told him why I know it will never happen."

"Why?"

"Because," she said simply, "I'm a cripple."

"Sidony. You're not a cripple. You walk with a limp, that's all. And you're pretty, smart—any man would be lucky to have you for a wife."

"That's just what Mr. Holyoake said."

"Well, then. Two wise old adults have given you excellent advice. I hope you listen to us."

Instead of returning her smile, Sidony looked troubled. "Now that's just it. How old a man would you say Mr. Holyoake is, ma'am?"

She thought. "Forty?"

"That's what I'd've said, too. But no, he bain't but thirty-five. I know because he told me last night when I asked. And here's the next thing. Last Sunday Bob Douthwaite asked if he could walk home with me from church. I said no thank you, and that night I asked Mr. Holyoake if I'd done right to say no."

"What did he say?"

Sidony turned her back to the river and perched her elbows on the stone ledge. "What he said—do what I think's right, all that—it's not really . . . that's not exactly what I wanted to tell you. The way he *looked*, the way he *said* I must do what was best for myself, so on and so forth—Mrs. Wade, you'll hardly credit it, but I had the strongest feeling just then that Mr. Holyoake might be fond of me himself. And not in the way of an old man caring for a child. The other way."

"I see." Rachel kept her face mild, to disguise her astonishment. But as the seconds passed and the idea had time to sink in, she grew less amazed and more intrigued. "Did he . . . say anything that would make you think he had feelings for you?"

"Not in words. To tell you the truth, I don't think he ever would. Ever will. He thinks he's old, and what's worse, he thinks I'm a little girl. No, that's not right—he thinks he *ought* to think I'm a little girl. I don't know why; it's part o' him being a gentleman, I suppose. But the truth is, Mrs. Wade, I stopped being a child a long time ago. I just don't know how to tell something like that to Mr. Holyoake. Or if I should. Or what I ought t' do. Or if I ought t' do anything a'tall." She heaved a massive sigh and turned back around, dropping her forearms over the bridge, gazing down into the river.

Rachel gazed down at it with her. Advice-giving was even newer to her than decision-making. Sidony seemed to want advice, but did she really need it? In truth, she wasn't a child; the longer Rachel knew her, the more she thought her wise, and certainly experienced in life's random cruelties, beyond her years. "How do you feel?" she asked hesitantly. "About William, I mean. Could you care for him as a man?"

"Oh, ma'am, I already do."

"Oh." Rachel smiled with surprise and pleasure. "Well, that simplifies things."

"Does it? But I don't even hardly know him. And how can I *get* to know 'im if he keeps on behaving to me like I'm twelve years old?"

Her frustration told Rachel the case was more serious than she'd thought. "Could you say something to him? Would it embarrass you to tell him how you feel?"

"Well . . . I don't mind being forward so much. What I'd mind is him *thinking* I'm forward."

"Hmm. But on the other hand, he might be relieved to have it out in the open. If you wait for William to speak first . . ."

"I might go to 'is funeral and then die an old maid myself," Sidony finished with a laugh. They lapsed into thoughtful silence. "The main thing I was wanting to ask," she said at length, "is if you think he's too old for me."

"Sidony, I can't tell you that. It's not for me to say."

"No, but—if you was to hear that me and Mr. Holyoake was together, like, and you didn't know anything else, just that. Would you be slanderized?"

"Scandalized? No," she said slowly, thinking she wasn't the best person to ask such a question. One dubious lesson penal servitude taught was a vast, perhaps an extreme tolerance for every human frailty except heartlessness. Still, the more she thought of sweet Sidony and sturdy, honest William together, the more the idea appealed to her. "No, I wouldn't," she said more forcefully. "Because I know you both to be good and decent people who would never take advantage of another, never betray anyone's trust. If I heard you were together . . . I would be glad for you. I would think, how grand that these two friends of mine have found each other. And I would wish you happiness."

When she smiled, Sidony's small, piquant face lit up like sunshine on a daisy. She reached impulsively for Rachel's hand and squeezed it. "Oh, ma'am. Oh, that's—I think it's just what I wanted to hear. Thank you. For listening to me rattle on, and for saying such a kind thing."

"There's nothing to thank me for." She'd have said more, but Sidony was backing away from her with a little dance step, looking like an excited pixie.

"I know where he is—in the stables wi' Collie. I'll go talk to him right now."

"Well, if you think you should—"

"Oh, now's the time, while I got my courage up! Don't worry," she called from the end of the bridge, "I'll go slow and careful. I wouldn't want to scare 'im to death!" With a wave, she whirled, gathered up her skirts, and dashed for the stables.

In a thoughtful mood, smiling to herself, Rachel began to stroll along the thin path that edged the far side of the riverbank. As unexpected as it was, the conversation with Sidony had cheered her. How lovely, really, if William and the dairy maid could find a little happiness together. But what a surprise! And how unpredictable life could be! Something else she'd acquired from ten years in prison was an inability to believe, *really* believe in the possibility of change—which must, she thought, be the very definition of despondency. But change was not only possible, it was constant—great, weighty, life-altering changes occurring all the time, not to mention the slighter, less dramatic changes you barely noticed. Her own circumstances proved it. The difference between the woman she'd become and the one she'd been four months ago was the difference between light and dark, hope and no hope. And for good or ill, regardless of whether it could last or not, she owed the change to Sebastian.

Lost in her thoughts, she saw that she'd wandered out of sight of the house. She had no watch, but by the August sky she reckoned it was about eleven o'clock. Time for her meeting with Monsieur Judelet. They met every morning to talk about the day's menu; or rather, she listened while he talked. She picked up her skirts and hurried back toward the Hall.

Cory, one of the stable lads, was loitering in the courtyard, holding the reins of two horses, one a swaybacked pony with a half-eaten tail. She recognized it; it belonged to Constable Burdy. She hadn't seen him in weeks. What would he be doing here? She crossed the courtyard uncertainly. As she approached the steps, Burdy and another man came backing out the door to the Hall; she had to sidestep smartly to get out of their way. She started when she recognized the second man. It was Chief Constable Lewes, the policeman she'd had to report to once a month in Tavistock.

The cause of his and Burdy's clumsy haste was Sebastian, who was bearing down on them like a baited bull. His voice preceded his black, angry countenance. "It's a mistake, I'm telling you. Even if it weren't, she's in my custody. It's not as if she's plotting an escape, for God's—" He stopped short when he saw her.

She came closer. "What's the matter? What's happened?"

Lewes was a stout, red-faced roman with small, black, unkind eyes. She'd disliked him on sight, and hadn't changed her opinion over the course of their acquaintance; the combination of callousness and stupidity with which he went about his job reminded her of almost every prison guard she'd ever known. "Mrs. Wade," he exclaimed, rounding on her. She stepped back involuntarily, but he closed the gap and stood over her. "Mrs. Wade, I've got here a warrant for your arrest."

She felt the blood drain from her face. Throwing a panicky glance at Sebastian, she asked, "Why?"

"On account of you violated the conditions of your release."

"No, no, I didn't."

"Where were you on Friday, then, and the last three Wednesdays running? And where's the pound and ten shillings you owes the Crown for your fine?"

She stared at him. "But I don't have to do that anymore!" She realized she was shaking. "My ticket of leave was remitted. I have a letter."

"What letter?"

"From the Home Secretary. It came—"

"If you got a letter from the Home Secretary, the sheriff would've got one, too," he said stolidly. "I'd've seen it, and so would Burdy. Nobody in the county knows nothing about a letter."

Sebastian stepped in front of her, and his tall, hard body blocking the constable steadied her a little. "If Mrs. Wade says she received a letter, then she received it. I wouldn't advise you to call my housekeeper a liar."

"Nobody's calling nobody a liar, my lord," Lewes said quickly, his ruddy cheeks turning redder. Beside him, Burdy seemed to get a little smaller. "I got this warrant for the woman, which I duly drew up on account of Mrs. Wade not abiding by the conditions of her release. Mayor Vanstone signed it," he added, jabbing the air with a folded piece of paper. "If there's a remittal letter, I'd like to see it, because otherwise it's my duty to execute this warrant."

"I'll get it," Rachel said before Sebastian could speak. She raced up the steps, leaving the three men in the courtyard.

It was silly to run, but she couldn't help it; by the time she reached her room she was out of breath and panting. She flung the door open wide and strode to her desk, jerked out the middle drawer. She kept her personal papers under the accounts ledger—not that she had that many, just her original release document and the two letters her brother had written to her years ago from Canada. And the Home Secretary's letter.

It wasn't there.

She searched again, feeling her palms dampen with perspiration. The two side drawers were for pens, pencils, stamps and envelopes, bills and receipts. She searched them anyway.

Not there.

She kept the housekeeping money in a strongbox. Her fingers trembled while she fitted the key into the lock—because she knew the letter couldn't be in there.

It wasn't.

Her mind went dangerously blank. She hated the tight, icy feeling under her breastbone, the chill vise of fear. They couldn't arrest her again; Sebastian wouldn't let them. He was a magistrate—he was a viscount! Anyway, the letter must be here, there was no place else it could be. She started her search over again, and when it was as futile as the first time, she widened it to her bedroom—the drawer in the little table beside her bed.

Nothing.

She made herself walk slowly back down the hall, calming herself with deep breaths. Outside, Sebastian and the two constables looked grim, as if they hadn't exchanged a single word since she'd left. They turned when they heard her in the doorway. Girding herself, she told them the news.

"I can't find the letter. It isn't where I put it."

Sebastian's mouth hardened; she couldn't tell what he was thinking. She needed to touch him—but of course she couldn't. Lewes, whose job was to take her into custody now, looked at once self-important and uncomfortable, as if the hazards involved in arresting Lord D'Aubrey's mistress were just occurring to him. "Well, now," he said uneasily. "In that case, it appears I've got no—"

Sebastian bit out a curse, turning his back on him. "Don't worry," he commanded softly. He took both of her hands and squeezed them. "Stay here." Then he pivoted, took Lewes by the elbow, and led him off a few paces to the center of the sunny courtyard. Burdy followed. She couldn't hear the words, only the low, fierce, implacable tone of Sebastian's voice. And for the first time since she'd seen Burdy's pony, she relaxed, because she knew she was safe. For now.

Without surprise, she watched the policemen nod one last time and walk off to their waiting horses. As they trotted through the archway, Sebastian said something to Cory, and the stableboy ran out after them, then turned and made a dash for the stables.

No privacy here. She wanted to run into Sebastian's arms and hold him until the helpless shaking subsided. She couldn't, of course; someone might see. So she kept her hands to herself when he approached her, and her voice low to ask him, "What can it mean? What will happen? The letter was there, and now it's *gone*."

Without speaking, he took her hand and pulled her up the steps and through the door, and in the dark, cool hallway he embraced her. "It's all right," he told her, and she tried to believe it. She was moved because he understood her fear without her having to explain it, but the only comfort came from the strong clutch of his arms around her. She pressed against him, fortifying herself.

Finally he let her go. "I've got to ride to Captain Carnock's. He'll sign a writ with me to delay this nonsense. Whatever Vanstone's up to, it's not going to work."

"The mayor? What do you mean? Why would he want to hurt me?"

"I don't know. I may be wrong, but I think something's rotten here. When I get back from Rye, I'll find out what it is. In the mean—"

"Rye? You're going home again?" Panic fluttered again.

He passed a hand over his eyes. "I didn't have a chance to tell you. While you were out this morning, a messenger came. My father's dead."

"Oh, *no*."

"It's only what we've been expecting."

"I know, but . . ." She touched his cheek. His eyes were downcast; she couldn't read his expression. "I'm so sorry. I know you weren't close to him, but still . . . it must mean something."

His smile was only a tightening of the lips. "It must," he said in an odd voice. "Rachel, there's very little time. I'll take care of this business with Carnock now. While I'm gone, will you pack a bag for me? I'll have to take the coach to Plymouth to catch the evening train for Exeter. Try not to worry—nothing will happen until I come back. You're perfectly safe. They won't touch you as long as you're in my custody." She nodded, hoping it was true.

But he must have seen doubt in her eyes because he gathered her close, murmuring, "Don't be afraid. I promise you, it's not starting over."

As soon as he said it, the panic overflowed. "But what if it is? Oh, God. I won't be able to bear it."

"Shh—"

"I won't. You don't know, you don't know! If they lock me up again—"

"They're not going to do that."

"But if they do—if they do, I'll find a way—*I will not let it happen again*—"

"Stop it. Stop." He gave her an urgent shake and brought his face down to hers. "You trust me, don't you?"

"Yes."

"Then believe me. I won't let them touch you. I will not." His big hands held her shoulders. "You're safe. Do you believe it?" She nodded, but he wanted the words. "Say it. Do you believe I'll protect you?"

"Yes."

They held on to each other for another minute. She wanted to tell him she loved him, had never needed to say it more. But she held back, because she was afraid. And because he already knew it. He must.

The clop of horseshoes in the courtyard finally parted them. Sebastian cupped her face between his hands and kissed her hard. "I'll be back in one hour. Pack a bag for me, or let Preest do it if you—"

"I will." It was hard to let him go; she kept his hand to the last second. As soon as he was out of her sight, all the dread came back.

She didn't stay to watch him ride off. She hurried through the house and went up to his room, intent on closing her mind to everything except the one task he'd given her. Preest was nowhere about, and she was glad; she couldn't have spoken to anyone. She found Sebastian's traveling case in his dressing room and began to put clothes into it. How long would he stay in Rye? Would he need two trunks? Three? She filled his case with shirts, trousers, waistcoats, cravats, jewelry, combs, handkerchiefs, two of his best black suits. When she ran out of room, she went to the storeroom on the third floor, found two more cases, brought them back, and filled them with more clothes. She thought of going for a fourth trunk when the reality of what she was doing suddenly hit her. She had a vision of his face when he saw what she'd done, and she laughed—then clapped her hand over her mouth, frightened by the manic sound of her voice.

In the bathroom, she ran cold water over her hands and wrists, staring at her white-faced reflection in the mirror. She couldn't disguise the fear; it lurked in her eyes, desperate as a cornered animal. *"Stop it,"* she said aloud, echoing Sebastian's command. This terror was crazy. A mistake had been made, that was all, and soon it would be rectified. She'd done nothing wrong, she wasn't guilty, she—

She whirled away from the mirror, hands dripping water, feeling drenched with dread. She'd been innocent before, but that hadn't saved her. A premonition of disaster made her shudder. How stupid to believe the nightmare was over—it would never be over! Sebastian couldn't help her, nobody could. Blind, she made her way into the bedroom and sank down on his bed, winding her arms around her knees.

"Stop, stop, stop," she begged, muffling the plea into her skirts. Had she *dreamed* the letter? Why hadn't she shown it to someone? No one had seen it but her, and now it was gone. Had somebody taken it? *Why?*

She lay in a tight ball of misery, alternating between despair and false confidence that everything would be all right, that Sebastian would return and tell her he'd made the nightmare go away. The room dimmed as afternoon shadows lengthened, darkened. At last she heard the sound of hooves on the stones below.

His horse was lathered and winded. He jumped from its back and handed the reins to Cory, speaking to him in a voice too low for her to hear. She couldn't tell from his face what he was thinking.

She put her hands on her hot cheeks, wishing she'd thought to wash her face, comb her hair—he would worry if he saw her like this. No time. She hurried out of the room to find him.

Sebastian had his foot on the first step when he saw her, rounding the curve in the staircase above him, holding her skirts in one hand and the bannister in the other. Her face told him everything. He waited for her to come to him, and at the moment she reached him he took her in his arms. She was brittle with fear; he held her gently, half afraid she would crack. "It's all right, Rachel, everything's all right. I've arranged it with Carnock. You're safe."

She murmured something, a low, fervent, inarticulate thanks, sagging a little.

Someone was coming down the corridor toward them. The formal drawing room was closest; he took her hand and pulled her inside, and closed the door behind them. But he'd no sooner embraced her again when a knock sounded at the door.

It was Susan. "My lord," she said, looking embarrassed—she must have seen them in the hall—"Reverend Morrell's here to see you."

"God rot it," Sebastian muttered.

"I'll go," said Rachel.

"No, stay." To the maid he said shortly, "Show him in," and she curtsied herself out.

"Sebastian, I should go."

"Why? Stay, Rachel, I want you here." He touched her hand, and his reward was her slight smile.

Christy Morrell's inopportune visit would have rankled if Sebastian hadn't liked him so much. As it was, he greeted the vicar amiably and accepted his gentle sympathies in good part, unsurprised by now that news of the old earl's death had reached his ears so quickly. Christy spoke kindly to Rachel, and if her presence at Sebastian's side surprised him, he didn't show it.

"So, my lord, you'll go to Sussex for the funeral?" he asked, accepting a glass of claret Sebastian poured out himself.

"Yes, I'll be leaving this evening. In about an hour, actually. No, it's all right," he protested when the vicar looked apologetic and set his glass down untouched.

"No, I've come at a bad time. I didn't realize you'd have to go immediately." He reached for his hat, which he'd set on a chair, and for half a minute he massaged the crown between his long fingers, looking as if he had more to say. He sent Rachel a level glance. "I've heard about the constables' visit," he said at last. "That they tried to arrest you, I mean."

"The devil you have," Sebastian exclaimed before Rachel could speak. "*How* did you hear of it? It only happened this afternoon."

"Not much stays a secret for long in Wyckerley," Christy said with a slight, apologetic smile.

Rachel had stepped away a little, distancing herself from them; she was squeezing her hands into fists at her sides, a subdued sign of distress Sebastian knew well. Going to her, he took one of her hands by force, pressing it flat between both of his, not giving a damn what the minister thought. He said, "Well, then you might as well know I've convinced Carnock to sign a writ countermanding Vanstone's warrant. They're saying she violated the conditions of her parole, but it's a lie. If you want my opinion, the mayor's up to something."

"Vanstone? Oh, I doubt that," Christy said seriously. "He's not an easy man, and I know he can be hardheaded, but upholding the law means everything to him. I've never known him to do anything remotely dishonest."

Sebastian grunted, unconvinced. Something was wrong with this whole business, but he didn't confide in the vicar his true suspicions. "Carnock's agreed to delay any proceedings against Rachel until I return. So she's safe. For now."

"Are you worried that they'll try to arrest her again?"

No point in minimizing the danger; Rachel knew the risk as well as he did. "I think there's a chance, yes. If she can't show them a remittal letter, she'll be in trouble. They'll call her a liar. I can delay the consequences, but I don't think . . ." He realized his candor had gone too far: Rachel's hand felt like a claw in his and her face had lost all color.

Christy looked between them for a long moment, his sympathetic eyes measuring. "Forgive me," he said softly. "I can think of a way you could protect Mrs. Wade."

"How?"

He smiled. "You could marry her."

Sebastian didn't move, even though it felt as if an explosion had gone off in his chest. "*Marry* her." He forced a hearty laugh, stunned, and too shocked to think of anything clever to answer. "*Marry* her," he repeated, stalling, filling his voice with wonder and amusement. He dropped Rachel's hand and faced her, willing her to smile with him. "Why, what an extraordinary idea. Really, Vicar, you amaze me."

"I beg your pardon." The minister was blushing, realizing he'd blundered. "I thought—it occurred to me that you might see that as a solution. Excuse me. It's just that, even if the mayor were up to something, as you suggest—which I doubt, my lord—I think he would lose his enthusiasm at the prospect of reimprisoning the wife of the Earl of Moreton. But I misspoke, I . . . misread the situation. I do beg your pardon."

"Not at all," Sebastian said meaninglessly. His mind had gone

299

blank. When he glanced at Rachel, he saw her staring at him with a weird fixity, a red spot glowing dully in each cheek.

"If you need anything," Christy was saying to her, "help of any sort, I hope you won't hesitate to tell me, Mrs. Wade. Or my wife, if you should need a woman friend."

She murmured, "Thank you," and bowed her head.

"I'll see you to the door," Sebastian offered. His voice sounded stupid to him, foolishly light, almost jocular. Christy went out. Following, Sebastian stopped in the threshold and turned back to say quietly, "Wait for me," to Rachel. Her colorless eyes were impenetrable. The first inkling of what he'd done began to seep in, like a cold rain down the back of his neck.

Christy's horse was tied in the courtyard. Walking down the long passage to the door, he broke an awkward silence to say, "I apologize again if I've offended you. I can see I made a mistake."

"No, no, you haven't offended me." Sebastian forced a chuckle. "Embarrased the hell out of me, perhaps, but . . ." He trailed off. Another joke gone flat. He ran a distracted hand through his hair, and finally said something true. "I don't know what I'm going to do about Rachel, Christy. I wish I did."

"Maybe it will come to you when you're in Rye," he said kindly.

"Maybe."

When they arrived at the courtyard door, the vicar said, "Did you know that Lydia Wade's aunt died last night?"

"Mrs. Armstrong? No. I'm sorry to hear that. I knew she was ill. What will become of her niece?"

"That," said Christy, frowning, "is a very good question."

After he left, Sebastian hurried back to the drawing room, but Rachel was gone. She had chores, duties; a servant could have come for her to solve some household dilemma. Otherwise she'd have waited for him. Of course she would have. They had things to talk about, Carnock's compromise, his trip to Rye, her—

"My lord?"

"What is it, Preest?"

"My lord, I've been informed by the maid that a light repast awaits you in the dining room, and by the groom that the carriage will be ready in the courtyard in exactly half an hour."

"Yes, all right." He glanced at his watch. "Am I packed?"

"Yes, my lord."

"Where's Mrs. Wade?"

"I believe she's in her room, my lord."

In her room. That meant nothing; she could have gone there for any number of reasons. "Go and get her, will you? I have to change clothes. Ask her to join me in the dining room in ten minutes."

"Very good, my lord."

Fifteen minutes later, he was sitting in his place at the table, debating whether to begin eating or wait a little longer. He sipped his wine; it tasted bitter, he could hardly swallow it. Five more minutes passed. He said to the maid serving him his soup, "Clara, leave that and go and fetch Mrs. Wade, will you? I think she's in her room."

He could have gone himself, but it seemed important to stay where he was, do nothing out of the ordinary. Take no initiative. Everything was fine.

Clara came back round-eyed. "Oh, sir," she blurted.

"Well?"

"Mrs. Wade says she's not coming."

"What?"

"She says she's not coming. She says—she says—"

"*What?*"

"She says to tell you to go hang!"

They stared at each other in utter astonishment, until Sebastian's wits came back and he had the presence of mind to send the girl away. Alone, he stared blankly at his soup for ten more seconds. Then he threw down his napkin and stood up.

He'd gotten to the doorway when they nearly collided. He started to laugh with relief. "There you are. Rachel, what—"

"I changed my mind." She kept moving; he had to walk backward to get out of her way. She went to the head of the table and stood beside his chair, as if waiting for him to resume it. Something told him it would be safer to keep his distance.

He leaned his hip against the edge of the table, twelve feet away, and folded his arms. He couldn't take his eyes off her face, which had an expression he'd never seen before. It wasn't only angry—although it certainly was that, finely, superbly angry, her cheeks blazing crimson, her eyes shooting sparks of ire. But something else tempered the anger, dampening any satisfaction he might have taken in it. With a sinking feeling, he realized the other quality was disillusionment.

"What's the matter?"

Her eyes narrowed on him in disbelief. "Do you have no idea? Not a single clue?"

"Why don't you—"

"I'll tell you what's the matter. You laughed at me." He started to deny it, but she lifted her fist and smacked it down on the table. "You *laughed*." Dishes rattled; a glass toppled, sloshing water onto his plate. *"Damn you."*

"Calm yourself. I wasn't laughing *at*—"

"I don't even want to marry you! *I will not be laughed at.*"

He could have kept on insisting she'd mistaken him, missed the point, taken it wrong—but the depth of the hurt he'd caused her wasn't to be denied. "I'm sorry," he said quietly, "I wish I could take that back. It was stupid and I regret it. You deserve much, much better. I swear it will never happen again."

He could have saved his breath, or given his apology to the wall. She sneered at him, and folded her own arms as if she were mimicking him. "No, you're right, it won't, because I won't be here. And I'm *glad* it happened, because for the first time since we met, Sebastian, I'm seeing you clearly."

He might have been alarmed, but her voice broke when she said his name, and her eyes glistened. He pushed away from the table. "Rachel. Listen to me."

She held up her hands, warning him away. "There's nothing you can say, nothing you're capable of saying that will mean anything to me."

"What do you want? Just tell me what you want."

"If you think this is about marriage, you're mistaken!"

"Then what is it about?"

She looked incredulous. "How can you ask me that?"

"How can I *answer* if you won't—"

"How could you not know?" She raised her voice, as if speaking to a deaf person. "I understand why you won't have me; you're a viscount and I'm a convict. But once you said you loved me—were falling in love with me."

"I—I—" He couldn't finish.

Disgust turned her eyes a frigid shade of gray. "I feel sorry for you. I do, because you're a coward. You laughed at me, and I can't forgive you for that."

He stared at her. "This is what you can't forgive me for? *This?* After everything else I've—"

"I gave you credit for decency and human feelings, a heart. But you've only been using me in some kind of—*experiment*. 'What an extraordinary idea,' you said. 'Really, Vicar, you amaze me!' "

"Rachel—"

"You make me feel cheap! You wanted to change me, and you have—but you don't even have the courage to see it through, or the decency to take responsibility for what you've done to me. *'What an extraordinary idea,'* " she said again, mocking him.

"There's something missing in you, Sebastian! I feel pity for you!"

He clenched his jaws, but anger wouldn't come to his rescue. "I thought you were happy," he tried in a reasonable voice. "You told me you were. You seemed to be."

"I am happy," she said grimly, "and it has nothing to do with you."

"That's good. I'm glad." He was anything but glad. He remembered the day he'd vowed to "resurrect" her, bring her back from the dead. He found it beyond ironic that he'd succeeded so well, she wanted to leave him now. He'd wanted her independent, but not *this* independent.

"I can't stay here," she was saying. "I could fool myself before that you felt something for me, but not anymore."

"What the hell are you talking about? How could you possibly think I don't feel something for you!"

At that moment Preest poked his head in the doorway. "The carriage is waiting, my lord," he said tonelessly, and vanished.

Sebastian closed the gap between himself and Rachel. "I have to go," he said, reaching for her stiff hand.

"How *convenient*."

"Rachel, I have a *train* to catch." He put a wounded note in his voice; he felt he'd finally caught her on lower moral ground, and he'd better take advantage of it. "My father's dead; I've got to go to my family."

"Oh, of course—the family you hold so dear to your heart— the father who meant so much to you. Go, Sebastian, no one's stopping you!"

He ground his teeth. "I don't have time to talk about this. You can't leave, and you know it."

"Why not? I could be someone's legitimate housekeeper. I'm grateful to you for that, at least—for making respectability mean something to me again."

"Will you listen? I'm sorry I hurt you. I wish I could take it back."

"I don't. You've opened my eyes." But the tears were back, mocking her bravado, and he was torn between compassion for her and gladness, because she didn't mean what she was saying.

"I'm sorry. We'll fix it," he promised, trying to pull her into his arms. "When I come back, we'll talk about everything. Some of the things you said—I can't deny them. But we can make it right. At least give me a chance to do better. You've taken me un-awares—give me a little time to think about the things you've said. That's fair, isn't it?" She turned her face away. "You can't leave me. Say you won't, Rachel. Come, say it."

She took a deep, quavery breath. "I don't know," she said miserably. "I don't know what I'll do."

He closed his eyes in relief, resting his forehead against her temple. She wouldn't leave him. "I'll miss you," he told her, holding her narrow shoulders when she would've broken away. "I'll come back as soon as I can. Sweetheart, won't you kiss me good-bye?"

"No."

They sighed in unison. "Let me kiss you, then." She craned away, but he held her and put his lips on her cheek. Her body was both stiff and yielding, ambivalent. That was the best he could hope for—but God, how he wanted her arms around him now. "You'll wait for me, won't you?" he asked again, holding her, pressing a kiss to the corner of her mouth.

"I don't know."

A thought occurred to him. "You have to stay—you're in my legal custody now. That's how I got Carnock to agree to a post-ponement of your arrest." She didn't answer, and finally he had to let her go. "Damn the train," he muttered, trying to make her smile; he'd have settled for a rueful smile, even a bitter one, but she wouldn't even look at him.

At the door, he glanced back. She was staring down at the hand she had gripped around the back of his chair, her eyes narrowed, her beautiful face taut. She seemed to be listening, not to the sound of his leave-taking but to something else. A voice in her own head, perhaps—probably the one telling her to go. A precarious second passed. The words that would have kept her for certain wavered on the tip of his tongue, but he didn't speak them. Couldn't. Instead he said, "Wait for me."

She didn't look up.

XIX

I OUGHT TO *feel something.*

But he didn't, even leaning over the open casket and staring intently into the Earl of Moreton's lifeless face. The rigid features were sallow, not pale, and too sharp, as if the corpse were a soapstone carving. Sebastian searched for something of himself in the still countenance, but there was nothing. In death as in life, father and son were strangers to each other.

Nothing? Really? What about that tight, unyielding look about the mouth? That looked familiar. Stubbornness, he supposed. Or maybe just a gritting of the teeth, a habit acquired from a determination to get through this business of life without feeling anything. If that had been the late Lord Moreton's goal, he'd succeeded admirably. *He never knew his son,* might be his epitaph. *And they both preferred it that way.*

Sebastian straightened, stepped back. He hadn't been that physically close to his father since . . . since ever. Every few years they ran into each other and shook hands. That was all. He had no memories of sitting on Dad's knee, being carried in Papa's arms; the idea seemed ludicrous, in fact, almost obscene.

The family chapel at Steyne Court was much grander than the one at Lynton, but exactly as musty and unused. Ashe, the parish priest, sat in a corner of the front pew, either praying or sleeping. What he was doing here at all Sebastian couldn't imagine, unless he hoped to ingratiate himself with the new earl, a feat he'd never managed with the old one.

Not that that was necessarily Ashe's fault. The old man lying in the mahogany coffin hadn't been one to socialize much with parish priests. An unintelligent man, oblivious, chronically unfaithful, Lord Moreton had had few passions in his life, although he'd filled it with desultory vices like gaming, drinking, and whoring. His dull days had occasionally lit up with flashes of spectacular decadence, but not often or brilliantly enough to lift him out of his own overwhelming mediocrity. Sebastian had never felt singled out by his neglect, since he'd neglected his wife and daughter equally, as well as his friends, acquaintances, tenants, and employees. If he'd been born a commoner, he'd have perished early on from the combined effects of stupidity, torpidity, and unimaginativeness.

"So much for you, Father," Sebastian said softly. He put his hand on the raised coffin lid. "I wish it could have been otherwise." As soon as he said it, an emotion finally entered his heart. It was grief, of a sort, not for the man but for the love they'd never felt for each other. For the gaping void of indifference they'd shared in place of friendship or affection. If there was blame to cast, Sebastian kept plenty for himself. "Good-bye," he whispered, and closed the lid of the casket with a final-sounding thud.

Reverend Ashe must have been listening for it. He sprang from his pew and advanced on the new heir with unseemly haste. He had long, luxuriant, yellow-white hair, a glossy mustache, and a monocle dangling by a silk ribbon on his chest. The ruby glinting on his smallest finger looked incongruous with his clerical collar. Christian Morrell wore simpler clothes, Sebastian reflected, and not only because St. Giles was a poor parish. He was a simpler man.

"Again, allow me to tender my most sincere sympathies, my lord, for your terrible loss. His lordship was a good man, a great man, respected by all who knew him. He will be sorely missed."

"Do you think so?" Once he'd have tweaked the reverend for this patent nonsense, labeled him a toady and a hypocrite, and done his best to embarrass him. He was an obsequious fool—but there were worse sins, and Sebastian had committed most of them himself.

"Oh, undoubtedly. I'm certain the funeral tomorrow will be well attended by your father's innumerable friends and loved ones."

"I suppose anything is possible," Sebastian conceded gravely. "Now, I won't keep you any longer; I'm sure you'd like to be at home, Reverend, working on your eulogy."

Reverend Ashe looked as though that thought hadn't occurred to him. But he recovered quickly and said, "Yes, of course, how kind of you, my lord, I will be running along. That is, unless you require my services, as it were, in a personal way before I go?"

"I beg your pardon?"

"If you would like to pray with me, or if you were moved to speak of your feelings on your father's passing—"

"Ah! No, no, thank you very much indeed." He turned away rather than grin in the minister's face.

They walked to the chapel door together and shook hands on the small porch. Reverend Ashe climbed into a smart green landau while his driver held the door for him. Sebastian thought of Christy again, and the chestnut gelding he rode in all weathers to visit the sheep in his humbler flock.

Across the park and the fountain pond, the massive stone pile of Steyne Court rose, its two mammoth wings spread out from the noble center more in the manner of barriers than welcoming arms. The house had been a sturdy, sensible Georgian mansion—he knew this from pictures—until his mother, newly married and flush with the power of sudden riches, had decided to have it rebuilt in the style of a French château. Now it boasted turrets and towers, battlements and balustrades, and fourteen separate chimneys vying for air space among the dormers, buttresses, corbels and cornices. It looked like a Parisian duc's summer residence, or Cardinal Richelieu's, and it was as out of place in rural Sussex as a tiara in a root barn, and about as useful. It had embarrassed him in his youth; later it amused him; now it irritated him, because the cost of maintaining the aberrant monstrosity had just shifted from his father to himself.

Inside, he found his mother in her second favorite place, supine on a Louis Quinze chaise longue in the tower drawing room. (Her favorite was in bed in her lavish boudoir, from which she rarely rose before three or four in the afternoon.) She was, as always, impeccably coifed, her stunning silver hair upswept and gleaming. And why not? She employed a hairdresser full-time; a Mrs. Peabody—she lived on the premises in a private suite, and traveled with her ladyship wherever she went.

At present her ladyship was either dozing or writing a letter, or possibly both at once, and the recipient of the letter would undoubtedly be one of her lovers. Sebastian wondered sometimes why his parents hadn't been happier together or liked each other better; they ought to have, considering how much they had in common. Lady Moreton was just as faithless as her husband, and only differed from him in that regard because she incorporated a soupçon of discretion into the conduct of her numerous love affairs. Sebastian had been fifteen when he'd discovered for certain that she was promiscuous, on the morning he'd walked into the stables and found her in a compromising attitude with not one but two undergrooms on the straw floor of a loose-box stall. He'd countered the shock by immediately seducing the housemaid, and after that, as many women as time and circumstances allowed, a habit he'd maintained steadfastly ever since.

Until Rachel.

"Is it dinnertime?"

The languid inquiry came from the window seat, where his

sister was slumped, drowsy-eyed, over a game of solitaire. That was industrious for her; normally she did nothing at all in her idle hours—which was most of them; the notion of Irene mending, sketching, or—ha—reading a book was quite unthinkable.

"Not that I know of," Sebastian drawled, whereupon his sister instantly lost interest in him and went back to her game.

He walked to the drinks table and poured a small glass of neat whiskey. Sipping it, he regarded his mother and sister, neither of whom seemed aware of his presence any longer, or indeed, of each other's. It was easy to imagine them sitting in this room for hours without exchanging a word. Sebastian had been home for half a day, and so far his mother had exchanged about five sentences with him. What an odd family they were—he supposed; since he'd known no other, he could only take it on faith that in other people's families people talked and listened to each other, laughed, cried, shouted, made up. Loved. He thought of the evenings he'd spent in Rachel's company—the public hours, not the ones in his bedroom. She liked to listen to him play the piano, and he liked to look at her face when she did. She would put her head back against the sofa and close her eyes, and presently a sweet smile would soften her straight, solemn mouth. Other times, she would read to him from her current book, and the rich, low, expressive sound of her voice was as sensually satisfying to him as piano music was to her. He'd taken those quiet, contented hours for granted, and now he missed them. Missed her.

"Where's Harry? Where are the children?"

Irene lifted her dark, sleek head and blinked at him. "Harry? He's at home, of course. With the children. Why would they be here?"

Sebastian shrugged. Why indeed? Irene was no more motherly than her own mother. If he asked her quickly and caught her off guard, he doubted if she could tell him how many children she had. Four, he thought, but possibly it was five by now. She was three years older than he. When he was twenty, he'd brought an Oxford chum home for Christmas holiday, and found him in bed with Irene on Boxing Day morning. "Join us?" she'd asked, stroking a bare breast to entice him. He'd declined the invitation politely. But from then on he'd had her measure.

Clearly, sexual licentiousness ran in the family, and Sebastian had spent the last decade or so trying to live up to his heritage. It occurred to him, not for the first time but more forcefully than ever before, that they might all fly to the arms of their illicit lovers in search of warmth, some human touch, a little companionship, commodities not noticeably abundant at home. Or was that only a rationale for cupidity?

The sun was setting over the Doric columns of the summer house at the edge of the deer park. He walked to the window to watch its slow descent. Lynton Hall had a derelict pavilion east of the house, no match for Steyne's pretentious "belvedere." Rachel had found the new dairymaid there one night, she'd told him, sleeping outside instead of in the house because she hated enclosed spaces. Sidony, her name was; her father had beaten and abused her. Here at Steyne, servants were faceless, nameless, interchangeable; if they had stories to tell, no one above-stairs ever heard them.

A sudden and unexpected wave of longing washed over him. In its wake he realized what it was: homesickness.

"Mother, what's your purpose in life?"

Lady Moreton turned her head in slow, increasingly incredulous degrees, while the pen in her hand made a spreading ink blot on her love letter. "My what?"

"You know, your reason for existing. Your raison d'être. You've heard of the concept, I'm sure."

Her handsome eyebrows arched disdainfully. "What an unpleasant person you've grown into, Sebastian."

"Yes, quite. But back to the question."

"Don't be impudent."

"Impudent?"

"Don't be an ass," Irene clarified, rousing herself to a sitting position.

He turned to her interestedly. "What's your purpose, Irene?"

She looked at him for a full ten seconds, her brows drawn together in ferocious thought. He saw the emptiness in her eyes before they could skitter away in pique. "What's yours?" she retaliated unkindly.

"I think it's to use the few talents I've been given to try to do something good in my small corner of the cosmos. And to be happy without hurting any more people than absolutely necessary."

Modest, even banal goals, but it was as if he'd said he wanted to become a vegetarian Buddhist monk. The family resemblance was remarkable when mother and daughter lifted identically elegant top lips and sneered at him, unanimous in their contempt. They might be in league against him for the moment, but only because it was convenient; usually they couldn't stand each other.

No question about it, his family was peculiar. Beyond eccentric; perverse. "Motherly love" was a given in other people's houses, but not this one, where her ladyship loved no one but herself, and had passed the proclivity on to her daughter. To her son, too, although lately he'd risen above it. There was someone now he cared for more than himself.

The butler came in then to announce dinner. During the brief, largely silent meal, no more was said about life goals, his or anyone else's.

Lord Moreton's funeral the next morning wasn't nearly as well attended as Reverend Ashe had prophesied, and all the mourners were dry-eyed. The widow couldn't be bothered to extend any hospitality to them afterward; they dispersed from the church (no one except Sebastian stayed for the interment) like aimless sheep, probably asking themselves why they'd come, since they hadn't gotten so much as a glass of sherry for their trouble.

In the afternoon, the lawyers read the will. There were no surprises: Sebastian inherited everything.

At a meeting with Sewell, his father's land agent, investment advisor, and the closest thing he'd had to a friend, Sebastian learned that "everything" was a sizable fortune. For such an irresponsible man, Lord Moreton had run up remarkably few debts, a testament to the business acumen of Mr. Sewell, Sebastian suspected, as much as to the magnitude of the Verlaine family fortune.

One of his lordship's few passions in life had been the petty one of keeping his family on a short financial leash, reveling in their bitterness and complaints. His wife and daughter had constantly badgered him for more money, bigger allowances, a larger dowry. But Sebastian couldn't stand giving him the satisfaction and had kept silent, living within his means, which by any objective standard were considerable. Now it was all his, the title, the houses, the farm estate, the investments, and all the capital.

Sewell was a smooth, sleek, well-spoken man who had grown wealthy in his own right as the old earl's chief steward. Sebastian couldn't help wondering in what other ways he differed from his own bailiff, William Holyoake, who was burly and rough-edged—and honest to a fault.

Two days and three nights later, after poring over half a dozen years of books, records, accounts ledgers, and receipts, he thought he had the answer: honesty was the only quality the two men had in common.

It was a relief. The longer he stayed at Steyne Court, the less he wanted to do with it; the fact that he could leave the management of it in Sewell's capable hands without worrying made his probable abandonment of his ancestral home much easier to justify.

Then, too, try as he might, he couldn't picture Rachel here, ever, under any circumstances. The coldness, the formality, his family's shallow heartlessness—everything about Steyne was antithetical to her. "Perhaps I would do better as your London mistress," she had said once. But in truth, he could only see Rachel at Lynton, in the pretty village that had somehow become his home. Wyckerley was the only place that deserved her.

The night before he was to leave, he called his mother and sister into the drawing room and told them what he had decided to do. To his mother he gave Steyne Court and all its valuable contents; he gave his sister Belle Pre, the house in Surrey. The London town house he would keep for himself, although they were free to visit it whenever they liked, as long as he wasn't in residence at the time. In addition, he was settling a yearly sum on them, forty thousand pounds for his mother, sixty thousand for Irene—because she had a family—which they would have in perpetuity, to do with as they wished. He advised them to use the money wisely, since it was all they would get from him.

They grumbled a little for the sake of form, but he could tell they were pleased. They ought to be. Not only was it a generous settlement, a fortune compared to what they'd been able to squeeze out of the old man, it had the added advantage of making further contact among the three of them superfluous indefinitely, for any but the most extreme social circumstances—the funeral of the next one of them to die, for example. It was perfect.

As he was leaving the room, it occurred to his mother to ask him what he would do now, where he intended to live.

"I'll live at Lynton," he replied.

"Lynton!" the two women exclaimed in unison. They looked appalled. "But I've heard it's a dreadful place," his sister protested. "Falling down, depressing, no society whatsoever. How could you mean to live there, Sebastian?"

He might have answered glibly, but it was a fair question; six short months ago, he'd have been in sympathy with Irene's consternation. "I mean to live there as well as I can," he answered. "Between my own investments and Sewell's, plus what's left from the rents on Steyne Farm, I should think I'll live very well indeed." That made sense to them; they nodded knowingly until he added, "I can demolish a lot of derelict Lynton tenant cottages now and build new ones. There's a prototype steam thresher I've been wanting to try out on the estate, and a pen of about eighty big Romney Marsh ewes I've had my eye on for a time. Holyoake, my bailiff, has been after me to repair the oast house and make some renovations to the dairy parlor. We need a new barn for castrating the pigs, too," he confided. "Last spring they kicked the old one to pieces."

Neither his mother nor his sister could speak.

"Well, good night," he told them, and went up to bed.

The journey home was interminable. He was obliged to ride to Dover for a direct train to London, and then he had to change in Reading, in Bristol, and again in Exeter. The farther he traveled from Rye, the more remote and unreal his family problems began to seem. Rachel had never been far from his thoughts, but as the train labored through the Black Down Hills of Somerset and entered the wooded river glens of Devon, she began to obsess them.

He thought he understood now what had drawn him to her in the first place. He'd seen her as the opposite of himself, and he'd wanted her to save him. Simple as that. She'd stood in his mind for survival, because she'd been through hellfire and come out strong and whole, indestructible. What had he ever suffered? Except for a drunken duel or two, he'd never faced death or even danger; in all of his wasted, numbing, unmanning life he'd never stood up for any principle except libertarianism. His plan had been to use her, but personally risk nothing. Take, but not give. He'd felt a perverse delight in her helplessness, the condition he'd relied on in cold blood to have her.

But her helplessness had become intolerable to both of them. He'd come to want her willingly, not under duress. Had he ever had her willingly?

He couldn't even tell her he loved her. He'd said it once, on a kind of exhausted sigh after they'd made love. Even then, he'd equivocated: "I'm *falling* in love with you," he'd said, and when she couldn't respond, he'd regretted his impetuosity—his insanity, as it had seemed to him then—and never repeated it. On the night he'd left Lynton for Rye, she'd needed to hear those words as never before, and he couldn't say them. He wasn't *falling* in love any longer, he was passionately in love, which made the admission even riskier. She'd called him a coward that night, among other things. Was it true?

A dozen more hard questions came to him on the endless journey, but only one answer. The red clay hills and the long green valleys were bringing him home, and in a little while he would see her. Certainly they had differences. She wanted changes and he wanted everything to stay the same. "If you think this is about marriage, you're mistaken," she'd said, but he thought her angry disclaimer was disingenuous. She was a woman—of course she wanted marriage. Because he was a man (or was it because he was a Verlaine?) he saw marriage as the end of everything.

But they could work out their differences. This was a crisis, not a catastrophe, nothing they couldn't overcome. They'd compromise, talk things over and make concessions, the way adults did. The first thing he would do was tell her he loved her. In a few days things would go back to normal, and she'd wonder what had distressed her so much. And then he would have everything.

*   *   *

He arrived home in a driving rain. No one greeted him in the deserted yard except the dog, who went into a fit of joyful barking when the carriage rolled through the archway. "What happened to you?" Sebastian exclaimed, trying to keep the wet, muddy puppy at arm's length. "Been rolling in the pig sty, have you?" He wasn't exaggerating; Dandy was a mess, filthy and neglected-looking, as if he'd been outside for days. "I'm telling your mother. Want to come with me?" Leaving Preest with the luggage, he sprinted through the downpour into the house.

He smiled at himself as he hurried down the dark stone corridor toward Rachel's room. She probably wasn't even there, and here he was, grinning and disheveled, eager as a schoolboy coming to court his first girl. At the closed door he paused to slick back his wet hair and straighten his necktie. But before he could knock, Dandy pawed at the door, and it swung open.

Empty. *Damn.*

"Rachel?" he called, in case she was in the bedroom. He wasn't surprised when there was no answer; the suite had an echoing emptiness that told him no one was here. Disappointment felt like a light slap in the face, sobering him.

He stopped in the act of turning to go, aware suddenly that the sitting room really was *empty*—bare, without the objects and adornments he associated with Rachel; no flowers on the windowsill, no book open on her desk, no shawl across the back of her chair. His slow footsteps sounded too loud as he crossed to the bedroom and pushed that door wide open. The evidence was everywhere—pictures gone, bureau bare, wardrobe half empty— but it was the silence rushing in on him, heavy as a pall of smoke, that confirmed his worst dread. She'd left him.

He shouted a ferocious obscenity and kicked the door against the wall. In the violent draft of air, an envelope fluttered off the bedside table and slid across the floor. He snarled at it, toying with the idea of letting it stay there. He already knew what her bloody note would say; the only emotional defense she'd left him was to ignore it, ignore her, counter her rejection with a show of indifference. He kicked the door again, and went to pick up the envelope.

> *I didn't lie to you. You asked me to stay, and I said I didn't know what I would do. It's still true, because I can't think here. I'm going someplace. When I know what I should do, I'll write to you.*
>
> *Sebastian, I don't blame you for anything, not anymore. In a way, I'm glad for what you said to Reverend Morrell. It's opened my eyes, and it's helped me to understand that in so many ways I can't keep ignoring, I'm still my parents' child— middle-class and conventional, the last woman on earth you should have taken for a lover. I hope you think the exchange has been equal, that we have both . . . I don't know what word you would use. "Enjoyed" each other, "taken pleasure" with each other. You've given me much more than pleasure, but I re- gret nothing, truly, not even the pain.*
>
> *If you could've loved me, perhaps I wouldn't have these scruples. Indeed, I think I would not. But that's a singularly useless speculation now.*
>
> *I mustn't write any more, I wouldn't make myself clear. Leaving you, the only thing that gives me pause is the thought that you might need me when you come home, because your father's death may hurt you more than you think it will. But I can't stay. I daresay you aren't used to being the abandoned one. And—I think you will miss me. That's a bittersweet con- solation for me, I confess.*
>
> *I love you. My task now, my new job, will be to stop loving you.*
>
> *Rachel*

Outside, the rain had slowed to a filthy brown drizzle. Ignoring the puddles, Sebastian ran toward the stables, with no plan and nothing in his head except a need for movement, industry, action. A girl was hurrying toward him; under her dripping bonnet, he recognized the piquant features of Sidony Timms.

"Where's Holyoake?" he demanded, stopping in front of her.

"M'lord, he rode to the moot hall to see the hearing. About two hours past."

"What hearing?"

Her eyes went wide. "Don't you know?"

"Know what?" He took off his hat and smacked it against his thigh with impatience.

"Oh, sir, it's Mrs. Wade—she was took up in Plymouth four days ago. They said she was trying to escape on a ship! They've had 'er in the Boro prison ever since, even though William—"

"Are you telling me she's in *gaol*?"

She nodded fearfully. "Today was 'er trial. They brought 'er up from Plymouth in a van. William went along to see if there were anything he could do. He sent you a letter, m'lord! He tried to tell you—"

He was sprinting for the stables; he didn't hear the rest. Panic and the need for haste made him clumsy. He spooked his fast stallion with rough handling, had to waste precious seconds calming him before he could get the bit in his mouth. Bareback, he cantered out of the stables like a madman.

In the lane, rain slashed his face and wind whistled in his ears. Over the roar of fear and the elements, he kept hearing the low, determined sound of Rachel's voice, the night she'd confided to him her grimmest secret: "If they ever tried to lock me up again, Sebastian, I couldn't bear it. I swear I would find a way to take my life!"

XX

Darkness. Even beyond her closed eyes, it was dark. *It's raining,*
Rachel remembered. And the remand cell had only one window,
dirty and high, the rain slithering down it in snaky rivulets. At
Dartmoor rain never touched her window, because it faced nothing but the prison's innards, its gray, institutional guts. This familiar room, dark and small and smelling of fear, was a step up,
then, because rain could slide down its one dirty window.

"Strum, Jonathan!"

She kept her eyes shut, didn't look up to see the third-to-last
prisoner stand and follow the constable out of the remand cell
into the moot hall. But before the door closed behind them, she
heard low voices and whispers, the hearing room in recess. Time
for the gawkers to tell one another what they thought of the last
prisoner's sentence, or credibility, or prospects next month at the
assize.

Would Burdy unlock the shackles on her wrists before he took
her into the courtroom? There was a chance, but she didn't count
on it. Didn't think about it. Didn't open her eyes, because she
couldn't bear to see her own clenched hands lying across her lap,
or the iron bands, rusty black, that covered her skin from the
base of her thumbs to the middle of her forearms. And she didn't
move, because she hated the sound; even more than the tiresome
pain of sharp iron on abraded skin, she hated the sound shack-
ling chain made when hands moved restlessly, thoughtlessly. She
didn't move at all, sat still on the smooth wooden bench, shoul-

ders hunched and eyes closed, and tried again to go back to the dark place.

She knew it well; she'd lived there for a long time, years ago. After she'd learned how to form the shell, the dark place had saved her. She'd learned how to be like an undersea mollusk, building the shell one slow grain of sand at a time, and when she finished she'd been flinty and impenetrable.

But she couldn't do it this time. She'd lost the knack, couldn't make herself blind and deaf anymore. Couldn't make herself invisible. She'd changed.

Sebastian's fault. How unkind of him to steal her best defense and leave her naked and soft-shelled, unprepared for her life's newest outrage.

She tried to concentrate on the worst thing that could happen. They wouldn't revoke her conditional release, not for only one month's delinquency. At most they would send her back to Dartmoor for a month or two. More likely they'd return her to the Tavistock gaol for a few weeks, to teach her a lesson.

That was all. Weeks, probably; months, possibly. What was that to her? Nothing. The blink of an eye.

I must not be cynical. I must not lose hope.

Hope was the most exquisite torture, but she wanted to embrace it anyway. Whatever they did to her, she wanted to face it directly this time, head-on, wide awake. She wasn't that bewildered girl anymore, reeling with shock as blow followed blow, horror upon horror. Everything had come true—she felt sick with fear because this room and this moment were the very essence of her nightmare—but still she couldn't go back. The fear had numbed her before, but this time it infuriated her.

"Mummer, Lewis!"

Deliberately, she opened her eyes to watch the second-to-last prisoner shuffle out of the room with Constable Burdy. Then the door closed, and she was left alone with the matron. Mrs. Dill was her name; on the ride from Plymouth, she'd sat in the front of the police van, the "black maria," with the driver and the male guard, while Rachel and one other prisoner, a boy no more than fifteen, had ridden in the back, hunched and handcuffed in their small, mean, separate stalls that smelled like urinals. Mrs. Dill had watched over her for the last four days in the Boro prison at Plymouth, too. She had the same beefy body and perpetually angry face of a matron at Dartmoor whom Rachel remembered well, a woman who had delighted in inflicting pain on her charges in small, indiscernible ways—the tiny squeezing of the flesh of the upper arm or the back of the neck, the pulling of a pinch of hair out of the scalp. But aside from obscene language and some rough shoving, Mrs. Dill hadn't abused her—yet. Rachel was fully conscious of her good fortune.

"Keep your eyes down, Wade. What're you looking at?"

She mouthed, "Nothing," and ducked her head. A second later her instantaneous, unthinking obedience appalled her. Had nothing changed, then, nothing at all? But she wasn't afraid of this hulking, stupid woman; she'd obeyed her out of habit, not cowardice.

To prove it, she lifted her head and said clearly, "Do you enjoy your work, Mrs. Dill?"

The woman stopped picking at a scab on her hand. "What?"

"Do you fancy ordering people about?"

"*What?*"

"Especially when they're handcuffed and helpless. Do you like herding them into dark cells? Locking them in and then listening through a grate while they weep with despair?"

Mrs. Dill came away from the high window and stood over her. "Shut up, you. You shut up or you'll be good and sorry."

Too late; she couldn't stop. She'd been a model prisoner for four days, but now the lid was off. She was boiling over. "What would make a woman take a job like yours? Tell me—I would like to know. Was it a lifelong ambition? Since childhood you've wanted to be a screw?"

Snarling, the matron made a grab for Rachel's shackled wrists and jerked her to her feet. "Insolent! Shut your mouth, you hear me?" She gave the irons a hard, punishing yank, then pushed her back down on the bench. "Silence!"

But Rachel felt mad, reckless; she waited until the matron was back at the window before she asked in a voice shaking with strange emotion, "What exactly do you think distinguishes you from the crazy, violent wretches you watch over? The ones you enjoy 'disciplining' by shoving and beating, shouting at them as if they weren't human at all—" She threw her hands up to shield her face, and the matron's fist struck the sharp metal edge of her manacles.

Mrs. Dill bellowed a curse, hugging her injured hand to her waist, breathing hard. *Now you've done it,* Rachel thought with dread and excitement, that dangerous mix that had resulted in dreadful punishments in the first year of her confinement. She'd thought that wildness had been annihilated long ago, by the prison guards and her own better judgment—but here it came roaring back with exactly the same violence and fury as before. Mrs. Dill's baffled rage egged her on. "Do you have children?" she asked her, pressing back against the wall, keeping her hands up. "Do you beat them, too? There was a screw at Dartmoor— she looked like you. She used to hold a pillow over her little boy's face when he wouldn't stop crying. It's true—she told me. She told me when she did the same thing to me!"

The next blow caught her on the elbow, and Mrs. Dill grunted in pain again, clutching her other hand. She had a truncheon in her belt; she was fumbling for it when the door opened and Constable Burdy called out, "Wade, Ra—" He stopped in amazement. "What the hell is going on here?" he demanded, staring back and forth between guard and prisoner.

"She was insolent!" Mrs. Dill accused, red-faced. "She insulted me!" *Stupid, stupid woman;* she might have said Rachel had attacked her, but she was too ignorant even to lie.

"That's enough now, that is," Burdy blustered, anxious to enforce the law but unable to credit the matron's accusation. Rachel couldn't blame him; in all their meetings he'd never seen her anything but docile and reserved, the perfect paroled convict. "Her case is up now, so enough o' this, whatever it is yer both about. It's time, I'm telling you." He took Rachel by her manacled forearm and helped her to stand, and she fancied his grasp was respectful, almost gentle. It helped to calm her, even though she knew it was respect for her erstwhile employer, not herself, that made Burdy touch her almost as if she were a lady.

Mrs. Dill couldn't resist a parting threat. Still rubbing her wrist, she muttered, "Afterward," close to Rachel's ear. Burdy opened the door, and the matron leaned forward to hiss, "Afterward, murdering bitch." Rachel flinched in spite of herself. Squaring her shoulders, she walked out of the remand cell and into the moot hall.

The strange euphoria evaporated as soon as she saw who was waiting for her at the end of the room. Her last hope died with it, and she was forced to acknowledge the foolishness of the fantasy she'd held in secret for four days—that Sebastian would come in time to save her. But only two black-robed justices sat behind the long table, Mayor Vanstone and Captain Carnock. The third chair was empty.

The courtroom was full, though, almost as crowded as the last time she'd been brought here. It ought not to have shocked her to see Lydia Wade among the spectators, but it did. She had her sewing basket by her side, one of her unwieldy squares of black knitting across her lap. Before Rachel could avert her gaze, she smiled at her in happy triumph. It was the sort of look a bride's dear friend might send her as she walked down a church aisle toward the altar. Except that Lydia's eyes had a half-mad sparkle, and behind her smile was raw, inimical glee.

Rachel looked away—and had a second shock. Across the aisle from Lydia, Claude Sully was twisted around in his seat, grinning a wolfish grin. His suave face unlocked a flood of ugly memories. She missed a step; Burdy caught at her arm, steadying her. Someone laughed. She knew that malicious sound. Looking up, she saw Violet Cocker, sitting on Sully's other side. She'd left Lynton over a month ago—were she and Sully together? But why?

Burdy let go of her and left her alone. Vanstone began to speak, reading from some legal document on the table. He was asking a question. Of her? She got out, "I beg your—?" before Burdy interrupted to answer; the question hadn't been directed to her at all. She looked down at the floor, flushing.

"No, Your Worship, accused still hasn't produced a ticket of leave remittal, which she claims to've got in the post from the Home Secretary on the twenty-fifth of last month. No one saw it but her, and she claims she can't find it."

Vanstone nodded judicially. Rachel cleared her throat, girding herself to respond, but he didn't look at her. "What are the precise conditions of her release that Mrs. Wade violated, Constable?"

"All of 'em, Your Worship, since five weeks ago. She failed to report to me fer four visits, nor the county constable twice running, and she's paid naught on 'er fine since the twentieth of July."

Heavy silence. They weren't going to let her speak. The mayor drummed his fingers on the table thoughtfully while Captain Carnock combed his bushy gray sidewhiskers, staring off into space. Behind her, she thought she could hear the click-click of knitting needles, fast and excited.

"Is the officer who apprehended Mrs. Wade here today?"

"No, Your Worship, 'e had court business in Plymouth this afternoon and weren't able to come. We have 'is affidavit."

"Tender it to the court, please."

Burdy handed the magistrate a paper.

Vanstone wore gold-rimmed half-glasses to read. He perused the affidavit unhurriedly, then gave it to Carnock.

"Mrs. Wade, a fugitive, was taken up by Officer Grimes of the Plymouth constabulary on Monday of this week," the mayor recited, speaking slowly so the clerk could write it down. "She was discovered at the Keyham Dock Yard, inquiring about the cost of clipper passage to Canada and America."

"Only to see—I was—"

Vanstone whipped his glasses off with a flourish, his pale gray eyes widening on her in indignation. "The prisoner will be *silent*," he commanded. She obeyed, but she didn't drop her eyes or bow her head in submission. She held his gaze steadily, without defiance, until *he* looked away. A minor victory, but it buoyed her.

"Is there anybody who can testify on her behalf?" Captain Carnock inquired, breaking the taut little silence.

No one answered.

Vanstone said, "In that case—"

"I would like to testify."

Rachel started, recognizing William Holyoake's voice. She hadn't noticed him before; he was in a far corner of the room. And now she saw that he was sitting next to Anne Morrell, whose lovely face was tight with worry. When her eyes met Rachel's, she smiled a quick, hopeful smile, trying to communicate support.

"Do you have information that relates directly to the circumstances of this case?"

"I have," William said.

"Come forward and be sworn."

William took the oath and went to stand in the witness box, a small wooden enclosure adjacent to the prisoner's bar.

"What have you got to say, Mr. Holyoake?" Vanstone asked him after he'd given his name to the clerk—a formality, since everyone knew who he was.

He held his hat by the brim and slowly turned it around in his big hands. Clearing his throat, he said loudly, "I want to say that Mrs. Wade weren't a fugitive. That is, she didn't try to escape, which is what I heard she got arrested for. I had a talk wi' 'er before she went away, and she weren't 'escaping.' She were just leaving, like." He darted a glance at Rachel, as if to say he hoped that would do her some good, then turned back to the justices.

Vanstone looked unimpressed. "Did she say anything in this conversation to indicate she was coming back?"

William had to say, "No. But," he added, "she didn't say anything to indicate she weren't."

"What exactly did she say?" asked Captain Carnock.

The bailiff screwed up his face, thinking. "I can't recollect word for word. Sommat like, 'I've got to go away.' And she shook my hand."

" 'I've got to go away'?"

"Mayhap not just like that. Mayhap, 'I'm going away.' "

" 'For a while'?"

"She didn't say for a while. But—"

"Did she take all her belongings?"

"As to that I couldn't say. *But*," he repeated louder, drowning out the mayor's next question, "she did say she were going to *Plymouth*. If she were *escaping*, why would she say that? She weren't escaping, I'm telling you, she was just going away."

Carnock shook his head while the mayor smiled a thin, cynical smile, more eloquent than words. "An interesting deduction, Mr. Holyoake. Is that all you have to say?"

William nodded unhappily.

He started to leave, but Carnock stopped him to ask, "Do you know anything about a letter rescinding Mrs. Wade's ticket of leave?"

"No, sir. Not until now, that is."

"You never heard anything about it before today?"

"No, sir."

"Would you say," Vanstone put in, "that you and Mrs. Wade are friends?"

William looked directly at Rachel and answered, "Yes, sir."

"Good friends?"

Seconds passed while he thought that over. "Yes," he said positively. "I would say we are."

Vanstone pounced. "But your good friend never told you she received a letter from the Home Secretary in Whitehall voiding the conditions of her prison release? A letter that, in effect, made her a completely free woman?"

Rachel looked down, unable to bear the confusion in William's plain, honest face. After a long moment, he mumbled something Vanstone made him repeat. "No, she never told me," he said belligerently. Then he was made to sit down.

Vanstone and Carnock put their heads together and began to whisper. Over the murmuring of the spectators, a woman's clear voice suddenly rose. "I have something to say." Anne got up from her seat a bit awkwardly, using Holyoake's shoulder for support. She wore a voluminous blue wool shawl over her gown, but it couldn't disguise the prominent swell of her belly. "Reverend Morrell had to go to Mare's Head on pastoral business, but I'd hoped he would be back by now. He wanted to come to this hearing and speak on Mrs. Wade's behalf. I would like to say something in his stead."

The mayor gave a gracious nod. "Does it relate directly—"

"It's not evidence, strictly speaking. I know nothing about Mrs. Wade's trip to Plymouth or the circumstances of her prison release."

"I see." Vanstone pulled on one end of his silvery mustache, then made a permissive, vaguely condescending gesture. "In that case, you needn't take the oath, Mrs. Morrell, and you may speak from your seat."

Anne bowed to him rather stiffly and said, "Thank you," without much warmth. "I only want to say that Reverend Morrell and I have come to know Mrs. Wade over the last half year or so, and we believe her to be an honorable woman—indeed, a *good* woman. It's clear that a mistake has been made, some clerical error, perhaps, a Whitehall mishap that's resulted in this unfortunate misunderstanding. I hope you will decide what's to be done with at least as much tolerance and understanding as—as strict adherence to the letter of the law."

"Is that all?" Vanstone asked politely.

"Yes. No. Is she going to be allowed to speak for herself?"

He smiled blandly. "Thank you very much, Mrs. Morrell. Mrs. Wade is fortunate in her friends."

He meant for her to sit down, but Anne persisted. "Excuse me. Is she allowed to say anything in her own defense?"

The mayor's professional smile didn't waver. "You may not realize, ma'am, that we're not an adjudicatory body. Mrs. Wade has no legal representative, and consequently no voice in these proceedings. Thank you. Thank you very much." With that, he turned from her and resumed his low-voiced conversation with Captain Carnock. Frowning, Anne finally took her seat.

Rachel agreed with Mayor Vanstone about one thing: she was fortunate in her friends.

"Mrs. Wade."

The magistrates' consultation was over. Rachel stood straighter and faced them. "Your Worship," she murmured to Vanstone, who was, as usual, the spokesman. She distrusted the look in his cold gray eyes, a combination of implacability and detachment that boded no good.

"The court finds that you violated the terms of your conditional release by failing repeatedly to meet with the parish and county officials to whom you were obliged to report, and also by neglecting to make restitution in a timely way on your outstanding debt. In addition, the court finds it reasonable to conclude that your removal to Plymouth and subsequent inquiries with regard to vessels bound for overseas ports constitute, at best, an attempt to circumvent the stipulations governing your release and, at worst, a plot to flee the country.

"Your sentence for the crime of murder was life imprisonment, with the possibility of release after ten years' servitude to be considered at two-year judicial intervals. Mrs. Wade, can you inform this body of any reason why it should not recommend to the assize court that you be returned to Dartmoor Prison for a period of time deemed appropriate by the servitude review office, such period of time not to exceed two years?"

Two years. She hadn't misheard, even though the light, measured voice had thinned in her ears like a wire turning around, twisting and twisting, stretching to the breaking point. Two years.

She watched her manacled hands reach out for the smooth wood of the prisoner's bar and grip it until her fingers ached, but she swayed anyway. The bar cut against her stomach and the bones of her hips. She wanted to sag against it, fold herself over it. She locked her elbows and knees and tried to bring Vanstone into focus, tried to remember his exact question. She couldn't retrieve it from the chaos of her brain—had forgotten how he'd phrased it. Was the proper response yes? No? What if she chose wrong?

"Your Worship," she got out before her throat closed. She shut her eyes and whispered, "Your Worship, would you . . . I'm not able to . . ." Low murmuring interrupted her; it seemed as if all the people behind her were talking at once. She sympathized with their impatience, but she wanted to get the answer right, and she wanted very much not to faint. "Your Worship," she tried again, a little louder.

An angry shout cut across every other voice in the room. "Why is she in shackles?"

Someone said, "Because she—"

"Release her!"

"She—"

"Release her!"

Constable Burdy slid a key in the lock of the iron on her right wrist, then the one on her left. The weights fell away with a rusty clank, and suddenly she was too light—ungrounded—she feared she might float up in the air. She imagined herself levitating over the crowded courtroom, and made another grab for the bar. Burdy turned his sloping shoulders sideways, out of the way, and she saw Sebastian.

He was dripping wet. He'd lost his hat. Water trickled from his hair and ran down his face, made dark stains on the shoulders of his coat, flattened his shirt to his chest. He stood between her and the magistrates' table, breathing hard, his eyes so hot she could feel the heat from here. She could feel his indecision, too; he wanted to go to her, touch her. But he stayed planted where he was, legs spread, hands in fists at his sides, while rainwater pooled under his boots. There was no doubt in her mind that he was close to violence, and that the battle he was fighting for self-control wasn't won yet.

"My lord," Mayor Vanstone said loudly, coming to his feet. "We were not aware that you had returned. We're—"

"Obviously." He snarled the word; the fire in his eyes became enmity, and he turned it on Vanstone eagerly, as if glad to locate a legitimate target for his anger.

"Perhaps you'll join us," the mayor said stiffly, "now that you've honored us with your presence." He touched his hand to the back of the empty chair next to his.

Sebastian ignored that. "Why was Mrs. Wade in chains?"

"My lord, she was apprehended while inquiring about vessels

leaving the country for foreign ports. Since then, she's been treated, not unreasonably, I think, as a potential fugitive."

"What rot," Sebastian enunciated, with so much scathing disdain that Vanstone colored. "Why shouldn't she be in Plymouth—or Brighton, or Dover—inquiring about anything she damn well pleases?"

"Because," Captain Carnock interjected mildly, "she was left in your custody, with the understanding that she would remain at Lynton until your return, my lord. At least, that was the understanding you and I reached on the evening of your departure."

Somebody chuckled with satisfaction. Sebastian whirled at the sound, and saw Sully in the second row of spectators. "You," he said slowly, moving toward him. "What are you doing here?"

Sully clasped one knee and leaned back on the bench; he was pretending to be at ease, but the glitter in his eyes gave away his excitement. "It's a public hearing, isn't it? Sebastian, my old friend, I wouldn't miss this for the world." Beside him, Violet Cocker snickered into her hand.

Sebastian looked coldly, murderously angry. If Vanstone hadn't distracted him at that moment, Rachel believed he would have attacked Sully.

"My lord, Mrs. Wade's defense rests on an apparently nonexistent letter from the Home Secretary voiding her conditional release. If there were such a document, the prison authorities, the lord lieutenant, and we, the jurisdictional magistrates, would have been informed of it. But we were not, and—forgive me, my lord—I'm quite certain Her Majesty does not make a practice of corresponding with convicted felons in secret. In the absence of any proof whatsoever—"

"The letter existed," Sebastian cut in.

"With respect, have you seen it?"

"No. I believe it was stolen."

"Stolen? How extraordinary. Do you have any proof of—"

"Who put you up to this? Sully? How much did he pay you to make sure she goes back to prison?"

The mayor's face turned bright pink; he drew himself up. "How dare you! By God, sir, that's a base lie! I demand an apology for it."

Sebastian turned on Sully, who smirked at him with undisguised delight—and, possibly, surprise. "Can't prove it, D'Aubrey. Wait, it's Moreton now, isn't it? The bloody *earl* of Moreton. But you still can't prove a thing."

Sebastian saw red. Over the muttering of the crowd, over the pounding of Vanstone's fist on the table for order, he heard a soft, insistent voice calling his name. He looked at Rachel. She had one hand on the wooden bar, the other stretched out to him, straining toward him, and the distress in her face brought him to his senses.

He couldn't help her like this. All he wanted was to get her out of here, by force if necessary—no, *preferably* by force; he was dying to smash something, anything—but if he lost control, he would be playing into Sully's hands. He mustn't let Rachel's fear, so heartbreakingly obvious, spread to him and cripple his judgment.

Deliberately turning his back on Sully, he demanded of the mayor, who was still sputtering from wounded dignity, "What are the charges against Mrs. Wade? Let me hear them again."

"She—"

"She missed a few meetings with Burdy, is that it?"

"And the county constable as well. And she—"

"Why wasn't she notified? If she wasn't showing up for her appointments, why didn't somebody complain about it?"

Constable Burdy spoke up. "She were sent a letter once, m'lord, by me, telling 'er she were remiss in her meetings."

"And?"

"She wrote back sayin' she was 'relieved of the obligation.' "

"And you didn't follow up after that? Except to arrest her?"

Burdy shrugged.

Sebastian muttered a disgusted curse. "What else?"

" 'Er fine, m'lord," he mumbled. "She quit paying on 'er fine."

"How much does she owe? Well?"

Burdy cleared his throat and pulled on his ear. "She 'ad to pay ten shillings a week. She missed four times running."

"She owes *two pounds*?" It was an effort not to roar it. He drew out his purse and snatched a handful of bills from it, and then it was an effort not to stuff the money down Burdy's throat. "Here," he gritted. "Now her fine is paid."

Vanstone had resumed his seat. Whether or not he was in league with Sully, Sebastian's accusation had turned him into a dangerous enemy. "Lord Moreton," he said with icy formality, "the most serious charge against Mrs. Wade remains—her attempt to flee. That cannot be dismissed lightly. It speaks for itself and it is grounds alone, in our opinion, for remanding her case to the assize."

Sebastian stared back at him thoughtfully. Gradually, not all at once, the solution came to him. He smiled at the simplicity of it. "But she wasn't fleeing, you see. She went to Plymouth at my suggestion, as it happens. To begin shopping for her trousseau. She inquired about passenger ship schedules because I asked her to—for our honeymoon. Mrs. Wade and I plan to marry at the end of the month."

Amid the gasps and exclamations, he turned his smile on Rachel. The shock he'd expected was there in her face, but not the gladness. He held her gaze, willing her to believe it. It was what she wanted, wasn't it? But there was nothing in her searching eyes but sadness. She gave a little shake of her head and looked away.

Vanstone must have noticed the byplay. When the noise died down, he leaned forward and asked pointedly "Is that true?"

Disoriented, sensing disaster, Sebastian said quickly, "Are you calling me—"

"No, it's not true," Rachel interrupted in clear, carrying tones. "His lordship is mistaken."

"Do you mean to say he's not telling the truth?"

"He's *mistaken*," she repeated. "There is no engagement. He's . . . mistaken." Finally her voice broke.

But when Sebastian took a step toward her she shrank back, letting go of the bar. He halted, shocked. "Rachel," he whispered. "Rachel, for God's sake." She wouldn't look at him; her frozen profile shut him out.

Vanstone was saying something. A woman laughed; he thought it was the maid, Sully's confederate, but when he looked up he saw it was Lydia Wade. She was clutching her knitting to her chest and muttering to herself. Had she gone mad?

He needed to sit down. He couldn't think. Rachel wouldn't look at him and he couldn't think what to do or say next. He slicked his dripping hair back with his fingers and used his sleeve to wipe the water from his face. Now Vanstone was winding up; whatever he'd said, it ended with "when the assize judges meet in September," and Carnock nodded heavily in agreement, muttering something about "unfortunate" and "no other choice." Two against one.

Was this the end, then? Was he going to just stand here while they took her away? Five months ago he'd gotten his way, in this same circumstance, through bluster and intimidation. They weren't working today—but the blow that completely defeated him was Rachel's repudiation. Her situation couldn't be more desperate, but she wouldn't let him save her. Wouldn't let him come near her.

Christy Morrell had come into the hall. Sebastian didn't notice him until he walked to the front of the room, drenched and dripping, leaving a trail of water from a closed black umbrella. He was out of breath. "Forgive me for interrupting. I'd have been here sooner, but I was delayed. May I speak to—"

"Excuse me, Reverend," the mayor broke in, "we aren't taking testimony in this matter anymore. Your wife spoke eloquently in Mrs. Wade's behalf, and we don't require any further evidence. Thank you."

"Let him speak," Sebastian burst out. "Whatever he's got to say, I'd like to hear it."

Vanstone threw up his hands. "Speak, then." He folded his arms and scowled.

Christy moved closer to the magistrates' table. "A matter has just come to my attention, gentlemen, something extremely important. I have to speak to you in private." He gestured to include all three justices.

"Does it bear on Mrs. Wade's case?"

"It does."

"Then take the stand and say it for the record," the mayor decreed, and for once, Sebastian agreed with him.

But Christy didn't move. "With respect, Mayor, this isn't something I can say in open court. I'd ask that you adjourn this hearing indefinitely."

"That's out of the question. If you have evidence that relates to the case, you can say it under oath, here and now. Otherwise, we're prepared to rule."

Christy shook his head. "That would be a mistake. I've misled you—what I want to say doesn't relate to this hearing."

"Then—"

"It relates to Mrs. Wade's original case. I've come into possession of evidence that she was wrongly convicted of murdering her husband."

Chaos erupted. Vanstone called for order, but no one could hear him. The spectators were on their feet, talking at once. In the confusion, Sebastian saw Sully edging toward the side of the room. On impulse, he made a dash for the door and cut him off.

"Going somewhere?"

Sully smiled his turned-down smile. "Looks as if the fun's over for now, and I've got better things to do. Stand aside, there's a good lad."

"Oh, not likely." Alert, spoiling for a fight, he moved in closer. "Where's your knife today, Claude? In your boot? Pocket?"

"Don't be an ass. Get out of the way or I'll—"

A woman's scream from behind Sully made him twist around. Over his shoulder, Sebastian saw Lydia Wade lift her arm in the air and slash it down. Christy Morrell jerked back in the nick of time, out of range, but his coat sleeve was torn and dangling. His wife screamed again.

But the minister wasn't Lydia's target. Sebastian watched in frozen, disbelieving horror while she scuttled around Christy, sharp, silver scissors high again in her fisted hand, and darted across the empty aisle to the prisoner's bar.

Nightmare. Sully wouldn't move—he was frozen, too. Sebastian half shoved, half tackled him, pushed him violently aside, and finally the way was clear. But only for a second; immediately bodies came between him and Rachel again. He saw her face change from confusion to terror just before the way was blocked again. He flung himself against a man's back, pushed someone sideways, stiff-armed somebody else. Over the bobbing heads and shoulders of more people, he saw the scissors rise and fall, rise and fall. Shouting, "No! No!" he lurched and twisted, throwing his body against the stubborn press, cursing flesh that wouldn't move, wouldn't move—

A break opened, big enough to punch through. He saw Lydia from the back, bent over Rachel across the magistrates' table, grappling, struggling to bring the scissors down in her face.

Rachel's frantic grip on Lydia's wrist faltered, slipped. Sebastian's heart stopped beating. He couldn't get to her in time.

Behind the table, Vanstone and Carnock were shouting, feinting, a blur of panicked, ineffectual fumbling. From nowhere, a huge body hurtled, heavy as a cannonball, through scarce empty space and smacked into Lydia's shoulder. The scissors soared in the air and stuck in the ceiling. With a grunt, she flew sideways and crashed against the wall. William Holyoake landed on top of her.

Rachel struggled up and tried to stand. Her knees buckled; Sebastian caught her as she was sliding to the floor.

They sat beside each other, halfway under the table, oblivious to the turmoil all around. "Are you hurt?" He couldn't see any blood; her eyes were still glazed and staring, but her hands clenching at his shoulders were strong. "Rachel, answer me, are you hurt?"

The question finally registered. She shook her head. "Are you?"

He gathered her up and held tight. His heart slowed its staccato pounding as the truth slowly sank in that she was all right. "No, I'm fine," he answered automatically, even thought it wasn't true. Setting her away from him, he fixed her with a baleful stare. "Why the hell won't you marry me?"

XXI

Dear Reverend Morrell,

By the time you read this, I'll be gone. I pray that God will forgive me for not having the courage to tell you this story while I'm alive, but it's too painful—I can hardly bear to write it. And I console myself that a few days or weeks longer won't make any difference. The terrible damage has already been done.

I'm not strong, and I must write quickly—but where shall I begin? The truth came to me so gradually, I didn't understand the full horror until a few months ago. My awakening coincided with Mrs. Wade's prison release, because that was when my niece's shaky hold on reality began to slip away completely, with no more brief but blessed periods of normalcy to disguise what was happening. At first I refused to believe it; she was raving, I told myself, the horrible things she said must be the work of a hysterical imagination. But the disjointed ramblings would not stop, and they were chillingly consistent. Then I read her journal—I admit it; I couldn't help myself, I had to know the worst—and finally I believed it.

Dear God, I can't bear to write this! But I have to. I haven't said the words in my own mind, and now I must set them down for strangers to read. It's this: Lydia and her father, my brother, Randolph Wade, were intimate. Physically intimate, I mean. I am saying they were lovers.

It began, I think, when Lydia was eleven, although per-

341

haps, poor girl, she was even younger. I know now, because I have heard, she has told me, some of the details of this wicked liaison, but I can't write them. And I swear before God that I knew nothing, nothing of it when it was occurring. Should I have known? We lived in separate houses; my brother and I weren't close; Lydia was strange, standoffish, never a warm or confiding child. These are my excuses, but you must know that my conscience will torment me until I die.

It's clear to me now that the perversions Lydia engaged in with her father began to affect her mind even before his death. She's grown worse over the years, but the real disintegration began when she learned of Mrs. Wade's release from prison. Before that, the only thing standing in the way of a total breakdown was her satisfaction in knowing that Rachel, whom she blamed for all her unhappiness, and whom she hated with an intense, fanatical bitterness, was suffering. But after Mrs. Wade's release, Lydia lost all restraint and all natural discretion. In her ravings, she told me something else, and it was worse, even more horrible. Ten years ago, driven mad by jealousy and grief, she killed her own father.

She has repeated to me the details of the ghastly scene again and again, details I can't bring myself to write, and the particulars never vary. There is absolutely no doubt in my mind that she is telling the truth.

So. It's over. I had expected to feel relief now, some measure of consolation after the burden of this dreadful knowledge was no longer mine to bear alone, but my sadness hasn't lightened. I think I will go to my grave as weighted down from the horror as always. Pray for me, Reverend.

Have I done wrong in waiting so long to tell the secret? I thought the worst was over, that nothing could bring back all the years Mrs. Wade spent in prison for a crime she didn't commit. But now I'm filled with doubts and second thoughts.

Even more, I worry for Lydia. And I beg you, Christy, don't let them abuse her. She'll have to be shut away someplace, I know that, but surely she deserves compassion, not punish-ment, because she is not in her right mind. *Evil has been done here, but not by that poor girl. My brother is burning in hell for his sins, and I cannot pray for him! God forgive me, but I cannot!*

I'm weak and ill; I must stop. Dr. Hesselius is coming in a few minutes. I'll give him this letter—that way it can't fall into Lydia's hands—and ask him to give it to you after I'm gone. Where I failed, I know that you will have the courage to do what's right.

God bless and keep you, Christy. And God help us all.
                                        Margaret Armstrong

For a long time after she read the letter, Rachel sat quietly, staring out the window of the Morrells' second-floor guest bed-chamber at the quiet village green, soggy and deserted because of the rain. A light hand on her shoulder brought her out of her reverie. Anne asked, "Are you all right? How do you feel, Rachel?"

Sebastian had asked her that, too, an hour ago when he'd brought her here. She hadn't been able to answer with any cer-tainty. She was glad, relieved, of course, because she had been exonerated, but it hadn't really begun to sink in yet. It was too big, still too much like a dream; she couldn't quite trust it.

"I'm all right," she answered. But she felt a nagging melan-choly, and next to it, an absurd hopefulness. Too much had hap-pened; her emotions were too tattered to react sensibly and correctly to events that kept coming and would not stop. The last thing Sebastian had said to her before Anne took her upstairs for a bath and clean clothes was that he wanted an explanation for why she'd refused his marriage proposal. "You must know," she'd whispered at the bottom of the staircase, and he'd all but snapped back, "No, I haven't a clue, and you *will* tell me."

"Are you hungry? Let me tell Mrs. Ludd to bring you some soup. Tea, then. Rachel, you really should eat something."

She roused herself to smile. "Anne, I'm not hungry. They did feed me in gaol, you know."

She made a face. "How *horrible* that must've been. God, if we'd known, if we'd had any idea—"

"You couldn't have done anything. Anyway, it's over now, and I'm fine." Her friend looked dubious. "Truly I am. You've taken such good care of me, I feel as good as new."

"William will be relieved to know that. He's downstairs, waiting to hear how you are."

"Is he?" She traced the pattern of the upholstered chair arm with one finger. "He's been a good friend. He saved my life."

"He saved mine once," Anne said unexpectedly. "Not quite so literally, but almost."

"I'll go down and thank him."

"You'll do no such thing. You'll stay here by the fire and rest."

Rachel smiled, thinking how lovely it was to be spoiled. "You're not a mother *yet*, you know." Her smile faded when she remembered how Lydia had attacked Reverend Morrell first, then Anne when she'd tried to help him. "Thank God you weren't hurt," she whispered. "Or your baby!"

Anne reached for her hand and squeezed it. "Thank God Christy wasn't," she returned with the same fervor.

"What do you think will happen to Lydia?" Rachel wondered after a pause.

"They'll put her someplace where she can't hurt herself. Do you feel sorry for her?" Anne asked curiously.

"Yes."

"Even though she ruined your life?"

"Yes."

She raised her eyebrows. "Well, I suppose I must believe you, but I'm quite sure I wouldn't be so forgiving if I were in your place. I leave all that sort of thing to Christy."

A knock at the door made them turn. It opened after the briefest second, and Sebastian strode in. His clothes weren't wet any longer, only damp and extremely wrinkled. He looked exhausted. But his eyes lit up when they met Rachel's, and in spite of herself she felt warmed clear through to her bones.

Anne jumped to her feet; Rachel started to rise, then stayed where she was. "Well," Anne said brightly. "I think I'll go down and see how Christy's doing."

"Don't leave on my account."

Sebastian's insincerity was so obvious, Rachel blushed. She stood up and said, "We'll go down with you. I'm perfectly fine now, there's no reason—"

"No, we'll stay put," Sebastian said firmly, and she frowned at him. Already he sounded like an earl.

Anne was smiling and trying not to. "Well, you two fight it out between yourselves. I'm going down. And," she added with a pointed look at Rachel, "I'm sending Bess up with a tray. Yes, I am, and I expect you to eat every bite." She put her hand on her bulging tummy. "How could you not be hungry? I'm *starving*."

After she was gone, Sebastian regarded Rachel in silence for a long moment. "Pretty dress," he murmured. "Pretty hair. You look . . . new."

An odd word choice,, but she understood what he meant. She ran a hand down the skirt of the lavender muslin day dress self-consciously. "Anne lent it to me."

"It suits you." He started to say something else, then seemed to change his mind. He walked toward her; she took a step back. He went past her to the fireplace. "The fire feels good," he said distractedly.

It seemed decadent to her, a fire in September, but Anne had insisted. "You must be tired from your trip," she said, determined to keep up her end of this ridiculous conversation.

He ignored that. "Sully's gone, raced off to London, no doubt. Not that it'll do him any good. He forged the letter from the Home Secretary, Rachel."

"How do you know?"

"Violet Cocker told me—told Vanstone and Carnock, rather, in my presence. At my insistence," he added meaningfully. "She denies sending you the Broad Arrows, and I believe her. That had to be Lydia. I've apologized to the mayor, by the way. He's a bit of an ass, but I must admit he took it in good part. Christy was right about him—he had nothing to do with Sully's plot."

Rachel put her hand on her forehead. "But—how did *Violet* know Sully sent the letter?"

"She's the one who stole it from you. Sully put her up to it— bribed her, gave her trinkets, probably seduced her. It was all just an elaborate prank, designed to make trouble for you. His way of getting back at *me*, you see."

He came closer, spoke more softly. "And it worked perfectly. When I couldn't help you today, couldn't make them listen to me, I wanted to smash things, kill somebody. I've never felt so precarious. So . . . imperiled. It was as if my life hung in the balance, too."

How tempting he was, half smiling, his blue-green eyes tender and intent at the same time. "As soon as you came, I knew I could stand it," she heard herself say. "Even if you couldn't save me, I knew it would be all right in the end. You can't know how that felt. Thank you."

"It's not really your gratitude I'm interested in."

She looked down. "Sorry."

"I told Christy to call the banns on Sunday," he said abruptly. "We can be married in three weeks."

"You what?" Her heart began to pound. "Sebastian, that was a *mistake*."

"You said that before. Explain yourself."

"I—I would like to explain myself somewhere other than in this bedroom."

"Why? Don't you trust yourself?"

"It's not *I* who . . . oh." She couldn't get used to being teased; she loved it, but most of his jokes on her still went over her head until he laughed at them. Oh, but he was dangerous! He knew a hundred ways to get around her strongest convictions. She girded herself for a fight.

He ambushed her by putting his hands on the sides of her face and holding her still in the soft trap of his fingers. His eyes were more stirring than a caress, and his wicked smile coaxed a helpless one from her. "I could tie you to the bed," he whispered. It took her a moment to hear that. She gasped, and he took a kiss from her lips, his hands on her face still the lightest of prisons.

She touched his chest, felt the warm, steady throb of his heart. "You can kiss me . . ." she breathed against his mouth. "You can kiss me," she tried again, "but it won't make any difference. I'm telling you . . ." One of his hands slid to her throat; she stopped its insidious downward glide by capturing his wrist. "Sebastian."

"Hmm."

"Your ability to seduce me has never been in question."

"No," he agreed.

"And it's not the issue now. I thought we were discussing marriage."

He rested his forehead against hers. "That's what I'm trying to discuss. I didn't do it very well before. Let me try again. Will you marry me? I love you completely. You'll be happy with me because I'll see to it."

She drew away, dismayed, elated. "I think you must be—the most arrogant man in the entire world."

"Well, I am an earl now, you know," he said deprecatingly.

"Exactly. Exactly. You needn't think those hasty words in the courtroom today, which you said out of kindness and—and duty, bind you to me in any way."

He looked amused. "I've never been accused of being kind and dutiful before. I have to plead not guilty." He trailed his fingers down the length of her arm, shoulder to wrist. "I'm a selfish man, Rachel. I want you because I love you. You're ascribing your own gentle motives to me, which is very sweet; but you're in error."

Her cheeks warmed. She turned her back on him. "You don't love me."

"Excuse me, I do."

"No, you don't. You proclaimed our imminent marriage in front of witnesses because you thought it would save me. It was an impulse, anyone could see that. Under any other circumstances, you would not have done it. Can you deny that?"

"Certainly."

She turned on him. "Really? You can't deny that a week ago, when Christy Morrell suggested you *might* marry me, you laughed in his face!" She felt like a fool when hot tears stung her eyes. Sebastian reached for her hand; she pulled away, but he held on and made her face him.

"Rachel, don't. Sweetheart, if I could take one thing back in my whole miserable, misspent—"

She yanked out of his grasp and backed up. His pained expression looked too much like pity, and she couldn't stand it. "Please don't do that," she commanded. "I do *not* need your sympathy or your apology. I'm sorry I brought that up again—I don't know why I did. It's ancient history. I don't think about it."

Before he could call her a liar, she rushed on. "I'm setting you free, here and now. To safeguard your honor, we'll say that you did your duty and asked for my hand, and I declined. I'm sure people will call me a fool, but that will be comparatively easy, since before now I've been called much worse."

She felt pleased with the cadence of that, if not the sentiment; she thought it sounded rather dignified. But Sebastian didn't look impressed. "I see," he said, nodding, smiling facetiously. "And what will you do with yourself? How will you make a living?"

"I'll find work."

"Housekeeper? You've experience there. Or a governess, perhaps?"

"Yes, perhaps. I can keep books."

"That sounds fascinating." His smile grew gradually less amused as he said, "You've gone through fire for ten years so that you can keep someone else's house, or books, or wipe the noses of their bratty children. That's brilliant, Rachel. So much more interesting and involving than being a countess and raising children of your own with the man you love." He closed in, backed her toward the window. "Deny that. Deny that you love me. Come, say it."

"I can't," she said tightly.

"No, you can't. Why is it so hard for you to believe I love you?"

"You didn't before. Why would you now?"

"Why not now? Who made it a rule that I had to love you 'before,' whenever that was—when I first laid eyes on you? Is that the rule? Then or never?"

"No, of course not. You know what I—"

"Well, I *did* love you then."

She had to laugh. "Oh, Sebastian."

"You don't believe me?"

"Certainly not. All you cared about was taking me to bed."

He opened his mouth to deny it, stopped, and finally shrugged. "Very well, but in no time at all—"

A tap at the door cut him off. It was the maid, carrying the tray Anne had promised. She put it on the table by the bed. Sebastian thanked her, and she curtsied and withdrew.

"Thank God it's not tea, it's wine. And about a dozen sandwiches. What's this, stuffed mushrooms? And a bowl of fresh bilberries and a pitcher of cream. A *feast*." He poured a glass of wine from the decanter and brought it to her. She took it, but when he went back to pour a glass for himself, she set hers down on the bureau without tasting it.

He sat at the foot of the bed and leaned back against the heavy post. She felt like a bundle of nerves; he looked completely at ease. A mask, she knew, at least in part. But truly, he did look lordlike; the mantle of earldom rested on him with annoying naturalness.

"I'll tell you when I first began to love you," he said, sipping his wine.

"That's not necessary."

"It was during one of our morning meetings. Early on, when I took such a delight in tormenting you. Pushing you, seeing how far I could go before you pushed back. Testing the depths of your stoicism, one might say. You had on your brown dress that day, and I'd gotten so used to the black, I thought it looked quite colorful. You stood in front of my desk, very quiet and demure, talking about cleaning the chimneys or some such thing. By then I wanted you constantly. I remember thinking your skin looked as if it would feel like chamois. I was fascinated by your hands. Your strict, sexy mouth."

Rachel changed her mind and reached casually for the wineglass on the bureau. Her hands weren't entirely steady; she used both of them to hold the stem and lifted the glass to her lips. The wine was sweet and bracing. She kept the glass, staring into its burgundy depths, pretending absorption.

"I wanted to see your hair in the light. I asked you to go to the window and draw the curtains wider."

She looked up, remembering. "It was raining."

"Yes."

A perfectly ordinary day. Nothing stood out; nothing had happened between them that she could recall.

"The maid came. Susan, the Irish one. She asked you a question, some household inquiry that couldn't wait. She was nervous—she knew she wasn't supposed to interrupt his lordship's morning conference with his housekeeper. I remember you smiled at her, spoke to her gently. Sweetly. She was afraid of me, but she trusted you. Loved you, I thought, because you were kind to her. When she went away, it struck me that I was jealous. I wanted you to smile at *me*. Speak gently to *me*."

"But how could I—"

"You couldn't. Of course. I knew it then, too. But I felt belligerent. 'I fired one of the stable lads yesterday,' I said—like a challenge. The servants loved you, I was sure, but they probably hated me. I'd discharged the boy because I saw him hit a horse, cuff a mare in the mouth with his fist because she wouldn't follow him into her stall. No one else knew why I let him go; I didn't mention it to anyone. 'I fired a lad,' I said to you, trying to sound as careless and mean as I knew you thought I was. With good reason. Do you remember this at all?"

She nodded faintly, but she was still bewildered.

"Do you know what you said to me? You said, 'Don't worry, my lord. Jerny told me Michael wasn't good with the horses. And he has family in Wyckerley, so he'll be all right.' "

She stared back at him, unblinking.

"It was—so inappropriate. So uncalled for. I knew you weren't a stupid or an insensitive woman. The only explanation for this bizarre show of sympathy and comfort for the man you had to

351

know by then was your mortal enemy was a superior heart. Don't look away, Rachel. A heart that neither cruelty nor perversion nor captivity had been able to crush. Had not even touched."

She closed her eyes, unable to look at him any longer. When she heard him get up from the bed, she turned around, to stare out the window, as if the dark, watery view fascinated her. "You are . . . too much for me, Sebastian," she managed to say, watching her breath condense on the glass. "I'm afraid of you."

He was standing directly behind her, but he didn't touch her. "What you're afraid of is being happy. And frankly, I'm disappointed in you. I believed you were stronger. I thought you hadn't a cowardly bone in your body."

"If you thought that, you don't understand me at all." She could feel his breath on the side of her neck, behind her ear.

"I understand you perfectly. Inside and out. Don't let your fear win this war. Be brave one last time. I dearly love you. I swear I'll protect you and care for you for the rest of our lives. Don't throw away this last chance."

She put her hands on the window ledge. She wanted to rest her head against the cool glass, but that would look too weak. Too cowardly. She felt a light touch on the crown of her head—a kiss?—and then Sebastian drew away.

She heard him moving furniture. She pivoted, and saw him drawing a chair up to the small table by the bed, and now he was sitting down and shaking out a big linen napkin. "You think about it while I eat," he suggested, and began to inspect the contents of all the sandwiches, sniff the mushrooms, pour himself more wine.

She folded her arms and started to pace, eyeing him uneasily. "You should think of yourself," she said. He cocked a questioning brow, his mouth full of bread and roast beef. "It's true I've been cleared of the crime I went to gaol for, but I'm still a fallen woman, and I always will be."

"How's that?" He bit down on a mushroom pensively.

"Not because of what I did, but because of what was done to me. I'm a character now, an—object of interest. All your soaps and scents can't wash away the stench of prison, Sebastian, or the memories people have of what Randolph did."

"Being a countess could, though. You'd be amazed at how much respectability a title can buy. My own past isn't exactly sterling, you'll agree, but no one's ever going to impugn me for it now."

"But I'm a *convict*."

"You *were* a convict. Now you're a martyr. Any day now I expect you'll be a heroine. And you'll be the toast of London when we go up in November for the opening of Parliament."

"The—what?"

"I sit in the House of Lords, you know. Occasionally. Now that I'm going to be respectable, a veritable country squire, I suppose I'll have to attend more often. Hurry and make up your mind, darling, because I've just thought of an extremely interesting use to which we can put these berries."

She flushed, feeling hot all over. "You have answers for everything," she muttered. "Oh, God, I don't know what to do!"

He stood up, and this time she didn't back away; when he took her hands, she let him press them between his, over his heart. "Marry me, Rachel. I want you with me at Lynton for the rest of our lives. Having our children. Both of us in Devon, in this pretty village, living and working with the people who depend on us. Growing old together. I've given the house in Rye to my mother because I need to be here, and I'm needed here. But if you won't have me, I don't care where I am. I love you, darling, and you love me. Say it."

"I love you."

"Will you be my wife?"

"Yes."

Patricia Gaffney

She came into his arms. They held each other, both trembling a little. She murmured, "I love you," again, and told him how much, freely, truthfully, not holding back. If they had wasted time, been afraid, made mistakes before this minute, it didn't matter anymore. Rain pattered against the window; the mantel clock ticked; embers snapped and sizzled in the fireplace grate. Their hearts beat together, and this moment was perfect.

He kissed her. They seemed to drift toward the bed, sink down on it without conscious thought. She kissed his hands when he let her, but he was busy with them, and he touched her in a new way, with a slow, urgent tenderness she could hardly bear. Her borrowed gown was half unfastened before she realized what they were doing, or about to do.

She brought his hands to her mouth to still them. "Sebastian, stop, we can't do this here," she whispered—as if someone might be listening at the door.

"Why not?" He grinned at her. His hair was mussed from her fingers, his lips pink from kissing.

"*Because.* This is the *vicarage.*"

"Christy won't mind. If we stay, somebody can put up a sign one day: 'A countess slept here.'"

She rolled her eyes. "I doubt that I would do much sleeping."

"Well, then the sign can say, 'A countess—'"

"Hush." She put her fingers over his laughing lips. Before he could reach for her, she stood up and backed away from the bed, smiling at him, buttoning her dress. "Let's go home."

"Home." The word convinced him. He said it again, "Home," as he rose from the bed and came to her, and she loved the sound of it in his voice.

They took hands. He opened the door for her. In the threshold he paused, and she turned to see him gazing back into the room. "What?" she asked, puzzled. "Did we forget something?"

"Definitely."

354

"What?"

"The bilberries."

Their laughter, his and hers, rang out as she pulled him from the room. The gay sound would follow them down through the years, keeping them company for the rest of their lives.

If you've fallen in love with Wyckerley, don't miss the other
marvelous novels in Patricia Gaffney's beloved trilogy.
Return to the place where enhancing romance
and unexpected passions meet. . . .

To Love and To Cherish

and

Forever and Ever

NAL TRADE PAPERBACKS
COMING IN SPRING 2003

Turn the page for a special early preview . . .

To Love and To Cherish

EVEN ON HIS DEATHBED, Lord D'Aubrey was a hard man to love.

God, give me patience and humility, prayed Reverend Christian Morrell, who was in the business, as it were, of loving the unlovable. Leaning over the bed but not touching it—ill as he was, the elderly viscount still bristled when anyone except his doctor got too close—Christy asked his lordship if he would take the sacraments.

"Why? So I can go straight to heaven? Do you think I'm going to heaven, Vicar? Eh? Think I'm—" He ran out of breath; his parchment-colored face turned blue until he sucked in a wheezing gulp of air. By now he was too weak to cough; he kept swallowing until the spasm passed, then lay exhausted, hands limp on his sunken chest.

Christy sat down again in the high-backed chair he'd pulled as close to the bed as the old man would allow.

Dr. Hesselius ought to be here, he couldn't help thinking. "Send for me if you need me, but I doubt that you will," he'd told Christy two hours ago, in this room. "He's not in any pain—they frequently aren't at this late stage. I doubt he'll live through the day. I've done all I can; old Edward's in your hands now, Reverend." Christy had nodded at that, gravely, calmly, as if the prospect didn't demoralize him.

In his own estimation, at least on good days, he was a reasonably effective clergyman, considering he was new at his calling and his best qualities were still only earnestness and perseverance. But he had numerous failings, and they had a perverse way of multiplying and combining at extreme times like this, when his deepest wish was to give comfort and consolation to the needy. Edward Verlaine offered a special challenge, and Christy despaired that he wasn't up to it.

Memories kept intruding on his best efforts to pray. In the sparsely furnished room, a dark, gilt-framed oil painting of Lord D'Aubrey's grandfather loomed conspicuously over the mantelpiece; a peculiar grayish blur under the haughty-looking ancestor's nose made Christy smile, albeit a bit grimly. He recalled the day, probably twenty years ago now, when he and Geoffrey, his best friend, had stolen into this room, giggling and shushing each other, giddy with nervous excitement. Christy hadn't really believed Geoffrey would do it, but he had: he'd stood on a chair and drawn a charcoal mustache on the scowling face of his great-grandfather. Faint traces still lingered, the charcoal having proven remarkably resistant to numerous efforts at removal. Christy wondered if Geoffrey still bore the marks from the thrashing his father had ordered for punishment—delivered by his steward, not himself, for even in his rages Edward Verlaine had kept his distance.

The words in Christy's Book of Common Prayer began to run together. He rolled his stiff shoulders, fighting off the sleepiness that kept dragging at him. He stood up and went to the window. Drawing back the curtain, he looked out past Lynton Great Hall's derelict courtyard toward the tall black spire of All Saints Church, half a mile away and all that could be seen from here of Wyckerley, the village where he'd grown up. It was April; the gentle, oak-covered hills were a brilliant yellow-green, and the Wyck, normally a placid little river within its steep-sided banks, churned down from Dartmoor with the force of a torrent. He and Geoffrey had fished in the Wyck year-round, ridden their ponies up and down every sunken red lane in the parish, left urgent messages for each other in a crevice of the gray stone monolith at the crossroads. They'd been all but inseparable for the first sixteen years of their lives—until Geoffrey had run away. In twelve years, Christy hadn't heard a word from him.

Until six days ago, when a note had come to the rectory. "Just tell me when the bastard croaks," Geoffrey had scribbled on the back of a tailor's bill—and that only after Christy had written repeatedly to the London address he'd finally gotten from Lord D'Aubrey's solicitor. "How the hell are you?" he'd scrawled in a postscript. "You're joking, aren't you? A *minister*? ?"

Christy wasn't surprised that his new vocation seemed like a joke to Geoffrey, considering all the times that, as boys, they'd made fun of Christy's gentle, pious father. "Old Vicar," the villagers called Magnus Morrell now, although he'd been dead for four years; and Christy, inevitably, was "New Vicar." Stories of Geoffrey's wild, decadent life in London and other worldly fleshpots were hard to reconcile with competing and almost equally incredible rumors that he was a mercenary soldier, ready to take up arms for any cause that paid enough money for his services. Christy had stopped missing him—even the deepest wound heals in time—but he'd never stopped wondering what had become of him.

A noise from the bed made him start. The viscount's face, yellow with jaundice, had turned on the pillow; he was glaring at him. "You." It came out an accusing croak. "Don't want you. Where's your father?"

"My father's dead, sir," he reminded him gently, leaning over the bed.

Recollection took the anger out of the old man's hard black eyes, but a truly ghastly smile curled at the corners of his mouth. "Then I'll see him soon enough, won't I?"

Christy fumbled with his prayer book, reconsidered, and laid it aside. He hated the pain he felt at this moment, and the inadequacy, and the trivial sound of all the things that came into his mind to say. He felt like a child again—like the boy who had grown up terrified of this dying wreck of a man, hating him on principle because Geoffrey, his best friend, had hated him.

He bent closer, into the old man's line of vision. "Would you like to pray?"

Out of habit, the viscount's eyes narrowed with contempt. A moment passed. He turned his face away. "You pray," he exhaled on a feeble sigh.

Christy opened his book to the Psalms. "The Lord is my shepherd," he began, prosaically enough; "I shall not want. He maketh me to lie down in green pastures; he leadeth me beside the still waters. He restoreth my soul—' "

"Not that one. Before that."

"The—"

"The twenty-second." His eyes closed in exhaustion, but the bloodless lips curved again, sardonic. "Read it, Parson," he rasped when Christy hesitated.

He scanned the seldom-read psalm in dismay. "My God, my God, why hast thou forsaken me? Why art thou so far from helping me, and from the words of my roaring?' " He read the prayer in a low voice, but it wasn't possible to soften the desperate message. "They cried unto thee, and were delivered; they trusted in thee, and were not confounded. But I am a worm, and no man; a reproach of men, and despised of the people. All they that see me laugh me to scorn . . .' "

A sound silenced him; he looked up. Edward's eyes were closed, his jaws clamped in a grimace; but, for all his efforts, tears trickled through his papery lids. Christy reached for one of his hands and held it tightly, while the viscount's weeping turned into weak, desolate cursing. The words became garbled as he grew more agitated. He gave Christy's wrist a feeble yank. "Do it," he muttered. "Do it, damn you."

He stared at him, baffled. "I don't—"

"Absolve me."

Christy looked down at the fierce, spidery grip the old man had on his hand. "Almighty God," he prayed quickly, "who desireth not the death of a sinner, but rather that he may turn from his wickedness and live, hath given power to his ministers to declare and pronounce to his people the absolution of their sins. Edward, do you truly and earnestly repent of your sins?"

"I do," he grated through his teeth, eyes closed.

"Are you in love and charity with your neighbors—"

"Yes, yes."

"And—will you lead a new life, following the commandments of God and walking from henceforth in his holy ways?"

"Yes!"

"Go in peace, then. Your sins are forgiven."

The viscount peered up at him in panicky disbelief.

"They're forgiven," Christy repeated, insistent. "The God who made you loves you. Believe it."

"If I could . . ."

"You can. Take it inside your heart and be at peace."

"Peace." His hand loosened and fell away, but he continued to gaze up with pleading eyes. All the hopes of his life had narrowed and funneled into this one hope; that he was loved, and that he was forgiven. Christy was learning that at the end it was all anyone wanted.

"My lord," he asked, "will you take the sacraments?"

A minute went by, and then the old man nodded.

Christy prepared the bread and the wine quickly, using the bedside table for an altar, reciting the words of the ritual in a voice loud enough for Edward to hear. He was to ill to swallow more than a tiny morsel of the Host, and he could only wet his lips on the edge of the chalice. Afterward, he lay utterly still, the flutter of the wilted lace on his nightshirt the only indication that he still breathed.

Time ticked past in the dim box of a room; the lamp wick began to sputter, and Christy rose to turn it higher. A choking sound from the bed made him turn back quickly.

Edward was trying to sit up on his elbows. "Help me . . . help . . . oh, God, I hate it . . . I'm afraid of the dark . . ." Christy put his arm around his thin shoulders, propping him up. "Geoffrey?" He stared straight ahead, unblinking. "Geoffrey?"

"Yes," Christy lied without hesitation. "Yes, Father, it's Geoffrey."

"My boy." His smile was rapturous, a little smug. "I knew you'd come." His head bobbed once and fell on his left shoulder; a long, ragged sigh rattled up from his chest, but he was already dead.

Christy held him in his arms a little longer before laying his slack torso back on the bed and gently closing his eyes. "Go in peace," he murmured, "for the Lord has put away all your sins." The unmistakable aspect of death had already seeped into the viscount's corpse; his soul was gone. Christy administered the last sacrament, the anointing of the body with oil, taking a melancholy comfort in the solemn rite. When he finished, he sank to his knees by the bed to pray, hands folded, his forehead pressed against the side of the mattress.

That was how Geoffrey found him.

Christy hadn't heard footsteps but something, maybe a change in the air, made him lift his head and look toward the doorway to the hall. A tall, dark-haired man stood in the threshold. Sallow skin, sunken cheeks, black, burning eyes in hollow sockets—for one grotesque moment, Christy thought it was Edward, returned from the dead in the semblance of his youth. But a second later, a flesh-and-blood woman materialized behind the man's shoulder, and Christy realized he wasn't seeing ghosts. He got to his feet in haste.

He met Geoffrey in the middle of the room. He would have embraced him, but Geoffrey held out his hand and they shook instead, clapping each other on the back. "My God, it's true," Geoffrey cried, his voice sounding shockingly loud after the long silence. "You've gone and become a priest!"

"As you see." His gladness gave way to concern as he took in his oldest friend's profoundly altered appearance. At sixteen, Geoffrey had been a strapping, muscular youth; when they'd wrestled together, they'd almost always fought to a draw, and on the rare occasions when Christy had won, it was only because he was taller. Now Geoffrey looked as if a well-placed blow from a child could knock him down. But his charming, wolfish grin hadn't changed, and Christy found himself smiling back, wanting to laugh with him in spite of the somber circumstances of this meeting. "Geoffrey, thank God you've come. Your father—"

"Is he dead?" He moved around him to the bedside without waiting for an answer. "Oh, my, yes," he said softly, staring down at the still corpse. "He's dead, all right, no question about that."

Christy stayed where he was, to give Geoffrey a little time to himself. The woman in the doorway hadn't moved. She was slim, tall, dressed sedately in a dark brown traveling costume; the veiled brim of her hat cast a shadow over her face. He glanced at her curiously, but she didn't speak.

Geoffrey had his back to the room; Christy tried to read his emotion from the set of his shoulders, but the rigid posture was unrevealing. After another minute, he crossed to the bed to stand beside him, and together they gazed down at Edward's lifeless face. "He didn't suffer at the end," Christy said quietly. "It was a peaceful death."

"Was it? He looks ghastly, doesn't he? What was wrong with him, anyway?"

"A disease of the liver."

"Liver, eh?" There was no hint of sorrow in his frowning, narrow-eyed countenance; rather, Christy had the unnerving impression that he was scrutinizing the body to assure himself it was really dead.

"He asked for your before he died."

Geoffrey looked up at that, incredulous, then burst into high, hearty laughter. "Oh, that's good. That's very good!"

Dismayed, Christy looked away. The woman had come farther into the room; in the shadowy lamplight, her eyes glowed an odd silver-gray color. He couldn't read the expression in them, but the set of her wide, straight mouth was ironic.

"I think he was sorry at he end," he tried again. "For everything. I believe he felt remorse in his heart for—" This time Geoffrey cut him off with a crude, appallingly vulgar oath that made Christy blush. The woman arched one dark brow at him; he'd have said she was mocking him, but there was no playfulness in her face.

Then Geoffrey flashed his charming smile, and the anger in his eyes disappeared as if it had never been. He spun away from the bed and draped his arm across Christy's shoulders, giving him a rough, affectionate squeeze. "How've you been, you ruddy old sod? You look . . ." He stood back and made a show of examining him, head to toe. "Christ, you *still* look like an archangel!" He ruffled Christy's blond hair, laughing, and under his breath Christy caught the unmistakable odor of alcohol. He stiffened involuntarily. All the things he could have said about Geoffrey's appearance seemed either tactless or hurtful, so he didn't answer.

"Come on, let's get out of here," Geoffrey urged, guiding him toward the door. Christy resisted, and Geoffrey stopped short, adjacent to the silent, motionless woman. "Oh—sorry, darling, forgot about you there. This is Christian Morrell, an old chum from my halcyon youth. Christy, meet my wife, Anne. Anne,

Christy. Christy, Anne. Shake hands, why don't you? That's it! Now let's all go have a drink."

"How do you do, Reverend Morrell," murmured Anne Verlaine, unsmiling, ignoring her husband's facetiousness.

Christy struggled to hide his surprise. Rumors about Geoffrey were always rife in Wyckerley, had been since he'd run away at sixteen and never returned. About four years ago Christy had heard that he'd married the daughter of an artist, a painter; but the next rumor had him off fighting the Burmese in Pegu, and there was no more talk of a wife. As a consequence, Christy had assumed that the marriage was just another in the colorful catalog of stories about the village's prodigal son that might not be true but never failed to entertain the natives.

"Mrs. Verlaine," he greeted her, taking the cool, firm hand she held out to him. She was younger than he'd thought at first, probably not even twenty-five. Her accent was English, but there was something distinctly foreign about her; something in her dress, he thought, or the penetrating directness of her gaze.

"No, no, it's not Mrs. Verlaine anymore, is it? It's Lady D'Aubrey! How does it feel to be a viscountess, darling? Frankly I can't wait for someone to call me 'my lord.' Come on, we must go and drink to Father's demise. It took him long enough, but better late than never, what?" Geoffrey's arm around his wife's waist looked steely; she resisted for only a moment, then let him lead her out of the room. Christy had no choice but to follow.

Forever and Ever

THE TOWER CLOCK on All Saints' Church struck the quarter hour with a loud, tiny thud. Connor Pendarvis, who had been leaning against the stone ledge of a bridge and staring down at the River Wyck, straightened impatiently. Jack was late. Again. He ought to be used to it by now—and he was, but that didn't make his brother's habitual tardiness any less aggravating.

At least he didn't have to wait for Jack in the rain. In typical South Devon fashion, the afternoon had gone from gray to fair in a matter of minutes, and now the glitter of sunlight on the little river's sturdy current was almost blinding. It was June, and the clean air smelled of honeysuckle. Birds sang, bees buzzed, irises in brilliant yellow clumps bloomed along the riverbank. The cottages lining the High Street sported fresh coats of daub in whimsical pastel shades, and every garden was a riot of summer flowers.

The Rhadamanthus Society's report on Wyckerley had said it was a poky, undistinguished hamlet in a poor parish, but Connor disagreed. He thought the authors of the report must have a novel idea of what constituted poverty—either that or they'd never been to Trewithiel, the village in Cornwall where *he'd* grown up. Wyckerley was friendly, pretty, neat as a pin—Trewithiel's opposite in every way. Connor had been born there, and one by one he'd watched his family die there. Before he was twenty, he'd buried all of them.

All except Jack. Here he came, speak of the devil, the folded, one-page letter. "Enough to cover the note of deposit I've just signed for our new lodgings."

"Well, that's a relief for you, counselor. Now you won't get pinched for false misrepresentation o' personal fiduciary stature." Jack chortled at his own humor; he never got tired of making up names for laws and statutes, the sillier sounding the better.

Connor said, "I had to pay the agent for the lease of six months. Thirty-six shillings." It wasn't his money, but it still seemed a waste, since they wouldn't be in Wyckerley past two months at the most.

"What's our new place like, then?"

"Better than the last. We've half of a workingmen's cottage only a mile from the mine. We'll share a kitchen with two other men, both miners, and there's a girl who comes in the afternoons to cook a meal. And praise the Lord, we've each got a room this time, so I won't have to listen to you snore the glazing out of the windows."

Jack cackled, going along with the joke. There were times when he kept Connor awake, but it was because of his cough and the drenching night sweats that robbed him of rest, not his snoring. "What do they say about the mine?" he asked.

"Not much. It's called Guelder. A woman owns it. It's been fairly—"

"A *woman*." Jack's eyes went wide with amazement, then narrowed in scorn. "A woman," he muttered, shaking his head. "Well, ee've got yer work cut out right and proper, then, 'aven't ee? The radical Rhads'll be aquiver wi' joy when they read yer report this time."

Connor grunted noncommittally. "The woman's name is Deene. She inherited the mine from her father about two years ago, and she owns it outright, without shareholders. They say her uncle owns another mine in the district. His name's Vanstone, and he happens to be the mayor of Wyckerley."

"Why'n't they sent you to that un? The uncle's, I mean. Tes bound to be far better run."

"Probably, and there's your answer. The Society hasn't employed me to investigate clean, safe, well-managed copper mines." No, but the selection process was still fair, Connor believed, if only because conditions in most Cornish and Devonian copper mines were so deplorable, there was no need to doctor reports or tinker with findings. Or pick a woman's mine over a man's in hopes of finding more deficiencies.

He put the envelope in his pocket and clasped his hands behind his head, blinking up at the sky. The June afternoon was lazily spectacular, and he couldn't deny that it was pleasant to sit in the shade while butterflies flickered in and out of sun rays slanting down through the tree leaves. In a rare mellow mood, he watched two children burst from a side door in the church across the way and run toward the green. A second later, out came three more, then four, then another giggling pair. Shouting, laughing, they skipped and ran in circles and tumbled on the grass, giddy as March hares. He'd have thought Sunday school had just let out, except it was Saturday. The children's high spirits were contagious; more than one passerby paused in the cobbled street long enough to smile at their antics.

Half a minute later, a young woman came out of the same door in the church and hurried across the lane toward the green. The school teacher? Tall, slim, dressed in white, she had blond hair tied up in a knot on top of her head. Connor tried to guess her age, but it was hard to tell from this distance; she had the lithe body of a girl, but the confident, self-assured manner of a woman. He wasn't a bit surprised when she clapped her hands and every shrieking, frolicking child immediately ran to her. What surprised him was the gay sound of her own laughter mingling with theirs.

The smallest child, a girl of five or six, leaned against her hip familiarly; the woman patted her curly head while she gave the others some soft-voiced command. The children formed a half circle around her. She bent down to the little girl's level to say something in her ear, her hand resting lightly on the child's shoulder.

"Look at that now, Con. That's a winsome sight, edn it?" said Jack in a low, appreciative voice. "Edn that just how a lady oughter look?"

Where women were concerned, Jack was the least discriminating man Connor had ever known; he liked *all* of them. But this time he'd spoken no more than the truth. This woman's ivory gown, her willowy figure, the sunny gold in her hair—they made a very beguiling picture. And yet he thought Jack meant something more—something about the long, graceful curve of her back as she bent toward the child, the solicitousness of her posture, the *kindness* in it that took the simple picture out of the ordinary and made it unforgettable. When Connor glanced at his brother, he saw the same soft, stricken smile he could feel on his own face, and he knew they'd been moved equally, just for a moment, by the perfection of the picture.

She straightened then, and the little girl skipped away to a place in the middle of the semicircle. The spell was broken, but the picture lingered; the image still shimmered in his mind's eye.

She took something from the pocket of her dress—a pitch pipe. She brought it to her lips and blew a soft, thin note. The children hummed obediently, then burst into song.

Smiling encouragement, her face animated, the music teacher moved her hands in time to the melody, and every child beamed back at her, eager to please, all wide eyes and happy faces. It was like a scene in a storybook, or a sentimental play about good children and perfectly kind teachers, too good to be true—yet it was happening here, now, on the little green in the village of Wyckerley, St. Giles' parish. Mesmerized, Connor sat back to watch what would happen next.

The choir sang another song, and afterward the teacher made them sing it again. He wasn't surprised; smitten as he was, even he could tell it hadn't been their finest effort. Then, sensing her charges were growing restless, she set them free after a gentle admonition—which fell on deaf ears, because the shouting and gamboling recommenced almost immediately.

"Looks like a little o' new puppies." Jack chuckled, and Connor nodded, smiling at the antics of two little towheaded boys, twins, vying with each other to see who could press more dandelions into the hands of their pretty teacher. Heedless of the damp grass, she dropped to her knees and sniffed the straggly bouquets with exaggerated admiration. Her way of keeping their rambunctious spirits within bounds was to ask them questions, then listen to the answers with complete absorption.

Just then the curly haired little girl, clutching her own flower, made a running leap and landed on the teacher's back with a squeal of delight. The woman bore the impact sturdily, even when the youngster wound her arms around her neck and hung on tight, convulsed with mirth. But gradually the laughter tapered off.

"She'm caught," Jack murmured when some of the children crept closer, looking uncertain. "The lady's hair, looks like. Edn she caught?" Connor was already on his feet. "Con? Wait, now. Ho, Con! You shouldn't oughter—"

He didn't hear the rest. Impulsiveness was one of his most dangerous failings, but this—this was too much like the answer to a prayer he'd been too distracted to say. He took off across the green at a sprint.

No doubt about it, the teacher was caught. "It's all right, Birdie," she was saying, reaching back to try to disentangle her hair from something on the little girl's dress. "Don't wriggle for a second. No, it's all right, just don't move."

Birdie was near tears. "I'm sorry, Miss Sophie," she kept saying, worried but unable to stop squirming. The music teacher winced—then laughed, pretending it was a joke.

The other children eyed Connor in amazement when he squatted down beside the entangled pair. Birdie's mouth dropped open and she finally went still. The teacher—Miss Sophie—could only see him out of the corner of her eye; if she turned her head, she'd yank the long strand of hair that was wound tight about Birdie's shirtwaist button.

"Well, now, what have we here?" he said, softening his voice to keep Birdie calm. He shifted until he was kneeling in front of the teacher, and reached over her bent head to untangle the snarl.

"It got stuck! Now I can't move or I'll hurt Miss Sophie!"

Around them the children had gathered in a quiet circle, curious as cows. And protective of their teacher, Connor fancied. "That's right," he agreed, "so you must hold very, very still while I undo this knot. Pretend you're a statue."

"Yes, sir. What's a statue."

A breathy laugh came from the music teacher. He could see only her profile and the smooth angle of her neck. She had cream-white skin, the cheeks flushed a little from exertion or embarrassment. Her eyes were downcast; he couldn't be sure what color they were. Blue, he thought. "The stone cross at the edge of the green, Birdie," she said, amusement in her low voice. "That's a sort of statue, because it never moves."

"Oh."

The snarl was stubborn, and Connor was as anxious as Birdie not to pull Miss Sophie's hair. "Almost got it," he muttered. "Two more seconds." Her pretty hair was soft and slippery and it smelled of roses. Or was that the sun-warmed linen of her dress?

"There are scissors in the rectory," she said, speaking to the ground. "Tommy Wooten, are you here? Would you go and ask—"

"Out of the question. I'd sooner cut off my hand than a single strand of this beautiful hair." And if that wasn't the most fatuous thing he'd ever said in his life, he wanted to know what was.

She sent him a twinkling, sideways glance, and he saw the color of her eyes. Blue. Definitely blue. "Actually, I was thinking you might cut off the *button*."

"Ah, the button. A much better idea."

"Shall I go, Miss Sophie?" asked a reedy voice behind Connor's shoulder.

"Yes, Tommy."

"No, Tommy," Connor corrected as the last strand in the tangle finally came loose. "Miss Sophie is free."

She sat back on her heels and smiled, first at him, then at the children gathered around; some of them were clapping, as if a performance had just concluded. Her laughing face was flushed, her hair awry—and she was so stunningly lovely, he felt blinded, hindered, too dazzled to take it in. He remembered to take off his hat, but before he could speak—and say what?—she turned away to give Birdie a strong, reassuring hug.

"Did it hurt?" the little girl asked her, patting her cheek worriedly.

"No, not one bit."

She heaved a great sigh of relief. "Look, Miss Sophie, here's what I was giving you." She held out one bent daisy, the stem wilted, the white petals smashed.

Sophie drew in her breath. "Oh, *lovely*," she declared, holding the flower to her nose and sniffing deeply. "*Thank* you, Birdie." The child blushed with pleasure. Then she was off, anxious to tell her friends about her adventure.

Now that the drama was over, the other children began to wander away, too. Connor was still on his knees beside the teacher. "Thank you," she said in her musical voice.

He said, "It was very much my pleasure." They both looked away, then back. He put out his hand. She hesitated for a second, then took it, and he helped her to her feet.